PRAISE FOR *DISSOLUTION*

"Ranchers and university students fight to survive after an economic crisis turns American citizens against one another in this thriller. An absorbing, realistic dystopian tale with a superb cast."

—Kirkus Reviews

"Gear conjures a frighteningly realistic dystopian future in his Wyoming Chronicles series launch. Gear's impeccable detail work and timely references to MAGA and coronavirus make for a dystopian world that feels immediate and all too plausible. This harrowing future is sure to linger in readers' minds."

—Publishers Weekly

"Hold on to your hat. This thriller introduces Sam Delgado to the literary landscape in a story rooted in the archaeology and practices of the Shoshones colliding with a modern catastrophe where perhaps the only safe place to be is high in the mountains of Wyoming with some ranchers at your side."

—Candy Moulton author of Roadside History of Wyoming and Chief Joseph: Guardian of the People

"No one reads a Gear novel without being transformed in beautiful ways."

–Richard S. Wheeler

FOURTH QUADRANT

✶✶✶✶✶✶

THE WYOMING CHRONICLES: BOOK TWO

W. MICHAEL GEAR

WOLFPACK
PUBLISHING
— EST 2013 —

WOLFPACK PUBLISHING
— EST 2013 —

Wolfpack Publishing
5130 S. Fort Apache Road, 215-380
Las Vegas, NV 89148

wolfpackpublishing.com

Hardcover ISBN 978-1-63977-301-5
Paperback ISBN 978-1-63977-103-5
eBook ISBN 978-1-63977-295-7
LCCN 2021953249

FOURTH QUADRANT

******

TO

KAT AND LARRY MARTIN

FELLOW EXPLORERS IN THE WORLD

OF BOOKS AND FINE WRITING

THE LIZARD BRAIN

***

There's part of the brain, the limbic system, that's old. Said to be reptilian. A relic of hundreds of millions of years of evolution that goes back to the earliest vertebrates. Consisting of the amygdala, hippocampus, and hypothalamus. In vernacular, it's called the "lizard brain".

When I look back at those days after the Collapse, I credit my survival to the lizard brain. That's what took over. Kept me breathing, fighting, and fleeing danger.

I did things. Committed acts that would have been so horrible and inconceivable, that the Lauren I was before the Collapse would have believed them to be impossible.

It's like I went out of my way to turn the rest of my brain off. If I hadn't, if I had tried to think rationally, I'd have died in the first days. Instead I have to live with the consequences.

Whatever nightmares are, I don't think the lizard brain has them. It just lurks down there on the bottom of the skull, hissing, flicking its tongue out, and demanding that you move on to the next meal.

- Lauren Davis

CHAPTER ONE

***

MRS. DUFFIELD STOOD BEFORE LAUREN DAVIS'S TELLER WINDOW AT SPRINGS BANK WITH her withdrawal slip in her hand. For the rest of her life, Lauren would remember that the seventy-two-year-old woman wore a white-cotton twill hat, flower-patterned blouse, and comfortable white pants.

It was the Friday before Memorial Day weekend. The moment Lauren got off work, she and Tyrell were heading to Moab on their motorcycles for some backcountry camping. It would be their first real vacation since moving in together a couple of months back.

In her teller's cage, Lauren was surrounded by faux brick and glass. The wooden counter in front of her was so shiny she could see her reflection in it. Her wavy, shoulder-length auburn hair and oval face were only slightly distorted by the unnatural gleam, but her cinnamon-brown eyes looked huge.

Lauren gave the woman a warm smile. "Good Morning, Mrs. Duffield. How are you today?"

"I'm doing great." Duffield's gray hair had a bluish sheen in the overhead fluorescent lights as she slipped a withdrawal form through the teller's window. "I need to take out a hundred dollars, please."

"Sure."

Lauren took the withdrawal form and tapped in the account number. When the data flashed on the screen, she found herself staring at eight million, four-hundred-fifty-three-thousand seventy-four dollars and twenty-seven cents. A considerable amount for a retired school teacher.

Lauren took a deep breath, having never in her life seen an account balance like this.

Muttering customers waited at four teller stations down the line. The other tellers seemed to be having problems. Keys clicked as tellers repeatedly entered numbers into their computers, frowned, and reentered them.

Lauren smiled at Mrs. Duffield and processed the withdrawal. As she handed the elderly woman one hundred dollars, she quietly said, "Mrs. Duffield are you aware that the FDIC doesn't insure accounts this large?"

"What?" The retired school teacher blinked up at Lauren through her bifocals. Her wrinkles rearranged into confused lines.

"I mean, have you thought about consulting our financial services department? They may be able to advise you on safer places to keep your money rather than in a simple savings account."

"The FDIC won't insure a measly thousand dollars?" Mrs. Duffield's voice tensed.

Lauren straightened and glanced at the monitor again. She'd just started work here two weeks ago. It was a very good summer job in a field where she hoped to work for the rest of her life: Finance. She didn't want to take the chance of losing it by angering any of the patrons.

Quietly, she leaned over the counter to say, "According to the computer, you have over eight million dollars in your savings account. You might want to at least speak with our bank president, he—"

"Is that a joke?" Mrs. Duffield asked in shock. "You're awfully young, dear. And new here. Did you input the wrong account number?"

"If so, I apologize. Let me try again." Lauren cleared the page and carefully re-typed the account number. She tried to smile at Mrs. Duffield while she waited. "The system's slow. Must be all the activity before the weekend."

The retired school teacher didn't seem to appreciate it. She gave Lauren a hostile look, probably the same one she'd used on students who'd underperformed in her classes. "Are you old enough to work here? You look sixteen. Maybe you should get someone, shall we say, more seasoned? to double-check your work."

"I just finished my freshman year at the university. Three-point-seven GPA."

"Studying what?"

"International finance."

"Umm," said Mrs. Duffield.

When the same amount, over eight million dollars, appeared on the screen, Lauren grimaced at it, then at Mrs. Duffield. "How much would you estimate your balance to be? Just ballpark?"

"At least a thousand and twenty-two dollars, dear." The way she said "dear" reeked of disapproval.

"Please, excuse me for a minute. I do need to get my supervisor. I'll be right back."

"Good idea." Mrs. Duffield glared at her over the rims of her glasses.

Lauren made her way past the whispering tellers and through the door that led to the offices. First on the left was Randy Howman's office, the assistant bank manager. To her relief, he was sitting behind his desk, staring fixedly at his computer screen. Randy's blond hair sported a perpetual cowlick that seemed to always stand up no matter how he tried to plaster it down. Tall, and slightly overweight, his best feature consisted of lively blue eyes in a ruddy face. As usual, Randy wore a white shirt, tie, and light-gray dress slacks. His blue suit jacket hung on the back of his chair; a half-empty cup of coffee rested to the right of his keyboard.

Oblivious to her presence, Randy whispered to the screen, "That can't be right. Why would the Federal Reserve even consider..."

Lauren knocked softly on the door frame and leaned in. "Randy? I'm sorry to bother you. I've got a problem with an account."

He looked up with a panicked expression. "Give me just a minute, Lauren. I'll be right with you." He hit several keys and stared harder at the screen.

Lauren folded her arms across her chest and gazed down the hall and out at the bank lobby.

Patrons had gathered in the middle of the lobby to talk in low voices. A mixture of emotions moved across their faces. One man kept glancing angrily at his watch, as though he was in a hurry. A woman paced back and forth with a disgusted expression.

The hostility was rising.

"Forgive me," Randy said, and forced a smile. "What can I do for you?"

She walked into his office and stood before his neat desk. Through the window, she could see Pike's Peak rising in snow-capped glory to the west. "I'm not sure. Mrs. Duffield says she has a little over a thousand dollars in her savings account, but our computer insists she has over eight million. I was hoping you could come and—"

"You're sure?" Randy's smile froze. He lowered his voice to just above a whisper: "You double-checked?"

"Well, yeah, of course."

Randy murmured, "Please, God, don't let this be happening."

He shoved to his feet and brushed past her. The muscles knotted in his jaw as he led the way back to her teller position. As they emerged the other tellers started calling, "Mr. Howman? Got a problem here." "Randy? You've gotta see this."

"Soon as I'm done with Lauren," he answered as he hurried down the line.

"Mrs. Duffield," Lauren said cheerfully over Randy's shoulder as he dove for her keyboard, "I'm so sorry for the delay, but Mr. Howman is going to see if it's a computer problem."

The other tellers were crowding in behind her and muttering about their accounts.

Mrs. Duffield didn't look appeased, adding, "I'd appreciate it if you'd be quick about it. I have appointments this afternoon."

Randy—focused like a laser—didn't even say hello to the woman. He input his security code, looked at the account number on her withdrawal slip, and began tapping the keys. When Mrs. Duffield's account came up, he swallowed hard and stared at it. Softly, he asked, "Lauren? This is the amount you saw?"

Lauren whispered, "It's gone up by about one hundred thousand."

Randy's voice was shaky. "This can't be happening."

Horrified, Mrs. Duffield asked, "It's gone up? What does that...? I mean, I'm an honest person. That's not my money. Why is it in my account? Are you people incompetent, or what?"

Randy tried to smile. Couldn't quite do it. "I know you're honest, Mrs. Duffield. I promise you, we'll get this straightened out. Computers can be finicky and this—"

Lisa—the second teller down—called, "Randy? Sorry to interrupt, but I really need you here. Got a second?"

The bearded man in work boots, with Ray's Plumbing printed on his blue shirt, looked like he was about to explode.

Randy clenched his fists, steeled himself, said, "Excuse me, Mrs. Duffield," and hurried to Lisa's booth.

"What's going on?" Mrs. Duffield shouted. "Come back here and fix my account first!"

Lauren flinched and turned to watch Randy.

Lisa quietly told him, "I keep reentering Mr. Krause's account, and his balance keeps coming up as zero."

The plumber, Krause, propped his thick arms on the counter, jaw muscles bunching. "I just deposited my paycheck. There's over three thousand dollars in that account! If you've lost my money, there's gonna be hell to pay."

Randy flushed as red as a cherry. "It's right here in the bank, Mr. Krause. I assure you, everything's fine. Just a computer hiccup. We'll get it straightened out." To Lisa, he said, "Process Mr. Krause's withdrawal."

"Sure. Okay." Lisa looked confused, but she started counting out twenties, smiling nervously at Mr. Krause as she did so.

Bank President, Bill Blassen, opened the door to the tellers' counter, stepped inside, and politely called, "Randy? We need to talk. Now."

"Certainly, sir." Randy walked over. Their backs to the patrons, a hushed conversation ensued. Blassen, from what Lauren could see, looked panicked. Randy kept nodding, going pale as if the blood had drained from his head.

Mrs. Duffield stood before the teller's window, arms crossed, looking really pissed. Three people had come to line up behind her.

Lauren looked up when Lieutenant Tyrell Ramirez, the love of her life, stepped through the bank's door and headed straight for her. To her surprise, he was in uniform, cover tucked tightly under his arm. Tyrell never wore a uniform when he was off base. With his beard and longer hair, people on the street would never have known he was CAG, that he served with an elite "Delta Force" team.

Lauren felt that rush of happiness and relief...until she noticed his expression.

This isn't good. Her thoughts went immediately to the news that morning. About Taiwan, and the Chinese landing troops there. And the two carrier groups that President Brown had dispatched to the South China Sea.

Please! Tell me we aren't going to war with China.

The way he moved in his ACUs reminded her of a hunting lion as he crossed the lobby. His black hair was sweat-soaked, plastered to his tanned forehead and cheeks.

"Hey," Lauren said when he crowded in ahead of Mrs. Duffield. "What are you doing here? Thought you were home packing for our trip to—"

"Lauren, can you come out for a second?" Tyrell had one of those authoritative voices—his officer's voice accustomed to giving orders—that spoke volumes even when he kept it low.

Mrs. Duffield turned to stare at him. "What's wrong, Lieutenant?"

Before Tyrell could answer, Lauren said, "Excuse me, Mrs. Duffield."

The older woman gave her a disbelieving look and glanced sidelong at Tyrell.

Lauren walked for the door that secured the tellers' positions and keyed in her code. The instant she stepped out into the bank lobby, Tyrell took her arm in a hard grip, and dragged her a short distance away.

"Hey, what are you doing here? And what's with the ACUs?"

Gaze taking in the lobby, he softly said, "Listen, we're activated. I've got an hour to get my first-line gear wired before they fly us out. Don't know when I'll see you again."

"God, tell me this isn't about Taiwan. I've been worried ever since the news—"

"Lauren, I don't know. Just got the word from the head shed. My ODD is active."

"This is our first three-day weekend. We've been planning this..." Words failed her. That's what living with a Tier One operator was all about.

Tyrell ran tender fingers down her cheek. "Just listen. And don't argue with me. I want you to get out of Colorado. But do not, repeat *do not,* even attempt to get home to your family in Maryland. Joint Base Andrews is locked down. The 316th Wing is on alert. That high school friend you talk about, Breeze Tappan. You said she comes from a backcounty family ranch in Wyoming, right?"

"Sure, but Breeze and I..." She swallowed hard. "You know about my brother and her."

"She's in Denver, right?"

"Well, yeah. Working for Seakliff Investments. She's—"

"You said she rides. I need you to take the KTM, not your Suzuki or car. Get to Denver. Whatever you have to do, *make* Breeze take you to her family's ranch." He smiled weakly. "If you have to get on your knees and beg. As long as—"

"Damn it, Tyrell, tell me we're not going to war over Taiwan."

As though making a difficult decision, Tyrell gave her a look that drilled down into her soul. He might have only been twenty-four, but he had seen some 'serious shit' in faraway places that he could never tell her about. Just how serious showed in the hard lines of his face. "Bad shit's coming down, honey. You hear me? I love you. Never doubt that."

She felt a sinking sensation in her gut. "Ty, so help me, if they're sending you off to die in Taiwan..."

"All I know is that my team is activated," he said, looking around the bank. Patrons were staring. "That's the truth. But I got a bad feeling about all this. You and Breeze, take the motorcycles; more maneuverable in tough situations. I'm leaving you my boogie bag. Strap it on the back of the bike, and don't—"

"Your boogie bag? Why on earth would I need a bunch of guns and explosi—"

He tightened his grip on her. "Lauren, strap my bag on the back of the KTM, pull out all the cash you can get your hands on, and smoke it up to Wyoming, understand?"

He looked scared. And Tyrell didn't scare easily.

Leaning closer, he placed his mouth against her ear. "Keep your .38 in your inner jacket pocket. Handy, understand?"

"Yeah."

While her mathematical mind correlated the available data, her gaze darted to where Randy and Bill Blassen talked. Then to the worried customers. "Does this have something to do with the bank—"

"Pay attention!" Tyrell hissed through gritted teeth. When he straightened to his full six-foot-four height, she had to look up at him.

"Cash. As much as you can get. And once you hook up with Breeze, stay out of cities. Not ever. *Any* city."

Her heart began to trip in her chest. "What about you?"

Tyrell gave her that secret smile. The one that meant he'd found a solution to a problem. "Unknown. When I can, I'll come find you at Tappan Ranch. That's the rendezvous."

"But, Tyrell, Breeze hasn't spoken to her parents in years. I *can't* ask…"

Tyrell pulled her close and kissed her like it was the end of the world. When he stepped back, he softly said, "Then find a cave in the backcountry where you can wait this thing out. You can hunt with my M4. Take good winter clothes. Do not waste another second. You have to get out of the Front Range and into a low population density area *pronto*. If I mean anything to you, do it."

"O-Okay." She nodded. Winter clothes? Whatever this was he thought it was going drag on into winter. "I don't understand, but I love you. Be careful."

He gently stroked her hair. "Could be months."

"I'll be waiting."

Tyrell hugged her like it might be the last time, pivoted, and strode for the exit. His booted feet struck a martial cadence as he crossed the polished wood floor.

Lightheaded, frozen in place, Lauren watched Tyrell shove open the bank door and vanish. Everyone in the lobby was looking at her. Some with suspicion, others worried. Mrs. Duffield with downright disapproval.

Mr. Krause strode up to the teller's position, slammed a fist on the counter, and shouted, "I want my damned money! Three-thousand-four-hundred dollars. I don't know what the hell's going on here, but I want to close my account!"

Behind her teller's window, Lisa turned to Randy and President Blassen and weakly inquired, "What do I do? Our figures say he has nothing in his account."

"I want to close my account, too!" a young red-haired woman shouted. A chorus of "me toos" echoed around the lobby.

While Randy and Blassen exchanged taut whispers, Lauren input her code on the keypad at the door and made her way to her window.

She didn't finish her paperwork, didn't log out of her computer. She didn't speak to Mrs. Duffield, who was watching her expectantly over the black rims of her glasses.

Instead, Lauren grabbed her purse from the shelf beneath her teller's window and withdrew her checkbook. She wrote a check for $929.00, which, except for twenty-seven cents, emptied her account. Processing the transaction without a word to anyone, she stuffed the cash in her pocket.

She'd ridden her battered Suzuki DR350 to the bank so that she could gas it up on the way home. Ready to leave that night for their three-day motorcycle trip to Moab. It was Memorial Day weekend, after all.

Four paces away, Randy Howman and Bill Blassen, were still deep in conversation; Randy kept shooting Lauren worried glances.

Lauren heard Blassen's order: "Lock the doors and process any customers as quickly as you can. Do whatever they ask, but by hand. Make paper records. Don't touch the computers." Then he turned on his heel and left the teller's cage, headed back to his office.

"Right. Sure thing." A smile was the only acknowledgment Randy gave Lauren as he hurried past her, out into the lobby, and locked the front doors.

On his way back, he asked, "What did Ramirez tell you?" His eyes bored through her like blue lasers.

"Well, Randy, it's...it's..." She'd never been a good liar. "Something I have to do for Tyrell. It's, um, personal. I'm sorry."

"Do me a favor? You heard Blassen. Process the withdrawls by hand and close out your teller position. Meeting in the conference room as soon as you and the other tellers are done."

The clock read: *10:32 AM.*

CHAPTER TWO

* * *

THE GENERAL PALMER ROOM WAS THE BANK'S BIG CONFERENCE ROOM. A HUGE OVAL-shaped tropical-wood table dominated the center. Western art featuring steam locomotives chugging through the Rockies spoke to the early railroad-builder's theme. The room was packed; Lauren, and most of the other junior employees, were relegated to stand along the walls while the older and more senior hierarchy of Springs Bank had chairs. Bill Blassen stood at the head of the table, a pensive look on his sixty-year-old face.

The bank was silent, the phones automated to take calls and explain that the bank was closed due to a computer malfunction. Security was covering the front doors where the growing crowds waited outside, sometimes slapping hands to the glass and demanding entry.

"It's all over the country," Blassen told them. "It's not just us, which is somewhat of a relief. All we know is that it's some kind of computer virus. What they call a Trojan malware. It rides on good code. The IT guys are trying to trace it. Figure out how it works. Stop it. It corrupts accounts."

"Corrupts how?" Vice President Clarisse Ali asked. She leaned forward in her chair to tap her long red fingernails on the tabletop.

Blassen spread his hands. "From what I've heard so far, it creates false balances in accounts. Apparently, it's only affected about ten percent of the accounts nationwide, but it's spreading." He made a face and ran a hand through his white hair. "All we can do is wait to see what..."

His phone chimed the opening notes of Beethoven's Fifth. While people whispered and glanced uneasily at each other, Blassen took the call. After listening he said, "Yeah. Thanks, Tommy."

He pocketed his phone, looked around the room. "That was Tommy Nelson. The Federal Reserve just shut down the system. Every bank in America has been ordered to close and cease any and all transactional activity. He confirms that it's a cyberattack. But on a scale we've never seen before."

Enrique Garcia held up his cell phone, "It's all over social media: Facebook, Twitter, Snap Chat. Check it out, man. They're all saying, 'Get your money out while you can.' What are we going to do about the crowd gathering out front?"

"I know, I know," Blassen raised his voice. "Look, people, we'll sort it out. It's just going to take time. A couple of days. That's all."

Randy Howman lifted a hand, was acknowledged, and asked, "Bill, so they fix the hack. I mean, I'm not an IT guy, but how do we reestablish those corrupted files?"

"We've got the backups," Bill told him. "We can reset the system in forty-eight hours. But we're not going to be able to reload that data until the hack is fixed. As I understand it, it's a Trojan malware, right? The virus could still be there, dormant, and it would just start all over again. Like I said, we just need time."

Lauren leaned her back against the wall, Tyrell's words rolling around inside her head. A chill ran down her spine. *It isn't just the banks. Can't be. If it's just the banks, why is Tyrell's Delta Force team being deployed?*

"What about when we open next Tuesday?" Enrique asked. "We've barely got a fifteen-percent cash reserve. It's Friday before Memorial Day weekend. People are pulling cash for the holiday."

"We've got bonds to cover that," Blassen waved a hand.

"If the bond market holds up," Randy noted in an ominous voice. "I mean, every bank in the country is going to try and unwind their assets to convert them to cash. And people are going to want to pull all their cash out, just in case this isn't a temporary glitch."

"Fifteen percent cash reserve? We're in noncompliance under Dodd-Frank," Clarisse said sharply. "We're in the Mountain Time Zone. We're two hours behind. Every bank on the east coast is going to be selling bonds to cover their reserves. Dodd-Frank puts us in a straightjacket."

"She's right. Bill," Randy said. "We've got to move on it. In a

couple of hours, when we mark our bond portfolio to the market, and
if it's down even twenty percent, we're screwed."

A faint sheen of perspiration covered Blassen's face despite the
air conditioning. "Way ahead of you. Call's been made. I've already
given settlement instructions to the broker along with our designated
account numbers."

Lauren took a deep breath. When she got home she'd see if she
could corner Carole. Get her finance professor's take on what it all
meant.

As the meeting broke up, Randy tried to sweep by Lauren, but she
gripped his sleeve to stop him. "How are we going to get out the front
doors without being eaten alive? There's a mob forming out there."

Randy had that deer-in-the-headlights look. "Bill has the code to the
rear security door. Maybe we can slip out one by one." He swallowed
hard. "Or maybe we ought to be proactive and call the police."

CHAPTER THREE

***

12:45

THE CHANGE IN COLORADO SPRINGS WAS SO PALPABLE THAT LAUREN FELT IT IN HER GLOVED fingers as she rode home on her ratty old '99 vintage DR350 Suzuki. She'd bought the bike for two grand. With less than six thousand miles on the odometer, it had been stored in a garage, and though in good mechanical condition, was difficult to start, and finicky.

The fact that Tyrell had told her to take his beloved KTM 790 Adventure instead of her Suzuki was almost as sobering as his dire warnings. Sometimes she wondered if Tyrell loved the motorcycle more than her. He kept the orange-and-black machine immaculate. In preparation for their trip to Moab, he'd had it completely serviced with a new chain, tires, and air cleaner.

One thing she knew: He'd been dead-assed serious about her getting the hell out of the Springs.

But Breeze? That was out of the question. Too many bridges burned. Not that Breeze would so much as see her. Being with her one-time friend would be a constant reminder of that horrible night when her brother died. Too much pain. More than Lauren could bear.

Breeze, you weren't the only one who loved my brother.

As she waited for a red light, she stared at a growing crowd in front of the Colorado State Bank. People were cupping their hands against the windows to lean close and peer inside. One fellow was pounding on the door. Even as the light turned, and Lauren motored away, a Colorado Springs Police cruiser pulled up, its lights flashing as the officers emerged and began to disperse the crowd.

Cottony clouds drifted through the blue sky over the Cheyenne

Mountain, not a care in the world. It was a surreal contrast to what she knew was brewing.

She turned into the apartment complex, rode down to their building, and parked the bike in its designated space. Unbuckling her helmet, she swung her backpack onto her shoulder and took the steps two at a time up to their second-floor apartment.

Strange. The apartment complex seemed unnaturally quiet. With all the bases around Colorado Springs, a lot of military personnel rented here. Usually at this time of morning, she could hear TVs blaring and babies crying.

Lauren unlocked the door and immediately noticed that Tyrell had left his boogie bag just inside, ready for her to pick up. The olive-green duffle held Tyrell's back-up for his first-line gear. She'd seen him sort through the heavy canvas bag many times: night-vision goggles, M4 rifle, two pistols, ammunition, camping gear, survival equipment, ration packs, trenching tool, signaling devices. Hand grenades. Just about all the necessities a lieutenant in The Unit would want.

"Why do you think I'm going to need it, Ty?"

God! Please don't let this be about Taiwan.

Unnerved, she shrugged out of her heavy Ralley jacket and tossed it on top of the boogie bag. After turning on the news, she aimlessly wandered around the apartment, trying to decide what she needed to pack.

The only thing on the news was Taiwan. The runner stated: **CRISIS IN THE SOUTH CHINA SEA. SECRETARY OF STATE ON WAY TO BEIJING.** They kept running clips of President Brown staring into the cameras, telling the Chinese to stand down.

At the bottom of the screen appeared the words: **BREAKING NEWS. SEVERAL MAJOR BANKS SUSPEND NORMAL BUSINESS OPERATIONS IN WAKE OF MAJOR ACCOUNT HACK.**

Lauren swallowed hard. Tried to distract herself.

The furnishings had come with the place, and neither of them had many possessions. Tyrell's imprint consisted mostly of photographs of his family and the guys in his spec ops team. In the center of his desk, photos of Lauren and Tyrell together created a semi-circle around his laptop.

Worried sick about him, Lauren walked to the bedroom. Her sleeping bag, tent, and small duffle were already packed for Moab. Ready to be strapped to the rear of the bike. Perfect in case she ended up in a cave in the Owl Creek Mountains.

My God, why would he tell me that?

Taiwan. Had to be.

Walking to the closet, she dragged out all their camping equipment, and carried it over to dump it on the bed. Almost as an afterthought, she ran her fingers over the taut bedspread, remembering cherished moments. She'd never fallen for a man like she had for Ty. Had never lived the sudden rush of total and encompassing love. Just being with him was like a drug. Touching him. Seeing that smile light his lips, and the twinkle in his dark eyes.

She couldn't quite convince herself to leave. Pulling out her cell phone, she called Tyrell's number, but she was shunted straight to voice mail.

"Love you. Just wanted to say it again. Stay frosty out there. I miss you."

She carried the camping gear to the living room, set it beside his boogie bag. Leave? And go where? Wyoming? Seriously? Sure, she'd spent the biggest part of her peripatetic life there, had friends there. But then what?

Tyrell told her that he'd find her at the Tappan Ranch.

Damn it, Ty didn't understand. Not only did Breeze hate her, blame her for Jim's death, but Breeze and her parents weren't even on speaking terms.

Both of us have fucked-up lives.

In a strange daze, Lauren walked to the tiny dining room just off the kitchen and switched channels; she found herself staring at the President of the United States: Dr. Anna Brown sat behind the famous desk in the Oval Office. Her voice sounded confident and unemotional: *"...no evidence that this is related to the situation regarding Taiwan. I repeat: There is cause for panic. The country has been preparing for a cyberattack like this for many years. Our financial system is healthy and secure. Yes, it's Memorial Day weekend. However, with most credit card purchases temporarily suspended, we are asking all Americans to stay at home. I understand that it's an inconvenience, but it's just one weekend. Come Tuesday, the banks will reopen. Meanwhile, just like with COVID, we urge all Americans to stay home."*

Lauren whispered, "Really? Then why are our spec ops people so scared?"

The screen switched to a journalist interviewing a financial analyst. The man said, *"...must have stolen all these numbers and PINs years ago and been waiting for the right moment. Corrupt just enough bank accounts, and Citi, Bank of America, Amex, Bank of Omaha, Chase... they can't trust the account information to verify credit card purchases. Which accounts are valid? Which are corrupted? It was perfectly engineered to paralyze the use of credit and debit cards."*

Almost unconsciously, she reached for the wallet in her back pocket. That's why Tyrell told her to get as much cash as she could. He knew.

The journalist said, *"Okay, so, this cyberattack is an inconvenience. It will hurt the economy. But once the bug is found and a patch worked out, everything will bounce back to normal in days, right? This won't be like COVID. Life will go on."*

The analyst paused in a professional manner. He looked like a professor. Thick wire-rimmed glasses. *"Oh, absolutely. I'm sure that's right. The major concern at this moment is that the crisis seems to be spreading across the globe. Cyber security people call this a "forest fire".*

"A forest fire?"

Lauren might have only finished one year of college, but she knew what a forest fire was. A cyber contagion, it could potentially infect every financial account that could be accessed via satellites through the internet. Even things like hotels, airline booking sites, and retail sites, every place that might have bank account numbers, credit card information, your birth date, your passport number, social security number...

Strangely, a red neon sign flashed in her head. She'd seen it on the internet six months ago: *Milestone: 6 billion people are now online.*

She flipped the channel to another "Breaking News" where a camera caught a mob rioting outside a bank in Tennessee. The reporter said, *"...people think their money is gone. Police were unprepared for this level of..."*

She flipped over to the business news. The anchor said, *"...a disaster the likes of which we've never seen in America."* In the background, a gas station had a big sign on the window stating: **CASH ONLY!** The clip then showed an angry man at the pump open the back of his SUV. The man withdrew a brick and threw it through the gas station window.

Talking back to the TV, Lauren said, "But the U.S. has a twenty-two-trillion-dollar economy. Even if this cyberattack cost the country five hundred billion, it's just a dent, not a death blow."

She turned down the volume, tuning out the **News Alert** of rioting in Chicago. Shaken down to her boots, she needed to just stop and think.

Cyberattacks were routine. Tyrell once had told her an unknown hacker had penetrated the Pentagon's secure network and stolen information on everything from ordinary personnel records to the location of every spy stationed around the world. Naturally, they'd all been hunted down and killed, not that most Americans knew that.

She'd heard that the Chinese military had accumulated more data on every American citizen than the American government. They'd done it by hacking government agencies from the IRS, Department of Justice, DoD, to the DHS and NSA, credit unions, mega-insurance companies, medical records, banks, Google, Amazon, Microsoft, and just about every social media platform. All for a special AI program whose very existence China refused to acknowledge.

And that didn't include the Russians, Iranians, North Koreans, Pakistan, or any of the other bad actors.

Everyone—especially our spec ops people—feared the hackers had gotten far more information than the government let on. Maybe top-secret technology or even the nuclear codes that would allow the hackers to launch U.S. missiles.

Barely audible, Lauren said, "Is that why you're on alert, Ty?"

Across the bottom of the TV screen, the latest news alert ran in silence: **Credit Crisis: Martial Law Declared in Chicago.**

She sat down hard at the kitchen table.

Still, she couldn't convince herself to leave. When she called her finance professor's number, she was shunted straight to voice mail. "Carole? It's Lauren. When you have a moment, could I talk with you? I'm hoping you can help me understand what's really going on. Thanks."

Over a supper of microwave pizza pulled from the freezer, Lauren sat glued to the TV, nervously sipping tea and trying to make sense of it all. Unbelievably, parts of Denver—just seventy miles to the north—were burning. It had started when credit cards had been refused at a grocery store in a low-income neighborhood. A curfew had been declared.

How could it get this bad this quick? Granted the country had been pulling farther apart ever since the 2020 election. And then there were the tensions sparked by COVID, the economic contraction as the SARS-CO-2 virus mutated into variants. But to see so much anger and violence over credit cards?

As if in agreement, the talking head said, *"By the time the government can finally act and open the banks, half the country is going to be on lock down. Attention is going to be on the streets, not how the government has repaired American banking and guaranteed the funds. Or how the credit card industry is once again functioning and solvent."*

Lauren considered the statistics she'd studied in Dr. Caroline Steppman's finance class. After the fudging of facts in the endless reports the government had produced—their free use of 'facts' and statistics to make the economy look strong—no one was going to believe anything the government told them.

"Call it critical mass," the analyst said. *"The attackers weren't really after the banking system. Their ultimate goal is social unrest. Scare people and see where the chaos leads. It's working."*

Lauren had chosen University of Colorado at Colorado Springs because Caroline Steppman taught there. Steppman had written the definitive text on international banking. Lauren walked over and pulled it from her neat stack of textbooks.

Shutting out the report of rioting in Philadelphia, Lauren reviewed the section on international banking and liquidity.

"There's so much of this I don't understand."

American banks were the lynchpin. That much she got. If they failed, within twenty-four hours, the South American banks would fail. After that, every bank in the Western Hemisphere would follow. They were all linked together, constantly loaning each other money to keep liquidity in the system and distribute risk among as many members and regions as possible. Steppman had an equation at the end of the chapter that would measure the impact of each closure on global stability.

"Even China—if that's who is behind this—with their supposedly isolated banking system, can't stand alone, can they?"

Feeling depressed, she walked to the cabinet and pulled down the bottle of tequila she and Tyrell saved for special toasts. Pouring a couple of shots into a glass, she walked back to the living room.

On the television, the news alert flashed: **PRESIDENT PONDERS DECLARATION OF MARTIAL LAW.**

"For God's sake, don't tell me this is 'America, may it Rest in Peace'." She raised the glass, and then took a sip. As the taste of the fine Reposado hit her tongue, she wondered if she was toasting the end of life as she knew it.

CHAPTER FOUR

***

7 AM SUNDAY

LAUREN MADE A FACE, STRETCHED UNDER HER WARM BLANKET, AND BLINKED UP AT THE ceiling as morning's first golden rays slanted past the blinds. The news hadn't gotten better throughout the day on Saturday. As report after report came in, she'd periodically glance at Tyrell's boogie bag. Several times, she'd made the decision to leave, only to wander back and change channels to a different news outlet. Depressed, she'd turned to the bottle of reposado again.

Too damned much tequila last night. She could hear birds chirping in the trees outside and traffic noises. All normal.

She sat up, pushed the blankets back and forced herself to get dressed and start the day. Maybe everything had been fixed? Maybe the world had settled down, and she didn't have to keep her promise to Ty and get the hell away from the Front Range?

Wearing the oversized T-shirt she slept in, she walked barefoot down to the bathroom. Fifteen minutes later—showered and teeth clean—she dressed in jeans, motorcycle boots, and a baggy blouse.

In the kitchen, she placed a pod in the coffee machine and punched the button, then walked over to check her cell phone on the kitchen table. She had a text message from Dr. Steppman: *I'll be out of contact for the next two weeks. Sorry.*

Lauren sighed, walked to the TV, turned it on and froze as the stunning images flashed across the screen...

Despite the exchanges being closed, the DOW was down twenty-three percent in afterhours trading. S&P and NASDAQ had similarly fallen like rocks. Memories of yesterday's news, of the president calling for calm, had a hollow ring now.

The financial analyst being interviewed by the TV anchor, said, *"If you ask me, this is an act of war. This thing was orchestrated perfectly to paralyze the use of credit cards."*

The anchor sat back in his chair. *"Okay. So? Sure, it's a pain, but once the bug is found and a patch worked out, everything will bounce back to normal in days, won't it? I mean, how long can people survive when every credit card is worthless plastic and the banks are closed so you can't get cash?"*

Lauren walked over to pull her coffee cup from the machine; her gaze moved between the screen and the olive-green bag and camping gear by the door. Of course, she was leaving. She kept telling herself that. She was packed. Ready to go.

But she still couldn't convince her feet to do it. This was her home. She had plans. She was going to finish college, marry Tyrell, and get a job she loved in international finance. She was going to find her place in the world. How could she give up that dream and head for the backcountry? Or worse…the Tappan ranch in Wyoming?

Yeah, hi! Sure, I killed Jim. Broke Breeze's heart. You wouldn't mind if I just moved in, waited here for my fiancé, would you?

She wandered around the apartment. Kept surfing the different channels. It was like an obsession. She had to hear all sides, not just the partisan garbage.

Her laptop on the kitchen table showed the local anchor talking to a Colorado senator. The anchor said, *"Oh, come on! This can't be happening in America. Don't we have the best cyber security in the world? How could our banking system be so vulnerable?"*

The senator across the table from him, replied, *"Look, this is the fault of the president. Don't you remember all that garbage she spewed during the campaign about how vulnerable our banking system was? Her own words directly resulted in a deterioration of public confidence in the banks. She—"*

"What are you talking about?" the anchor exploded. *"We were attacked! This is an act of war!"*

The senator lifted a finger to get the anchor's attention. *"Try to listen. The attackers want people to believe that their money is gone. They played on the president's fear-mongering, and there she sits in the Oval Office, looking like a duck hit in the head by a thrown rock. Meanwhile, people tear each other apart. The violence is cascading as we speak, and she's doing nothing about it!"*

Lauren thought about the mob that had instantly formed at the Springs Bank and carried her coffee to the kitchen table to look at the local Colorado Springs channels. KKTV was making a point of showing the bright side, how the downtown merchants were offering "Cash Only Days" discounts and sidewalk sales. How the 'temporary disruption' had led to an increase in visitation to local parks, which, after all, didn't require either cash or credit cards. A cheery young reporter narrated each story, smiling, tone of voice upbeat.

Lauren switched to social media. It was telling a very different story: Video after video posted to Facebook, Twitter, YouTube, showed people crowded around supermarkets guarded by police, or shop owners with rifles standing before their stores. And the other stores—not so lucky—with streams of people erupting from their smashed windows, carrying TVs, cases of liquor, or pushing shopping carts piled to the top with groceries, as fights broke out in the parking lots.

"Couldn't get police protection. Lost it all," one store owner in South Boston had written over the posted photo of his looted and burning grocery.

The Denver TV stations showed fires burning downtown. Police lines and rioters appeared to have reached a stalemate. Shots of ambulances with flashing lights arriving at crowded emergency rooms looked worse than at the height of COVID; they were intercut with an angry crowd outside of a King Sooper's store in Lakewood being held back by a deputy sheriff with a riot shotgun cradled across his chest.

Another clip—backed by the mayors of Denver, Aurora, and Lakewood—kept calling for calm, insisting, "People, I have been assured that the banks will be open Tuesday morning. For the time being, 'Shelter in Place.' Stay in your houses. This is only a temporary inconvenience."

Airlines were no longer booking flights. Amazon had taken its entire site down with a disclaimer stating it would be back just as soon as credit card service was restored.

A UK story titled "Get it While You Can! Why the US Govt Won't Fix It!" had gone viral. According to the story, the meltdown was a sinister US government plot to justify bankruptcy, so it could wipe out its staggering national debt. The post showed a man with an AR15 over his shoulder pushing a grocery cart away and the caption, "I got mine. You gonna get yours?"

The Fox affiliate in Fort Collins showed clips of cars stalled and out of gas because the drivers hadn't been carrying enough cash to fill up on their way home.

A film crew from Boulder had footage of a vehicle at an intersection on Pearl Street that had the windows smashed in, the interior set on fire by youths angry that it had blocked their way.

Lauren chewed her lips, tossed down the last of her coffee, and thought, "Yeah, Tyrell. I promised you."

She swung around when there was a knock at her door. "Lauren?" Randy Howman called. "You in there?"

Surprised, she trotted to the door and pulled it open.

Randy Howman stood nervously on the other side with his blond hair shining in the sunlight. His pale complexion had taken on a rose-pink hue. Down in the parking lot, next to Tyrell's KTM, she could see his Kawasaki motorcycle leaned on its kickstand.

"Hey, Lauren."

"What's up?"

Nervously, he licked his lips. "Can I come in?"

"Sure. 'Course."

"You all right?" Randy asked as he stepped inside. "Everything okay?"

She gave him a curious look. "You've never come to my apartment before. What's wrong?"

"I just…" Randy made an airy gesture with his hand. "I wanted to tell you that you don't have to come in on Tuesday morning. Neither do I. Just needed to let you know."

"How long will the bank be closed?"

"Guess the Feds are going to monitor the situation. Try to figure out how the hackers got into our secure systems. Word is this virus, it's worse than we thought."

"Got it. Right. So, you're riding your bike around to every employee's house to tell them this?"

Randy glanced at Tyrell's boogie bag, her sleeping bag and tent, the backpack, all sitting beside the door. "What else did Lieutenant Ramirez tell you?"

"What do you mean?"

He gestured to the boogie bag. "He told you to go to Wyoming. This is worse than we think, isn't it?"

Now she understood why he was standing at her door. "Why would you think that?"

"Well, for one thing, I heard a news report that said the computer virus is mutating as it sweeps around the world. Some kind of AI that's rewriting itself."

She shifted her weight to her other foot. "Rewriting itself? How can a computer virus do that?"

"Apparently, it has the ability to adapt. Like, it's monitored by some AI program somewhere. When it breaks into a new system, the AI learns better how to defeat the next one, and so on. There's lot of speculation, but nobody knows where it came from or how to stop it."

"Someone will figure it out. We're Americans. We have the best cyber people on earth."

"Do we?" Randy's eyes narrowed as he looked out the door where Cheyenne Mountain rose in the distance. "Then why did Ramirez tell you to get the hell away from the Front Range?"

Stunned, she asked, "How do you know he told me that?"

"You were standing right in front of the security camera. Sounded pretty bad. Ramirez told you to go to Wyoming."

"Yes, he did, but—"

"What's happening, Lauren? Please tell me."

"I don't know, okay?" she cried, venting her frustration. "Just what Ty said."

He hesitated a second, as though afraid to ask. "You heard from him since?"

Lauren took a deep breath. Through the open door, morning cloud shadows could be seen as they crawled across Cheyenne Mountain.

"No. Not a word." She narrowed a suspicious eye. "Randy, what do you want?"

"Not long after you left, things started getting ugly outside the bank. Cars roared into the parking lot. Patrons pounded on the locked doors. Broke out the glass."

"Did you call the police?"

"Blassen did. They told him they had their hands full and couldn't get to the Springs Bank for hours. If then. Then they ordered him to get everyone out of the building ASAP." Randy ran a hand through his hair and shook his head. "Blassen told me not to come back until he called me. So, I guess we're all out of work for a while."

"Sorry to hear that."

"It's worse. Actually." He shrugged awkwardly, his face burning crimson. "Remember when Enrique said we only had fifteen percent cash reserve? That we'd cover it with bonds? We took a beating. I mean, we got less than fifty percent mark to market. We're not even close to covering our mandated reserves."

"That bad?"

"I was on the phone with a colleague in the Caymans. With the bond market in free fall, tens of thousands of bonds went through several different accounts...most of which were finally bought by the Chinese and Russia at less than twenty cents on the dollar."

"Holy shit," Lauren whispered in shock.

"Yeah," Randy told her. "Looks like we're just at the beginning of what's going to be a really ugly future."

"What can Blassen do?"

Randy gave that inoffensive shrug again. "Springs is gone. Once the regulators turn their noses our direction, Bill and the board of directors will have to sell assets. FDIC will cover the deposits up to $250,000. Someone else will pick up the accounts." He winced. "I think."

Lauren tried to reason it through. "The Fed shot all of its arrows with easy money starting in 2009 and accelerating the easing because of COVID. The country's over twenty-five trillion in debt. The only way they can raise money..." Something clicked. "Just a minute."

She walked over to the dining room table, pulled up Safari and typed in Banco Santandar de Brazil. She pushed enter, and waited, choosing the most pertinent search return.

Randy was staring over her shoulder as the Fox Business News headline came up: "Banco Santandar de Brazil, in a rare Saturday move, proclaimed that they would be closed indefinitely."

"We're screwed," she whispered, going back, typing in Banco Santandar de Chile. Essentially, the headline was the same, along with the news that long lines of people were forming outside the bank doors throughout South America and Mexico, demanding that they open, Saturday or not.

"Dominoes are falling." Lauren's knees went weak.

"What are you going to do?" Randy was still staring at the screen.

When Lauren laughed, it sounded as hollow and mocking as she felt inside. "Try to go back to the one place I never wanted to go again."

"Where's that?"

"Wyoming. Bad things happened there. But I guess if anywhere qualified as home, it would be Wyoming. In all the bouncing around, being a military brat, I lived there the longest."

"That's right. Your father's a general in the air force. You talked to him?"

She shook her head. "No."

To change the subject, she said, "Even if the government can reopen the big six banks on Tuesday, it'll be too late. Europe will be going down by then. The fever will be catching all over the world."

Lauren stepped over to the door and looked down at the parking lot. His shiny Kawasaki was only a couple of months old. He barely knew how to ride it, but its square saddlebags were piled high with a pack, sleeping bag, and tent.

"I'm going to ride home and spend time with my family in Seattle,"Randy said. "Can I ride with you as far as Wyoming?"

"'Course."

"Are you gassed up?"

"That's the first thing I did, right after I emptied out my bank account."

"All right, then, let's go."

"This instant?"

Randy frowned at her. "If we're lucky, we'll hit Denver at around 9 AM and miss the worst morning traffic. That way, we can blast straight up I-25 into Wyoming and be there by noon. I'll buy you lunch at Little America."

Lauren lifted her heavy yellow tour jacket from where it lay across the boogie bag and shrugged into it.

"I guess I'm ready. I…" She looked around their apartment again, seeing Tyrell everywhere. *Get out of Colorado. You hear me?* "Yeah, hell, let's go. If it's not as bad as they say, it's only a day's ride to get back."

Randy gave her a toothy smile. "Once we're in Cheyenne, maybe we can relax a little. Don't know what it was like on this side of town, but things got pretty crazy around my house last night. Guns going off. Looting."

Lauren lifted the heavy boogie bag and slipped the strap over her shoulder, then reached for her small backpack. Her sleeping bag and tent were already strapped to it.

Following him out, Lauren locked the door and headed for the stairs. Didn't bother to look back.

It wasn't the first time she'd left an entire life behind.

CHAPTER FIVE

* * *

IN THE SLANTING MORNING SUNLIGHT, LAUREN PULLED THE COVER OFF TYRELL'S KTM Adventure. The saddlebags were already packed with camping gear they'd expected to use in Moab: stove, propane, ground tarp, tire-repair kit, Tyrell's rain gear, tool kit, 12 volt air compressor, and other stuff.

Lauren stretched the bungee cords around Tyrell's big army-green pack as she secured it to the luggage rack. The taut cords barely sank into the tightly packed material. The backpack with tent and sleeping bag went on the passenger seat.

"You look like you've done that all of your life," Jennifer Markman—one of the neighbors—said, as she trotted down the stairs with one hand up to shade her eyes.

Lauren took a deep breath and squinted up at the looming bulk of Cheyenne Mountain where it rose to the west. The steep slopes— studded with trees—had a rugged and resolute look as the first shadows deepened in the valleys and beneath outcrops. In the distance she could hear the sound of sirens. And then a far-off pop. Gunshot? Really? On Sunday morning?

"The general, my dad, taught me military survival skills. He started me on horses. Once you've got packing an elk with a diamond hitch down to a science, everything else is a piece of cake."

Jennifer stepped closer, glanced at Randy, who'd just thrown a leg over his motorcycle, and her brown eyes turned serious. "Both of you work at the bank, right? Are you leaving town?"

Lauren tried to smile. "For a few days."

"Seriously? I just saw the news. The futures market is crashed. South America's banks are gone. What are the chances that the government is going to pull a rabbit of its hat, and that after Tuesday morning it's all going to be put back the way it was?"

Lamely, she responded, "I'm worried too, but I'm sure the government will figure this out."

"Tyrell know about this?"

"Yes, Jennifer." Not that it was any of her business. "He told me to go."

"But, Lauren, Fort Carson is here and Peterson Air Base, not to mention Cheyenne Mountain. The military isn't going to let things get out of control in the Springs. But out on the road? Anything could happen. It'll be like the law of the jungle."

"It's one-hundred-and-seventy miles to the Wyoming border. Call it three hours if traffic is bad. After that, once we're past Cheyenne, it's a straight shot. Another five hours—including pee stops—and I'm safe on a friend's ranch. I have enough cash to get there." She lifted a suggestive eyebrow. "You and Thorn could come."

"Oh, sure. Me and Thorn. On a ranch. That's rich."

"Toss out the perishables in your refrigerator, throw a couple of suitcases into the trunk of your fancy Jaguar, and call it a vacation."

"Leave? Just like that?" She snapped her fingers.

"Why not?"

"Lauren, I'm a city girl. I design websites and Thorn...well, Thorn can't boil water." Jennifer reached out and hugged Lauren. "Besides, I'm not as brave as you."

At the sound of Randy's thumping big single, Lauren looked over at his green-and-white KLR. He was clearly getting impatient to be on the road.

"Besides," Lauren said, "it's not like I'm going alone."

Jennifer asked skeptically, "How's Tyrell going to like that? You... and Randy?"

"It's not like that. I said I'd get him across the border. After that, he's headed on to Seattle."

She gave Jennifer another quick hug, zipped her touring jacket all the way up and rolled her helmet over her head. She was pulling on her gloves as Randy accelerated for the road and came within a rat's whisker of dropping the bike.

"Good luck!" Jennifer waved as Lauren punched the starter and the KTM purred to life.

Lauren motored over to where Randy had just stalled the Kawasaki at the stop sign. He over-revved the engine as he eased out the clutch and stalled it again.

It would be a miracle if the guy didn't kill himself before he got out of the Springs, let alone to Seattle.

She put that from her mind. He'd either make it or he wouldn't.

CHAPTER SIX

***

AS LAUREN AND RANDY NEARED CASTLE ROCK ON INTERSTATE 25 THE TRAFFIC SLOWED TO a creep, then stopped dead. People were opening doors, standing on the sills to see what lay ahead. Not that there was much to see but the square backs of stalled semi-trailers.

Lauren led the way as she and Randy maneuvered their motorcycles around the stalled vehicles that blocked the lanes, but it was stop-and-go, and agonizingly slow work. Sometimes they had to ease between bumpers to find an opening.

She and Randy definitely were not going to make Cheyenne by noon. He was having real trouble with his bike. He'd dropped it twice; the only damage consisted of scratched body work and a bent front brake lever. Each time, however, she'd had to stop and help him repack his load. The miracle was that he'd survived the first upset without losing anything, and he always looked so grateful when she took over and showed him how to balance the load and tie it securely to the bike.

When a man opened his door ahead of her and stepped out of his car, Lauren clamped on the brakes and stopped just in time to avoid hitting him.

The man, in his fifties, yelled. "Hey, I'll give you five hundred bucks for your bike."

"Not for sale," she shouted back.

He left his door open, blocking her path, and walked back to her. "How about seven-fifty. That's all I got."

Randy pulled up and stopped to her left, gave the man a hard look, and said, "What's the problem?"

"No problem," the man said. "Will you take seven-fifty for your bike?"

Randy shook his head. "Are you nuts? It's a brand new KLR. I paid more than seven grand for it."

"I need to get out of here!" the frustrated man half-yelled. "I've been sitting here at a dead stop for three hours! I'm trying to get to my family in Greeley."

"So you tried to get out of Colorado Springs early this—"

"Colorado, hell," he said. "I drove up from Albuquerque last night. It's mayhem down there. I filled my tank and took off, everything was fine until I hit this mess!" He flung an arm out at the traffic snarl. "The only way to get through this is on a bike. I'll give you a thousand bucks for that motorcycle."

"No." Lauren shook her head. "Let's go around him, Randy."

She put both feet down and started backing up. Randy followed her lead, backpedaling his KLR.

"Hey! I'll give you two thousand!" he shouted at them as they veered wide and sped away.

Lauren swerved onto the right shoulder and started passing cars.

She finally understood why Tyrell had told her to leave her ancient Toyota Camry behind. The section of I-25 from Monument to just north of Larkspur, Colorado, was a solid block of stalled traffic. Made sense. People couldn't get cash. Credit cards were declined. People had driven as far as their tanks of fuel would take them, and just rolled to a stop. Sitting on empty fuel tanks, they didn't have a chance of moving forward, which meant that 18-wheelers couldn't get around them. And once the big rigs stopped moving, so did everything else.

A few people stood outside their vehicles, arms propped on their hoods, waiting for rescue. Voices sounded angry. Curses laced the air.

Lauren flinched when a Dodge pickup truck roared up alongside her, dove off the shoulder, and plunged down through the highway ditch, then climbed up the other side and blasted through the fence that separated the highway from the frontage road. After that it was like a flood. Four-wheel drive vehicles bounced through the ditch and up the other side in pursuit of the big Dodge.

Lauren waved to Randy, then pointed to the hole in the fence, rode off the shoulder, and followed everybody else. When she hit the black top of the frontage road, she accelerated to sixty and glanced at the stalled traffic on the highway. Angry people shook fists in her direction.

Trucks and SUVs flew past her doing eighty, apparently in a hurry.

A few miles to the north, she discovered why. The drivers must have been on their cell phones, or listening to traffic reports, and were trying to get ahead of this.

Lauren and Randy, however, were completely unprepared for the people climbing over the highway fence and blocking the frontage road.

When she slowed down, Randy rode up beside her, lifted his helmet visor and shouted, "This is a mob, Lauren. What do you want to do?"

Stunned, she watched a woman hurl her empty gas can at the windshield of a passing SUV, and scream, "I just want a ride to the nearest gas station. Goddamn you, I got thirsty kids in my car!"

When a pickup slammed on its brakes to avoid running over the woman, the truck was mobbed. Fists flying, people scrambled into the bed of the truck.

One man yelled at the driver, "I'm not getting out until you take me to a gas station!"

Lauren extended an arm to the rutted dirt road that cut across the grassy meadow to her right, and pointed.

She and Randy wobbled their way through the uneven grass, onto the dirt road, heading east. Hit a county road and took it north.

Pines dotted the rolling hills. This was urban sprawl. Expensive houses on ten and twenty-acre tracts. While she sucked in a deep breath, she watched a flock of cawing ravens sail through the sky above her.

At a crossroads, two pickups were pulled up. Men with hunting rifles stood beside them. When Lauren rolled to a stop, one, dressed in faded jeans, work boots, and duck-hunter's vest, walked forward, pointing. "Go back to the interstate. This area is closed to travel."

The guy didn't look the least bit chatty, so Lauren jerked a nod, and took the left, headed back west. She braked to a stop as they hit I-25 again. The north-bound lane here was open. Only dotted by occasional stalled vehicles. South-bound, headed back to Colorado Springs, was wide open. An SUV was even headed south on the left lane.

Randy pulled up beside her, killed his bike, and lifted his visor.

"Don't think we're making Cheyenne tonight, Randy. Maybe tomorrow. If we're lucky."

His blue eyes looked tormented. Like he couldn't bear to be out here in the wilds of Colorado, when they were supposed to be headed to a restaurant and hot food in Wyoming.

"So, what do we do?" He expelled a breath and squinted out across the plains. Wildflowers spread across the hills in a variegated yellow and purple blanket.

The road back south to Colorado Springs was open. She could head back. Looking north, in the distance, she thought it looked like another snarl. Didn't look like the eighteen-wheelers were moving. But she couldn't be sure.

Reluctantly, she nodded to him, took the on ramp, and headed north. As she sped up, wind whipped loose strands of auburn hair around inside her visor. The Rockies stood like warning sentinels in the distance.

Did I just make the worst mistake of my life?

CHAPTER SEVEN

* * *

9 PM

AS DUSK FELL, SHE WAS IN FIRST GEAR, THREADING BETWEEN THE STOPPED CARS ON I-25, when two men trotted out into the narrow apron between the Jersey barrier and the side of the semi-trailer. The first guy waved a jack handle. The other carried a two-foot-long length of steel pipe.

"This can't be happening," she whispered to herself. The thirty-eight caliber revolver tucked inside the pocket of her coat suddenly felt warm and heavy.

The big guy with the pipe ran out in front of her and shouted, "Get off the fucking bikes. Right now!" As he said it, he smacked the pipe into his left hand. "You may have helmets on, but I'll still beat your brains out! Off the bikes!"

"I heard you!" Lauren shouted back over the soft thumping of her exhaust. Slipping the gearbox into neutral, she put her feet down and coasted to a stop. With her left hand, she unzipped her coat. She'd always considered herself to be pretty tough. After all, she'd been raised by a man who insisted she be competent at every survival skill in the military book.

But this was different. The fear tickle was loose in her guts.

When Randy came to a stop beside her, he threw up his hands. "What the hell is going on?"

"We want those bikes!" the big guy shouted. "Right now!"

"Get out of our way!" Randy shouted back.

The man with the jack handle stomped up to Randy, and yelled, "You heard him! Off the bikes, or I'm going to break every fucking bone in your body, asshole!"

Lauren used the distraction, pulled Tyrell's revolver from her pocket. Leveled at the man with the pipe. "Move out of our way!"

Illuminated by Randy's headlight, people could see her clearly. Yells rose, followed by blaring horns.

"Get back!" the man with the pipe yelled. "She's got a gun!"

"Way back! Other side of those cars in the middle lane. Move it!" She could hear the terror in her own shaking voice.

The men scrambled over the concrete barrier and vanished behind the line of cars stopped on the far side of the highway.

"Randy!" she called as she shoved the revolver back in her pocket. "We're taking back roads from now on!"

Putting the bike in gear, she accelerated down the narrow highway apron. Headlight wavering in her mirrors, Randy got started, and pulled out after her.

Adrenaline was burning through her muscles like a drug.

Then she got the shakes.

CHAPTER EIGHT

* * *

LAUREN TURNED OFF THE ROAD INTO A MOUNTAIN CAMPGROUND IN THE PIKE NATIONAL Forest and headed for the space with the huge blue spruce tree. Behind her, Randy's headlight followed. The tang of conifers perfumed the cool night air. Pulling up next to the picnic table, she killed her engine and used her heel to lower the side stand. Randy's headlight, coming slowly flicked back and forth as he wobbled along the dirt trail to the camp spot and killed his engine.

"Breathe," she told herself as she gazed up at the stars sprinkling the sky overhead. "Just breathe."

Unstrapping her helmet, she removed it and hung it on the mirror, but for several moments, she just sat there, so emotionally drained she felt numb. Turned out that Lauren Davis wasn't nearly as tough as she thought. She could face a grizzly bear in the wild, but facing men intent on hurting her was another thing entirely. Her entire sense of identity had been shattered in one awful night. She wondered how long it would take to piece herself back together.

The forest was filled with the sounds of wind through the trees and crickets singing in the grass.

She finally got off the bike. On unsteady legs she walked over to sit on top of the picnic table.

Everything felt surreal. She and Tyrell had camped up here. God, she wished Tyrell was with her. She had never missed him as much as she did now.

The campground was in a secluded location despite being just south of Denver. To her surprise, only a few of the camp sites were occupied.

Tonight, however, the place had a strange dreamlike shimmer from the adrenaline pumping through her veins.

"Where are you, Ty?" she whispered. "Flying over some godforsaken place?"

Randy kept fumbling for the Kawasaki's side stand. Got it down and leaned the bike, asking, "You all right?"

"Dead tired, Randy."

"Me, too. Glad you stopped."

Stepping off his bike, Randy walked with mincing steps, as if unsure that his legs would support him. Sighing relief, he propped his butt on the tabletop beside her. He didn't take his helmet off, just sat there staring off into the distance, as though disoriented and trying to find his bearings. When he finally unbuckled the strap and removed his helmet, he set it on the table between them with a thump. Ran a hand through his blond hair. For once the cowlick was plastered flat.

"What are we doing, Lauren? We've been riding for fourteen hours straight and are less than fifty miles from Colorado Springs. I thought we'd be five hundred to the north by now." He swallowed hard. "If you hadn't had that gun in your pocket... That last bunch. They would have killed us. It's a nightmare I can't get out of my head."

Reminded, she unzipped and reached into her pocket. Pulling out the .38, she opened the cylinder, ejected the empty brass. Fishing around, she found a loose cartridge and reloaded the empty chamber. Snapping the cylinder closed, she slipped the Smith & Wesson back into her pocket.

Randy watched with morbid fascination.

I shot at another human being. The thought—kept at bay since leaving I-25—kept rolling around in her head. It had been too close. They'd had to find another way north, and she'd taken the first exit.

Randy rubbed his face. "God, I can't believe it. I keep reliving the guy with the knife...and that last guy who tried to grab your elbow as you rode by. When his friend aimed that rifle at my belly, I thought it was over."

"That was a close one, all right." Lauren couldn't stop the shiver that ran through her. They'd been winding through that last knot of stopped and stalled traffic. It seemed like a fucking nightmare. Like it couldn't have been real.

Randy's voice sounded small, "When you fired that shot at his feet, you saved my life."

The scent of the creek carried to her, sweet and pure. In the back of her head, she could hear Tyrell say, *That was really stupid. Never use a firearm to try to scare someone away. Aim to kill. Otherwise, you give your assailant time to kill you first.*

Not that the guy would forget; he'd be picking slivers of lead and fragments of bullet jacket out of his feet and ankles for days.

"Maybe." She shivered harder this time. "I don't know if he would have actually shot you."

"That's because you weren't looking him in the eyes. Believe me, he was going to kill me. You saved the bikes. Maybe my life."

"Under other circumstances, I'd have just said, 'Okay, take the bikes, just don't hurt us.' I mean, it wouldn't have been worth the hassle of shooting someone. Instead, you just fill out the police reports, file the insurance, and it's a few days' irritation. Shoot someone over a motorcycle? That's another thing. I'd be arrested, there'd be lawyers, a pile of worry, and maybe in the end, because it was a robbery, I wouldn't get charged. But the guy I shot, he could file a civil suit. I might be morally right, but that's not enough. Not in the world we used to live in anyway."

"Used to?" Worry etched his face.

"You think the police are going to go looking for a couple of thieves who stole our bikes? They have bigger priorities right now."

"True. Not only that, Lauren, what would have happened to us? We would have been left on foot on the highway. The cash in our pockets would have been gone in a heartbeat. Either to pay for a ride, or food, and water, or beaten out of us by some desperate person."

Lauren took a deep breath and held it for a second. What would she have done if the thieves had killed Randy and turned the rifle on her? She had no idea what she was capable of in such a situation. Or...more importantly...what she was *not* capable of. Tyrell had once told her that no one knew who they truly were until they were staring death in the face and there was no way out. You had to choose: you or them.

Randy pulled his phone from a pocket, checked it. "No service here. Weird. You'd think this close to Denver we'd at least get a bar or two."

She checked her iPhone, found no service, then shut it down to save the battery. "At least we're still okay. And we have our bikes. We'll get to Wyoming tomorrow."

"Really?" He let out a deep breath. "I can't believe how bad this is. It's only been two days since the cyberattack, and the country is worse than it was in the midst of the banking crisis of 1933."

Lauren turned to stare into his starlit eyes. "I haven't had that class yet."

Without a word, Randy walked to his bike, unzipped the tank bag and pulled out two cans of Coke. As he walked back, he handed one to her.

"Thanks," she told him. God, her stomach was like an empty hole. She really needed to eat.

Randy braced his feet, opened his can and took a long drink, as though he needed a sugar fix before he could tell her. "It was the middle of the Great Depression. By 1933, over nine thousand banks had collapsed. In February of that year, Americans, frightened that their bank would be next, panicked. There was a run on the banks. People emptied out their accounts."

"Like what happened at our bank."

He nodded. "But in 1933, it caused a chain reaction that spread like wildfire. More banks failed because they didn't have the cash they needed for daily operations. And with less money in circulation, prices soared."

"Inflation?"

"Right. People couldn't buy as much, so they didn't. When people stopped buying, factories and farms cut back production. Stores reduced their work forces. Millions were thrown out of work."

Photos of the Great Depression flitted behind Lauren's eyes. She'd seen them in a textbook: hungry people standing in food lines; overloaded cars, some with cages of chickens strapped on top, packing the highways, headed to California, where desperate people hoped to find work. The label beneath the pictures in the book was: *The Great American Exodus.*

"All of it was caused by people pulling their money out of banks?" she asked.

Randy walked over and perched on the table again. "Most of it. When Franklin Delano Roosevelt walked into the Oval Office on inauguration day in March of 1933, he completely shut down the banking system, suspending all transactions. He'd proclaimed it a 'bank holiday', but everyone knew what it really was: a desperate act to save the country."

Lauren studied his shadowed face, then looked out at the pines swaying in the night breeze. "President Brown pretty much did the same thing."

"Correct. Thank goodness she did it immediately. Maybe the government actually learned the lessons of 1933."

Lauren popped the top on her Coke. "Will it work?"

"I..." he shook his head, "I don't know. It's a different world today. Money isn't just paper. It's digital numbers on a computer screen. If you can't trust the numbers, how do you maintain a stable financial system? Even if we print money to keep cash in circulation—like Roosevelt did in 1933—we still have the same problem. Until we figure out the virus, or whatever it is, and stop it, we can't trust the numbers."

In the darkness, he was a mere silhouette against the background of conifers and empty picnic tables. Lauren took a drink from her can. It tasted sweet and delicious.

Randy said, "Frankly, after what we've been through, I've never been so damned scared in all my life. How 'bout you?"

She gripped her can with both hands. The wind had changed direction, and she could hear the creek thirty paces away. It was a soft gurgling that she found soothing.

"Can't we just go back to doing it the old way? Paper money and written records of deposits and withdrawals?"

"How do you run a massive global financial system on paper records, Lauren? I don't think it's possible."

The vast implications of what he'd just told her seemed beyond her exhausted mind. She needed time to process all this. "Hey, I'm hungry. Let's eat. There are MREs in my saddle bag. Meals-Ready-to-Eat. Want chicken and rice?"

Randy laughed softly. "Sure. Thanks. God, I'm so hungry I'd eat skunk and boiled okra."

CHAPTER NINE

***

MORNING CAME TOO FAST. LAUREN BLINKED AWAKE IN THE EARLY PREDAWN, LISTENING
to the birds singing in the trees. The smell of green grass mixed with
the tang of pines. Where...oh, right. They'd stopped for the night at a
campground in the Pike National Forest. Up in the mountains.

She rubbed her eyes. She'd slept with her revolver clutched in her
fist, ready to defend them, which meant every tiny sound had awakened
her. To make matters worse, Randy snored.

Turning, she saw the bikes standing side-by-side on their kickstands.
A faint breeze conjured rustling from the aspen leaves along the creek.
They were safe. Everything was all right.

She unzipped her sleeping bag, rose, and walked over to unstrap
her backpack from the KTM. As she carried it to the campfire ring,
she scanned the forest, unconsciously searching for hidden threats.

She powered up her iPhone, still no service. Which was weird. She
remembered that she'd checked her email the time she and Tyrell had
camped here.

The bottom of the fire ring was filled with chunks of old charcoal,
and a small pile of branches lay to the right. Standard camping
procedure in the West. If you had time, you always left wood for the
next person. Methodically, she pulled kindling from the pile, then
steepled wood around it. From a saddlebag on the KTM, she retrieved
a can of lighter fluid. Then she reached into her coat pocket for the
matches she kept handy. At a touch, flames began to lick through the
tinder. Felt good. It was a chilly June morning at this elevation. She
could see her breath frosting the air.

While she dug around in the saddlebag for the collapsible coffee
pot, she glanced at the tufts of fog drifting over the creek ten yards

away. Sun wasn't up yet, but the mist had a lavender pre-dawn hue.

Lauren pulled out the coffee pot, then dug deeper for the water bottle and bag of coffee. After she'd poured water into the pot, she filled the basket with coffee, and set it at the edge of the flames to heat.

Tyrell? It's supposed to be you and me drinking this somewhere in the canyon country outside of Moab.

An emptiness sucked at the bottom of her heart. She glanced up at the lavender pre-dawn. How had their world gone so wrong so fast?

"Randy?" she called. "Sorry to wake you, but we've got a hard day ahead of us. We're not taking any main roads today."

Randy groaned, made a face. Then, with a start, sat up. "I don't think I slept at all last night."

"Then you play-acted with all that snoring."

"Oh. Sorry about that. I snore when I'm having nightmares."

Trying to make a joke, she said, "Nightmares? Really? After our lovely ride yesterday?"

He crawled stiffly out of his bag and used his fingers to comb his tangled hair. First thing, he, too, checked his phone, mumbled, and stuffed it back in a pocket.

Lauren pulled another branch from the wood pile and gently placed it on the fire. Sparks whirled upward. "Well, I think the Front Range is too dangerous. A smarter route would take us west through the mountains."

Randy said, "My God, I feel sorry for those poor people sitting in their cars waiting for rescue. They make perfect targets. They've got cash in their pockets, jewelry. Some of them still have fuel in their tanks. It's a candy store for monsters."

As the fire crackled and the blaze grew, Lauren shifted the coffee pot, pushing it deeper into the flames. "That's why they want our bikes. The bad guys can go anywhere and take anything they want."

Randy hesitated a beat. "Maybe we should use our cash to get hotel rooms and hideout until things settle down?"

Lauren didn't answer right away. Instead, she walked over to stuff her sleeping bag into its sack, then carried it to the KTM.

Randy patiently watched her standing before her bike. After a time, he asked, "Did you hear me?"

"You're not the only one who has thought of that, you know?"

He frowned. "I don't get your drift?"

As she stretched her bungee cord over her bag and hooked it beneath the luggage rack, she said, "By now, lots people have decided to abandon their cars and walk to the nearest town. I'm sure there are no available hotel rooms along the major roads."

Randy gave her an odd look. "What about small hotels along the back roads?"

She tried to think like Tyrell. What would he tell her to do?

"You're welcome to go find a hotel, if you want to. I'm not doing it. Once the highways are stripped, the bad guys are headed straight for the lesser-used roads. They'll kick down the doors of any house or hotel in their path and take what they want."

Randy hung his head and seemed to be glaring at the old pine needles that littered the ground around the fire. "But it'll take a while for the bad guys to get there, Lauren. Maybe we'd be all right for a few days."

Strange how Tyrell's stories of faraway places echoed in her mind. She could hear him say, '...the flood of fleeing civilians was like a tidal wave, and the warlords were right behind them...'

Where had that been? Afghanistan? Sudan?

Inhaling a deep breath of cold air, Lauren said, "I'm walking down to the restroom. I want you to stay here and guard the bikes. Soon as I'm done, you can take your turn. Then we're rolling out of here."

Randy looked shocked by her tone. He saluted her. "Yes, ma'am."

That made her stop and stare at him. She'd unconsciously used Tyrell's tone of voice. Cold-edged and hard. Giving orders. Tyrell's shut-the-fuck-up-and-do-as-I-say tone.

"Sorry. Didn't mean it to sound that way."

As Randy lowered his hand, he smiled, a little embarrassed. "It's okay. We're both strung out."

She nodded and strode for the restroom.

Think, Lauren. What's the smart play here?

For the time being, people in Denver, Longmont, Loveland, and Fort Collins—all eight to ten million of them—would do as they were told. They'd been trained by the pandemic. Shelter in place. Wait for the government to fix the problem.

What she and Randy had experienced on I-25 was only the first domino falling in the collapse. People trying to get home who'd become trapped. In the sprawling urban areas, people still had lights, water, food, and locked doors to live behind in their mostly safe neighborhoods.

But eventually, they'd realize help wasn't coming. That this was more than supply-line disruptions; the distribution networks had broken. All those semis she and Randy had passed, weren't going to be delivering goods. When that happened, people in Colorado would look to the mountains. Figure they could find food and shelter, hunt a deer, drink water from the creeks. That was Colorado. How they thought here.

But when they started coming, the folks who lived in the mountain communities would react. Pull out their guns. Shut down the roads.

We've got to make it through before that happens, Lauren told herself.

When she got back, Randy took his turn. Out of habit, she checked tire pressures, made sure the oil was full, and jiggled the Kaytoom's chain to check the slack. Kaytoom. That's what Tyrell called the bike. The coffee had started to perk and smelled really good.

"I checked my cell phone," Randy announced as he plodded back in his heavy motorcycle boots. "There's no service. You think it's just up here in the mountains? Or have the Feds shut down cellular and satellite services to prevent more cyberattacks?"

"I didn't think of it until now, but… They must have. It's standard operating procedure in case of major cyber breach. The internet becomes the enemy."

"How do you know that?"

She gave him a don't-be-stupid look.

"Oh," he said. "Right. Ramirez is Delta Force. He's probably been briefed on every possible national security scenario."

Randy walked to his sleeping bag and started stuffing it into its sack. Suddenly, he squinted at the morning sky. "Lauren… Have you seen any planes in the air? We're not that far from Denver International Airport. There should be contrails and planes crisscrossing the sky everywhere."

"Randy, planes use commercial satellites to navigate. I'm sure they're all grounded."

He whirled around to look toward Denver. As the dawn had brightened, a smoke pall was now visible where it rose into the heavens up north.

"I was…remembering…" He let the sentence dangle and squinted as though the rest was unthinkable.

"Remembering what?"

"Do you recall a few years ago when that security researcher found the codes for thousands of airplanes publicly accessible online and downloaded everything he could?"

A cold wave ran through her. "2019, yeah, I do. His name was Santamarta. He said that, for a hacker, the flaws in those codes could represent one step in a multistage attack. Tyrell was terrified hackers would take over the controls and use the planes like guided missiles, sending thousands crashing into targets around the world all at once."

Randy picked up his sleeping bag and rose to his feet. "I—I guess I'm drowning in worst case scenarios this morning. Didn't mean to worry you."

Behind her eyes, the grand governmental buildings of London, Paris, and Berlin, all vanished in an instant. How strange that her brain could not bear to imagine the rubble of the White House or capitol Building in Washington, DC.

Changing the subject, she said, "Right now, I'm more worried about what's happening out there in the financial world."

His expression slackened, which made his blue eyes look huge. He walked over and strapped his sleeping bag on his Kawasaki. "Me, too. By now, the rest of the world is going down. They can't stop it. They rely on American loans for daily operations, and the Feds have shut off the money. By tomorrow afternoon, there'll be rioting in the streets across Europe. If it isn't already happening."

Slowly, he walked back and knelt before the fire. Lauren poured two cups of coffee and handed him one.

"Thanks." He took it and stared down into the steaming black liquid.

"What do you think is happening in Asia?"

He took a long drink of coffee before he answered, "I suspect…"

A pair of fighter jets shot through the morning sky above them. Seconds later their building roar could be heard as they left vapor trails across the sky. Their thunder echoed across the mountains.

Randy watched them. "I guess the military is still flying."

"Thank God." The words were a prayer.

"I'm hungry," Randy announced. "More MREs?"

Lauren drank coffee while she considered their options. "Let's keep them for a reserve. We're going through Deckers, across the South Platte, and over to Bailey. Should be a convenience store open. We'll fuel up, choke down a microwave burrito, and head west to Fairplay. Pick up Colorado 9 north to Kremmling. If we make it that far, and depending upon the situation, we've got three options to cross the Wyoming border."

"Which is the safest?"

"There's nothing safe. We have to get that through our heads."

Randy laughed in a panicked way and closed his eyes for a second, as though trying to absorb the truth.

While they finished their coffee, Lauren thought about Breeze and the Tappan ranch in Wyoming. It was a beautiful place in the mountains. Suddenly, begging her best friend's forgiveness for her part in Jim's death didn't seem like such a hard thing.

But Breeze is in Denver. Her eyes went to the smoke pall where it glowed brown and ugly in the morning sunlight. It seemed to hang over the city like an evil and malignant pestilence.

Breeze? You all right up there?

She tried to second guess how Breeze would react. Last Lauren had heard, Breeze had a BMW 650.

Come on, Breeze. Be smart enough to realize how this is coming down.

Lauren prayed that Breeze was already headed north. Hell, she could have made it all the way back to the ranch by now. With that thought, Lauren emptied the dregs onto the fire and kicked dirt over it to smother the coals.

As she walked to her bike, Lauren tightened her helmet's chin strap and paused. Instead of pulling her right glove on as usual, she tucked it into the tank bag, along with her cup, and zipped the pocket closed. She had almost dropped her S&W last night, fumbling because of the heavy glove. The thick padding had jammed in the trigger guard.

From here on out, she couldn't afford to take any chances.

She started the bike, flipped the switch for the heated grips to compensate for the loss of her glove, and gave Randy a nod. After creeping through the traffic last night, he'd learned a lot about the use of his clutch, but he still bobbled as he pulled out in her wake.

Today makes us, or breaks us.

CHAPTER TEN

***

AFTER A HARROWING RIDE PAST STRANDED MOTORISTS, LAUREN ROLLED UP BEFORE THE gas pump at the Pay-N-Pak General Store in Fairplay. The sign read: **$20.00 a gallon. Cash Only!!! Pay inside.**

She used her heel to lower the kickstand and stepped off, feeling a bit of monkey-butt: that numb sting that reminded her she'd been riding on a dual-sport bike with a skinny and under-padded seat. By now, she suspected, the first wave of exodus would be starting from Denver. Despite the occasional cars and trucks they'd passed, roads had been clear enough that she'd ignored the stop in Bailey and pushed on to Fairplay.

In the vacant lot across the street, it looked like people were living in their cars. Hastily scribbled cardboard signs in the windows read: **Need Cash! Any donation helps!** and **PLEASE FEED OUR CHILDREN!**

Randy killed his engine a foot behind her and pulled his helmet off. "God, I'm cold." He pulled off his gloves, blowing on his fingers, and asking, "How'd your butt ever get to be so tough?"

"Doesn't feel very tough at the moment," she replied as she glanced at the high mountains around them. This early in June, patches of snow still stood out white against the gray granite peaks where they jutted into the clear blue mountain sky.

Randy promptly gave her a sheepish look, then pulled his phone to check for messages.

She walked up to the station door and went inside. A woman— maybe mid-forties with red hair—sat behind the counter. A big TV screen hung on the wall over her head, but it was turned off.

"Where'd you come from?" the woman asked.

"Up from Deckers."

"How's it look?" she asked.

"Road's still open. More than I can say about I-25 between Colorado Springs and Denver."

"Headed far?"

"Trying to get to Wyoming."

"You got a ways to go, then. Need to fuel up?"

"Both bikes. Shouldn't take more than four gallons."

Lauren handed her a hundred dollar bill, which the woman held up to the light.

"You'll get your change if there's extra."

"Thanks."

While Randy hit the Men's room, Lauren walked back outside, topped off their tanks, and went back to buy two microwave burritos. As she carried them to the counter, Lauren studied the almost empty store shelves, and thought about the TV being off. National TV used satellites to beam their broadcasts around the country and world. So, was the whole world in chaos?

Placing her chicken burritos on the counter, she asked, "What do you hear about the roads up north into Wyoming? I'm figuring on taking 9 through Breckenridge."

The woman's brows lifted. "Well, I heard they were going to close Interstate 70 at the Eisenhower Tunnel last night. Heard it's passable west of the tunnel, but don't try Denver. Governor cracked down with a total curfew. Lot of shooting last night. This credit card thing is really playing hell. Stores won't take the food stamp cards. Government cards. Nothing except cash."

She gestured to the parking lot outside. "Like them folks living in their cars. Just had credit cards and not enough cash, so they're waiting it out. Figure the cards will be accepted sometime on Tuesday, and they can gas up and get home."

"Anything on the national level?" She couldn't keep the dread out of her voice.

"Not much. TV, phone, even most radio has been shut off by the government 'cause they're afraid of another cyber hack, but we heard the president's big address last night on our shortwave radio."

"What did she say?"

The woman gave Lauren a disgruntled look. "You ask me, she's a broken record. Keeps repeating the same old garbage. Things like, 'This lawlessness must end,' and, 'I've called up the troops to put down violent protests,' followed by a plea to be patient, communications will be up and running again in a few days, and this will all be over soon. 'Shelter in place, shelter in place. The government will fix this.' Over and over."

"You think it's true?"

"Damn well better be. We've got people huddling in their cars all over town. Stranded, waiting for the credit card machines to go back online."

"I understand."

The woman gave Lauren a skeptical look. "Bet you don't. You don't have any kids with you. Most of those people out there in the cars do, and they're terrified. They can't even buy a bottle of milk for their screaming babies." The woman counted out Lauren's change. "That's what's left of your hundred dollars."

"Thanks."

Stuffing it in her pants pocket, Lauren glanced up at the dark TV screen. It was habit. "Why was there so much shooting in Denver?"

The woman pointed to her head. "Never understood those folks on the Front Range. People have gone crazy. Man in the gray Chevy out there said they made it out in a nick of time 'cause they knew all the back roads to take. Said the governor called out the National Guard, but half the soldiers didn't have cash to buy gas. The rest couldn't get across Denver to report for duty on account of the abandoned cars on the roads."

"So crime is running wild?"

"The way I hear, it's a free-for-all. Word is that the murder rate has climbed two thousand percent and scared people are barricading themselves in their homes."

The woman tipped her chin toward Randy, who was fiddling with his phone as he stood in the door. "You and your friend might want to get on those bikes and as far from here as you can." She paused. "Got enough cash?"

Cautiously, Lauren answered. "Hope so."

"Good, 'cause I don't think charity is going to be in any kind of oversupply in the coming days."

After Lauren and Randy walked back to the bikes, he said, "At least there's phone service, but it's all National Security Alert stuff from the Department of Homeland Security. Like they preempted the system. The whole page scrolls down with all these new rules and regulations. No unnecessary travel. Shelter in Place. Obey all military and police instructions. Do not hoard food. Do not do this, do not do that. God, it's like a freaking bad movie."

Lauren pulled out her own phone, finding the same thing. Prominently displayed, a line of text from her provider told her that by order of the President and the Department of Homeland Security, during the current emergency internet access and phone service would be temporarily interrupted. A whole list of laws, executive orders, and the applicable regulations followed.

Like, who the hell cared about that, right?

When she tried her email, the screen remained blank. Same thing when she tried calling Tyrell. Just...nothing. The effect that had on her was as upsetting as anything to date.

"Talked to a guy while you were getting gas," Randy told her as he put his phone away. "Denver sounds like what happened in downtown Kabul when we pulled out."

The images that flashed through Lauren's mind made her grit her teeth: *Little girls being dragged out of houses...boys and men shot down in the streets...bodies with nooses around the throats hanging from windows.*

Lauren handed Randy a burrito and unwrapped hers. She ate fast and washed it down with a bottle of water from her pack. Tyrell had told her about Afghanistan. About how the different tribal regions stayed in an almost constant state of war, raiding each other, burning fields, taking hostages. After twenty years of freedom, resistance fighters were everywhere, struggling to win back their country from the Taliban. Maybe it hadn't been a waste after all.

Lifting her helmet from her mirror, she pulled it down over her ears and threw her leg over the motorcycle. When she hit the ignition key, the Kaytoom came alive.

She said, "Gangs are a lot like tribes. Let's hope the country isn't headed that way."

Randy looked around the parking lot where people were waiting in their cars. "All these folks think the problem's going to be fixed in a day or two."

Lauren nodded. "President Brown keeps promising."

As she accelerated across the lot and headed for the junction with Colorado 9, she wondered if there was anything that anyone could do.

CHAPTER ELEVEN

* * *

AT FRISCO, EXPECTING TO CONTINUE NORTH ON COLORADO HIGHWAY 9 THEY TOOK THE onramp to I-70 East. A quarter mile later, a Colorado Highway Patrolman at the checkpoint turned them around, informing Lauren— in no uncertain terms—that travel any farther east or north was "prohibited". He motioned her to take the crossover to the west bound lane, sending them back the way they'd come.

Relegated to Interstate, she and Randy made their precarious way to Wolcott, where they talked their way past an Eagle County deputy sheriff to head north on Colorado 131.

At the junction in Toponas, Lauren twisted the throttle open when several men who'd been leaning against a pickup tried to flag her and Randy down. It was a pattern she quickly adopted. A motorcycle moving at a hundred miles an hour made an effective ally.

But Lauren was smart enough to know she couldn't run the next roadblock. They'd made it to the turnoff where Colorado 14 turned off of US40. A Jackson County deputy sheriff sat with his car straddling the centerline. A small knot of men stood next to a pickup behind him. Some wore billed caps, others were in cowboy hats. Most were carrying rifles. Their gun barrels glinted blue-black in the slanting rays of afternoon light.

As she approached, the black-haired deputy flipped on the flashing lights and stepped out into the road, calling, "Can I help you?"

Lauren killed the bike and instinctively removed her helmet. The deputy's expression changed perceptibly, obviously expecting a man.

"We're headed for Wyoming, trying to get to a friend's ranch outside of Hot Springs," Lauren told him.

Randy shut his Kawasaki down and removed his helmet, too.

"Can I see some ID?" The deputy was giving them a squinty-eyed look. Maybe trying to look tough?

Lauren and Randy handed over their licenses.

The deputy's eyes narrowed. "Says you're residents of Colorado Springs."

"I was studying at the university there. Randy, here, is from Seattle. We worked at a bank in the Springs."

The deputy arched an eyebrow. "You have cash?"

"A little," Lauren said. "Enough to buy us a meal and get us to Rawlins up in Wyoming."

"How much fuel you got in those tanks?"

Lauren pushed back on the bars and studied him. In his twenties, he kept one hand propped on the pistol in his belt holster. "Like I said, we're just passing through. We've got enough gas to get us to Rawlins, so we're not going to be any trouble for you or the other officers."

"You're already trouble. You probably haven't heard, but they've declared a National State of Emergency. No unnecessary travel." He gestured to her motorcycle. "Which is what you're doing."

"Look, we're just trying to get across the Wyoming line. After that, we've got family who'll take care of us."

"Uh-huh." His lips twitched. "Well, you're not going to. On top of President Brown, your governor up in Wyoming is a son-of-a-bitch. He's closed the borders. Says he doesn't want to be overrun by people fleeing the cities in surrounding states." The deputy worked his jaws as if he was chewing on something. "It's going to cost you a hundred bucks."

"Excuse me?"

"To get past us. Call it a toll. You know. Like a toll road. We got families, too."

Careful.

Lauren winced. "How about twenty-five. It's not like we're rich."

"Seventy-five." The deputy said. "I got a heart. But that's my last offer. Pay up, or turn those bikes around and get out of here."

Lauren took a deep breath, pulled out her wallet, and shelled out seventy-five dollars. Let the deputy see that doing so pretty much cleaned her out. The rest of her cash was in Tyrell's bag strapped to the back of the bike.

"Thanks for your business," the deputy told her. "Oh, and just so you know, I'm radioing your tags ahead. You'd better be across the Wyoming line or in the refugee camp by midnight."

"Refugee camp?"

"That's what they're calling all the vehicles that are stalled-out up on the Laramie road just south of the Wyoming border."

"All right," Lauren told him and clamped her helmet onto her head. The deputy stepped back as she started the KTM. She toed it into first and motored past the rifle-toting men, then accelerated down the long slope into North Park with its world-renowned hay fields. The fragrance of new-cut grass hay carried on the wind—curiously clean and fresh in contrast to what they'd just endured.

Five miles on, Lauren eased onto a pullout. Killing the bike, she stepped off and waited for Randy to shut down.

"I'll pay you back, Lauren. I can't believe we really just had to bribe a deputy." Randy said in disbelief as he rolled up beside her.

"Yeah, well, it has me thinking. You're wearing that fancy ICON touring jacket. It's got a hidden pocket, doesn't it?"

"Sure. Down in the back under the lining."

"How much money are you carrying?"

"Three thousand four hundred and change." When her mouth gaped, he added, "Like you, I figured maybe I'd better close my account."

"All right. I suggest you put all but about fifty bucks in that hidden pocket. Call it insurance in case we get shaken down again."

Stunned, he said, "Right. Okay."

While he did it, she pulled fifty from the envelope in the boogie bag and slipped it into her wallet. Almost as an afterthought, she reached into Tyrell's bag and moved the loaded .45 pistol to the tank bag in front of her. Call it added insurance.

"Jesus, Lauren! How many pistols do you have?"

She gave him a flat look. "How many people have tried to wave us down today? Not to mention the guys stopping us last night? Now a cop just shook us down."

"What else is in Tyrell's bag?"

"A broken down M4. Night vision goggles. Survival equipment. Ration packs, signaling devices. Entrenching tool. Hand grenades. Just about all the shit a Ranger-patched lieutenant in Delta Force would need."

Randy stared out at the mountains on either side of the shallow valley. Through a shaken exhale, he said, "Son of a bitch."

She slapped a hand on the side of the KTM's tank. "If Governor Agar really has closed the borders, it means the situation along the Wyoming-Colorado border—"

"Has turned medieval?"

"Good description. The governor has pulled up the drawbridges around the castle and plans to defend the walls at all costs."

"But what could possibly have happened that would—"

"Maybe Wyoming was attacked."

"Attacked?" he said in disbelief. "That's nuts. Who'd attack the state of Wyoming?"

"Don't know."

"Damn." His gaze seemed to have gone hollow. "Nothing's going to be the same, is it?"

"Doubt it."

In the golden light of the high-country sun, Randy's face took on the pale translucence of a Renaissance angel. But it was his eyes that riveted her attention. They were enormous, owl-like, and glittering with fear. The police shakedown had scared him more than thieves with guns.

"Lauren, seriously. How bad do you think it is?"

"Governor Agar is nobody's fool. I suspect the situation along the Front Range is going to shit. Come on, we have to get out of Jackson County, and I don't think it's going to be easy."

CHAPTER TWELVE

***

APPARENTLY THE CONVENIENCE STATION IN THE CENTER OF WALDEN HADN'T HEARD THAT travelers couldn't buy gas. Lauren and Randy topped up their tanks, paying only ten bucks a gallon. Then they wheeled the bikes to the side and stopped to eat a sandwich. The bald heavy-set city cop at the table across from them said, "Headed to Wyoming, huh? You know the border is closed?"

"Yeah, we heard. We're still trying to get our heads around the notion," Lauren replied.

The cop used his plastic fork to stir his packet of microwave macaroni and cheese. "Guess, like us, they're worried they're going to be overrun by hordes of folks fleeing Denver. Not that we're bad people, but where are we going to put a hundred thousand refugees? Seriously. How do we feed them? Where do they stay? From what we get on the police bands, the looting's already Biblical in Denver and Salt Lake City."

Lauren took another bite of her cold turkey sandwich, chewed, and said, "Is that why Governor Agar closed the border? Looting?"

"Oh, hell, no." The cop took a bite of his macaroni and swallowed. "When the first wave of people got out of their stalled cars and started walking north up I-25, adding to the ones already stranded on I-80 and I-25. They couldn't buy food, started begging from the locals in Cheyenne and Laramie. Stealing things. Making threats. Word is that Agar figured it was just the tip of the iceberg, and he didn't want the state to be the Titanic. The president gave him the legal authority with the travel ban. Made it legal."

"What about the rest of the Front Range?" Lauren was thinking about Breeze. Wondering how she might be doing.

"Folks are starting to trickle out of Fort Collins and Greely. The Larimer County Sheriff's Office report people have started shooting livestock, then they shoot the ranchers trying to protect their animals. Guess it's getting ugly."

"Shooting livestock?" Randy wondered. "What do you do with a dead cow laying in a field?"

"Cut it up, keep a couple of steaks, and trade it for things you need." The deputy lifted an eyebrow. "We're not going to allow that in Jackson County. Listen, I already checked. Your tags are in the system. You've got about three hours to be out of the county."

"That's our plan."

He considered Lauren. "You a ranch girl?"

"Spent summers on a ranch with a friend. She taught me to push water, stack hay, hunt elk, and vaccinate calves with the best of them."

The cop pursed his lips. "Okay, listen. I don't know if the Carbon County deputies are going to let you across unless you can prove you're from Wyoming. You got a way to do that?"

"They can call the Tappans up in Hot Springs. That or I have a lot of friends in Laramie and Cheyenne."

"No, they can't," he said. "Feds shut down all communications except old-fashioned radio. Anything with an internet or satellite connection is dead."

"Well, I'll think of something."

The cop—Parker, according to his name tag—nodded, skeptical eyes on Randy. "Listen, here's the thing: There's a line of cars at the border. Don't try for Laramie on 127. At the junction north of Cowdry, head for Encampment. The line is shorter there."

"Thanks. Really. Appreciate it."

Parker shrugged nervously. "I got a daughter your age in Houston and, last I heard, Houston is eating itself alive. I'm worried sick about Amy, her husband, and my little granddaughter."

Lauren stood up and stepped out of the small booth. As she wadded up her sandwich wrapper, she motioned for Randy to get up, and he instantly climbed to his feet.

Parker pointed to Lauren's jacket. "That pistol making a bulge in your coat pocket... You know how to use it?"

"Yes, sir. Dad's career Air Force. Had me shooting tin cans when

I was eight."

"Okay, so I want you to listen close. Our deputy has his roadblock at the junction north of Cowdry. Anything beyond that to the Wyoming border is essentially a No Man's land. If anyone stops you, there's no law. No one to help you. Get my drift?" He narrowed one eye.

The way her chest contracted made it hard to draw breath. "Fallen that far, has it?"

"Don't stop for any reason until you run into the Carbon County deputies. Hear me?"

"I do. Thank you, sir." Lauren gave Parker a grateful nod. "I pray that your daughter's family is all right."

His smile filled with longing. "Guess that makes two of us."

Out at the bikes, Randy glanced up at the slanting afternoon sun. "Can this get any more depressing?"

"If it's this bad in po-dunk Jackson County, what kind of chaos is tearing up urban America?"

Randy was silent. Finally he said, "You really think Wyoming is going to be any different than 'po-dunk Jackson County'?"

"Maybe. It's a different ethic across the line. According to the old saying, Wyoming is just one small town with really long streets."

"Yeah, but that was before the end of the world. What's it like now?"

Lauren straddled her bike, donned her helmet thumbed the starter button. "We'll find out in another twenty-four miles."

CHAPTER THIRTEEN

***

AFTER TAKING COLORADO 125 WEST AT THE COWDRY JUNCTION, LAUREN AND RANDY entered what Officer Parker had called the No Man's land. A line of cars and trucks were pulled off at the side of the road on the south-bound side. People congregated in knots. Most were gesturing for Lauren and Randy to turn back. Apparently, Wyoming wouldn't let them cross the line, and Jackson County wouldn't let them go back to Walden.

Riding a bike with Colorado plates, how do I prove I'm from Wyoming? The question rattled around in Lauren's head as she accelerated down the narrow blacktop road. Behind her, Randy stuck close, his Kawasaki filling the mirror.

What did she make of him? The guy was older than she was, should have been more experienced, but he sort of reminded her of a marshmallow. A bit squishy. She had to wonder: where in this new world, did Randy Howman fit? He'd have made a great banker, or maybe an affable financial advisor. How the hell would he ever make it all the way to Seattle?

They shot across the low rocky headland, following the narrow strip of asphalt down into the North Platte Valley. Sagebrush, outcrops of black rock, and scattered pines gave way to lush meadows glowing iridescent green in the slanting afternoon light. Wildflowers in all the colors of the rainbow carpeted the fields. Overhead, the scudding clouds glowed eerily around the edges as they raced eastward against a blue sky.

The border was easy to see. A line of vehicles had been pulled off the side of the road. Looked like fifteen or so. They gleamed in the stark high-county air.

Two families had set up camp in the right-of-way beside the

barbwire fence. The children were crying. One of the cars had Ohio plates, a couple from California, Kansas, and some she didn't have time to make out. A Nevada pickup pulling the camp trailer was parked defiantly in the middle of the north-bound lane. A collection of coolers, suitcases, and thermoses, were stacked up like trophies beside the trailer. One pickup with New Mexico plates seemed abandoned, as did a company truck with oil field decals on the door and commercial plates. The rest of the pickups had Colorado plates.

The expressions of the four Nevada men who watched her and Randy ride past really set Lauren on edge. They had the look of predators, eyeing her and her bike as she rolled up to the Carbon County sheriff's cruiser that blocked the road.

The **Welcome to Wyoming** sign looked like a beacon—blue with a bucking horse and rider.

She shut the bike down.

From behind the cruiser's door, one of the deputies approached. A second deputy lay across the hood of the patrol car with a pump shotgun at the ready. Beyond them, a stock trailer had been pulled across the road into Wyoming. Four men with rifles emerged and stationed themselves around the trailer.

"I'm sorry, but the border is closed until further notice," the deputy announced as he approached, one hand on his unsnapped side arm.

"I'm Lauren Davis. This is Randy Howman, a friend of mine. We're headed north to Hot Springs."

The deputy stepped wide, and Lauren was eerily aware that the man leaning across the hood was pointing the shotgun right at her.

"Hey, could you point that thing the other way?" she called.

The deputy behind the cruiser didn't shift his aim so much as a millimeter.

The first deputy—with Miller on his name tag—stepped back. "You've got Colorado plates on both bikes. I can only pass Wyoming citizens and their families."

"I am a Wyoming Citizen. I'm going home to Tappan Ranch up in the Bighorn Basin. I've been going to school in Colorado Springs. I also have a Colorado driver's license, just like Randy."

The deputy gave her a wary look. "No matter where you're from, we're under orders to close the border at seven sharp. That's ten minutes ago. No exceptions. If I let you through, these other people are going to throw a fit. I can't risk getting my deputies killed."

She glanced back at the line of cars and the four Nevada men who watched with apparent interest. "What do they think they're going to find in Wyoming? We can't feed and shelter them, any more than their own state can. Food and fuel are in short supply everywhere."

"Guess they think it's a place to hide out until this blows over."

Randy said, "If this blows over. Have you heard any news reports?"

"Not much." Deputy Miller shrugged. "President's put a travel ban in place. Governors across the country have called up state National Guards, trying to keep the peace until the banks reopen. Agar has called for the militia."

Lauren said, "Wyoming has a militia?"

"Does now."

Lauren pointed to the side of the road. "Okay, so, how about Randy and I sleep right there? Then, in the morning, when the border opens, we'll be first in line?"

"No way!" the deputy with the shotgun cried. "Lady, you're not exactly blowing my skirt up by saying you're from Wyoming while riding a bike with Colorado plates."

"Listen!" she cried. "I'm from a military family. We moved around a lot, but I lived in Casper most of my life. Graduated from Natrona County High School before I went off to college."

"Yeah, yeah," Deputy Miller said, raising his hands. "Can you prove it? We're not supposed to pass anyone. And don't fall back on that Third Quadrant horseshit."

Lauren blinked at him like he was speaking a foreign language. "What's the third quadrant?"

"The governor has divided the southern border into quadrants. Wyoming is about four hundred miles wide, right? So when President Brown's order came to prohibit all unnecessary travel, the governor was looking at a map. He broke the southern border into four parts starting with the First Quadrant in the west around Evanston. Second Quadrant south of Rocks Springs. We're the Third Quadrant, administered out of Rawlins." Miller made a face. "But I'm with Agar. Only Wyoming residents allowed across the line. So, prove you're a Wyoming girl."

Lauren pointed to the bucking bronco on the **Welcome to Wyoming** sign. "See that horse? His name was Steamboat. He was foaled in Chugwater, Wyoming. The cowboy riding him was Guy Holt. Not Stub Farlow no matter what he said later in life. Now, here's the curious irony. Steamboat was injured at a rodeo in Salt Lake. When they brought him back to Cheyenne, the horse was dying. Charlie Irwin put the horse down with the pistol that had belonged to Tom Horn." She paused. "And if you never heard of Tom Horn, Deputy Miller, you're not—"

"Yeah, yeah. Tom Horn. The famous outlaw."

The deputy behind the patrol car stood, letting the shotgun drop. "Hell, that's more than I know, and I was raised in Saratoga."

"So we can cross?"

"Can't let you," Miller shook his head. "Not until eight in the morning. Our orders are no exceptions. If God was standing here, I'd tell him the same thing."

"All right," Lauren sighed and turned around, trying to figure out where they could camp for the night. The rolling sage covered hills were darkening with shadows as the sun dropped toward the mountainous horizon.

Miller stepped closer to her. "Pay attention. You and your friend here had better turn your bikes around. Darrell, the Jackson County deputy back the junction, won't let you go back to Walden. So someplace between here and there, get well off the road to sleep for the night. Someplace where those four Nevada guys can't find you." He lowered his voice. "You get my drift here?"

Lauren looked at the Nevada men. "Yeah, I get it."

"Pete and I would just as soon step out of our Wyoming jurisdiction and into Colorado, so we could hammer the shit out of those dirtbags, but the governor says we can't. They've looted the rest of these poor folks, siphoned their gas, and hauled two or three young women into that trailer. Not sure it was consensual, but not sure it wasn't, either. It happened at night, and we didn't see it."

Lauren glanced back at the four men who still watched her with smirks on their faces. "Shit."

"Yeah," Deputy Miller told her. "So you go hide, and I mean hide. We'll see you at eight in the morning, right?"

"Right."

She punched her starter, gave Randy the "go around" signal, and motored back down the road. As they passed the Nevada outfit, she met the leers the men were giving her with a hard stare.

CHAPTER FOURTEEN

***

LAUREN LED THE WAY FOUR MILES BACK TO WHERE A RANCH ROAD RAN WEST. SHE STEPPED off the KTM to take down the wire gate. After wheeling her bike through, and letting Randy motor his way past, she refastened the gate. Riding down the two-track, she kept going until they were well into the sagebrush and out of sight of the highway.

She stopped, raised her visor and looked around. The two-track dropped into a low dip here, what looked like exfoliated granite outcrops rising on all sides. Scrubby limber pines and juniper dotted the outcrops a stone's throw to the north and west.

"What do you think?" Randy asked as he stopped beside her and killed his Kawasaki.

"That flat on the other side of the fence looks good. Not many rocks, and there's space for the bedrolls between the sagebrush."

Shutting the KTM down, she snapped the side stand out and leaned the bike as she crawled off.

She and Randy tossed their bags over the barbwire fence. As Randy was unpacking, Lauren studied the thunderheads in the east. "It's raining over the Medicine Bow Mountains. My call? We put up my tent."

Lauren had to show Randy the way to climb over a barbwire fence without neutering himself. Took a couple of trips, but in the end, the tent, complete with rain fly, was ready.

From Tyrell's bag, she took a length of parachute cord and ran it from the back tire of her KTM through the tent door. Last, she tied a loop in the cord.

She'd read about it in the history books. Whites and Native Americans alike had tied a picket rope with one end knotted around their horse's foot and the other around their wrist. If anyone tried to make off with the horse during the night, the owner would be awakened and at least have a chance to dispatch the thief.

As night fell, Lauren seated herself in front of the tent. Nighthawks took to the purple-and-indigo skies. They dove and darted, wings rasping in low moans through the air.

Crickets began their song, and to Lauren's delight, a lilting, quavering yipping could be heard in the distance.

"Coyotes," she called. "Thought I'd never hear them again."

"Guess we're about as far from trouble as we can get," Randy noted as he rolled out his sleeping bag inside.

She looked up where the first stars were visible. "Peaceful here. Hard to believe the world's falling apart."

He took a seat beside her and retrieved his water bottle to take a sip. Then he tried his phone again. All it would do was flash that same list of orders, regulations, and warnings. In the dim light she could see his expression; the guy was looking anything but happy.

"You all right, Randy?"

"Up at the border, it hit me. I really don't have a chance, do I?"

She frowned, trying to fit what he was saying into any logical framework. "What do you mean?"

"To make it to Seattle."

She pulled her hair back, combing it with her fingers. "Well, it's not going to be easy. But sure you do, if you're careful."

Randy's blond hair ruffled in the night breeze. "I'm not a brave guy, Lauren. Not like you and Ramirez. If it had been me? We'd have lost the bikes when those guys jumped us outside Castle Rock. If you hadn't had that gun... Do you really think I can make it across Wyoming, Idaho, and western Washington by myself?"

She filled her lungs with the sage-scented air while she thought about him calling her brave. She was scared right down to her bones. "You have a good map. If you take all back roads—"

"I was raised surrounded by millions of people in Seattle. I don't know all the backcountry tricks you do. I'd have never gotten us past the roadblocks or thought to bargain with that deputy. You made him think we really didn't have much cash. If he'd had a clue as to how much we're carrying... Well, I don't even want to think about it. Then, going through that gate and over this Jeep trail to find this spot? Get far enough away that we were safe? Wouldn't have even occurred to me."

"If I'm so smart why did it take me so long to figure out we needed to stash most of the cash in case we got shaken down hard?"

He ignored her. "And then, all that stuff about the bucking horse? How did you know that?"

"My best friend, Breeze, was a champion barrel racer. Steamboat was her hero. She taught me a lot of Wyoming history. I even tried rodeo for a while. Didn't work out."

Didn't work out? That could have been her personal motto.

He shook his head. "See? That's what I mean. I'm not going to make it to Seattle."

Lauren filled her lungs with the cool air. "I don't know how to tell you this except the blunt way, but I suspect that as bad as Denver was, Seattle is going to be worse. By the time you get there, a few more days will have passed. Long enough for people to be truly desperate."

"I've been thinking the same thing."

At the subtle pleading in his voice, she said, "Look, if you want to, you're welcome to come with me to the Tappan ranch. No guarantees. I'm not even sure they'll take me in, but they're really good people. You could give it some time. See what happens in the country."

He gave her a skeptical look. "The Tappans don't know me."

"Hey, listen, you'll have to pitch in. Work. Pull your weight. You okay with that?"

"Yeah, sure. Thanks." He didn't sound convinced.

She studied him. Imagining Randy on Tappan Ranch immediately brought up memories of Breeze's twin brother, Brandon. Pure, whipcord-tough cowboy. Lauren had just turned eighteen, and Brandon had swept her right off her feet. He'd been Lauren's first in so many ways, and not just sexually. The thing between Jim and Breeze had been getting serious, and she and Brandon had just seemed like a good fit. Until a black-haired beauty of a break-away roper from Absaroka, up in Montana, caught his eye.

In a sense, though, Brandon had defined the kind of man she wanted to spend time with. Next had come Vinich and then Ty. Each fully male, competent, and capable in his own way.

But Brandon and Randy? Comparing the two was like putting cast bronze up against gray silly putty. Hard angles, grit, and competence versus round soft white curves and wide-eyed jello.

She asked, "Randy? Why'd you come to my apartment that day? You could have stayed in the Springs. Probably had a better chance. It's a military town, after all. With all the bases there, it's not like the brass at Fort Carson, Peterson Air Base, Cheyenne Mountain and Piñon Canyon are going to let things get out of hand."

At the serious tone her voice, he sighed. "Because I was being stupid."

"Don't get me wrong, if I thought leaving was stupid, I wouldn't have done it."

"That's not what I mean." He bent his head back, staring up at the darkening night. "Listen, ever since you started at the bank... I mean I know you and Lieutenant Ramirez were a couple. Still..."

She winced. God, no. Not this. But a lot of things began to make sense. The help he'd given her at the bank. Why he'd suddenly bought a motorcycle. His sometimes awkward attempts at conversation.

He shrugged slightly. "Hey, I know I don't measure up." Chuckled. "Really know it now. But, even that being the case, I didn't want you riding off by yourself. Thought it would somehow be safer for you if there were two of us."

"Randy..." She steeled herself.

"No, Lauren. Don't say it. I don't want to hear the 'I think you're a really great guy, but...' speech." He juggled the soil in his hand. "You see, the last couple of days have been a real eye-opener. And being on the bikes—"

"Listen, I don't—"

"Let me finish, Lauren." He took a deep breath. "Being on the bike all day. You're locked inside your helmet. And the only person you have to talk to is yourself. A lot of time to really be honest with yourself, right?"

"I guess."

He laughed softly. "So, I'm scared to death. I've got to see if I can learn how to survive. Figure out if I've got any chance to just keep breathing."

"Randy, it all comes down to doing what you have to do next. You don't think about it, you just do it."

He nodded. "I'm figuring that out, Lauren. Just like I've figured out that I need you as a friend. And just a friend. Lieutenant Ramirez? That's the kind of man you're going to end up with. Until you find him..."—he turned to her, grinning—"I'll do my best to do whatever comes next."

"Yeah, 'just friends' is good," she told him, giving him a fist bump. "You know, takes a lot of courage to look inside, and admit what you see."

He looked up at the stars, cocked his head at the coyotes singing in the distance. "How about you? You seem like you're made of steel. Ever have doubts? Make mistakes?"

"Yeah. The kind that can't be forgiven." And with that, she turned and crawled into the tent to find her bedroll. "See you in the morning, Randy."

Slipping into her sleeping bag, she curled into a ball, thinking, *If you only knew.*

CHAPTER FIFTEEN

***

JUST BEFORE DAWN, LAUREN AWAKENED HEARING THE LILTING CALL OF THE MEADOWLARK. Faint hints of dawn light sifted through the mesh window. She shifted, groaned, and sat up.

Randy's sleeping bag was empty. Reaching over, it was still warm inside, so he hadn't been up long.

After she untied the cord from her wrist, she grabbed her coat and shrugged it over her shoulders. Just for good measure, she adjusted the pistol in her inner pocket. Then she crawled outside, delighted to see the gray profiles of their bikes on the other side of the barbed-wire fence. Still there.

Behind the bikes, across the rolling juniper-whiskered hills, the distant peaks of the Medicine Bow Mountains stood in dark silhouettes against a blood-red sky. She'd seen that color before. It was the gaudy color of prairie wildfires and air thick with smoke. Something big was burning along the Front Range. Fort Collins? Loveland? Greeley, maybe smoke from the fires in Denver blowing north?

Randy squatted a short distance away, checking the map spread over his knees, his breath frosting in the morning air. To her surprise, flames flickered and snapped behind a ring of stones.

Randy glanced up, calling, "I started a fire. 'Bout five minutes to hot oatmeal."

"Good, I'm starving." She walked over to warm her cold hands above the flames. Sagebrush—twisted from the ground—was piled to the side. She could smell its perfume-like aroma in the smoke.

As he refolded the map, Randy said, "Lauren, be honest with me, okay?"

"Sure."

He tucked the map into his tank bag, then looked at her. "Washington's really a pipe dream, isn't it?"

She looked back at the crimson sunrise. "That red sky? That's from fires all along the Front Range communities. Maybe not Colorado Springs because of the bases, but everywhere else, people are scrambling for what's left of the food, gasoline, medicines, and water. Seattle's bigger, denser. More packed together."

"So..." He took a deep breath, as if to steel himself. "I know last night's Tappan ranch talk was to make me feel better. Besides, I'm not a cowboy. What do you think I should do? Where should I go? I'm feeling lost."

The pressure in her bladder was growing. "Let me think about it. Right now, I have to pee."

She walked up the ridge to a granite outcrop, unsnapped her pants, and squatted down behind a juniper. A few feet away, a cottontail rabbit broke cover and dashed off through the long shadows cast by the sage.

"Nice ass," the man's voice said behind her.

She froze, heart thundering in her chest.

"Got a rifle on you," he casually informed her. "I could break your arm. Smash that left elbow with a bullet. Wouldn't do a thing to mess up that nice ass of yours. So, how about you stand up and turn around."

"Who the hell are you?"

"Butch Masterson. You passed us last night."

"From Nevada."

He chuckled. "That's right. We got a reputation, huh? I'm the short one with the brown hair. Took me most of the night to find you. Now, you going to stand up, or do I have to lay you down? For good."

Lauren rose, pulled up her pants, and fastened them. When she turned, she saw the rifle. Bolt action, scoped, and he was holding it like he knew how to use it. A six-inch Bowie knife with an ivory handle hung from his belt. His shoulders reminded her of thick slabs.

"What do you want?"

He grinned. "Somehow I ended up last man out. Only three of the girls was worth a shit. I could have taken one of the moms, or the little girls, but I figured providence would eventually provide. Then you and your boyfriend come riding by. And on bikes, no less. Better for scouting and getting around roadblocks, don't you think?"

Lauren studied the way he carried the rifle. He had a tendency to shift his eyes to the left, as though accustomed to threats coming from that direction.

"Tell your boyfriend to come over here, and if his hands aren't empty, I'm shooting you, bitch. Keep your hands high over your head. Hear me?"

"Randy?" Lauren shouted as she lifted her hands higher. "Walk over here. He's got a gun on me."

She watched as Randy appeared in the trees with a horrified look on his face.

Masterson grinned. "Okay, let's stroll down to the bikes nice and easy, all right? You two go first."

With every step she took, Lauren's terror built until it felt like her ribs would explode. Randy walked beside her, his hands high over his head. From his expression, he was about to throw up. Masterson followed a few paces behind them.

"Who is he?" Randy whispered.

"One the Nevada guys the deputies warned us about. Guess we didn't hide well enough."

"Guess you didn't," Masterson said.

"Castle Rock all over," Randy whispered. "At least you're not wearing gloves this time."

The pistol in her coat pocket seemed to be calling her, vibrating, or maybe it was just the fact that she was shaking.

"Not a bad place for a camp," Masterson called. "Nice and out of the way. Lots of trees. Maybe we'll spend the day here. Now, what's in those bags on your bikes? Got any cash?"

"A little," she told him. "Right saddlebag on the KTM, but it's locked."

"Well, maybe you ought to be nice and give me the key." Masterson used a smarmy voice. "I been walking most of the night. A reward would be good about now."

Lauren swallowed hard.

When I pull the pistol, I'll have a half second before he realizes. A half second to kill him before he can pull the trigger.

Which, of course, was lunacy. He was going to kill her.

Lauren stopped walking and turned to face him. "It's in my pocket.

Can I reach for it?"

"Slow and easy."

As she lowered her hand, he swiveled the polished rifle muzzle so that it aimed at her chest.

She slid her hand into her pocket; her fingers tightened around the pistol's grip, index finger finding its way to the curve of the trigger.

As she withdrew the pistol, Randy screamed and rushed the guy.

Masterson pivoted on his right foot, swinging the rifle. The muzzle blast deafened as the gun went off.

Masterson rocked back in recoil as Randy hit the ground hard.

Masterson spun back to Lauren.

"Don't!" she cried, ears ringing.

He was staring at her pistol with surprised eyes when Lauren shot him in the face. He dropped as if his cords had been cut.

Masterson's rifle clattered to the ground, and Lauren stumbled forward, blood racing, lungs panting, desperate for air.

Masterson sprawled on his back, his face a mess, the back of his head spewing thick dark blood and bits of brain. She felt sick to her stomach. On the verge of…

"Oh, my God." Randy sounded stunned.

She turned. His left leg lay oddly tangled in the sagebrush. He had fallen on his side. Was clawing weakly at the ground. A rush of blood drained from his riding pants, spreading across the ground.

"Randy?"

For a disbelieving moment, she just gaped, trying to understand. Adrenaline flooded her brain. She couldn't seem to put anything together.

Through gritted teeth, Randy said, "Lauren, I—I'm shot. He shot me."

She dropped at his side. Randy looked up at her with tears running down his cheeks. "He sh-shot me, Lauren. I'm shot," he kept repeating. His pupils had dilated, his pale skin a sickly white. Probably going into shock.

She glanced around, searching for any other threat, then shoved her pistol back into her pocket. "Just stay still. You're okay. Try not to move. I need to see your wound."

So much blood. *Think!*

She ran to jerk the Bowie knife from Butch Masterson's belt, and charged back. Slitting Randy's pant leg open, she got her first good view. The bullet had blown through his thigh. Blood was rhythmically pumping from the holes in front and back.

Femoral artery. How long do I have to stop the bleeding? A minute? Less?

Frantically, she looked around for something to use as a tourniquet. The parachute cord. She had to vault the barbed-wire fence. Cut the crap out of her palm on a barb.

With thick fingers, she cut the cord from the bike's rear wheel.

"Come on, damn it!" She tried to steady her quaking fingers. Blood from her sliced palm made her left hand sticky. Tears silvered her vision as she clambered back over the fence. The cord caught on the barbed wire. Almost pulled her over backwards.

Whimpering, Lauren tore the cord free and landed on her knees beside Randy. She pulled his leg straight, horrified at how heavy and loose the limb felt. Bone broken.

With all her might, Lauren lifted, worked the cord through the blood, and pulled it as high as she could in his crotch. She tied it off. Looked around for something to use to twist the tourniquet tight.

The rifle.

She scrambled for the gun, shoved the barrel under the loop and spun the long gun around in a circle until the parachute cord bit deeply into Randy's pants.

Eyes on the spreading pool of blood. Lauren held her breath.

"Thank God," she whispered. "It's stopped."

To keep the binding tight, she propped the rifle.

"Randy? Can you hear me? You're going to be okay."

"Lauren?" he said in a sleepy voice. "Where are we? Wyoming?"

"Not yet. But we'll make it today. Border's only six miles up the road."

As if dismissively, his head fell to the side. He might have been waiting for the morning sun to peer over the distant peaks.

Lauren kept the tourniquet tight while her heart hammered in her chest. "Randy?"

Slowly, his body went limp, and his mouth fell open.

"Randy?"

No response.

"Randy!"

Releasing her hold on the rifle, Lauren dove forward and placed her fingers against his throat. Nothing. No pulse. His heart wasn't beating.

"Randy, no!"

In between giving him mouth-to-mouth and performing chest compressions to try and get his heart to start beating, she glanced at his leg. The bleeding was barely a trickle. She refused to give up for another fifteen minutes, kept breathing for him and pushing on his chest.

Randy's eyes had turned a curiously crystalline blue behind the widened pupils. The way his lips parted reminded her of opening flower petals. Canted at an angle, his blanched face caught the first rays of morning sun to break over the distant silhouette of peaks. The entire sky now burned a muddy red, as if the heavens were as bloody as the ground on which Randy lay.

Lauren swallowed hard. Her heart had become stone in her chest.

When she touched Randy's left eyeball, he didn't blink.

She'd seen old Bill Tappan do this with a dead cow. No need to check for a pulse or feel for a breath.

Out beyond the camp, bees buzzed in the sunlit air, flitting across the blue-and-yellow mosaic of wildflowers that flowed over the slopes.

CHAPTER SIXTEEN

***

WHAT THE HELL DID SHE DO NOW? BRAIN-SHOCKED, UNFEELING, LAUREN WIPED HER BLOODY hands on her pants and bent to untwist the Remington 700 from the parachute cord. Working the bolt, she ejected the spent case, and found two in the magazine. One she chambered in case any of Masterson's friends suddenly appeared. Next she went in search of the entrenching tool she knew was in the boogie bag.

The grave wasn't much. When a man sacrificed himself to save a woman, he deserved better. No amount of additional labor was going to penetrate the bedrock she encountered a foot and half down. After taking Randy's personal possessions and money, Lauren rolled him onto his sleeping bag and dragged him into the grave. Using it for a shroud, she covered him with the crumbled soil. As a final touch, she left his helmet for a tombstone.

Masterson's billfold surrendered three hundred and forty-two dollars that Lauren stuffed into her coat. She kept the slick-looking Bowie knife and left the rest for the coyotes and magpies.

After she had repacked her tent, bedroll, and the entrenching tool in the boogie bag, she took a moment. Stared at the hump of earth marked by the shining white helmet. Glanced at Masterson's body where it lay face up. Flies feeding on the gore.

It all seemed so God-damned senseless.

Slinging the Remington over her shoulder, she heeled the side stand up, started the KTM, and wheeled it around Randy's Kawasaki. Numb, Lauren rode down the bumpy two-track. After refastening the gate, she turned north.

Nothing was inside her. Everything…hollow.

With one hand on the pistol, the other on the throttle, she passed the line of cars. Considered shooting holes in the camper from Nevada. Would have shot the other men down in cold blood had they stepped out, but the only people were the pale-faced campers along the right of way.

Lauren pulled up to the Carbon County Cruiser.

Her arrival was a little after eight that morning. As she tossed Deputy Miller the Remington 700, she told him: "That will serve you better than those shotguns. Four point six miles back, on the west side of the road, is a ranch gate. If any of your people want a brand new Kawasaki KLR, they'll find it sitting a couple hundred yards to the west, fully loaded, with the keys in the ignition. No sense in letting it go to waste."

She didn't give Miller time to speak as she added, "The man in the shallow grave is Randy Howman. Leave him in peace. The piece of shit with the back of his head blown out is Butch Masterson. He's one of the Nevada bunch. Leave him for the magpies and maggots."

Deputy Miller's eyes narrowed when he fixed on her blood-caked hands. Took in the glassy intensity of her stare. "He found you, huh?"

"Yeah," she answered hoarsely. "For all the good it did him."

She ground her teeth, glanced back at the Nevada pickup and trailer. "You seem like a decent man. You might want to sneak down tonight and rescue the three girls Masterson's buddies are raping in that trailer. Evil runs free when good men do nothing. You get my meaning? I don't give a good goddamn about the governor's orders."

He nodded. "You're right." A pause as he considered the trailer. "They partied pretty late last night. Lot of screams. Might be we'll just walk down and wake them up."

She put the KTM in gear, gave Deputy Miller a respectful nod of the helmet, and motored past the cruiser into Wyoming.

Alone now.

She can't pinpoint the moment she crosses over. It's like warm water engulfing her body. Buoyant, floating in a sparkling torrent. Wind stirs, and the clouds sailing above swallow the sunlight. Shadows fall.

Hold on.

But her grip grows as fragile and delicate as a spider web.

Hold on.

CHAPTER SEVENTEEN

* * *

LAUREN'S FINGERS ARE LOCKED ON THE KTM'S GRIPS, HOLDING ON FOR DEAR LIFE EVEN though she knows she's hurtling for oblivion and there's nothing she can do to stop it.

She is headed to Laramie on the back roads, refusing to dare I-80. Here, paralleling the Colorado border, butchered carcasses from the occasional cow occur with some frequency on the other side of the right-of-way fence. Familiar sight now. Animals slaughtered to feed the burgeoning hordes of refugees finding their ways into the state. She passes individual people and parties walking along the road. Most just let her pass, others try and wave her down.

That may be a dead body. A living human wouldn't be covered with fluttering magpies.

One of the ranchers who tried to protect his livestock? Or someone the ranchers shot for killing stock?

The world flashes by, but she barely notices.

There's nothing alive in her head.

It's broken.

An eggshell after the chick has flown.

No movement.

No memories.

And it's getting worse.

Just the road ahead.

Watch the road.

The two-lane strip of black asphalt winds between sagebrush as she flogs the KTM down winding blacktop on the Snowy Range Road. Pastures and green irrigated fields of alfalfa lie to either side. The creek bottoms are thick with willows, the water sparkling in the sun. Distant snow-capped peaks to the south rise against a robin's-egg blue sky, only to fade into a sickly brown haze off to the east.

The Front Range continues to burn.

The staccato of the KTM's exhaust and the wind whipping past her helmet are the only sounds. She's headed for Laramie. Not Tappan Ranch. Just a short detour. To see her friend. To sit for a while and talk. Remember who she is. Or maybe who she was.

She remembers Tiffany. Why can't she remember high school?

It's as if her entire world has been cleaved in two, divided into before and after, and before has ceased to exist. Except for Tiffany. Scares her. Tiff still works at the Country Kitchen Café in Laramie, doesn't she? Got an email. Just a few days ago, right?

Or was that last year?

Hollow.

All broken open. Nothing left inside.

No. Oh, no…

CHAPTER EIGHTEEN

***

CARRYING THE HEAVY BOOGIE BAG OVER HER SHOULDER, LAUREN PICKED A BOOTH NEAR the front of the Country Kitchen. The eatery sat just off the Highway 287 interchange on Laramie's outskirts. Mostly it catered to I-80 travelers. Now it was occupied by a handful of stranded folks with just enough cash left to buy them a cup of coffee.

The table, being next to the window, provided a clear view of the parking lot and the KTM leaned on its side stand. She didn't dare let the motorcycle out of her sight, not now, not ever.

Lauren lowered the bag into the booth, then slid in beside it and waited for the blonde waitress to come over. Before the waitress could ask, Lauren ordered, "Coffee. Sausage and eggs, over easy."

"That'll be thirty bucks. I'll need to see the cash first."

"Sure." Lauren shifted, pulled out her billfold and laid the bills out on the table. "That good enough?"

"Want toast with that?"

"Sourdough." A pause. "And one last thing: Does Tiffany still work here?"

"Yeah." The waitress shot an evaluative glance. "She'll be in at eleven. But if you're thinking she'll vouch for you to get a job here, we ain't hiring."

Lauren stared out the window at Tyrell's bike and the colorful signs on the buildings across the street. Lot of the businesses were boarded up. It was new plywood. Were there so few cash customers that business owners had just closed their doors? What good did it do to keep paying employees to come in when no one could buy anything? On the other hand, maybe their employees had walked out and gone home?

Dear God, what's...

Lauren jumped when the waitress set the breakfast plate in front of her with a clatter.

"You awake?"

"What?"

"Looked like you'd fallen asleep with your eyes open. I've seen long-haul truckers do that. They stare at the wall like zombies. Just like you were doing."

"No, I... That was just fast. I mean, I just ordered," she said a little breathlessly.

"Really? I was going to apologize for the how long it took. Glad you're not mad. I'd refill your coffee, but we're selling it by the cup. You know, Sysco's no longer delivering. No telling how long supplies are going to last."

Lauren blinked at the table. How long had that coffee cup been sitting there? "No. Thanks. It'll be okay."

"Sure thing."

The waitress left, and Lauren watched the eggs steam in the cool café air. Grabbing her coffee in both hands, she steadied it as she lifted it to her mouth. Stone cold.

How much time had she lost? Twenty minutes? Thirty?

Kept seeing it over and over again: shooting Masterson. The way the man's head and eyeballs seemed to puff out while a red spray blew out the back.

Awake, asleep, it was right there. Over and over again, she relived the last moments as Randy bled to death. How it felt to reach out and touch his dead eyeball. Each time, she experienced the same visceral fear and nausea.

While she ate her sausage and eggs, her gaze drifted. Almost everyone—including the cashier behind the register—wore a pistol on his or her belt. Just like Lauren who wore the .38 Smith & Wesson openly. Civilization was wilting.

The tree of liberty was dropping its leaves one by one. If the government didn't get the financial system back on line soon, people would stop taking paper money. How many days did she have left before her cash was no good, and she'd have to start trading ammunition for food? Precious ammunition.

Her hand quaked as she lifted a forkful of egg to her mouth. Riding, she'd bungeed the HK .45 to her tank bag; all it took was a yank with her left hand to free it. She needed her right to control the throttle and steer. Twice on her ride over the Snowy Range Road, she'd had to brandish the pistol when bands of people stranded in the middle of the road had tried to wave her down.

They were probably all decent folks just wanting to ask her to send a message to the authorities, or to ask her to give them a hand.

But maybe they were another version of Butch Masterson.

Similar events had to be playing out all along the Wyoming line. No wonder the governor had used President Brown's order and closed the border. Check points—she'd heard—had been established. Some even as far south as The Forks on Highway 287 in Colorado. It was a chokepoint that controlled all the forest service dirt roads that led north to Wyoming.

If the Larimer County Sheriff's Office down in Fort Collins objected, they'd sent no one to the road block to complain.

The eggs, sausage, and hash browns were no doubt average. Discount restaurant fare. The same food, cooked on the same kind of grill, with the same cheap cooking oil that was sold across the entire United States. As far as Lauren was concerned, it was the finest meal she'd ever eaten.

She fought to stay focused. Any illusions she might have had about the world returning to normal were gone.

As she finished breakfast and reached for her coffee cup again, she glimpsed Tiffany Bishop riding her bicycle into the parking lot. Her gaze clung to her friend, as though if she could just see Tiffany, everything was okay. *I'm Lauren Davis. Tiffany is my friend. 'Member?*

Tiffany glided to a stop in front of the restaurant, stepped off, and chained her bicycle to one of the posts outside. She had her brunette hair in a ponytail, wore blue jeans and a red T-shirt.

They'd gone to high school together, graduated and gone to different universities. Tiffany had been there for Lauren when her friendship with Breeze had shattered in the wake of Jim's death.

When Tiffany opened the café door and saw Lauren sitting in the booth, her eyes went wide. "Lauren? That you? Good Lord! I've been worried sick about you."

"Hey, Tiff."

Tiffany hurried across the floor and bent down to give Lauren a hug. "What are you doing here? You okay?" she asked as she slid into the booth on the opposite side. "How on earth did you get out of Colorado? We hear it's like Armageddon down there?"

"B-Back roads. Got across the border south of Encampment yesterday. Was headed north. Maybe Tappan Ranch. Then, all of a sudden, I wanted to see you. So...I came here instead. Got a room."

With Butch Masterson's money. Dickered the price down to three hundred a night.

She inclined her head toward the hotel across the street. "Needed a shower and a good night's sleep. Thought I'd catch up on the news, but it's just government announcements on the radio. How many times can they tell people to stay home and not panic?"

"I can't believe this is happening."

Lauren shook her head, images of Randy behind her eyes. "Like a nightmare that you never wake up from."

Tiffany shoved loose strands of hair away from eyes. "Is it as bad as they say in Colorado? Did you see the rioting and looting?"

"I went wide around Denver. Had a close call on I-25, so I steered us for the back roads." She waited while Tiffany ordered coffee, then asked, "What about here? Cheyenne? Casper?"

"Hey, it's Wyoming. When the police got overwhelmed, the store managers called all of their relatives with guns and took over their own security. Meanwhile, enough people in Laramie pitched in with a food drive. We're talking ten thousand people pulling precious cans of food out of their pantries to help others."

"Grocery stores?"

"Empty. Well, but for stuff like knick-knacks, greeting cards, and novelty googaws like Welcome to Wyoming coffee cups."

"And we thought nothing could be worse than COVID?" Lauren shook her head.

"People are out hunting when they can get gas. They donate part of each animal to the local food bank, which distributes it to the needy. So far everybody's okay. There's no rioting."

"Banks are still closed, though." Lauren tilted her head toward the sign at the cashier's check out: **Cash Only.**

"That doesn't look to change any time soon. Europe's crashed. Even places like China, which I hear have huge gold reserves, are fighting mobs in the streets. Serves 'em right if they triggered this. I hope the whole house of cards collapses around their ears."

Lauren swayed slightly in her seat, suddenly lightheaded. She had to grab for the table to steady herself. "Is that what people are saying? It was China? How do we know..." What had she been talking about? She'd lost her train of thought.

Tiffany studied her with thoughtful brown eyes. "You okay?"

"No, I—I lost a friend. Just need some time."

"What happened?"

Lauren took a long drink of cold coffee, hoping the caffeine would help. "My fault. Should have hidden us better. Been farther off the road. He saved my life."

Worried, Tiffany asked, "Tyrell?"

"No. He's deployed somewhere. This was someone I worked with at the bank." She clamped her jaw to keep her lips from trembling. "Sorry, it's still too close."

Tiffany nodded, glanced out the window to give Lauren time to compose herself. Then asked, "What about Breeze? When this broke, I tried to call but didn't get through. She's working for that company in Denver. Did you guys talk? Did she tell you what she was going to do?"

Lauren stared woodenly at her. "What would I have said, Tiff? Hi, former-best-friend. Now that the world's ending, I thought I'd call. I know you hate me, but—"

"Water under the bridge, Lauren. We all make mistakes. Breeze knows that. God knows, she made enough of her own. Give her a chance."

"See, that's just it, Tiff. I haven't forgiven myself for getting drunk and slamming into that tree. I fucking killed my brother, okay? You think I can ever forget that? That I don't miss Jimmy every day of my life? She *loved* him. They were going to get married."

"If you would just talk to—"

"Enough about me." To change the subject, Lauren said, "What's happening in your life?"

Tiffany's knowing expression changed to a smile. "I'm engaged to Trevor Phillips. He was driving a truck for UPS, but that cratered as soon as the crash hit. So he signed up with the new Wyoming State Militia. Three month hitch. He's south of town holding the line down at the The Forks. Governor Agar has patrols monitoring the whole length of the southern border." She paused. "Funny isn't it? It used to be the state line, now it's 'The Border', as though the surrounding states are enemy nations."

"Don't know how long Agar can keep that up," Lauren said it bitterly. "There's only six hundred thousand of us in the whole state. There's eight million of them just across the line."

Tiffany nodded. "That's the point. We can't let them in. We'll be overrun in a heartbeat. They'll take everything we have. Kill all the farm animals. Rob our houses. I know it sounds heartless, but we're spread out all over the state in small towns. What would you—"

"I'd do exactly the same thing Agar has. I've seen what's happening out there. Lived it." She closed her eyes; Butch Masterson grinned out from her memory.

"Sorry," Tiffany whispered.

"No. I'm sorry. I...I'm sort of coming apart, Tiff."

Tiffany reached across the table to grab her hand. "I'm right here, Lauren. And you're going to be okay. Wyoming's holding the line."

"Good," she exhaled the word. "That's good. I...I'm just a little confused right now. I used to think I knew who I was."

"Really? I'm still trying to figure it out. Sometimes I think I know who I am. Other times I hope not."

Lauren smiled and massaged her forehead with a nervous thumb. "Yeah, me, too."

Tiff patted her hand and released it. "You heard about Mike Vinich?"

"No. How's he doing? We were like the four musketeers. Heard he was selling cars in Douglas. Half-owner in his dad's car lot or something." After she and Brandon Tappan broke up, Lauren had been half in love with Mike until he'd taken up with the gorgeous Pamela Starwood.

She asked, "He still with Pam?"

"She threw him over for a lawyer in Casper. Mike was in the Wyoming National Guard. Got called up first thing. He's in Cheyenne. Governor Agar is in the process of deploying the Guard all along the line. Hey, it's just the beginning of this thing, right? People are still scrambling to set up what they call Observation Posts from the east to the west. Places where people will try and cross. Some of the stories..."

"Like, what stories?"

"Probably nothing. Just, Trevor says things are getting worse every day. They're trying to figure out what to do if thousands of refugees swarm the border. How do we stop them? Open fire? Shoot down women and children?"

Lauren clutched her cup in both hands. Barely audible, she said, "Who'd do that?"

Tiffany leaned back in her seat. "Hopefully, no one. Hopefully, the government reopens the banks tomorrow, and we all go back to whatever remains of our lives." A pause. "You remember that big buffalo ranch south of Cheyenne?"

"Sure. Beautiful animals."

"Well, when the first rush of people fleeing Denver hit the I-25 checkpoint on Sunday, they started crawling over the fences and shooting buffalo. Then they camped on top of the carcasses to eat their way down to the bones. While the ranch got what they could catch of the herd rounded up and shipped out, a thousand more people were stopped at the border where the state patrol was trying to enforce the president's travel ban. A bunch got around the roadblock and made it to Cheyenne. Word is they were pissed off about the roadblock. Blamed it on Wyoming and took it out on the businesses. But it was awful. I mean, really ugly. Lot of people died.

"That's when Agar militarized the border. Called out the National Guard and stopped all traffic on I-25. It's President Brown's order, right? No unauthorized travel without a permit unless you can prove you're a Wyoming resident. People have been filling up that buffalo ranch ever since. Agar won't let 'em into Wyoming, and they don't have anything left to go back to down in Colorado."

Lauren paused to suck in a deep breath before she said, "Dear God."

"Yeah." Tiffany moved her coffee cup around the table top. Her brows drew together. "Trevor says if they get into Wyoming, they'll kill every one of us to take what we have. And you know Wyoming people. We'll fight back. It'll be a blood bath."

Lauren said, "It's all coming apart, Tiff. I don't think right and wrong exist anymore. The only thing left is survival."

"You had friends in Colorado Springs?"

"I *have* friends in Colorado Springs. They must be all right. The military is there. They'll be keeping the city from imploding."

"You sure? I heard tens of thousands of refugees from Denver headed south, too. And the roads into the mountains are flooded with people. That's why Wyoming invaded Colorado."

"We invaded Colorado?"

"Had to. I told you about The Forks, that bar and restaurant? It's a headquarters now. Guard is hauling rations down in those big desert-tan trucks with the gnarly tires. But no one gets up 287 past that point. The biggest camp is just south of Cheyenne. That's where Mike is stationed."

"How many people do we have guarding the border? What happens if these big camps decide to swarm across?"

"Trevor says we're just going have to suck it up and open fire."

These are fellow Americans. People I know.

Everything goes glittery…

There again. Floating. Life drains from Randy's eyes.

Lauren looks at her hands and goes quiet, letting the warm darkness swaddle her insides. Despite the shower she had this morning, blood clings around her fingernails. She scrubbed and scrubbed them. Randy won't go away.

She drifts, listening to Tiffany's voice, telling stories… *try-outs for the women's Olympic shooting team…you were way better than me… that time you stole our eighth-grade teacher's…* The sentences don't connect. Nothing makes sense. Time stretches like a rubber band until the world around her quivers, ready to break.

"Maybe I will go to Cheyenne," she manages to say, and Tiffany looks up as though Lauren just interrupted her. "I—I'd like to see Mike. Be good to see him. Good to see what he's up against."

Tiffany's eyes narrow. She knows something's wrong, really wrong.

Lauren tries to find words, but it's like her brain can't function. It just runs afterimages of Masterson's head exploding growing, filling the universe.

Tiffany studies her for a while, then slides out of the booth, rises, and walks over to slide in next to Lauren. They hug each other.

"You're going to be okay, Lauren. You are."

She nods, tightens her hold on her friend and closes her eyes.

Hold on.

CHAPTER NINETEEN

***

LAUREN PARKED THE KTM OUT FRONT, TOOK OFF HER HELMET AND HUNG IT ON HER MIRROR, then she walked uncertainly to the door of the Wyoming National Guard headquarters outside of Cheyenne.

They'd established it at the Port of Entry south of town on the north-bound lane of Interstate 25. The place where semi trucks used to weigh and obtain permits had become an armed camp with a couple of Bradley tanks and host of machine-gun mounted Humvees. Pickups, marked **Wyoming Militia,** were relegated to the rear. The motto "Always ready. Always there" hung over the front door.

She stopped to study the corral full of horses to the left of the headquarters. A big stack of hay stood nearby. Beyond them, vast tent camps and abandoned vehicles cluttered the rolling grassy hills.

When she opened the door and entered the WNG headquarters, she saw a familiar white-haired man sitting behind the desk: James Ragnovich. The Ragnovich family had deep roots in the state's history. The captain's great-great-grandfather had come from the old country to mine coal in Rock Springs at the turn of the Twentieth Century. Since then, Ragnovichs had served in the legislature, run for governor, built ranches, made and lost fortunes speculating on Wyoming's boom and bust cycles, been indicted and served time, and generally prospered along with the state.

"Morning, Captain Ragnovich."

Ragnovich looked up and squinted as though he thought he knew her. "Hey! You're Lauren Davis, aren't you? I served with your father back in the early 2000s. How is the general?"

"And I remember you, too, sir. Dad said you were one of the best soldiers he'd ever served with. He considered you to be a good friend."

Ragnovich grinned. A three-day growth of snowy beard barely hid the deep lines that webbed his mouth and cheeks. His ACUs looked like they hadn't been washed in a week. "What are you doing here? Carrying messages for your father? I heard he was back east somewhere."

Lauren shook her head. "Actually, I'm looking for my friend Mike Vinich. Heard he's stationed here."

"He is. Currently distributing rations to the buffalo ranch down on the border. He's a sergeant now." Ragnovich made a face. "Lord knows when, or even if, it will ever become official. The Department of the Army had been remarkably silent no matter how many attempts we make to contact them."

"You're providing rations for buffalo?"

"No. Refugees camped there. I know feeding them is a stop-gap measure, but if they decide to rush the border again I guarantee you there isn't enough tear gas and rubber bullets in the world to stop them." Ragnovich lifted a hand in a helpless gesture. "I don't even want to think about the alternatives."

Lauren walked closer to his desk, and Ragnovich said, "Sit down. Tell me the news. You still haven't told me about your father."

"Thanks." She sat. "Haven't heard from the folks. Just that they were in Maryland when this broke. Where are you getting the rations? Store shelves are bare everywhere."

"Warehouse east of Cheyenne is filled with FEMA emergency rations. Agar's fighting with the DHS director in charge of the state. Guy named Edgewater. Big power play over who now runs Wyoming. Not my problem. That food's supposed to be used to feed the people of Wyoming in case of a disaster. Which is what this is. I guess."

Lauren thought about that. "I heard it was bad."

"Getting worse, Lauren. Yesterday a mob stormed the capitol in Denver, killed the governor, and ransacked the place. Folks in Colorado are terrified. Most are locking themselves in their homes. But some are running. I have a presidential order that there's to be no unauthorized travel without a permit. What permit? That's supposed to be issued by the military. Which military? Or is it DHS? Who?"

"I thought Agar closed the border."

"Yeah, Agar jumped on President Brown's order after that bunch got past the roadblock and started looting downtown. Agar called out the Guard, began issuing orders to us and created the Wyoming Militia. What am I supposed to do? I can't let a million refugees into Wyoming. And I can't let 'em starve in front of my eyes."

A chill ran down Lauren's spine. "They murdered the Colorado governor?"

The captain nodded. "Mob of about ten thousand. Colorado National Guard troops refused to fire on their own citizens. It's the law of the jungle down there."

"How big are the camps?"

Ragnovich shrugged his shoulders. "Hard to get a good count. Thirty thousand, maybe, scattered across two or three dozen camps along Wyoming's southern border. But every day that number grows. Not only that, we're trying to feed refugee camps inside the border, too. You know, people stranded on the interstates when the credit cards stopped working. Didn't have cash to go on. Or, if they did, thought it was too dangerous. Got one camp in Frontier Park for stranded travelers here in Cheyenne."

As the enormity of the situation dawned on her, Lauren shook her head. "This is Friday, isn't it? It's been a full week. When is this going to end? Why hasn't the government solved this cyber problem?"

Ragnovich leaned across his desk and laced his fingers on the polished wooden top. "Agar says they're stymied. They keep running patches, fixing things, and an instant later the virus knocks 'em for a loop, and comes back stronger."

"Was it China? Do we know?"

Ragnovich lifts one shoulder. "Not for sure. Speculation runs the gamut from China to Iran to North Korea."

"Not Russia?" Lauren asked incredulously.

"Well, doesn't matter at this point. Agar says it's like being on the Titanic. The country is sinking, and there aren't enough lifeboats. Agar has chosen to protect the people in this lifeboat. In Wyoming. Lauren, I'm siding with him. Even if it means going head-to-head with Edgewater and the DHS."

The scent of coffee wafted through the air, and Lauren saw a corporal in camo walk by carrying a bright blue cup and a stack of folders.

"Other states doing the same thing?"

"Those that can. Most of us are holding our borders. We've been flying reconnaissance, interrogating refugees. It's bad out there. Colorado is the worst, but the Salt Lake Valley's a mess, too. Up and down the highways, anything goes. Travel south of the line is impossible. Most people along the Front Range—and we're talking millions—barricaded themselves in their houses and are waiting for the government to come save them. Maybe another million have fled west into the mountains."

She wondered how the lady at the gas station in Fairplay or Officer Parker in Walden were doing.

Lauren's gaze moved over the service ribbons on Ragnovich's chest, the commendation plaques on the wall. "Just before TV went down, I saw pictures of Pennsylvania and New York. Looked like war zones."

"Still does, I hear. Same for the west coast. All the big cities are in chaos. Military and police were overrun almost immediately. Nobody could stop the rioting. Then the electricity grid went down."

"How are you getting news?"

"Shortwave radio, mostly. Anything that doesn't require a satellite to work. Governors in the Rocky Mountain west and northern Plains talk back and forth. Some news trickles in from Warren Air Base, but they are locked down tight. Even before, they were staying pretty tight-lipped about what's really going on out there."

"We get word from people who make it through. Usually on motorcycles, which I guess isn't news to you."

"What are the horses for? You starting a pony express?" Lauren looked out the window at the spring grasses moving in the gentle wind that swept the plains beyond the camps. Like waves upon a green ocean. It was so peaceful. She wondered if, like the Pony Express, it was still ten days' ride from St. Louis to Sacramento?

"For the time being the militia's using them for mounted patrols. We don't know how long we can keep the refineries running." Ragnovich frowned. "Don't I recall your dad saying you were majoring in accounting and banking down in the Springs?"

"That was the plan." A pause. "Once."

Ragnovich stared hard into her eyes. "So...how do you think this happened? How could America be so vulnerable?"

Lauren gave him a blank look. "I've been thinking a lot about that. You remember all those hacks the Chinese were behind? All that data their military was accumulating on Americas? The security breaches at Equifax, Yahoo, Marriott, the airlines, Amazon, PayPal, the Pentagon, IRS, and others that stole the data of hundreds of millions of people?"

"Yeah."

"Did you ever put a credit freeze on your accounts, change your passwords, ask for a new credit card number?"

Ragnovich arched a suspicious eyebrow. "Never had any problems, so I figured—"

"I suspect the hackers finally decided to use that data."

"Use it how?"

Lauren shifted in the chair. "I had an economics and society course where we examined the vulnerabilities of 'the internet of things'."

"I don't know what that is."

"It refers to the fact that there are tiny computers everywhere, and they're all hooked together: laptops, phones, webcams, microphones, speakers, remote monitors to reduce traffic congestion and regulate overhead lights, stuffed animals, pressure sensors, TVs, self-driving cars, drones, airplanes. If hackers have the passwords, they can wait years to take control of tens of billions of devices, then establish their own malicious software, and recruit the devices into a botnet army."

"A botnet army?" He looked uncomfortable. "Sounds like science fiction."

Lauren nodded. "It's not, though. I suspect the hackers who initiated the cyberattack have been compiling stolen data for years. Then you design and release the Trojan malware and a sophisticated artificial intelligence to constantly adapt it, and it's sort of like a digital COVID. Within the blink of an eye, it's all over the world."

Ragnovich didn't say a word, but the lines at the corners of his eyes tightened.

Lauren broke the uneasy silence. "Captain, is there something I can do to help you? You said Mike's delivering rations. Maybe I could pitch in for a few days?"

"A few days? How about enlisting? Smart woman like you? There wouldn't be any risk. I'll make sure you're assigned to the office.

God knows, even without any direction from Washington, we're still drowning in paperwork. It's driving Colonel Mackeson to drink."

Drowning in paperwork? An office? Not if I can help it.

Aloud, she said, "Thank you, sir. But I really have to be in Hot Springs in a couple of days. I just thought, maybe, until you get things set up, you could use an extra—"

Ragnovich called, "Corporal Baker. See that Ms. Davis has a spot on tomorrow's provisioning run."

Then he glanced at the HK pistol on her hip. "We don't expect trouble so long as we keep giving them food, but you'd better take that along. We all know they're just trying to get away from the insanity down south, find a safe place for their kids, but if we let 'em through, we'll all be dead. You understand?"

Lauren blinked. "You mean because it'll be like a swarm of locusts eating everything in sight?"

"Worse. We've done the math. It'll take less than a month before Wyoming's resources are gone. Even if we don't die in the onslaught, it'll be from starvation when winter comes."

CHAPTER TWENTY

***

LAUREN CHECKED INTO A ROOM AT THE PLAINS HOTEL ON CENTRAL AVENUE JUST A BLOCK from the Hilton in downtown Cheyenne. She'd known the historic property from when her father was stationed at Francis E. Warren Air Force Base. He had taken Lauren, her mother, and Jim out for the occasional fancy meal in the restaurant. She'd always loved the grand lobby, the tiled floors, and stained-glass ceilings.

Now, with cash almost non-existent, travel at a standstill, and the economy dead, she was able to barter the manager down to a week's stay for two hundred bucks. Cash. Paid in advance. And she did her own housekeeping.

Better, there was parking for the KTM out front and she could chain it to a light pole.

In the room she took stock of her worldly possessions: The boogie bag, three changes of clothes, her laptop and iPhone—none of which worked without internet and cell service—her riding gear, camping equipment and weapons.

Wow.

Walking to the window, she stared down at the bike. Wondered where Tyrell was. A part of her hoped he was blowing the shit out of whomever had released the Trojan malware. Another part of her prayed he was somewhere safe. Maybe guarding an island in the Aleutians or Hawaii where no one would shoot at him.

"You out there, Ty?"

So, tomorrow, she'd ride in the supply truck with Mike Vinich. See the sprawling refugee camp herself. Then what?

The offer to enlist still stood.

Colonel Mackeson was in command of the Wyoming National

Guard. Colonel Steadman was in charge of the 153rd Airlift Wing with its aging fleet of C-130s and three Blackhawk helicopters. According to the rumor, all he'd heard from his commanding officer were conflicting orders that seemed to reflect confusion from above.

As she stared at the empty street below where traffic should have been bumper-to-bumper at this time of day, she wondered if enlisting in the Guard was what she wanted. Her father, the general, might even be proud. She'd be serving.

"Shuffling papers," she whispered. Tried to draw a mental image of that. Day after day. Sitting at a desk. While the action was outside.

"Then, what happens if Tyrell appears at Tappan Ranch, and they tell him that last they heard, I was in Colorado and probably dead?"

She walked to the bed, gaze fixed on the boogie bag. No, there wasn't any sense in rushing north to Hot Springs and the Tappan ranch. Wherever Ty was deployed—and given the length of his enlistment— her fiancé wasn't showing up on the Tappan's doorstep anytime soon.

The clock on the nightstand read 6:37. Ragnovich had sent word to Vinich. Mike was supposed to meet her at the bar at seven after he got off duty.

She took a deep breath, checked herself in the mirror. The jeans and cotton blouse were wrinkled from being stuffed in the pack. She looked like she'd lost five pounds since that morning she'd ridden away from the Springs. Good thing she had a belt.

"Not bad," she told herself as she pulled her hair back into a ponytail. But she worried about the tension in her eyes. Brandon Tappan had called them 'cinnamon brown', a name Vinich had picked up on. She'd never shared that with Ramirez, now she wondered why.

Wear the .45?

She chewed her lip as she considered. It was a freaking fancy hotel. She and Mike were having drinks and supper. Not the sort of place to go packing a pistol.

"So, you're leaving the HK and bag full of guns, ammo, cash and gear unguarded in a hotel room?" She sighed, hearing Tyrell's voice: *How stupid can you get?*

Lauren slipped the .38 Smith & Wesson into the back pocket of her jeans. Winced at the way the pistol's outline stood out where the denim hugged her ass. Call it post-apocalypse chic. But she sure as hell wasn't leaving the gun in the room; nor was she wearing her heavy riding jacket to a nice dinner. The HK .45 she stuffed into the boogie bag, slung the heavy duffle over her shoulder and headed for the door. That bag wasn't leaving her sight.

Who would have ever thought that women's fashion during the collapse could be so complicated?

Lauren descended the stairs from her second-story room, crossed the ornate lobby with its century-old opulence, and entered the classy bar with its cut glass, polished brass and waxed wood. Stepping into it was like the collapse hadn't happened. Just a little slice of life as it had been. Patrons were talking over drinks, the bottles all neatly stacked on the back bar, the server hurrying back and forth between tables.

One of the small booths along the wall was open, and Lauren slung the boogie bag onto the seat and slid in beside it. When the server asked what she wanted, Lauren ordered a glass of oatmeal stout from one of the local breweries.

She'd barely sipped the rich brew before Mike Vinich walked in. He was in uniform, wearing ACUs, pants dressed in the tops of his boots. He glanced around, fixed on Lauren, and beamed a smile.

She stepped out, gave him a big hug, and pushed back. "Damn, it's good to see you."

"You, too, Lauren. God, when I heard you were here? Well, call it a gift from the gods." He studied her with soft eyes, as though truly glad to see her. Except for the uniform that hugged his muscular body, he didn't look much different than last time she'd seen him: Brown hair, brown eyes, square block of jaw. That little scar on the right cheek and the bigger one on his brow. She remembered that his older brother had talked him into shooting their dad's scoped .338 Winchester from a bench when Mike was eight. When the big magnum's recoil had blown the boy back, the scope cut a deep crescent in his forehead.

Families were like that. Like the time Jim... *No, Lauren don't let yourself fall down that rabbit hole.*

She slipped back onto the seat. After ordering an IPA, he settled across from her, asking, "How the hell did you get out of Colorado? That's where you were. The Springs, right?"

"Ty told me to go when this all came down." She took a deep breath, fingers rotating the glass of stout. "I hung on until Sunday morning. Figured, despite what Ty said, that it would blow over. Then my supervisor from the bank showed up. Said it was all going to hell. So we made a run for it."

"Glad you made it."

"I did. He didn't. A guy shot him down south of the line." She felt a fist tighten around her heart. Fought to keep Randy's face from forming in her thoughts. "Listen. I don't want to talk about it. How about you?"

The look he was giving her was unsettling. Worried. Studying her intently.

Absently, he replied, "Not much to tell. Dad wanted more time fishing, so he let me take over the dealership. Then the chip shortage hit. Small, low-volume, dealership in Douglas, Wyoming? We didn't have the clout the big urban dealers had, so we got one, maybe two new vehicles a month. Whatever they wanted to send us. Most were sold before they hit the lot. And then there were none. For a time we did a bang-up job with used trucks and SUVs. Until people figured out that there was nothing to replace their current rides. Doesn't matter what trade-in value is if there isn't anything to upgrade to."

Mike shrugged. "Since the car business was going nowhere, I joined the National Guard. One weekend a month, two weeks duty a year, and a paycheck. Then, wham. I'm in Cheyenne, made a sergeant, and put in charge of the food program at Buffalo Camp."

"That's the refugee camp, right?"

"Yeah, it's on the buffalo ranch south of town. They trucked the last of the bison off to a place up around Iron Mountain somewhere, and people now have a home where buffalo roamed, but without the romance of the old West song."

She took a sip of stout; Mike's sensitive smile had always reassured her. "What about Pam? Tiffany said she dropped you cold for a lawyer in Casper."

Vinich took a deep breath, eyes on his beer. "To use an automotive analogy, Pam's like a hot Italian sports car. Great to look at, fast, classy, and she'll make your heart race. Hot, with fantastic curves and body work. But she's an expensive investment, and you'd better be ready to pony up. What you'd call way-high maintenance and really temperamental."

He paused, glanced away. "She's in it for herself, and only for herself. As soon as she figured out that the car business was gone, so was she."

"And the lawyer?"

Vinich snorted. "The guy's twenty years older than Pam is. Ditched a wife and three kids for her. She married him the day the divorce was final, and now she's living in a million-dollar house up Garden Creek at the base of Casper Mountain."

"Sorry."

"Don't be. The best lessons are the ones that are hardest learned." He arched an eyebrow. "How about you and Tyrell Ramirez? Last time I talked to Tiffany, she said you were engaged? That still on?"

"Yeah." She played with her stout glass. "You'd like him, Mike. He's a lieutenant in a Delta Force team. Grew up in Los Angeles. Has a wicked sense of humor. Likes a lot of the things I do. Camping, outdoors, hunting. The plan was that I'd get my degree in business, then wherever he was deployed, I'd have the skills to just pick up and go. I'd always be able to get a job accounting, in a bank, managing a business, whatever."

Mike was giving her that intent inspection again, and she could see the doubt.

"What?"

"Thought you and Breeze were going to be high-stakes financial gurus. Wasn't that the deal? You'd both be millionaires living in Manhattan, traveling to France, gambling in Monaco? Kick off your dusty Wyoming shit-stained boots and don Jimmy Choo's for the stroll down Wall Street?"

She avoided his gaze. "Yeah, well, Breeze and I planned a lot of stuff once upon a time."

He let the silence hang, then said, "Lauren, life's a complicated business that's full of mistakes you can't see coming. Yeah, Jim was your brother. But he was one of my best friends, and he and I talked a lot. About all kinds of things. If you'll recall, his string of mottos consisted of, 'Shit Happens', 'Stuff goes sideways', 'Nothing's for certain'. You grew up with him. You know he'd be really unhappy that you're punishing yourself like this."

Lauren tightened a fist. "When I took hold of the steering wheel that night, I assumed the responsibility and I—"

"Bullshit!" Mike's jaws clamped, his eyes narrowing. "Those are the general's words. Coming right out of your mouth. God knows, if Jimmy had been driving that night..." He waved it away. "Lauren, living comes without a warranty. You were eighteen. Drunk. And Jim's not exactly a blameless victim in all of this."

She bowed her head, pinched the bridge of her nose. "He comes, you know. Talks to me at night. Tells me about all the things I've fucked up." She paused. "Sometimes I wake up in the darkness, sweating, my heart racing."

"That's your brain making stuff up. The guy I knew would never punish his sister that way." Vinich smiled, shook his head. "Lauren, if Jimmy were around, he'd tell you that he loved you. You and Breeze were his life."

He read her disquiet, smiled, and asked. "Enough of the past. How'd you know I was here?"

"Saw Tiffany in Laramie."

"Yeah? Spoke to her just before the phones went dead. What about Breeze?"

"Tiffany says she hasn't heard anything."

"But you haven't heard from her?"

"Some things just can't be undone," Lauren whispered.

"You know, you're not the only one carrying a cross up Golgotha. Breeze is bearing part of that load, too."

"You trying to pick a fight?"

"Nope. I'm trying to help a friend see past her own blinders. That's horse talk, by the way. I do more than just car analogies."

She glanced up, shared his smile, even if she didn't feel it. "So, what about Buffalo Camp? What do I need to know?"

His smile faded. "You ever heard the term TEOTWAKI?"

"Yeah, shorthand. Stands for 'The End Of The World As We Know It'."

"Call it your introduction to The Line."

CHAPTER TWENTY-ONE

***

IT WAS CALLED A MEDIUM TACTICAL VEHICLE, OR AN MTV. LAUREN WONDERED WHY THEY didn't call it an ugly 5-ton cab-over truck. She rode in the back of the bouncy thing, perched awkwardly atop boxes stamped with an American eagle and labeled "FEMA Emergency Food Supplies". The six-cylinder Caterpillar C7 engine roared as they barreled down I-25 at a barnstorming fifty miles an hour.

Vinich sat on a crate across from her—sort of wedged in between the boxes and the tailgate. Within his reach, a battered black M16 hung from the bouncing truck's side rack. They had just passed under the interchange that once hosted the Wyoming Welcome Center.

"Lauren, you still sure this is a good idea?" Vinich asked as they passed a group of people walking resolutely north on the other side of the right-of-way fence. Two of the men carried rifles, and the women and children looked haggard and hungry.

"I thought you needed help. And I want to get an idea of what's going on."

"We do, but I'd just as soon you went somewhere safer."

"I will. Eventually."

"Think Tyrell would approve of you going into a refugee camp to toss out boxes of food?"

"I doubt it." She grinned. "Not unless he was here to keep an eye on things. Maybe help toss out a couple of boxes."

Vinich nodded in approval. "Then he's a good guy."

"A very good guy." She repressed the emotion in her voice.

Climbing to her knees, she squinted into the wind and looked south past the cab to the dark-brown haze. Whatever was burning in the Front Range communities should have been consumed long ago. Instead, the smoke just seemed to get darker, more malignant as it drifted east across the Plains.

As the truck crested the rise and headed down into the old buffalo pasture, Vinich said, "Good Lord, there are more people today than yesterday."

When Lauren saw the cars, tents, and make-shift shelters that spread across the rolling grass-covered hills, it took her breath. There had to be ten thousand in this one camp alone. People were living in the lines of vehicles; they'd been pulled into rows that glinted in the sunlight. Looked like some bizarre flea market or Renaissance fair.

"Any of the bison left?"

"No. Some of the big bulls hung on for a while. Magnificent old guys. I guess they get feisty when a lot of strangers start crowding around them. Some idiot figured he'd kill one and use it to feed people. So, the damn fool stands in front of the buffalo, shoots it in the head with a little .22 pistol, and the buffalo charges and kills him and half his family. Right there on the spot."

"What happened to the old bull?"

"Another refugee with an aught-six put him down. Same for all the others they couldn't round up. Thank God they got the rest shipped out to Iron Mountain. They'll be out of reach of the refugees. Unless, of course, we can't hold the border."

"Any other ranches sending animals up there?"

"Yeah. A few of the ranches close to the line. They know what's happening to livestock in Colorado. People are figuring out that all those cows, sheep, and horses are edible. I hear it from the refugees. If you can shoot a farmer's cow, get it back to the city, you can trade the meat for just about anything you want."

"How are the farmers and ranchers taking that?"

Vinich gave her a dead look. "They're shooting back. Heard an outfit down on Owl Canyon Road drove an entire herd north, crossed the line over on Harriman Road. Just left their whole ranch behind. Said it was too dangerous."

"Hard to believe we'd ever see people stoop to this."

"What would you do if you were down there, electricity off, water doesn't work. Stores are empty. You're on your last tank of gas, assuming no one carjacks your wheels, how far would you go to feed your children?"

"Don't know." She'd already killed Masterson. Maybe she had a better idea than Mike did.

"Yeah, well, those are the kind of questions folks in Fort Collins, Loveland, Longmont, Greeley, and on south are asking themselves these days."

Vinich pointed to the west where black thunderheads rose over the Rockies. "If that comes over, those poor refugee bastards are sure going to be miserable."

"Why's that?"

"We only had five hundred tents in the government inventory. The people who showed up with gas in their tanks were allowed to park their cars and live in them, then we set up the tents in the pastures. Lot of the others, people without any kind of shelter, are in the corrals. But most of them sleep out in the open."

"How many people will be waiting for food today?" Lauren asked, watching the verdant pastures as they passed. It was a beautiful day for June.

"Hard to say. Numbers keep climbing. Just looks like a sea of people," Vinich told her.

"Where are they all coming from?"

"They come from all over, walking up the interstate, carrying whatever they've got on their backs. Some come on ATVs. The lucky ones carry guns to keep from getting mugged. And the armed ones can always hijack some other poor bastard's ATV. When they arrive, they're given a choice: They can turn over their weapons at the gate or turn right around and head back south."

"Do they?"

He gave her a grim smile. "Most spout the Second Amendment and head back south, at least far enough that they can cut or jump the right-of-way fence and try to circle around through the ranches in an attempt to cross the line in a different place. Didn't take us long to figure that out. We've got drones monitoring the easiest routes. After a couple of attempts, most head south for good."

"To do what? There's nothing to the south but—"

"To prey on others, Lauren." Vinich looked defeated. "That's how it works now. Whatever somebody needs, a coat for their kid, a blanket, they take it from another refugee. Nothing we can do to stop it."

A moment later, he pointed. "There's the distribution center."

Lauren climbed on top of the ration boxes and hung onto the steel rack to get a good look at the big barn that had once housed pens, alleys, and the squeeze chute. Being a buffalo ranch, the perimeter fence was higher than in a normal cattle operation, and— though mostly barbed wire—the fence had an electrified high-tensile wire running along extensions wired to every third T-post. Humvees with mounted machine guns were parked every two or three hundred yards along the outside of the fence.

"Call it built to order," Vinich told her. "Not only was it fenced, but that electric wire? We monitor it constantly. Any time someone shorts out a section of fence, it alerts us as to where the breach is. We can have a squad on it before the infiltrators get fifty feet beyond the wire."

People stood in lines waiting for food, and the lines stretched for as far as she could see. Two privates with M16s guarded the barn doors. She prayed there were more soldiers inside. If this crowd decided to erupt, those two privates would be dead in a heartbeat.

The truck rocked and bounced, forcing Lauren to hang onto the rack with both hands.

The tents on the northern end were not government-issue, but colorful camping and backpacking tents. People gathered round them in little clusters. Then the numbers increased and ranks of heavy dark-green military tents covered the trampled grass. Beyond them were the pens that used to be the feedlot. These were filled with cars, trucks, trailers, and motor homes. All in neat lines.

"What about sanitation?" she asked.

"We scoured Cheyenne for porta potties. Wasn't even close enough. Ragnovich finally requisitioned the rancher's backhoe. We're digging slit trenches."

He made a face. "At this rate, we've got four days of rations left in the warehouse. Maybe less. People are still coming. We've flown recon, Lauren. Denver's a nightmare. Burning cars, burning buildings. Gangs in the streets. Entire city blocks with barricades protected by people with clubs and knives. That's what bothers me most, the ones hanging out in their houses praying for a miracle. Lambs waiting for slaughter."

Neither spoke while the truck rocked over the ruts in the road.

She shook her head, voice breaking. "The hackers were brilliant. They hit us where they could do us the most damage. The money system."

"Speculation is that the computer virus went everywhere."

"It would have," she replied. "Banks around the world are all connected. Tens of millions of transactions pass across the internet every day—"

"What does that mean?" He sounded frustrated.

"Basically? Means the Federal Reserve is helpless."

They turned into the ranch entrance, passed the tourist cabins and restaurant. In the southern sky Lauren could see the sickly looking brown smudge that smeared its way east. She'd seen Denver smog before, this was different: a dense, dirty plume that boiled through the blue.

A couple of ATVs with loaded luggage racks waited to be processed at the main gate. The people dealing with the armed guards turned to stare longingly at the MTV as it passed.

The truck rumbled across the cattle guard and past the first fence with its guards; people came from all sides to line the road, watching the truck, faces hopeful, many waving, all calling for food.

Lauren had seen scenes like this in the movies, in newsreels from places like Syria, Iraq, South Sudan, and Pakistan. In real life, here, within miles of Cheyenne, it tore a hole in her soul.

So many of them!

What stunned her was the view from her elevated perch on the ration boxes. To the south, it was a virtual ocean of humanity. All desperate, praying for salvation.

"So, here's the routine," Mike called over the roar of the truck. "We unload the ration boxes into the barn, then we get the hell out of there before anybody tries to steal our truck. Understand? Crew in the barn handles distribution. That's not our job."

"Got it."

A low roar built in the east, like a brutal thunder, rising, filling the sky.

"Holy shit," Vinich murmured as the first of the long formation of aircraft streaked from east to west across the sky to their north.

On either side, the crowd had gone silent, eyes fixed on the northern horizon.

Hutch Daniels—the private driving the truck—slowed to a stop and leaned out the driver's window to call, "You see that? Those are A-10 Thunderbolts!"

"Fuck me," Vinich answered.

At the sight of the air armada, Lauren tried to swallow, couldn't.

"A-10s were built to attack tanks." She could hear her father's voice saying those words.

His eyes on the fading Thunderbolts, Mike squinted, and said. "Yeah."

CHAPTER TWENTY-TWO

***

CHEYENNE'S HISTORIC PLAINS HOTEL HAD BEEN REQUISITIONED BY THE GOVERNOR FOR ALL personnel associated with military operations. In essence, Lauren concluded, the state was becoming a "State".

Sitting at a table in the restaurant's back corner after her final ration run for the day, she nursed a bottle of beer. Which used to be a crime. For another two days, she was twenty years old. Underage drinking? Who cared? With so many soldiers and militia members under the age of twenty-one being armed and sent to the newly established "Observation Posts" on "The Line", trying to enforce the law had become laughable.

She looked around and sighed. Outrageous room rates only lasted as long as cash did. With the travel bans in place, the constant east-west flow on Interstate 80 had vanished. In the entire city of Cheyenne only three venues for lodging remained open.

Her thoughts drifted to Tyrell, as they always did when she was alone. She missed him. Missed his laugh, his strength. Where was he? Some faraway place, probably. Tyrell could handle anything life threw at him. She knew that.

Keep thinking that way. He's alive.

She took another drink of beer. Was he hungry? Cold? She was sitting here with a full belly and a bottle of beer, when he could be hunching in a cave on the outskirts of Beijing, starving.

"You doing okay, Lauren?" the redheaded waitress, Lucy, called. "Need another beer?"

"No, but thanks."

Truckers couldn't buy fuel to carry products across the country, so the supply of national brands was drying up, but local beer, wines, and spirits continued to be made. And would as long as there were grain fields in Wyoming. At least until the refugee hordes broke through the border and moved across the land like plagues of locusts.

As for the rest of the goods brought by truck, things like shampoo, soap, toothpaste, windshield wipers, blueberries, light bulbs, and you name it, people had better find something else that worked.

She took the last bite of tender steak—another locally produced food—and pushed her plate back.

Leaning her elbows on the table, she dropped her head into her hands and massaged her temples. Memories flashed behind her eyelids like horrible cinema. Masterson, Howman…her mother's wounded voice demanding, *'Are you really that stupid? You got drunk and killed your brother?'*

"This chair taken?" a familiar voice asked, "Or is there already enough misery at this table?"

She looked up. Mike Vinich stood there smiling, looking exhausted enough for both of them. His uniform was rumpled and sweat-stained.

"Sit down. I can use the company."

Dropping into the chair opposite her, he sighed as he stared longingly at her beer.

She handed him the half-full bottle. "Here. Drink until you get your own. Then I want it back."

He gave her a big smile. "Thanks. How were the runs today?"

"Tense, thank you. Hope you enjoyed your day 'taking inventory' and hanging out with Captain Ragnovich. That last run today? It was like dangling a spark over a barrel of dynamite."

Lauren watched him down several swallows and waved to get the waitress's attention. When Lucy came over, Mike said, "I'll have whatever she had."

"Steak, beans, and beer?"

"Sounds good."

"Sure thing, Mike." Lucy headed for the bar.

Vinich gave Lauren a cautious look. "You know the governor called the legislature back into session last week? Guess it's going to take a while to get the legislators here. Some of them took their families, packed their horses, and headed up into the mountains, biding their time until this blows over. But it means Breeze's grandfather should be here sometime soon. Maybe her Dad and brother, too."

Lauren's heart actually ached. She missed the Tappans. Couldn't help but wonder what had happened to Breeze. How it would break their hearts if she just vanished in the maelstrom that was Colorado's Front Range. "What's happening?"

"Agar's working on a bill to allow the state to print its own currency."

Lauren laughed before she thought about it. "Backed by what? Gold? Coal? Otherwise, it's only paper."

Vinich made an airy gesture with one hand. "Agar's got to have something in mind to back them with. What will be a unit-of-value in Wyoming's economy? A cow? A bucket of coal? A barrel of crude?"

"No clue," Lauren said softly, trying to think it through.

The waitress returned and set the beer in front of Vinich. "There you go, Mike. Steak won't be long."

"Thanks, Lucy," he said.

Lauren tilted her head skeptically. "Maybe each Wyodollar will be redeemable for a steak? Come winter, that might be all the wealth in the world."

Mike took a sip of beer and a sublime expression came over his face. "Hope to hell there's beer in heaven."

Dust shimmered across his forehead and cheeks. He'd been in the warehouse all day. "Figured you would have headed out to Buffalo Camp. What are you doing in town?"

"Lieutenant Metz has the camp tonight. I came in with the captain. He's meeting with the governor. Planning session. And I wanted to tell you that Tiffany is going to be here."

"How do you know?"

"Militia truck came in early this morning. One of the guys was carrying a message from Trevor. He wanted me and you to know Tiff was coming in tomorrow, and now I've told you."

"What's she up to?"

Mike shrugged. "We'll ask her when she gets here. She's riding in on a militia truck. Going to meet us at Sanford's restaurant around seven tomorrow night. The good news is, it's still open."

As more people entered the restaurant, the noise level rose.

Mike lowered his voice. "Listen, you should know. We have to start splitting the rations we give the refugees."

A thread of panic went through her. "Jesus, Mike. What happens after the last ration box is delivered to the barn?"

"That's why Ragnovich is meeting with the governor." Mike took a deep breath. "We've got two or three days left. They processed another five hundred and sixty people today, and they just keep coming. They've heard that Wyoming is a sanctuary. Wish to hell we'd never started feeding folks. That was a mistake. Now there's thousands of half-starved crazy people flocking up I-25 toward Cheyenne."

She blinked, trying to visualize it. Each morning, noon, and night when the Guard MTVs pulled up at the big barn, people were already lined up, waiting in the alleys where the bison used to run, walked through the chute—if you could imagine—and were handed their rations. It wasn't meant to be demeaning, treating them as if they were livestock, there just wasn't any other way to safely and fairly distribute the rations. Despite that, fights frequently broke out. They'd had several fatalities, caused when somebody jerked a ration box from the hands of another refugee and tried to run away with it; sometimes they didn't make it very far.

She clenched her fist. "Is Colorado doing anything to help us?"

"Governor Agar delivered an ultimatum to the interim governor down in Denver. Word is that she did take action. Finally. Colorado National Guard is establishing a refugee camp east of Denver at the DIA airport. We'll start broadcasting the news all over the camp. Maybe some will start to leave."

Lauren ran nervous fingers through her hair, pulling it back. "That's a hundred-and-thirty-mile walk, Mike. Families. Kids. Babies. They've been robbed of everything but the clothes on their backs. Now they have to walk over a hundred miles to get food and water? Given that choice? They're not leaving."

"Colorado refuses to send buses up. Says they'd need to be escorted by military to keep them safe. And they don't want to waste the fuel. Nothing we can do."

She felt sick. "It's going to be a disaster, isn't it?"

"'Course. They're human beings. You know. You've seen. And, my God, the things some of them have already survived? Rape? Beatings? Robbery? They'll do whatever they have to, even if it means murdering you and me and walking over our dead bodies."

She gave him a hard stare.

"I'm not kidding, Lauren. This morning, a bunch of fools started shooting at one of our patrols about ten miles west of town."

"Anybody hurt?"

"Turns out the militia guy is a long-range shooter with a 6.5 mm Creedmoor who competes in F class. He went prone atop the Suburban they were driving and took out four of the attackers before the rest had enough and beat feet south across the hills."

He took a long drink of beer and set his bottle on the table with a thunk. "Don't know if you've heard the worst news."

"The worst?"

"Yeah, from General Kyzer at Warren Air Base."

"No. I've been busy with food runs all day."

"This is just a rumor. Understand? I can't verify it. None of us can."

Uneasy, she said, "Okay."

Mike looked around the restaurant, noting the positions of the other patrons, before he leaned across the table to whisper, "There's been no word from Washington. The Pentagon. Joint Chiefs. Nothing."

Fear wormed its way through her belly. Mom and Dad? Were they okay? "What do you mean, nothing? Military communications have been ongoing, despite the shutdown of the satellites."

Mike looked her hard in the eyes. "They've gone silent. Like no one's home. Rumor is that we're fighting Chinese on the west coast. San Francisco and Seattle."

Too stunned to speak, she just blinked at him. Finally, she softly asked, "America has been invaded?"

"It's a rumor, Lauren. That's all."

"Shit," was all she could think to say.

Giving her a piercing look, Mike told her, "You said that Tyrell left an M4 in that boogie bag? Starting tomorrow, I want you to take it with you. Every run, Lauren. I think things are going to start getting really hairy."

CHAPTER TWENTY-THREE

***

LAUREN AND MIKE FOUND TIFFANY WAITING ON THE SIDEWALK OUTSIDE OF SANFORD'S
Grub and Pub, hugged, laughed, and walked into the restaurant. It was
a fun place. They filed past the T-rex wearing the saddle and were met
by a young woman with a stack of menus and a name tag that read: Jo.

"Three of you tonight?"

"Yep, three," Mike answered.

"Gotcha. Follow me, please."

She led them through the almost-empty restaurant to a table across
from the bar. Tiff and Lauren took chairs on one side, while Mike
sat on the other. The walls were covered with cool memorabilia,
framed historical photographs, and rusty parts from old cars and farm
equipment. The rich smells of Cajun spices wafted through the air.
Lauren wondered what the place would smell like when the last of
the spices were used up.

The waitress handed out hand-printed menus. A far cry from the
old ones with fifty different entrees. She asked, "What can I get you
to drink?"

"Iced tea for me." Tiffany smiled up at her.

"I'll take coffee," Lauren said. Beer would be around forever, but
coffee was short term. Then there would be no more. Also forever.

"Got a Corona back there?" Mike asked hopefully, and when the
waitress shook her head, he said, "Then I'll take whatever you've got."

"On Belay IPA from Lander Brewery? That do ya?"

"Yeah, love it."

"Be back in a sec."

When she was gone, Lauren stared at the few items and soaring
prices. She had Randy's cash, plus her own money, and the two

thousand that Tyrell kept in his boogie bag, but she'd already spent over a thousand dollars, and, at this rate, the rest wasn't gonna last long. "Forty-five dollars for a hamburger? Sixty-five if it's made of buffalo? Who can afford this?"

"It's called inflation," Mike said.

Tiffany looked around at all the empty tables. "Be grateful that someone in the state still has buffalo to slaughter. What are you having?"

"My favorite is the Black Magic buffalo burger with parmesan garlic fries. Looks like this may be the last time I get to eat it, though."

Tiffany's brow furrowed. "I'm going to have the Voodoo Skillet. Even if there's no shrimp in it anymore. Jeez, I don't think I've ever paid this much for dinner in my life."

Mike looked up. "Why don't you let me treat you two to dinner? I just got paid. Not only that, Lauren's birthday is day after tomorrow. Let's make this her early birthday dinner."

"I'll take you up on it," she told Mike. "Thanks."

"Good. Happy Birthday. How 'bout you, Tiff?"

"Can't turn down an offer like that." Tiffany closed her menu and shoved it aside.

The waitress returned and set their drinks in front of them. "Have you decided?"

After they ordered, Tiffany lifted her glass. "Happy twenty-first birthday to Lauren! Wow. You're legal now."

They clicked glasses, or in her case, coffee cup.

"I'm so glad you're both here to help me celebrate." She smiled.

"I've been planning to buy you dinner anyway," Mike said. "But it's an added bonus that Tiff is here. Couldn't ask for better friends."

"Here's to the three of us!" Tiffany said and lifted her glass again.

While they made small talk, Lauren's gaze drifted over the colorful bottles of beer that lined the shelves behind the bar. Most were empty, just for décor now, she guessed. In the old days, she and Tiff had come in here and fantasized about the day when they'd be old enough to sit around with friends and taste some of those beers.

Tiffany asked, "You believe the rumor about China invading the west coast?"

"No," Lauren said.

"I don't either," Vinich fiddled with the cuff of his sleeve. "Last I heard, they were busy trying to take Taiwan. It would have taken a massive naval force. Not to mention months of prepositioning, troop movements, and logistics. Our spy satellites would have seen them prepping for war."

"Who says they didn't?" Tiff asked. "I'm just a civilian, but I think all this happened so fast the military was caught off-guard."

Sinking back into her chair, Lauren's thoughts tumbled over one another, trying to imagine how the U.S. military could possibly have missed it? Tyrell had said nothing. But then, he wouldn't have. Still, he had *not* been on alert prior to the cyberattack. No. He had not known. She was sure of it.

Tiffany looked around the table. "If there's any more bad news, tell it to me now, okay? So I can have fun for the rest of the night. How are you doing, Mike?"

Mike gritted his teeth for a moment. "Not an easy day to be out on The Line."

"What happened?" Lauren asked.

Mike hunched over his glass of beer. "Bunch of women shot at one of our patrols about five miles west of town. Guess they thought the Militia wouldn't fire back. Guys had no choice. They took out three before the rest ran off."

"So, we're shooting women?" Tiffany made a face.

"Tiff, put yourself out there. Say it's kids. Bullets start whizzing by your head, and you know the next one might blow out your heart. What are you going to do?"

In a hollow voice Tiffany said, "Guess I'd shoot back."

Please, God, I don't want to kill anyone else. The thought hit Lauren out of the blue.

Mike reached across the table to take her hand in a warm grip. "Next couple of days...anything could happen while we're out there. Stay close to me. You understand?"

Lauren looked down at his hand on hers. His touch made Lauren feel good, safer...and as though she were betraying Tyrell. Smiling so as not to offend him, she gently pulled her hand back, and said, "Sure, Mike. I'll stay close enough to keep you safe."

The joke broke the tension, got laughter all the way around.

"Yeah...thanks," Mike muttered wryly.

They turned when Jo brought their dinners. She set his Cajun ribs on the table. "That's extra bar-b-que sauce on the side. Don't waste it. Once it's gone, we're not getting anymore."

"Thanks."

Then Jo carefully placed Tiffany's Voodoo Skillet down and handed Lauren's buffalo burger to her.

They'd barely dived into their plates when two more Guard soldiers came in and took the booth behind Lauren and Tiffany. A man and a woman, she had corporal's stripes on her sleeve.

The woman softly said, "Can't be true. I don't believe it."

The man replied, "Maybe not, but Captain Ragnovich was scared when he came out of that meeting."

Tiffany seemed oblivious, just eating her dinner, but Lauren and Mike exchanged knowing glances.

The private asked, "So the captain told you straight out that America was at DEFCON 4? We're at war?"

Mike's face slackened. He quietly put his knife and fork down.

"Nope." There was a pause, then the man said, "He didn't say a word to me, or anybody else. Just walked into his office and locked the door."

"Probably didn't want you to disturb him. You can be really annoying."

The guy chuckled. "Yeah, maybe."

"Where'd you hear the part about DEFCON 4?"

Mike rose from his seat, walked to their booth, and said, "Mind if I sit down?"

"Hey, Sergeant Vinich, course not. Sit."

Lauren wasn't Guard and didn't feel like joining them anyway, but she listened carefully to every word.

Tiffany had caught on and was listening, too.

In a low voice, Mike asked, "Any more on San Francisco or Seattle?"

The woman said, "Guys out at Observation Post Delta Bravo said they'd heard General Kyzer cancelled all leaves. Even the civilian contractors and employees. No one in or out."

Mike exhaled the words, "You seen any evidence that Warren is mobilizing? Hard evidence? Not just bullshit rumors."

The man, barely above a whisper, said, "Yeah. They're sending teams out to the missile silos at night. Looks to me like…"

Two more people entered the restaurant, and the folks at Mike's table went silent. Then the conversation dropped to whispers that Lauren couldn't understand.

Her gaze drifted around the restaurant. The bartender stood behind the bar, polishing glasses, while Jo rushed from table to table taking and delivering orders. One of the tables was filled with people in business suits. Probably government employees. A few soldiers had come and sat with their eyes downcast, focusing on their food. The rumors must have been making the rounds, keeping everybody on edge, thinking about the future.

Mike came back and reseated himself across from her. Twenty-three years old, lines already carved the corners of his eyes and etched his forehead. Picking up his glass of beer, he took a drink, and quietly set it on the table.

"What'd they say?" Tiffany whispered.

Leaning back against the booth, Mike took his time. Studied Tiffany and Lauren, his gaze oddly intent, searching their faces, as though trying to memorize all the details he'd forgotten in the last couple of years.

"Lauren, do you remember the day we met? You were twelve. Junior High. Jim and I came barging in. You were on the basketball court…"

The lights flickered off, came on again, and the fluorescent gleam turned his brown hair faintly blue. People muttered throughout the restaurant. Mike hadn't even blinked. Just kept staring at Lauren.

"I remember. Lunch break. I was shooting from the free-throw line, tripped on my own feet and fell on the hardwood. I was crying. One of boys laughed at me. You hit him in the head with the basketball."

A tender smile came to Mike's face, but when the soldiers started talking again, it faded. "You got any body armor in that bag? Tyrell leave you a vest?"

"No. Why?"

"I'll loan you mine. For our next trip out to the camp."

Tiffany glanced between them, and said, "Okay, enough scary

shop talk. I want Lauren to tell us all about Tyrell. He's in special operations, right?"

Lauren's gaze remained locked with Mike's, but she replied, "Delta Force. What they call "The Unit."

Mike asked, "You said he's from LA? Born and raised?"

"He was born in Santa Fe, New Mexico. His folks moved to L.A. when he was six. Loves hot food. I mean really hot, fiery stuff." Talking about him made her miss him even more. "Wish I knew where he was."

"If he's Delta Force, he may not tell you for another twenty years," Mike said. "One of these days, you'll be sitting around the breakfast table with your five grown kids, and he'll look over and say, 'Okay, I can tell you now.' And boom, you'll find out he was in Africa eating worms while he hunted down terrorists."

"Wouldn't be the first time. You should hear his stories about Yemen. One time, he had to choke down meat squirming with maggots."

"Dear God!" Tiffany cried. "My Voodoo Skillet is filled with slivers of onion. You know what they look like now?"

Mike and Lauren howled with laughter.

And some of the puzzle pieces in her life started falling back into place, filling in the picture of who she was and how she'd gotten here. For the first time since she'd walked out of the bank, she felt whole. Raw, wounded, but whole.

CHAPTER TWENTY-FOUR

* * *

RAIN FELL AS LAUREN RODE OUT IN THE RATION TRUCK WITH MIKE THE NEXT DAY. AFTER this run, there were only three more truckloads of food before the warehouse ran empty. Some of the people had already begun to head south to the refugee camp at DIA in Colorado, but there were still thousands left. Today's rations should feed five thousand people. If there were ten thousand waiting in line, what would happen when the soldiers at the barn ran out of food?

Everybody was scared. Really scared.

She tucked Tyrell's M4 rifle beneath her yellow rain coat to keep it dry, and watched Mike, who crouched on top of the ration boxes on the opposite side of the elevated bed. Tension—tight as a stretched wire—creased his face as he gazed out at the huge camp. He had his M16 clutched in tight fists.

The ballistic vest Mike had loaned her was bulky and awkward. Heavier than she remembered from the last time Tyrell had let her try his vest on. It ate into her shoulders.

As the truck bounced over the cattle guard, people started running across the pasture to intercept its course. Looked like an army coming. Many carried weapons. They looked miserable. Children were sopping wet, even the toddlers hanging onto their parents' hands, dripped rain. Their hollow, hungry, eyes…

"We're starving out here!" a woman shouted at Lauren. "Where's the rest of the food? You Wyoming bastards keeping it all for yourselves?"

Hutch, the truck driver, didn't even slow down, just kept the MTV moving at a steady pace down the road toward the barn, which forced the woman to run along behind the truck, calling curses.

"Throw out a box now!" a teenage boy with a hunting rifle called.

"I'm not walking through those buffalo chutes again! I almost got trampled to death last time. Throw me a box now, goddamit!"

When Hutch suddenly hit the brakes, he hurled both Mike and Lauren over the ration boxes into the steel rack.

"Sergeant Vinich?" Hutch called. "I don't see any guards in front of the barn. Doors are wide open."

Mike scrambled to his feet to look over the rain-wet cab with worried eyes. "Something's wrong."

Lauren stood up. Massive crowds huddled in the rain around the barn. The ocean of humanity began to rise, pointing, calling out to someone inside the barn. Like a slow wave, they started toward the truck.

Mike said, "I don't like this. I don't see any WNG people. Did they get orders to clear out and we don't know about it?"

"Doesn't seem likely."

Mike turned and pointed sternly at Lauren. "You keep that M4 handy."

"I got it." She gripped the gun more tightly. Turned where the teenager was trying to grab hold and climb the high tailgate. "Hey!" she cried. "Get your ass back down!"

"Fuck you! Bitch. Toss me a food box!"

People—a lot of them—were headed their way from the tents and parked vehicles. Those in the rear were running to catch up.

"Hutch?" Mike called. "Move!"

Hutch started inching toward the barn again. The surge continued, people shouting insults, begging for food.

"What are we going to do?" Hutch called, hanging half out the driver's window. "We can't offload the ration boxes with all these people swamping the truck. We'll never make it!"

Mike had begun nervously glancing around. "Jesus-God-Almighty. Turn around, Hutch. Get us out of here!"

Hutch cranked the wheel so tight Mike almost lost his balance as the MTV spun in the mud.

Three bearded men—dressed in camo and carrying what looked like M4s—emerged from the barn and started calling orders. Then four more appeared, brandishing a collection of scoped rifles.

Over the distance and the MTV's diesel, Lauren couldn't make out the words, but she was getting a crawly feeling in her gut.

The four with the scoped rifles shouldered their weapons, all pointed at the retreating truck. Lauren instinctively hunched in anticipation of being shot.

All around the truck, people started picking up rocks, trash, even the rusty chunks of metal. The eyes of the women scared Lauren the most. She had no doubt but that they would do anything to get food for their children.

A black-bearded man in a dirty blue coat yelled, "No one needs to get hurt! Throw your weapons on the ground and step out of the truck. All of you! And keep your hands up! We just want the truck."

"Where's Lieutenant Metz? Where's Corporal Baker?" Mike demanded, climbing up onto the ration boxes so that he could see better. "And the guards, Dewey and Simms?"

"They tried to be heroes. Now, are you going to get out of that truck, or are we going to drag your dead bodies out?" Black Beard said as he ran to keep up with the slowing MTV.

Slowing? A glance showed Lauren that too many people blocked the way ahead. Even as Hutch slowed to keep from running over them, they crowded closer.

Every muscle in Lauren's body went rigid. The tremble came from deep inside, tickling around her intestines, weakening her knees and arms.

A woman with a baby in her arms looked at the armed civilians, then screamed up at Vinich, "Don't give them the truck! They've been taking what they want from everybody in the camp, then selling it down on the highway to the south. I need my rations! My kids are hungry!"

Lauren heard a *pow-slap* as a high velocity round smacked the truck. She dove for cover behind the tailgate just as Mike Vinich flopped down onto the ration boxes three feet away.

"Hutch!" Vinich screamed. "Drive, damn it! *Drive*."

Hutch laid on the horn. The diesel howled and roared. The MTV lurched forward with such force that ration boxes toppled and shifted. Lauren fought for balance, almost lost her footing.

Screams rang out. Bullets smacked into the ration boxes and the cargo rack's steel rails. Over the racket, she barely heard Mike shout, "Lauren, they're coming!"

The wave of men, women, and youths carrying guns or make-shift weapons surged after the truck. They were gaining. Hutch was barely crawling forward. Trying not to drive over the people blocking the way.

"Lauren, shoot!" Mike ordered. "Anyone with a weapon!"

Lauren unhooked the M4. Yanking the bolt, she let it slam home and flipped the safety to burst. It was a struggle to brace herself on the steel rack.

The black-bearded man was no more than ten feet behind, trying to aim his rifle as he ran. When he fired at her, Lauren triggered the M4. Her burst took him in the chest and spun the man behind him as well.

People kept coming, running and shaking fists, shouting curses. The crackle of gunfire was accompanied by the slap and pock of bullets hitting the MTV's sides, rack, and smacking into the ration boxes.

Mike screamed, "*Drive, Hutch! Drive, damn it!*"

Hutch screamed back, "I can't! People are blocking the way!"

"I don't give a damn! Drive, or we're dead!"

Hutch stomped on the accelerator and the MTV pitched forward. The sound of the screams changed, the timbre shifting from rage to terror as the big truck hit the wall of bodies.

The scene suddenly became chaos. The stuff of nightmares. Muzzle flashes flickered in the crowd as people fired at the truck, and a barrage of rocks and debris struck the racks and cab. Something hit her in the face. Rock? A thrown chunk of metal?

The truck lurched from side to side, bouncing with such force it slammed Lauren against the tailgate. She caught herself, settled the M4 on the men shooting at her, and fired.

Tried not to think about the screaming and broken bodies that appeared as if magic from beneath the big 5-ton truck. Littering the muddy ground, some scrambled to their feet, dazed and terrified to have been knocked flat and survived. The ones crushed by the tires didn't; they had a distorted look, like caricatures. Just human shapes, writhing and dying where they'd been pressed into the mud.

And then they disappeared, as if engulfed and trampled by the wave of pursing humans. Buried in the crowd, they caused not even a ripple.

Tyrell's disembodied voice kept repeating in her head, *sight picture. Breathe. Trigger.*

Short burst by short burst, she killed anyone who pointed a gun at her. For a second, she couldn't understand why the M4 had stopped. Or why Mike wasn't firing.

Throwing down her empty M4, she spun to look at Mike. Found him sprawled on his back across the ration boxes. He was gasping for breath. Blood bubbled at his lips.

"Mike?"

Three men were trying to climb up the rack, wild-eyed and awkward because of the pistols clutched in their hands. Lauren clambered over the ration boxes, grabbed Mike's M16. The bouncing was getting worse.

The screams.

The image didn't register.

Couldn't register.

That human beings were being crushed to death under the tires defied the brain.

Hutch had the accelerator floored and was weaving drunkenly down the road. Why the hell didn't he shift up?

A bullet cut past Lauren's ear as one of the men climbing the rack reached over the top.

When the truck swerved wildly, she thrust the M16 at the shooter and fired point blank. The man fell.

Stepping over, swaying for balance, Lauren shot the next climber. As he dropped, the third—a blond-headed man—gave up and jumped free. But there were more in the surging crowd, waving pistols, hunting rifles, semi-automatics. Men and women. Even boys, teenagers. And running in their midst, some in tears, others scared, were children. Too damned many children.

Like the fist of God, Lauren was punched in the side. She hit the tail gate. Fell flat on the ration boxes. Couldn't breathe.

It took a split second to realize a bullet had hammered her vest. Mike's vest.

Lauren couldn't get air into her lungs. She rolled to her knees, gasped. People were swarming the back of the truck. She caught an image of hands grabbing the slats. Faces peering between the rails. Shouts of rage and fear.

Bullets clanged against the rack and boxes. A sharp fragment of metal tore through her sleeve. Terror charged her muscles. Far back in her mind, Tyrell's voice said, *You never know what you're capable of until you're staring death in the face...*

Flipping the control lever to auto, she clambered to her knees. Swung the M16 in an arc. Brass flew, and the muzzle blast deafened.

Saw them. Men. Women. And the children.

Dear God, she was killing children.

All of them crumpling, toppling to the ground.

What stunned her was the rage in their eyes as they fell. Rage against her. Against Mike and Hutch. Dear God, they'd been giving them food!

The bolt locked on empty.

In desperation, she began tossing ration boxes out the back.

Why the hell was Hutch driving so slow?

The horde of people kept chasing them, screaming in hate, firing at her each time she lifted her head above the tailgate to shove out another box. Then another, and another. She attacked the stack, tossing box after box, and the cracking of bullets slowed, though the shooting kept popping and banging behind them.

She'd emptied half the load when suddenly the truck blasted forward, Hutch desperately trying to get away.

Lauren continued tossing out boxes, many of them soaked with Mike's blood. His body had slipped down, fallen onto the MTV's bed.

Lauren, fighting for breath, the ache in her side having grown unbearable, threw a look over the tailgate. Tried to make sense of the melee and chaos behind them. The mob was fighting over the ration boxes like some cannibalistic monster intent on devouring itself. Fists flew, people shrieked, and through it all guns kept popping. The animal savagery of it would haunt her forever.

But no one was pursuing the truck. They might have been forgotten.

Sobbing, shaking, she crawled to Mike and pulled his head into her lap. "You're all right," she told him. "We're almost back. Hang on."

"Lauren?" Mike mouthed the words, lips bloody. He started coughing. Blood. So much blood.

Heart hammering, she looked down into Mike's tired eyes. Too tired, barely able to keep them open. She held his hand. "You're all right. Hospital's five minutes."

"Five?" He tried to mouth the word.

He was fading. She could see it. She'd seen the same look in

Randy's eyes. Mike's grip on her hand was relaxing. He looked up and smiled at her as though glad she was there with him in his last moments. A bloody bubble formed on his right nostril, expanding and contracting with each gurgling breath.

"Stay with me!" she shouted. "Mike?"

By the time Hutch passed the armed guards in front of the FEMA warehouse, her ribs hurt so badly she could barely breathe. The truck lurched to a ragged stop. To her amazement, the rain continued to fall, soft and gentle, as if indifferent to the carnage.

A lieutenant climbed into the back of the truck, looked at her, then at Vinich. Before he could speak, she cried, "Get Sergeant Vinich to the hospital. Now, Lieutenant!"

In moments, men leaped into the bloody cargo bed, picked Mike up, and carried him away. She was shaking so hard she couldn't think, couldn't move. Finally, she grabbed Tyrell's empty M4 and stumbled out of the truck.

That's when she saw the two soldiers dragging Hutch out of the cab. The private was limp as a rag doll, covered in blood, his eyes half-lidded and empty.

In shock, she staggered off to the side.

The world spins.

Takes about five seconds for the bottom to drop out.

Falling.

Falling inside.

She's never felt this way before. The rain cools as it patters on her body. The scent of truck exhaust stings her nostrils. She's toppling headfirst into some strange abyss and can feel the bottom rising up to meet her.

The pain in her chest, from the bullet, increases until it feels like an iron band pulling tight around her ribs.

"Hey, Davis?" someone calls from an eternal distance. "You okay?"

It happens in slow motion. The world spins, flips upside down... her head hits the mud...

CHAPTER TWENTY-FIVE

***

LAUREN HUNCHED ON THE EXAMINATION TABLE WITH HER LEGS DANGLING. DEAD INSIDE, she wanted to break down and weep. Her body hurt.

Wished the bullet would have killed her.

Wished she didn't have to live with the memories of those people.

God, was that really me?

She gasped when the nurse wrapped another length of gauze bandage around her middle. In addition to the examination table, the tiny room had two chairs and a desk.

White.

Everything was white.

White rooms, long white halls, shiny steel that reflected the fluorescent lights. And nurses in pale-green scrubs constantly hurrying past the door.

Images—like some perverted Italian art movie—replayed in her brain: The vibrations and recoil of the M4 as she shot fellow human beings down. The shock in their eyes as the bullets blew through their flesh and snapped their bones. How they flopped face-first into the mud and puddled water.

A keening started deep in her soul.

"Where's Mike Vinich?" Lauren flinched when the nurse tightened the gauze bandage. The bullet had struck the vest low on the right side, but the massive bruise covered her entire chest.   The nurse glanced up briefly. She had brown eyes and bleached blonde hair with black roots. "In surgery."

"Is he going to make it?"

"I can't answer that until the surgery is over."

"What about Hutch, the truck driver? Just before I passed out, I saw soldiers pulling him from the cab. Did they bring him here?"

"Sorry, but I don't know a thing about him. Pretty sure he was not brought to the hospital. But so many people came in. Hell, we're still processing the wounded from that business at the refugee camp."

Lauren tried to breathe; pain knifed through her.

The woman finished the bandage, stood back to check her work, and then pointed a finger in Lauren's face. "Now, you listen to me. The hospital is overwhelmed, so I've been ordered to turn you loose. You're free to go, but don't think you can resume your normal activities. You should find a bed and sleep for a few days. Without that vest you'd be dead. Your liver is badly bruised, as are your ribs. You hear what I'm saying?"

"Yeah. I hear."

"You'd better," she said in a hostile voice, as though she expected Lauren to disobey and already resented her for it.

Lauren slid off the table, stifled a cry, and went over to pick up her shirt from where it lay on the chair. While she finished dressing, she watched the nurse clean up.

Just before the woman left, she turned and said, "Captain Ragnovich is outside. He wants a word."

"Okay." Careful of her side, Lauren eased down onto one of the chairs to wait. Mindless, hollow. The M4 kept vibrating in her arms, the brass flying, bodies breaking, jerking, falling...

When Captain Ragnovich stepped in, he met her eyes, nodded, and took a position by the door. He was wearing damp and mud-stained ACUs, his cover under his left arm.

A curious fluttery sensation tormented her stomach. Of their own accord her shoulders and fists knotted. She was about to pay for her actions. For the murder of all those people.

"Ms. Davis," Ragnovich said, and indicated the other chair. "May I?"

"Sir, yes, sir."

He dragged the chair around so that it faced her and sat. For a moment, he studied her thoughtfully. "How you feeling?"

"Fine. Nothing broken."

"You saved Vinich and the truck out there."

"No, I—I didn't. Hutch, he-he..." She stammered to a stop. "He got us out of there. Without him, we'd be... We'd be..."

"Take it slow. I want to hear your side of the story. Tell me exactly what happened."

Lauren swallowed hard, sick to her stomach. "When they started shooting at us... I mean, the bullets snapping past my head. Hitting the truck. I was so scared. Shaking. It was just instinct. Mike and I started shooting back."

"Wait, go back. What happened before the shots were fired?"

"Mike had climbed up on top of the ration boxes. He knew something was wrong. Barn doors were wide open. Guards were missing. He ordered Hutch to turn around. That's when the men came out of the barn with guns."

"They fired first?"

"Yes, sir. Told us to surrender the truck. Mike ordered Hutch to turn around. Then they started toward the truck. Started shooting. I mean there were people all around us. They didn't care. And I...I..."

She closed her eyes, fought a sob that speared pain through her ribs. *I murdered all those people.*

Ragnovich ran nervous fingers through his hair. "All right. I'll make a report to Colonel Mackeson. As far as I'm concerned, this is over. You were defending yourselves. Anything you want to add?"

"There were women and children."

"I'm aware of the body count. My understanding is that they were going to mob the truck. That true?"

She jerked a nod. "They just kept coming."

Ragnovich's voice softened. "You know what would have happened if you hadn't acted? All three of you would be dead. They'd have taken the MTV."

She shook her head, wondered if the surreal sensation clouding her thoughts was there to stay. "Nurse said Mike is still in surgery. Is he going to be okay?"

Ragnovich's wrinkles rearranged into worried lines. "They had to remove one of his lungs. It was shot to confetti, I guess. But surgeon says he's got a real chance."

Behind her eyes, she could see Mike looking up at her with blood foaming on his lips. He must have thought he was dying, but he hadn't cried or thrashed around in panic. He'd just focused on her face like it was a lifeboat.

"Lot of people are calling you a hero," Ragnovich said gently.

"Me?" The word stunned her. "Hutch was the h-hero. He got us out of there. I was just scared shitless, doing whatever I could to keep the truck from being overrun. There were women. Kids. I just…I had to…"

Ragnovich leaned back. "I know. There will be a final report."

Despite her pain and weariness, Lauren caught his meaning. Dear God… She stared at him with empty eyes.

"Believe it or not, I know how you're feeling. Been there myself. Back in Afghanistan," Ragnovich said in a kind voice. "But people were shooting at you. We counted nearly two hundred bullet strikes in the body of the truck. It's a miracle you're alive."

"I shouldn't be."

"Lauren, our intelligence tells me they were planning on stealing the MTV, using it to spearhead an assault on the north fence. We'd have probably stopped them before they got to Cheyenne. But most of the rest would have come flooding through the hole they tore in the perimeter. It would have been a blood bath. The dead and wounded would number in the thousands. Which is a whole lot less than died at the camp today."

She frowned at the tan vinyl flooring. "Captain, what happens next? With the camp, I mean."

"After today's events?" He shrugged. "What happened today was a catalyst. The perimeter fence is like a war zone. They've started shooting randomly at our people. We return fire. A lot of people gave up after today's incident. Decided they'd be safer somewhere else and started south. Others went east. We'll monitor them with drones."

Lauren shook her head. "There's nothing to the east or south except death and misery."

"True. And that really sucks the big one, doesn't it?" Ragnovich paused. "Anyone tell you that Hutch is dead?"

Lauren sagged forward. "What?"

"He kept driving, trying to get you and Vinich out of there, even though he had four bullet holes in him. You're right when you call him a hero. Tough as they come."

The antiseptic smell of the hospital suddenly nauseated her. She searched for the words. Couldn't find them.

Ragnovich said, "A car's waiting outside to take you back to the hotel. Take a few days and get some rest. From here on out, the Guard will be covering your room and meals. I'll have your bike brought over. You'll need time to heal."

She nodded dully.

Ragnovich rubbed his hands together. "Got some good news for you today. Breeze Tappan rode in out of the blue. She made it, Lauren. Got out of Colorado."

Lauren closed her eyes, tears rising hot and wet to break free and trickle down her cheeks.

Breeze? Alive?

Lauren's thoughts turned to her last conversation with Breeze. Her best friend had been crying, heartbroken that Jimmy, the love of her life was dead. Shouting that Lauren had murdered him. Screaming she should have never gotten behind the wheel.

All things that Lauren believed herself.

God, I'm a worthless human being.

Ragnovich rose from his chair. "When you're ready to go to work again, report to the supply depot. They'll tell you what to do."

"Yes, sir."

He pivoted and left the hospital room.

Lauren braced her elbows on her knees. When she closed her eyes, trying to block out this world, and the images that skittered and flashed white. Human beings blown apart. By her.

Something slithering around inside her.

It felt alive.

The despair.

CHAPTER TWENTY-SIX

***

WHEN DARKNESS CAME AT THE PLAINS HOTEL, IT GOT WORSE. THE NIGHTMARES TOOK ON a vivid new twist until several times she woke screaming, the sheets twisted around her sweating body.

Each time, she climbed out of bed. Stared out the window at the night. Looked down on Central Avenue, deathly quiet, devoid of traffic. Not even a pedestrian passed. When the tears threatened, she crawled back in bed and tucked the pillow tight.

She dreamed of Tyrell, of her arms around his warm and muscular body. Forced herself to feel his lips on hers, his hands moving reverently over her face, down her throat. She fantasized that they made gentle love.

Until the next nightmare blasted through the dream…

And it started all over again.

"Where are you, Ty?"

A reddish-orange morning light burned through the now-constant brown haze. It just kept blowing in from the west, sometimes blanketing the mountains, always carrying a faint stink, like burning plastic.

She sat up and reached for her jeans where they lay across the foot of the bed. She almost screamed at the pain. Felt like her chest was broken. She'd been kicked by a horse once during her rodeo days. So, yeah, she knew how badly bruised ribs could hurt, but nothing like this.

She walked over to the pill bottle. Pain killers. Paracetamol. Which was probably worth a bloody damn fortune given that when the last of the supplies in Cheyenne were gone, there would be no more. She still had four left.

Save them. Tough it out, woman.

What time was it? Was it the same day? Or two days since the battle? Each hour seemed to bleed into the next.

Blinking back tears, she finished dressing and strapped on her gun belt.

Was Ty off fighting Chinese invaders? Were Seattle and San Francisco really invaded? Or were those just the insane inventions that crazy minds had turned into rumors with a life of their own?

Lauren left her room, closed the door behind her. Ribs aching she made her way step-by-step down the stairs to the restaurant.

The chalk board outside advertised, "Homemade bread."

From here on out, that was the only kind there would ever be. There were three specials: beef sandwich with boiled rice, steak with beans, or a bowl of chili. The whole place smelled like hot grease.

Lauren entered and went to sit in her regular booth. She was still full of pain killers and felt lightheaded and stupid.

"Hey, Lauren," the waitress, Lucy, said as she strode up. "What can I get you?" She wore her red hair pinned into a bun tonight. Her freckles looked huge.

"The sandwich sp-special," Lauren stuttered. "And a Coke."

The waitress wrote it down, but hesitated. "You okay? Heard you got hurt out there."

"I'm fine. Just hungry."

She started shaking. Couldn't stop. She'd be all right for a few minutes, then another bout would accost her.

Lucy said, "Honey, you sure you don't want a whiskey? Might settle your nerves."

"No. Thanks."

Lucy gave her a worried look and left.

When the plate was set before her, Lauren blinked in surprise. She'd lost several minutes and had no idea where they went. She stared blankly at the cold beef sandwich. White rice.

"Get you anything else?" Lucy asked.

"I'm good."

Lauren had to grip the Coke can in both hands to get it to her mouth to drink. Tasted sweet and cold. Then she set the can down before her shaking hands sloshed it empty.

She knew she'd better enjoy every sip. Supplies around the city were vanishing. Word was that salt would be available through trade with the factories on the Great Salt Lake in Utah, but condiments like black pepper, vanilla, and cinnamon would soon be memories. Along with chocolate. What kind of world would it be without coffee and chocolate?

Prices on so many things were already rising beyond even a hint of credibility.

Normal things. Think of normal things.

She took a bite of her sandwich and leaned back in the booth. Another bite. Swallow. Dear God, was that her ribs hurting, or was that her liver?

Don't think about the look in Mike's eyes. The blood bubbling on his lips.

She chewed and tried to focus on conversations going on in the restaurant around her.

Normal things.

A WNG captain sitting with a lieutenant at the table five feet away said, "You think that's crazy? I heard that one of the executives at the refinery east of Cheyenne offered ten thousand barrels of gasoline for a case of insulin for his diabetic daughter."

The lieutenant shook his head. "What did the governor say?"

"Guess Agar got the message loud and clear. He ordered a twenty-four-hour armed guard on all pharmacies."

"Good move. A single bottle of antibiotics is already worth a fortune, but I feel for the exec at the refinery."

"Me, too, but what else you gonna do?"

"Heard that Agar ordered the chemistry department at the University of Wyoming to start working on how to make insulin from scratch."

She glanced up when two people walked into the restaurant. The man was obviously Wyoming Militia—maybe a logger or a construction worker before the collapse. He had that durable and muscular look to him. Maybe thirty. Scuffed lace-up boots. Beard—which had become the new normal—worn jeans, ball cap on his head, and longish hair that didn't quite fall to his collar. The rifle over his shoulder and bandolier of cartridges spoke eloquently as to his current occupation. Must be guarding the border.

The woman behind him had long black hair in need of washing. Her once-pretty face had a gaunt look, smudged, but traces of makeup remained. Lauren figured her for early thirties; the muddy hiking boots on her feet would have set her back a couple of hundred dollars at REI. She wore two-hundred-dollar designer jeans with half of the sequins missing. The knees had recently had the mud scuffed off. A tailored jacket hugged her shoulders and conformed to her thin waist, and a couple of buttons were missing from her form-fitting white cotton shirt. She must have been some kind of professional in the big city.

"Tory, you sit here," the man told her, pointing to the table next to Lauren's booth. "Don't move. I'll go get us a room."

The woman nodded, worked her lips, and dropped into the chair. She didn't watch him leave the room, but stared down at her hands, at the broken nails that had once been painted red.

When she glanced Lauren's way, it was to fix on the sandwich with a longing that almost vibrated the air.

Lauren leaned over and handed her the remaining half. "Here. If you're fast, you can chug it down before he gets back."

"Thank you. Really." The woman grabbed it the way a starving wolf took a baby rabbit, devouring it in five big bites, while she watched the door.

"Where you from?" Lauren said softly.

The woman's eyes widened with panic. "Boulder, Colorado."

"You're lucky. You made it across The Line."

Tory nodded, relaxing, her slim fingers lacing together. "Yeah. Just...never thought I'd be...here."

Lauren tilted her head in the direction of the militiaman. "You think he's worth the price?"

"I'll live." A pause. "More than I can say for Jill and Aleesha." She stared into some private hell.

"Pretty bad down south?"

"You have no idea." A pause. "I got on my knees and begged. Can you imagine? I did that. I told him I'd do anything to get across the border."

"People do what they have to."

Images flashed. Like video replaying in Lauren's head, visions of the human beings she'd shot down in the camp. The crushed human bodies that Hutch had run over in their desperate escape.

Tory said, "I had dreams once. Good dreams."

Lauren managed to take a deep breath. "What did you do in Colorado?"

"I was a professor before the cyberattack shut down the university. Dr. Tory Sanders. Taught Law." The woman dusted the bread crumbs from her fingers onto the floor. "Equal opportunity law. Women's issues." Her mouth trembled. "Is that rich, or what?"

"Right now all that matters is you're alive." The room shifted, spun slightly. Lauren rubbed her eyes, praying the disorientation would go away.

"Dear God, what happened to us?"

"Us?" Lauren looked up.

"Americans! What happened to us? It's only been a couple of weeks and we've turned on each other like animals."

Absently Lauren stared at her right index finger. She could almost feel the M4 vibrating. Hear the screams. She fought the flashback. "We are animals. I am. You are. All of us."

Tory frowned, then looked away for a solid minute. Finally, she asked, "You come up from the south?"

"Colorado Springs. I worked at a bank."

"How did you…? I mean… What did you have to do to get across the border?"

"I killed a man." Without a trace of emotion Lauren went back to her plate and finished the rest of her potato chips.

"You hear that the North Koreans invaded Los Angeles?"

Lauren blinked. "I…I heard it was Chinese in San Francisco and Seattle."

"Where was our military? Why didn't our Marines push them back? Is America so weak that we can't defend our own people? Why didn't they do something?"

The militiaman appeared in the doorway, and Tory instantly went still. The guy called, "Come on. Got a key." He held the card up so that it glinted in the restaurant lights.

Tory whispered, "Take care."

"You, too."

As Dr. Tory Sanders slipped out of the booth, she softly said, "I'll be okay. After what I've been through, servicing one more man's no big thing. And I don't have to do it on the ground with an audience."

Lauren watched her leave. The weight in her chest was now leaden. *There, but for the grace of Tyrell and Randy Howman, go I.*

Swirling the dregs in her Coke can, she no longer had the strength to finish it. Clutching her ribs, she rose and strode out of the restaurant as though on a mission.

She almost made it up the stairs to her room before the next flashback hit. The stairwell filled with screams. Her knees went weak. Lauren sank down on the steps and dropped her head into her hands.

CHAPTER TWENTY-SEVEN

***

WITH TEETH GRITTED AGAINST THE PAIN, LAUREN STOPPED THE KTM IN THE PARKING LOT and put a foot down. She killed the ignition and winced as she used a heel to swing the side stand down. Overhead, the sky was blanked by that endless smoky haze. She'd seen the like before. When giant forest fires had raged in California and Oregon a couple of years back.

The speculation was that these were cities burning, and the faint stench—like incinerated garbage in a dump—lent credence to the notion. Unlike the tang of wood smoke, this smell made her stomach turn.

Lauren used a heel to drop the side stand; she couldn't help but gasp as she swung her leg over the seat and steadied herself against the bike.

Any kind of good sense argued against riding this soon. Nevertheless, she marched—or at least hobbled—to the hospital doors. Guards with hostile eyes, rifles at the ready, watched Lauren unsling the M4 from her shoulder. She held it up with one hand, calling, "Just visiting a patient." Her other hand was in the air. Everybody was on the ragged edge. Especially at the hospital with its precious medical supplies. The two guards scanned her face.

"Lauren Davis," she called. "Here to see Sergeant Mike Vinich."

When she reached the rope that cordoned off the hospital, the first hard-eyed soldier, maybe eighteen, patted her down, and asked, "You the Lauren Davis from the Buffalo Camp?"

"Yeah. I guess that's me."

"You're a hero," the other private said in awed tones.

Lauren squinted, trying to understand the reverence in the Guardsman's expression.

"Sorry, Ms. Davis. You'll still have to turn over your weapon.

Orders, ma'am. You can pick it up when you leave."

Ma'am?

"Yes, Corporal." She flinched as she handed him the M4.

At the desk inside, Lauren asked the nurse: "Where's Mike Vinich?"

The nurse shoved a clipboard across the counter. "Sign in."

Lauren filled in her name, the date, and time of her arrival, and slid it back across the counter.

The nurse read it, glanced up meaningfully at Lauren, and her tone softened a little. "Second floor, Ms. Davis. Room 242."

"Thanks."

Lauren started down the white hall, headed for the stairs that led to the upper floors. Armed guards stood at the hall, monitoring the packed lobby.

When she reached the stairs, she took them a slow step at a time, and pushed open the door to the second floor. Another guard watched her pass as she strode for Room 242.

Silently, she stepped through Mike's open door and stood looking down at him. He was asleep, tied to monitors and being fed and hydrated through an IV. They had some kind of cannula that covered his whole nose strapped to his face. After they'd removed his lung, the doctors had kept him sedated and in isolation. An hour ago, Ragnovich had informed her that Mike had just been moved to the Intensive Care Unit, and the doctors were allowing visitors.

"Hey, Mike," she softly called. "It's me."

Easing into the chair at his bedside, she quietly examined him. He looked pale. Tubes looped around him. Brown hair limply framed his face. His breathing was shallow and tortured, and it broke her heart to listen to him.

She reached out to lightly place her hand on top of his. "Bet you wish you hadn't given me your vest, huh?"

His fingers felt cold. She drew the blanket up to keep him warmer, and whispered, "It saved my life, Mike. Doctor said if I hadn't been wearing it, the bullet would have chowdered my liver and blown out my spine."

His eyelids fluttered, but did not open.

"That's all right, Mike. Just rest. I'm going to be here for a while."

Sinking back in the chair, she reached for a magazine to pass the time. Felt strange, reading month-old news stories about a senator accused of an illicit affair with an aide. Seemed so trite in light of current affairs.

Mike jumped and gasped as he blinked at the ceiling.

"Hey," she said, "you're okay. You're in the hospital."

He inhaled a ragged breath, as though trying to confirm her words, then his gaze drifted to Lauren, and he whispered, "Ragnovich was here. Said you saved my life."

"Hutch saved your life. He was the hero."

A faint smile turned his lips. "Anyway. Thanks."

She reached up to touch his forehead, testing for fever. "You're hot. How you feeling?"

"Short of breath…all the time."

Trying to cheer him up, she put on a happy face. "The captain talked to the doctors yesterday. They said that will go away when your one lung gets used to the new load it has to carry."

He gave her a slight nod, and his gaze moved slowly over the white walls, stainless steel tables, and numerous tubes running into his body, then came back to her. "Keep waking myself up. Panicked. 'Cause I can't breathe."

She reached out and took his hand again. "Think on the bright side. It hailed yesterday. Quarter-sized stones. At least, you're not out there on The Line getting your brains beat out."

Weakly, his hand tightened around hers. "I will be. Soon as I can. Tell everyone."

"I will. They all send their regards."

A smile turned his lips, then vanished almost immediately when he struggled to get a deep breath.

The doctors had told her in no uncertain terms that Sergeant Vinich would never be on The Line again.

Lauren squeezed his fingers. "We got a report from Ragnovich this morning. He says the governors of Nebraska and Kansas have sent boatloads of armed men down the Missouri with orders to ascend the Ohio River to see what's happening on the East Coast. Since they figure the highways are closed, maybe they can make it by water. No word yet, though."

Mike grunted his assent.

"Big news is that the legislature has given Governor Agar special powers. He has a team organizing fuel rations, and he's keeping the refinery running. Trucks get priority on diesel as long as they're hauling crude. Everything's being prioritized. Electricity and energy production first, agriculture second, food distribution third. Then police and security. Medical and stuff like that next, and so on."

"West Coast?"

"Word came. Supposedly from Sacramento. Some woman who claims to represent the California governor. She said the whole coast had been overrun by the enemy."

Mike's eyes narrowed. "Chinese?"

"She said North Koreans, but after Colonel Mackeson questioned her, it was pretty clear she didn't know how to tell the difference. And she couldn't identify anything on their uniforms when Mackeson showed her photos. Some are wondering if she's a fraud."

Mike closed his eyes for several moments, as though pondering that news. "That's for sure? They're wearing uniforms?"

"Camo. That's all the woman could say for sure. But she said the United States is fighting back. Said the high Sierras are full of starving people eating pine trees to stay alive and keep out of the way of the troops."

Mike nodded feebly. "Means the enemy is trying to push inland. Toward us."

"Yeah. Everybody's talking about it." She patted his hand and released it.

"What's General Kyzer say?"

Lauren lifted a shoulder. "The officers at Warren Air Base are supposed to be having detailed conversations with the governor, but, if so, Agar is keeping quiet about it."

Mike shifted and coughed hard. It brought tears to his eyes, his face tight with pain.

"You okay?"

He nodded. "Yeah. Good."

When one of the hanging bags started dripping faster, Mike seemed to melt into his pillows, and Lauren wondered if that bag contained a sedative, or maybe a narcotic pain medication like morphine.

"You need your rest, Mike. I'm going to go. I just wanted to come and see if you were awake."

When she started to stand up, he gripped her hand and wouldn't let go.

"Lauren?" His raspy voice turned dark and serious. "Leave Cheyenne. Do what Ty told you to do. Head for the backcountry. Before it's too late to get out."

But it was too late. Bending down, she planted a light kiss on his forehead. "Thanks for worrying, but I'm not leaving until you're on your feet."

He lost the battle to keep his eyes open. In a drowsy voice, he said, "Looking forward to it."

Lauren walked out, but once she reached the hall, she closed her eyes, leaned against the wall.

Mike's alive because I killed all those people.

If she could just keep telling herself that, maybe it would be all right.

Yeah, sure.

CHAPTER TWENTY-EIGHT

* * *

STORIES HAD STARTED CIRCULATING. THE LINE OF OBSERVATION POSTS WERE BEING established from the east, starting outside Pine Bluffs and running the entire length of the Colorado border, past the Utah line to Evanston in the west, and then north to the Idaho line.

Most of the posts and personnel were concentrated here, in the Fourth Quadrant, south of Cheyenne and stretching over into the mountains below Laramie. This was the area of highest concern, where the millions suffering along the Front Range might surge north. A similar worry centered on the far west along Interstate 80. The border lay no more than seventy-five miles from Salt Lake City, Ogden, and the teeming population up and down the valley. So far that threat hadn't developed.

If the rumors could be trusted, part of that was due to the influence of the Latter Day Saints. For the time being—again according to the stories—most refugees from the Salt Lake Valley were fleeing south toward Price, Kanab, and Cedar City.

Lauren got up that morning, eased out of bed, and looked out her window to check the KTM; the orange-and-black bike rested faithfully on its side stand, rear tire chained to the light pole.

Holding up her jeans, Lauren wondered if she should wear them. "Ruin these," she told herself, "there are no others."

Supplies had been bought out as soon as people figured out that clothing made in Asia—or even as close as Mexico—might have been made on the moon. The same was true of most of the other stores, including the Walmarts.

Once the toilet paper was gone, they'd be washing rags in the sink. With homemade soap.

She pulled on her riding pants, muttering, "And now we pay the price for Amazon, internet sales, and UPS bringing whatever you want right to your door."

Because, sure as hell, there wasn't a single textile mill in the whole of Wyoming. The thought made Lauren wonder what people were going to be wearing a year from now. Assuming there were still people left to worry about it.

Donning her white blouse, she slipped into her riding coat, snagged up the boogie bag with a painful grunt, and headed for the stairs.

Lucy had kept Lauren's usual booth open, and she slung the heavy bag onto the seat before sliding into the bench. The place was full, mostly with Guard and various government officials.

She overheard one of the two guys in suits across from her say, "Lot of people dead."

"Sounds like it was a close-run thing," the other—a younger guy with close-cropped blond hair—agreed. "Still, how do you get your head around it. First the Buffalo Camp, then the I-25 check point? What the hell is happening to us? Fifty to sixty dead? Another hundred or so wounded and dying?"

Lauren made a face against the pain as she leaned out. "Hey, what happened?"

The two men shot her curious, somewhat dismissive glances. The young one said, "Last night. Just around dusk, an armed group. Some of them still pissed off that Buffalo Camp was closed, made a push on the I-25 checkpoint. Shot down the guards and tried to overrun it."

The older man, maybe in his fifties, added, "Figured they'd punch a hole in The Line for anybody wanting to get out of Colorado. Guess they hid their weapons until they walked up to the Militia guarding the checkpoint, pulled their guns, and started shooting. No warning. Just started killing."

"How many of our people did we lose?" Lauren asked, a sinking in her gut. Normally the I-25 checkpoint was manned by about twenty Guard with Militia backup. She knew a lot of those people. Admired them for taking the shitty job of turning back desperate fellow human beings.

"I guess fourteen," the young man said. "Another five are in the hospital. Some won't make it."

"Would have been a disaster," the older man told her. "Guess our people have a machine gun mounted on the Humvee down there.

From what we heard, some line rider, a girl, leaped up on one of the Humvees after the gunner has shot. Took over the machine gun and drove the whole horde of them back. Mowed down the front ranks like they were wheat in the field."

The young guy added, "I hear that the ones who survived are still running. Only the bodies and dying were left for our guys to pick up. Them and all those abandoned cars stretching down the highway clear to the Rock Forts this side of Wellington."

"Said the girl who stopped the attack was cool as ice. She just stood atop that Humvee, even as the attackers tried to swarm up and shoot her. Bullets were whacking past her, and she never so much as flinched."

Lauren ground her teeth, flashbacks from Buffalo Camp flickering in her mind.

"Breeze," the young guy said. "Breeze Tappan. That's her name."

"Makes you wonder, doesn't it?" The older man picked up his coffee cup. "Seems like all of our heroes are girls these days. Like that little gal out at Buffalo Camp. The one that saved the rations after they murdered the distribution team."

Little gal? Girls?

With effort, Lauren unclenched her fists, swallowed hard. Standing, she reached for the boogie bag, slung it over her shoulder, and stalked out of the restaurant, hardly aware that Lucy stopped short, a cup of coffee in hand to watch her depart.

Out at the bike, she dropped the bag, leaned on it with both arms propped on the seat.

God, Breeze...?

Lauren struggled for breath, lightheaded, scenes from Buffalo Camp swirling in her memory. The sounds, smells, the expressions on the faces as refugees swarmed around the...

"Hey?" a voice asked warily. "You all right?"

Lauren glanced up. The woman, maybe fifty, wore a brown Wyoming Cowboys T-shirt and white duck-cloth jeans, her feet in tan trainers.

"Yeah. Just needed to catch my breath."

"You're not sick, are you? You're sweating like you've got a fever." She stepped back, reflexively pulling a mask from her pocket. "Be just like our luck to have an outbreak from a new variant. So if you're feeling hot and—"

"I'm fucking fine, okay!"

"Yeah, right," the woman sounded anything but reassured as she turned and hurried down the sidewalk. She kept throwing scared looks back over her shoulder.

Lauren straightened, wiped at the dampness on her brow and cheeks. Her heart dropped back into a normal beat, and she unhooked her helmet from its lock. Then she freed the chain, wrapping it around the luggage rack before she strapped the boogie bag down.

The ride out to the Port of Entry might have been an anticlimax. No traffic but the occasional bicycle or ATV, and a couple militia vehicles with the letters painted or made of strips of tape on the pickup doors. The morning, however was dull and overcast, the sun burning down with a reddish glare through the perpetual brown haze overhead. She could barely make out the mountains to the west.

She took the crossover from the southbound lane and parked the KTM beside a white Ford F-350 dually with a flatbed. As she stepped off the bike, she realized the deck on the flatbed was covered with dried-and-caking blood. A lot of it.

While Lauren gave it a wooden stare, one of the Guard privates walked past, saying, "It's not ours, Lauren. They used that truck to pick up the bodies around the checkpoint."

"What did they...?" She gestured at the Ford. "I mean, where?"

"Used the backhoe at the Buffalo Ranch. Dug a trench next to where we put the others."

He didn't have to explain who the others were. She knew. The people she'd shot down; the ones Hutch had run over, along with those who had been killed in the fight over the ration boxes she'd thrown out.

She kept it together as the private walked past. Didn't let the shakes possess her. Steadied herself against the bike and fought the sudden urge to throw up.

Breathe. Just breathe.

Took her a couple of minutes, but she got her balance back. Stepped away from the flatbed so she could fill her lungs with fresh air, June air. Rich with the smell of grasses and wildflowers. All she got was that faint tinge of burning hair and plastic that came on the west wind.

"God, Lauren. Get a grip." Jaw knotted, she climbed the steps to the office, and opened the door.

No one sat at Ragnovich's desk, but Lieutenant Virginia Barrow and two privates were standing before the long strip of map they'd taped up to cover one entire wall. A makeshift thing, it showed the entire Fourth Quadrant: all the roads; topography; ranches; and drainages from Pine Bluff to Virginia Dale on the other side of the Albany County line. West of there, it was Captain Dykstra's responsibility to cover The Line out to Mountain Home where the Third Quadrant began.

Barrow was saying, "I need you to hustle out to OP Bravo Delta, here, on the butte. You know how to find the Chalk Bluffs?"

"Yeah," one of the privates told her. "South from I-80 on Wyo 217, then across Porter Creek."

"Then get to it. Be sure your wheels are gassed up and you've got water and rations. We'll try and get relief out there in a couple of days. And, hey, stay frosty. No one's tried The Line that far east yet, but they're going to get around to it."

"Yes, ma'am," one of the privates told her as they both saluted, turned and headed for the door.

At sight of Lauren, the first elbowed his friend, whispering, "You know who that is?"

"Breeze Tappan?" The other was giving Lauren a wide-eyed stare of wonder.

"Lauren Davis, you idiot." The first grabbed his friend by the sleeve, almost jerking the private off his feet as he headed for the door.

Lauren caught herself, forcing icy control. Kept her hands from shaking. Managed to step up to where Lieutenant Barrow was scowling at the wall map.

"It'll fade," Barrow said softly. "They'll forget as other events pile up." She gave Lauren a sidelong appraisal. "What can I do for you, Ms. Davis?"

"Tell me about being a line rider."

Barrow turned when a crackle came over the radio and a voice called, *"FOB? This is Cramer out at OP Charlie Echo. We've got a guy on horseback here, says he's a rancher from off Owl Canyon Road south of the line. He and his family want to bring sixty-five head of cattle across the The Line. Says we can have them if we'll let him pass."*

Barrow stepped over to where Private Brenda Smith sat at the radio and took the mic. "Charlie Echo, this is FOB. Let them pass. Repeat, let them pass. Tell them they can keep their cattle and graze their way north on highway right-of-way until we can find them pasture."

"Roger that. Let them pass."

Barrow turned back to Lauren. "That's the second time. Word's getting around that Colorado ranchers can bring their stock north in return for safe passage. Beats having their cattle and horses shot or being shot themselves fighting to protect them. And the raiders are getting a lot better at killing ranchers and farmers before looting their places. Now what was I saying?"

"Line riders. Tell me what to do." Lauren crossed her arms, adopting a defiant stance as Barrow—a woman in her thirties with dark-brown eyes and a much-too-delicate-looking face—studied her.

"Lauren," her voice dropped, "you've done enough. The riot down at Buffalo Camp almost killed you. The captain would have my ass if I sent you out and anything happened to you."

"Well, the captain tells me that you were in Afghanistan during the pullout. That you were recommended for a medal after you went into Kabul and brought a bunch of trapped Americans out from under the Taliban's noses. Why didn't you just go home to Lingle? Go back to work in the auto parts store with your family? Why'd you immediately enlist in the Guard?"

Barrow's brown-eyed stare seemed to look right through to Lauren's backbone. "I guess I couldn't let it go."

"Neither can I."

At that moment a building roar could be heard, then the entire building shook as an airplane—something big and way too loud—thundered low over the roof.

Lauren couldn't help herself, she ducked, shoulders hunched, waiting for the crash. But the sound just faded.

"What the hell?"

Lieutenant Barrow had barely flinched. "Governor Agar and Colonel Steadman. You know who Steadman is?"

"Yeah, he's in command of the 153rd Airlift Wing. They fly Wyoming National Guard C-130s out of the Cheyenne airport. That was him?"

"Them. The colonel and Governor Agar," Lieutenant Barrow told her as she reached back and rubbed the nape of her neck. "They're taking another reconnaissance flight down south. After the firefight at the I-25 checkpoint last night, it's probably even more important to know what's happening down yonder. See if they're regrouping to hit us again."

Lauren had resumed her crossed-arm stance, trying to adopt an adamant expression. "You didn't stay away, why should I?"

Barrow cracked a weary smile, turned, yelling, "Hey, Steve? What have you got?"

"OP Alpha X-Ray, LT. Battery's dead on the Humvee. One of the yo-yos forgot to turn everything off. They need one of the portable jump-start chargers."

"Roger that." Barrow turned back to the map, pointing for Lauren's benefit. "Here's the layout. Starting at the Nebraska border is OP Alpha Alpha, then Alpha Bravo, Alpha Charlie, Alpha Delta and so on until you get here, at Thunder Basin Road, where the next OP is Bravo Alpha, Bravo Bravo, Bravo Delta, and on west to where the Charlie OPs start and run through the call signs all the way over to Delta, and so on."

"Got it."

"Each one is placed on a road, choke point, or elevation with an overlapping field of view with the next post."

"I see."

"Think you can find Alpha X-Ray? They're here, south of Carpenter Reservoir on Dump Road."

"Piece of cake. Where do I find a battery charger?"

"Stores. Take one of the portable units. It ought to strap on the back of your bike."

"What about my boogie bag?"

"I'll lock it up here until you get back."

Lauren knocked off a salute. "Thanks, LT. Tell the guys I'm on the way."

Walking out, Lauren stared up at the brown-hazed skies. She was a Line Rider. Maybe now, having a purpose, the nightmares would go away. The memories of Buffalo Camp would fade. All she needed to do was keep busy. Keep the ghosts at bay.

CHAPTER TWENTY-NINE

***

ANOTHER DAY, ANOTHER MISSION. LAUREN LEANED THROUGH THE CURVES, RIDING HER bike toward Observation Post Charlie Able with cases of bottled water and MREs strapped to the back. Lauren's thoughts were on Tyrell. His M4 hung from her left shoulder. His pistol was holstered on the top of her tank bag where all she had to do was yank it free with her left hand.

Down in the dead part of her heart—where horror festered—she'd convinced herself Tyrell was dead. It was her way of protecting herself. If she kept thinking that, maybe it wouldn't be so hard when the news finally came.

If the news finally came.

Cell service was just as dead as ever. To the point that even the most die-hard phone-obsessed among them no longer bothered to pull their devices and try to scroll through text messages or email.

Her mind kept trying to imagine different possible futures. A future if he came home, and four or five if he didn't. Which way would she go? What would she do without him? After the firefight at Buffalo Camp, she'd been trying to figure out who she was and her place in this new world. She still didn't have a fricking clue.

Only one thing for certain: supporting the troops, making sure they had food and water, made her feel useful and needed. And that was something. Without which, there was nothing.

It also comforted her to talk with the men and women on The Line. Fragments of news from the West Coast continually filtered through the ranks. Snippets heard on shortwave radios, or from refugees, or Express Riders.

People were supposedly eating each other in the Sierras—just like the Donner Party in the 1800s—while the U.S. battled North Koreans or Chinese or Iranians. Maybe Russians, too. Nobody knew how much was true. But if any of it was, Tyrell was sure to be right in the middle of it.

Lauren's eyes scanned the green pastures on either side of the barbed wire fences. Her skin prickled; a nervous energy added just a tickle of adrenaline to her muscles. The KTM's front tire searched slightly on the gravel, and periodically the bike squirmed on the loose stuff. Behind her, her path was marked by a rooster tail of curling dust.

She still felt raw, like her insides had been clawed bloody. No matter how exhausted she was, she couldn't sleep. Just as soon as she started to drift off, she was back in the truck with Mike and Hutch, fighting for her life. Each night she gunned those same people down. Watched their faces as bullets tore their bodies apart; so filled with terror and adrenaline that she had to get up. So, she wandered her room half of every night, listening to her heart pound.

Instinctively, she knew this craving for action stemmed from the emptiness that plagued her. Doctors at the hospital called it the "soldier's curse". PTSD. Survivor's guilt.

Hutch was dead. Mike had lost a lung. But she was fine. Why? There was no one looking out for her. God was dead, just as dead as the people she'd shot down at the camp.

Cresting a rise, she saw six people walking along the roadside. Three men, middle-aged, two women, maybe in their thirties, and a teenage boy. Somehow they'd made it past the border guards and into Wyoming.

When they waved their hands and yelled at her to stop, Lauren downshifted and veered wide to go around them. Before she could speed up again, two men ran into the center of the road. One pulled a handgun from his waistband.

"Stop, or I'll shoot you!"

She barely fixed an image of a red-bearded young man, clothes in rags, face hollow and filthy. His companion, taller, older, wore a torn suit coat, dirt-splotched dress shirt unbuttoned to the navel. His Dockers would have horrified a homeless bum.

Probably wouldn't shoot her. Just trying to feed their family, but she had no way to know that for sure.

The old familiar tension tightened her chest; the pounding of her heart energizing her muscles. Would it work? She clamped on the brakes, slid the rear tire to a halt. In one fluid motion she slipped the M4 off her shoulder and brought it up to her cheek. Fire control flipped to semi-auto, she fired two rounds past the young guy's right ear.

He shrieked, tossed the handgun, and outraced his companion to the fence. The wires bent and vibrated as he scrambled his way through the slicing barbs. The second man nearly tore what was left of his pants off his body as he, too, scaled the fence in clumsy panic. Then they were off, pounding their way down the grassy slope.

The women and teenager fell to the ground screaming, their hands over their heads.

Lauren gunned the bike and sailed past them.

On the other side of the hill, she passed a ranch house set back from the road. Lettering on the mailbox proclaimed **Johnson Ranch**. The hand-painted sign at the gate bluntly stated: **Keep Out! Trespassers Will Be Shot! No Warning Will Be Given!**

Ten minutes later, she pulled into OP Charlie Sierra and killed her engine. The post was located on a ridge top with a clear view across the drainage below and south to the next ridge, which lay in Colorado. Purple wildflowers dotted the green grass.

What passed for the OP consisted of two foxholes hammered down through the sandstone bedrock, each manned by four people. Two Humvees—with M249 5.56 machine guns mounted on top—were parked to either side with overlapping fields of fire that covered all approaches to the OP. At the thumping sound of her engine, the four men had risen from their foxhole and waved to her. Binoculars hung from the sergeant's neck.

A woman sat atop the Humvee, scanning the valley below with a pair of binoculars.

"Who're you?" a private with Edmond stenciled on his shirt asked.

"Lauren Davis. Captain Ragnovich sent me out. He said you were running out of food and water. I'm your resupply."

"You're the one from the fight at Buffalo Camp." The second private—Fanta on his right pocket—was grinning. He was in his twenties, blond, with a lady-killer smile.

The kickstand snapped down under her heel, and Lauren stepped off. She started to unstrap the case of bottled water and MREs from the back.

"Captain wants you to save the bottles, so we can refill them," she told them. "Won't be any more after these are gone."

"Got it," the third man, Tully, replied. Like the others, a thin film of dirt coated his face and uniform.

Fanta trotted over and carried the crate of water and MREs to the foxhole.

While they chowed down and joked with each other, Lauren walked to the edge of the bluff and looked over the valley. Scattered Ponderosa pines whiskered the slopes to the west as the divide rose toward a summit that gave way to the Laramie Basin. With her bare eyes, she could just make out a glint in the distant trees. If she remembered the map in Ragnovich's office, that would be OP Charlie Tango.

To the south, the next ridge gave way to yet another, stretching all the way to the high hogbacks that guarded the tree-dark slopes of the Medicine Bow Range with its snow-capped peaks. The same peaks she'd been looking at from the west when Butch Masterson had rudely interrupted her by calling, "Nice ass."

It might have been a different lifetime.

Looking southeast, she could just see the high smokestack from the Rawhide Energy Plant in the distance. Governor Agar had sent a full company of WNG down to hold it no matter what. Essentially, Wyoming had annexed the electricity generating plant to keep the lights on in Cheyenne and Laramie.

"Any action?" she asked, stepping back from the edge to look down into the foxhole. Every man had a mouthful of food or was gulping water.

"Heard some shots from up north," Fanta slurred around a mouthful of food. "Maybe ten minutes ago. Was that you?"

"Yeah, two guys jumped me near the turn off from Goose Creek Road."

"You kill 'em?"

"No. Just scared 'em off."

Odd how routine that sounded. Just an ordinary day at the office, dear. I shot at a man who pointed a pistol at me.

She gazed south again. Colorado was morphing into something alien and dangerous. Where it had just been another state—the place a person went when they needed to go to the big city—now it instilled terror. Somehow Colorado and its citizens had become the "enemy".

"You hear how long we're going to have to be out here?" the man with Muirhead stenciled on his pocket asked.

"No idea, sorry."

"So, like, what's your place in all this?"

"Just a delivery girl." She made a dismissive gesture. "Like the rest of the line riders, I shuttle emergency supplies out to the OPs."

"Good old Ragnovich," Fanta started, "he's..."

Something snapped and tore the air off to one side. A half second later the distant crack of a rifle sounded; Lauren hit the ground on her belly, scrambling head-first into the foxhole with the other soldiers.

"Shit," Edmund muttered as he squirmed up to the rim of the berm and raised his binoculars to glass the south. "Vasquez? Where'd that come from?"

"Way out there. Other ridge, I think," the woman who'd been sitting atop the Humvee answered, then she leaped off the vehicle and ran to dive into the other foxhole.

"Took the sound of the shot a half second to get here, didn't it?" Tully asked.

Edmund said, "Yeah, 'bout that. Shooter must be around five hundred yards away."

A bullet made *ping-whup* sound as it splattered on one of the Humvees. A fragment of the copper jacket danced across the trampled soil and bounced into the foxhole no more than a foot in front of Lauren's nose.

Fanta picked it up, howled, and dropped it. "Fuck! That's hot!"

Edmund leaned down and looked at it. "Thirty caliber. Wish I had a 300 Win Mag. With, like, a four-by-twenty scope on it. I could knock something down way out there."

Another bullet blew over Lauren's head, followed a half-second later by the rifle's distant report.

"What are they doing?" Lauren asked.

"It's suppressing fire. Supposed to keep us down while a party makes a try for the border. That, or sometimes they feel lucky, like they can tag one of us, or make us so miserable that we'll change our minds and decide to just let them pass by."

A bullet whacked dully into dirt just under the crest of the foxhole.

Tully muttered "fucking son of a bitch" under his breath, crawled up and glared. "You know what the hottest trade is out here? It's a 6.5mm Creedmoor."

"A what?" Lauren asked as another bullet cracked past in its supersonic path.

"Long-distance cartridge," Vasquez told her. "Hell, I'd never heard of one either. The good news is that there's no shortage of them among civvies. Lots of makers. Remington, Ruger, Savage, Winchester, you name it. And most folks put big scopes on 'em. Now, if we had a 6.5 Creedmoor or Weatherby we could take that evil little son of a bitch out."

Edmund searched the hills through his binoculars. "There they are. Yellow ATV. About halfway between us and Charlie Tango."

"All right," Tully said. "Who's going?"

"I am." Vasquez leaped out of the foxhole and scurried for the closest Humvee, opened the door, and jumped inside.

Lauren heard her key the radio and call, "Charlie Tango, Charlie Tango. This is Charlie Sierra. We've got a shooter about five hundred yards at two-hundred-sixty-five degrees from our position, and a scooter trying to split the difference between us. Request a rebuke from Ma Deuce. Over."

"Roger that. We're on him. Clear."

"Watch this, Ms. Davis," Fanta called.

She lifted a hand to shade her eyes from the haze-choked sunlight. The yellow side-by-side ATV was racing north across the grass-filled valley.

Dirt erupted in a flurry just in front of the distant vehicle. The driver jacked his wheel, almost flipped the ATV as he made the turn on two wheels.

Lauren heard the popping of a far-off machine gun mixing with the barely audible putter of exhaust as the ATV raced for safety. Moments later, it climbed the ridge and disappeared.

"Gotta love a .50 caliber," Tully said with envy. "Wish we had one."

"Thought you wanted a 6.5 Creedmoor?" Lauren reminded.

"One of them, too," Tully told her.

Another angry bullet tore overhead. Maybe as a rejoinder.

"Why do they keep trying?" Lauren asked.

"'Cause they've got nothing left," Fanta replied. "Last refugee we captured said it's mob rule down there. Nobody goes out after dark. Power's off. Stores have all been looted. He said people are sitting in their houses in the dark starving."

Another bullet was followed by a distant gunshot.

"Will the shooters try you again after dark?"

"Might," Edmund told her. "That's when we spread out. Use the night-vision gear. It's a whole lot safer. We can see them, but they can't see us."

"Yeah," Tully said sourly. "And that's when you can see the kids, hear them begging. I hate this shit. I mean, what are we doing? They're Americans, too, aren't they?"

Lauren gave him a shrug. "Is anyone an American now? Or are we Nebraskans, Coloradoans, and Wyomingites? It's like saying German, French, and Dutch. State identities have replaced national identity."

"Dear God, I hope not," Tully said.

Fanta gestured with his chin. "Well, the shooting's over for now. They're headed back south. None of those people left home expecting to fight a war. They took their guns for self-protection. Maybe to shoot a deer or some farmer's cow to keep their bellies full. It's not like some sexy babe on a bike is going to show up like a miracle with a couple hundred rounds of 5.56 ammo." He gave her a suggestive wink.

"Bet you say that to all the girls who show up out here." She laughed for the first time in days.

"Hell," Fanta told her, "after looking at Muirhead for the last week, I was starting to think he looked like Kim Kardashian."

She laughed again, hard. Then harder. As if some dam had burst inside her. She laughed until her stomach hurt, and every person in the foxhole was howling with her.

Foxhole laughter. That's what Tyrell called it. The crazy mirth of soldiers under unbearable stress. He said it was the only medicine for madness.

"All right," Edmund said when the amusement started to die down. "Enough fun for one day. Back to business. Tully, clean up those empty MRE packets. Don't want people tripping over 'em next time we're hit."

"Yes, sir."

As Tully gathered up the trash, Lauren leaned back against the dirt and smiled. She was becoming one of them. A soldier, of sorts.

Was that her path? To be a soldier? Right after she'd fallen in love with Tyrell, she'd considered enlisting in the army, but decided against it. She'd really wanted to finish college.

But now?

Somehow, serving alongside these people on The Line felt more meaningful. Life had purpose when you were fighting to protect the other soldiers in your foxhole—and fighting to protect the people of your state or country who could not protect themselves. The sick, the elderly, the children. Someone had to fight for them.

Lauren could do that. Couldn't she?

CHAPTER THIRTY

***

THE SMOKE HAD BEEN TOUGH THAT DAY. DARK, OBSCURING THE SUN; LIKE A BLOODY RED orb it rose high in the sky. And the air stank. The "burning garbage" smell, as it was referred to, had an acrid sear that hurt the nose and burned the back of the throat.

Wearing an N95 mask cut the worst of the burning sensation. As did her helmet when she rode with her visor down.

Talk around the Guard warehouse centered on whether this was smoke from a burning Salt Lake City, or if it had come from farther

West. Maybe San Francisco, Portland, or Seattle. The great California forest fires of the early 2020s had proved just how far a thick smudge could crawl across the sky.

After Lauren made it back to the hotel, she chained the Kaytoom to its light pole, took a quick shower, and donned her jeans and white cotton shirt, thankful to be rid of the stench.

She grabbed up the boogie bag and trotted down the stairs to the bar, entering with a weary swagger. Only to find someone sitting in her booth. Seeing the top of the woman's head over the back of the booth, Lauren stopped short, shot a "what the hell" glance Lucy's way.

The barmaid raised an eyebrow, then tilted her head toward the booth in a "You'd better go see" gesture.

Lauren rocked her jaw and started forward, stepping up next to the booth and staring down into Breeze Tappan's tanned face. Her old friend had both hands clasped around a half-empty glass of stout. That old familiar Tappan glare was still the same. Breeze's dark-brown irises blending to tawny-centers that gave way to hard black pupils. The tanned lines of her face seemed to blend with her dark-brown hair. A hardness lay in the set of her lips and jaw.

She wore a blue-denim, short-sleeved shirt that exposed tanned and muscular forearms. Slim Levi's clung to her legs. A 9 mm 230 SIG Sauer rode in the holster at her hip.

"Hey, Lauren."

"Breeze." Lauren's gut twisted itself into a double knot. "What are you doing here?"

"Take a seat." Breeze gestured with a long-fingered hand.

Seeing the familiar pattern of scars left by ranch work sent a shiver down Lauren's back.

Breeze told her, "That barmaid, Lucy? She's got your back. I had to swear on a stack of Bibles that I was your friend before she'd let me sit here."

"Yeah, well, Lucy's got a really low bar when it comes to this booth. That's why she lets me use it."

Lauren tossed the boogie bag in next to the wall and slid in beside to it. On the edge of the seat. In case she had to run for it. "So...like, how are you?"

"Fucked. How about you?" Breeze's lips quivered, tried to make a smile, and failed.

"'Bout the same, I guess." Lauren couldn't figure out what to do with her hands; they kept knotting and rubbing together like nervous rodents. She could have kissed Lucy when she set a cold glass of stout in front of her. Lauren took a sip, thankful for the rich taste on her suddenly too-dry mouth.

"Saw Mike today." Breeze lowered her gaze to where she tapped slim fingers on the table. "Said we needed to talk. Said you're going to get yourself killed. That you think I hate you."

"How's he doing? I haven't been by in a couple of days. They've had me busy."

Breeze fiddled with her glass. "Me, too. Figured we'd run into each other in the FOB. Can you believe? The Port of Entry's now a forward operating base? Where the hell did that come from?"

"It's military. Tyrell always talked about the FOB, how it was sort of the center of their world. He, um..." The words just faded away. She was staring into Breeze's eyes, heart beginning to pound.

"Must be a hell of a guy." Breeze tried to smile. Couldn't quite pull it off.

"Yeah. You seeing anybody? I mean, before all this..."

"Nope." Breeze paused, her brow lining slightly. "Something about the guys at University of Denver. Then the investment firm I was working in. I don't know. It's something about how they've never had dirt or blood under their fingernails. You know what I mean?"

Was that why she'd taken to Tyrell with such a passion? Because he didn't define himself by whether or not his team won on Sunday night football? By the kind of car he drove? Or because he could work out for forty minutes in the gym?

At the silence, Lauren asked, "How'd you get out of Colorado?"

Breeze had a haunted look. "Back roads through the mountains. Four of us started. On bikes. I'm the only one who made it as far as Woods Landing. Got lucky. The Militia at the checkpoint let me pass. Might have gotten nasty but there were two women with them. And it turned out I knew more about Wyoming history than they did. Can you believe they were raised in Rawlins and don't know who Big Nose George Parrott was?"

"Well...it's been a while since anybody in Rawlins has hung an outlaw from a lamp post on Spruce Street and then buried his body in a barrel in their back yard." Lauren paused. "And, as I remember, the governor of Wyoming wore a pair of shoes made from a chunk of hide he skinned off of old George and tanned."

Breeze nodded. "Sort of makes you think Rawlins isn't quite the same fun and rollicking-good-times-not-to-mention-jolly place that it was in the 1880s, doesn't it?"

"Change is the only constant." Lauren sipped her stout. "Heard you saw Tiffany."

"Yeah. Right after I crossed the line." Breeze was running her fingers along the sides of her stout. "She told me Mike was in charge of feeding Buffalo Camp. I kind of fell into the line rider thing. Didn't have anything else to do."

"What about the ranch?"

Breeze looked around at the fancy bar. "When I got accepted to University of Denver, I figured I'd never set foot in Wyoming again. Unless it was to attend the Jackson Hole Economic Policy Symposium. You know, for when the chairman of the Fed called me over for advice. Or maybe to go skiing at Teton Village after I made my first million."

"How's that going?"

"Pretty shitty. You?"

"'Bout the same."

Breeze gestured around. "Yet, here I sit. In a bar in Wyoming. Where I never thought I'd be." She shook her head. "When all of this broke, I was in the middle of a business lunch at a swanky place in south Denver. Shit just got worse by the day. And as it did, all I could think about was getting home. Back here."

Breeze paused, frowned. "I waited too fucking long, Lauren. Should have left that weekend. By the time we pulled out, it was all we could do to get the bikes past the wreckage in the roads."

"What about the roadblocks?"

"Took 40 to Granby. Took two days before Felix and I could trade for another tank of gas for his bike. Cost him a gold Rolex. But it only got him as far as a roadblock on top of Willow Creek Pass."

"The Jackson County deputies? They shook us down for seventy-five bucks."

Breeze met her stare with dead eyes. "If there were ever any Jackson County deputies they were either fled or long-dead. No, this was an ambush. It... Damn it, they shot Felix for his bike. Would have taken me for the fucking, but I shot 'em, Lauren. Had a pistol."

"Yeah," Lauren whispered, Masterson's face hanging behind her eyes. "You still see them? Like, some part of them got sucked inside? Maybe like you inhaled their souls and can't get rid of them?"

Breeze was watching her with that hard-eyed Tappan stare. "I guess I... No, damn it. Not really. I mean, they'd set themselves up on top of that pass. Felix and I weren't the first. The ditch on the downhill side? It was full of bodies, Lauren. Men, women, children. Only...the women were naked. And behind the roadblock? Twenty vehicles. Their cache."

Breeze looked away. "It should bother me, Lauren. Only it doesn't. Maybe I'm soulless. Hell, I felt worse when I was a kid and shot coyotes that were killing the sheep." She swallowed hard. "And then came the I-25 checkpoint. And women and children. And now I know I'm a monster. Because I just shot them down. That machine gun just keeps firing, the brass spitting out the side. And those people, human beings, keep falling, tumbling, screaming, and...and..."

"Yeah," Lauren whispered hollowly.

"Hey," Breeze stood, grabbing up her jacket. "I gotta get out of here. See ya on The Line, Lauren."

"Yeah, you, too."

Lauren didn't see Breeze leave. She was too busy staring at her clenched fists.

"Lauren?" Lucy asked from some impossible distance. "You okay?"

She croaked, "I think I need a whiskey."

And then another.

And another.

CHAPTER THIRTY-ONE

***

"HEY, YOU'RE SITTING UP," LAUREN SAID AS SHE WALKED INTO MIKE VINICH'S HOSPITAL room. She shrugged off her riding coat and propped her helmet on a chair.

Didn't matter that it was late afternoon. Her head still felt like someone had driven ten-penny spikes into her brain. Lauren had spent too much of her night with her head hanging in the toilet, her stomach trying to pump itself out past her teeth like a prolapsed cow.

Knowing the consequences, she'd drunk as much water as she could hold after each bout of the heaves. And, thankfully, breakfast had stayed put.

Propped on a mound of pillows with a hunting magazine in his hands, Mike's eyes lit up when he saw her. The weird nose-covering cannula was supplying oxygen, but the hanging bag with the feeding tube was gone. All the stainless steel sparkled as though freshly polished, and she smelled the distinctive odor of cleaning fluid.

"Yeah. Sitting up. Not sure I like it, either. My chest feels like someone yanked it in two and ripped out one of my lungs."

"That about sums it up." Lauren took the chair at his bedside and smiled at him. "You look better, though. Are they letting you have solid food?"

Mike laid the magazine on the bedside table, and she could see the majestic six-point elk on the front cover. "Mashed carrots and vanilla pudding. Tasted like baby food."

"Better than the fare provided by a feeding tube."

His mouth puckered. "You think?"

Lauren laughed and propped her elbows on the bed to look at him more closely. The fluorescent lights shone on the pink-and-healing scar on his right cheek, where he'd slammed into the truck rack as he fell. "Well, I hope you enjoyed the vanilla. All traffic on the highways has stopped. Truckers aren't delivering supplies. So think of it as the last vanilla you ever get."

Mike smoothed one hand over the white sheet at his side, while he considered that. "I heard they're jerking truckers out of their cabs and murdering 'em for their loads. I wouldn't risk it either."

Lauren's smile faded. "Agar's on it. Trucks now get Militia escort. Unlike Guard, they don't worry too much about shooting people. Truck jackings have become a high-risk venture or a quick way to suicide."

His brows drew together. "But armed escorts, that's just local, right?"

"And sanctioned. Gotta have state pass to prove what you're hauling is one of the authorized loads. Stuff critical to keep the state operating. Otherwise, you don't make it past the highway check points. And there's no fuel at any price these days. People took every bottle and tin can they had down to their local service station, filled them, and buried them in their back yards."

"Any way that will ever change?"

"Yeah. The refinery is now running full bore. As long as they can get crude. Word is that they'll be starting deliveries to service stations by the end of the week as the kinks are worked out of the supply line from the oil fields.

Manufacturing has stopped. Stores are boarded up. Jobs have vanished.

Mike reached out and took Lauren's hand in a half-unthinking intimacy. "How are things going out there on The Line?"

"Everybody's holding on by their fingertips. Waiting for the next disaster."

As he laced his fingers with hers; she was aware of the warmth and gentleness of his touch. After a second or two, he lifted his gaze, and his brown eyes shone. "What happened out there today?"

She stared at him. She could tell he'd heard some rumor, "Nothing."

"That's not what the guys who've been coming to see me say." He hesitated for a while, his face tense with worry. Then he cautiously said, "Private Zachary told me you got ambushed out by OP Charlie Able. That true?"

Lauren didn't answer right away. He was still in frail condition. Getting his heart rate up, and his breathing going, might put an unnecessary strain on his one lung.

"Nothing I couldn't handle, Mike. I don't want to talk about it, okay?"

Lauren tightened her grip on his hand. The bones felt large and awkward entwined with hers.

"Okay. I get it. Just… Be careful, Lauren."

"I'm always careful."

The ghost of a smile came to his face. "Don't forget, I knew you in high school. You'd ride the rattiest motorcycle or jump off a building if somebody dared you to. I don't want you to take any chances. You hear me?"

Their gazes held, and it occurred to her that she was a fool for coming to see him every day. Their old friendship was growing into something more. Something she cherished and feared. The least she owed Tyrell—out there fighting for the life of his country—was loyalty.

"Breeze was waiting for me in the bar last night. Said you'd sent her."

"How'd that go?"

"I don't know who she is anymore. I mean, the old Breeze, she'd charge Hell with a bucket of water just to see if she could do it. The woman I sat across from last night…?"

"None of us are the same, Lauren. Least of all, you." He arched an eyebrow, which twisted the cannula on his nose. "So, did you two talk about Jim?"

Lauren shook her head. "Never got that far. She was talking about how she got out of Colorado, and it sort of morphed into the firefight at the I-25 checkpoint." She chuckled humorlessly. "God, Mike. She was the strong one. Now she's as fucked up as I am."

Mike released her hand and brought his clenched fist back to his lap. "You didn't answer me," he pointed out. "About when I asked you not to take chances?"

"I won't take any chances." She crossed her heart. "Hope to die."

His mouth quirked. "That didn't exactly ease my fears."

"Oh, right. Sorry."

"Too late. I'm already rattled."

They both laughed, and Mike instantly winced and squeezed his eyes closed in pain. "Oh, God, that hurts."

A nurse wearing green scrubs rushed into the room, went straight to his heart and blood pressure monitor, and said, "What happened, Sergeant? Your heart monitor just rang at my desk. You didn't try to get up, did you?"

Through gritted teeth, he answered, "No. I just laughed."

"Well, stop it. The bullet that took out your lung also clipped your heart. It doesn't need the stress. Understand?" She had an authoritative voice, and when she glared at Lauren it was downright scary.

"I'll be good," Mike said in a contrite voice and exchanged an annoyed glance with Lauren.

"It was my fault," Lauren told the nurse. "I—"

"Visiting hour is over, Ms. Davis," the nurse informed her. "Go home. Sergeant Vinich needs to sleep."

Lauren shoved to her feet. "Sure. No problem. I'll be back tomorrow, Mike."

"Before you go, militia guy came in to deliver a message from Trevor. Tiffany is supposed to be coming to Cheyenne tomorrow night."

The relief that filled her made her lightheaded. "Yeah? What time?"

"Don't know yet." He shifted in bed, as though to ease some pain. "I'll send word when I hear."

"Thanks."

Lauren leaned over to kiss his forehead, but stopped herself. She was looking into his eyes from less than a hand's breadth away when she straightened up. "Why didn't you tell me that the bullet had grazed your heart?"

His head waffled back and forth. "Why would I? You have enough to worry about. Besides, it's healing. See you tomorrow?"

"Promise to eat your baby food?"

He fought not to chuckle. "Got no choice. Steaks are off the menu. Unless you're planning to sneak me contraband?"

"Nope." She smiled and turned for the door.

As she strode down the long white hall, she wondered why no one had told her that the same bullet that had destroyed his lung had also damaged his heart? She felt like she'd just been struck in the belly by a hard fist.

CHAPTER THIRTY-TWO

*** ***

"I LOST MY JOB AT THE COUNTRY KITCHEN," TIFFANY SAID AS SHE LEANED BACK IN LAUREN'S booth at the Plains Hotel. She'd cut her brunette hair short, and it fell in attractive layers around her face. Her turquoise blue turtleneck perfectly accented the cut, making her neck look longer. "There's just not enough travel on I-80 to justify it. You're lucky The Plains is still open."

Lauren shoved her glass of beer around the table, thinking about that. A half-empty plate of nachos sat between them. The cook had been grinding his own corn and making tortillas to keep the popular item available.

Lauren told her, "Governor Agar is subsidizing both the Plains and the Hilton. He has to. He's designated the Plains for military personnel and the Hilton to state government. Folks from out of town, anyone who comes to Cheyenne on official state business, has to have a place to stay."

Tiffany looked around the restaurant. Practically every table tonight was filled with people in uniform. "Makes sense. There has to be someplace people walking the high-wire can go to let off steam."

That was when Breeze came tromping in, her motorcycle boots thumping on the antique-tile floor. She shot a nervous glance at Lauren but grinned from ear-to-ear as Tiffany leaped up to hug her despite Breeze's thick rally-style motorcycle jacket.

"Sorry I'm late. Had a run that took me all the way over to Alpha Delta. My first passenger run. I had to take a replacement out to fill in for a yo-yo who was fucking around with a rattlesnake and got bitten."

"Yo-yo?" Tiffany asked.

"Somebody who does something stupid on The Line," Lauren told her. To Breeze she asked, "Any action?"

"Slow day. Word is that there's a lot of raiding down in the Pawnee Buttes country south of the line. Ranchers down there are trying to keep their cattle safe. They're giving it all they've got, but there just aren't enough of them. A couple of riders representing the ranches down there came through the OP at Alpha Sierra. They want to see if they can evacuate their herds north. Corporal Symonson took them to see Agar in the OP's Humvee."

"If they do, it'll leave that part of The Line open," Lauren noted. "As it stands now, those ranchers are keeping refugees away from the eastern end."

"Yeah, the east side's everyone's preferred duty. Nice and safe," Breeze said. Then, voice dropping, she added, "Valerie Ivenson quit today."

Lauren stiffened. "She say why?"

"Who's Valerie?" Tiffany asked.

"Line rider," Breeze told her. "Like us. Val runs stuff out to the OPs." To Lauren she added, "She says it's getting too dangerous. Showed LT Barrow two fresh bullet holes in her fancy ICON Overlord jacket. Said it's the last close call she's going to have."

"That just leaves you, me, Audra and Salina," Lauren said woodenly.

Very few civilians understood how dangerous it was to hold the border, but Tiffany got her news firsthand from Trevor. She was nodding thoughtfully.

Breeze—obviously changing the subject—asked, "Speaking of which, how's Trevor?"

"Okay." She didn't sound like she meant it. "He's just worn down to nothing. The Militia is stretched so thin along the southern border that it can't do its job. But it's the psychological cost. They're being ordered to turn back hungry and defenseless families. Starving women and children. People in rags who are just like them, who but for an unlucky break, happened to have lived south of The Line."

Tiffany paused, her normally soft brow lining. "Do you know what that's like? What it costs our guys? People don't talk about it, but the Militia's ripe with desertion. Men and women who just can't bear to force innocent people back down south at gun point. It's killing their souls."

Lauren said, "Yeah, we've heard. It's not so bad on our part of the border. We're not face-to-face like in the mountains."

Tiffany cried, "Don't get me wrong. They do the best they can with what they've got, but raiders are constantly harassing them. Testing The Line to see where it's vulnerable. And then there's the corruption. Want across? Just fork out the money. Or offer sex. Maybe it's drugs or booze. Jewelry. It's like a sieve in the Medicine Bow Mountains south of Laramie."

Lauren pulled out a cheese-covered chip and chewed it. Cheese made from fresh milk was a whole different thing than the stuff she used to buy in the grocery store. Fresh cheese was richer and creamier. And damned expensive.

After a couple of seconds, she said, "What are you going to do now that you're out of a job?"

"You got fired?" Breeze cried.

"No work, Breeze." Tiff shrugged. "I'm looking at a job with the elementary school. Or I may go north and sign on in the coal mines. They're hiring. They don't pay much these days, but it's better than no paycheck at all. Trevor doesn't want me to, but—"

"Of course, he doesn't," Breeze muttered. "Last I heard, he was planning on marrying you."

Tiffany's expression tightened. "Yeah, hope so. If everything is all right between us when the date finally rolls around."

Lauren wiped her hands on her napkin. "I don't like the sound of that."

Tiffany pulled a chip from the stack of nachos; she didn't eat it, just stared at it. "He...he won't sleep with me, Lauren. I..."

Breeze growled, "What the hell? Any man in his right mind would kill to have you in his bed."

"We had a bad night, and it scared him. He started screaming and reached over and grabbed me around the throat."

Glimpses from Lauren's own nightmares ran through her mind like an agonizing film: Jim's lifeless body illuminated in the ambulance and patrol car headlights; Buffalo Camp, staring into the eyes of the children and women as they died; the back of Masterson's head exploding in a red haze. How many times had she awakened screaming and reached for her pistol? Flashbacks were more real than the real world. The trauma never went away.

Lauren said, "Give him some time, Tiff. Once this is over—"

"Will it ever be over?" Tiffany shook her head as though denying what she'd just said and glanced around the restaurant, worried someone might have overhead. Lowering her voice, she said, "He didn't mean to hurt me. He was reliving the last fight with the raiders. I guess it was pretty desperate. One of them, a big guy, wrestled Trevor to the ground and put a gun to his head. Trev grabbed him around the throat."

Lauren took a deep breath and let it out slowly. Trevor was alive, which meant he'd probably choked the guy to death with his bare hands, and the fight kept replaying in his nightmares.

Breeze slipped a reassuring arm around Tiffany's shoulders. Gave her a hug. "Just about everybody on The Line has a story like that, Tiff. They're all walking wounded."

Lauren reached across the table and twined her fingers with Tiffany's. "Trevor's tough. He's going to make it through this, and you two are going to live happily ever after and raise great kids."

"Trevor says having a child today would be an act of cruelty."

Lauren tightened her hold on Tiffany's hand, then released it to pull her beer over and take a drink. Tiffany had always talked about having children, longed for the day when that dream came true. Her heart must be breaking, both for Trevor and for those lost babies who would never smile up at her.

Breeze was staring woodenly at the table. Whispered, "He might be right."

Tiffany said, "That's grim, Breeze. But, I mean, how are you doing?"

"Actually, I…" Breeze swallowed hard. "I'm thinking of enlisting. Probably with the Guard."

Lauren started. "Enlist? You kidding? Ragnovich would own your butt. You'd have to follow orders."

Tiffany's eyes narrowed. It wasn't quite disapproval, but close to it. Tiff took another drink of beer as though she needed a few seconds to mull over her response before saying, "You're one of the best rifle shots in the state, Breeze. But…are you sure that's what you want?"

Lauren shifted uncomfortably in her seat. "I don't think you should. The guys on The Line, they'd miss you."

"Naw," Breeze told her with a wry smile, one that hearkened of a different time in the past. "They've got 'The Hero of the Camp' to keep them in bottles of water, ammo, and batteries." She inclined her head suggestively. "Besides, Lauren, your motorcycle's bigger and faster than mine."

"Then maybe I ought to enlist, too? Leave them all hanging," Lauren quipped.

Somehow, Tiffany missed the humor. "Maybe you should wait until Tyrell gets back. You know? Make the decision together."

A nauseating mixture of fear and grief stuck in her throat. I mourn him every day. "I don't think he's coming back, Tiff."

"Stop that," Tiffany said sharply. "Of course, he's coming back. He told you he'd meet you at the Tappan ranch, and he will. He could be there right now, you know, waiting for you, worried sick about where you are."

"Tappan Ranch?" Breeze snapped, straightening. She was suddenly looking daggers at Lauren. "You want to tell me about this?"

"It's not what you think." Lauren's panic began to rise. "That Friday, when Tyrell was deployed, he said, if it all went to shit, he'd meet me there when this was all over." She raised pleading eyes. "Honest, Breeze. He didn't know. About the history, I mean. And, and, well..."

God, of all the scabs to have picked off. Lauren didn't have a clue about what had gone wrong between Breeze and her family. But just the mention of the ranch had Breeze almost smoldering.

"Give it a break, Breeze." Tiffany pointed a finger. "Lauren wouldn't anymore get into your shit than you'd get into hers. And you're both too damned fragile to think straight. Like this 'enlist in the Guard bullshit'."

Lauren watched the water droplets run down the outside of her beer glass. They glittered in the overhead lights. God, why did Tiff have to bring Tappan ranch up? Like throwing gas on the prickly glowing coals that lay between her and Breeze.

In a toneless voice, Lauren said, "If Tyrell had showed up at the ranch and learned I'd never made it there, he would have moved mountains to get to Laramie. He knows that Tiff is my best friend. That if anyone knew where I was, it would be her."

Tiffany's face was somber as she said, "I mean it, Breeze. Cut Lauren a little slack."

Breeze relented. "Hey. Water under the bridge. It's okay, Lauren. No harm, no foul."

But it wasn't. Just a glance at the strain in Breeze's face, the fire in her eyes, was proof of that.

The overhead fluorescent lights flickered, and every person in the restaurant glanced up to watch them until the electricity stabilized again. The strobe-like effect gave the faces at the tables a surreal quality, here, then gone, and back again.

Tiff glanced up. "You don't think the restaurant is trying to tell us it's closing time, do you?"

Lauren laughed in an attempt to relieve the sudden tension. "No. Believe me. Lucy comes out and orders everyone to go home. It's a lot more effective than dimming the lights. It is getting late, though. When do you have to catch the Militia truck back to Laramie?"

Tiffany lifted her wrist and glanced at her watch. "Trevor said they'd be finished loading up supplies around nine. So, another forty-five minutes, I guess. They're going to pick me up here."

Lauren nodded. "Wish you didn't have to go. The only time Breeze and I feel really normal is when you're around."

"I'll be back on the next supply run. Unless I get hired to help herd little kids at the elementary school, it's not like I have a job to keep me busy. In the meantime, let's finish these great nachos. They cost a small fortune, and they're too delicious to waste."

They both reached for a cheesy chip, but Breeze seemed oblivious, her gaze locked on eternity. She'd clamped the muscles in her jaws, always a bad sign.

Around a crunchy mouthful, Tiffany asked, "How's Mike Vinich? Trevor said he's still in the hospital holding on."

"He's getting better." Lauren tried to make light of it, as aware of Breeze as she'd have been about a lit stick of dynamite.

Cautiously, Breeze said, "Is he?"

"Yeah. Why?" Lauren shifted her gaze.

Breeze took a deep breath. Seemed to decompress. "Probably nothing."

Lauren sat back against the booth. "What did you hear?"

Tiffany held her latest chip, hesitating, as if waiting for the second shoe to drop.

Breeze shrugged, eyes lowered. "One of the nurse's told me Mike's having heart problems, but I'm sure it's a minor thing. The hospital staff will get it figured out."

Lauren sat there with blood pounding in her ears. "What else did the nurse say?"

"I haven't heard much more than that. I guess Mike's had some bad episodes of V-tach. Once, his heart even stopped, and they had to jolt it—"

"Jolt it?" Lauren felt suddenly helpless. "How can you apply electricity to a heart as frail as Mike's? He can't even laugh without a nurse rushing—"

"Look," Breeze met her gaze, "the medical staff is giving him VIP treatment because of what happened at Buffalo Camp. He's going to be okay."

Lauren propped her elbows on the table and dropped her head in her hands. She'd lost Tyrell. She didn't know if her mother and father were alive or dead. And now she might lose Mike?

"Hey," Tiffany said and reached across the table to put a hand on Lauren's arm. "Stop imagining the worst. Everything's all right."

Lauren stared at the darkness behind her eyes for a few seconds longer, then took a deep breath and lowered her hands. As she gazed across the table at Breeze, she said, "Thanks for telling me. Really. I mean it."

Jaws still clamped, Breeze nodded. "Yeah. Life's just one fucking minefield after another, huh?"

CHAPTER THIRTY-THREE

***

THE KTM'S THUMPING EXHAUST WENT QUIET AS LAUREN SHUT THE ENGINE OFF AT THE EXIT
342 checkpoint on I-80. The checkpoint was little more than a collection
of orange Highway Department barrels filled with sand that funneled
traffic into a sinuous lane on the east-bound side; the tight curves were
supposed to keep anyone from blasting through at high speed.

Checkpoint 342 was manned by a Laramie County deputy and four
members of the Wyoming Militia: three men and a woman.

Roadblocks and checkpoints like this had been placed all along
the length of I-80 in Wyoming. The major ones—like those outside
Cheyenne—were staffed by the Highway Patrol. Word had it that the
HP had become Governor Agar's right hand when it came to keeping
the state tied together. They sure didn't have to worry about valid
license plates, moving violations, or checking big rigs these days.

Checkpoint 342 had quite a view looking east and north across the
rolling plains. Geologists called this "the Gangplank', a long incline
of land that rose to the Sherman Hill summit in the Laramie Range.
Past that lay the Laramie Basin and one of the easiest crossings of the
continental divide. The gentle slope had originally drawn the Overland
Stage route, and then the Union Pacific railroad.

From here she could see seventy miles or more with the needle-like
peaks of Vedauwoo rising to the north.

"Hey, Lauren," Deputy Brad Tolland called as he stepped out from
his cruiser. Around fifty, he was a big muscular guy, six-foot-two, who
had a bullet-shaped head covered with gray buzz-cut hair. Tolland's
deeply lined forehead gave him a perpetually worried look. A shotgun
and an AR15 lay on a pad on his hood. Off the apron sat a Chevy
three-quarter ton with Platte County plates. As an addendum, the word

Militia had been painted on a piece of tin bolted to the bumper.

"How's it going, Brad?" She glanced up as a convoy of four pickups passed them in the westbound lane. The occupants honked and waved. "Looks like traffic's picking up."

"Yeah, governor has people coming in from all over the state. Legislators. And others. I was here yesterday when a delegation from the Sinclair refinery arrived. Governor Agar's trying to figure out how to keep everybody on the job. As long as Wyoming can produce enough gasoline, diesel, and natural gas, we can keep the coal mines, oil fields, and farms and ranches working. The latter being the most important. We have to be able to feed people."

"I know. I heard the silos across the state are almost empty. We're going to need those grain crops as soon as the harvesters—"

"You're Davis?" a young militiaman walked forward.

"I am," Lauren answered.

If he was old enough to drive, it was just barely. Dark-haired, he wore a black Resistol hat, faded denim shirt, jeans and scuffed western boots.

"I'm Kyle Rogers." The boy looked almost worshipful. "People tell stories about you. You're a hero. People are mighty grateful to you for braving the roads alone to take care of soldiers up and down the Fourth Quadrant." He stuck out his hand. "Pleased to meet you."

Lauren shook it, and said, "I'm not the only line rider, and I'm no hero, but thanks."

The youth just ducked his head and backed away.

Tolland said, "I see your bike is packed with supplies. Which OP is it this time?"

"Delta Alpha is out of water. They're getting a little frayed around the edges out there. Captain Ragnovich is trying to figure out a rotation. Get the people off The Line for some rest."

"If they'd let the Militia pick up more of the responsibility, we'd button up the entire border," Rogers insisted proudly.

Lauren gave him a weary look. "Not a good idea. I know most of the Militia is decent people. But you have some really bad apples in your ranks, too. There's a lot of anger over what you—"

"What do you mean?" Rogers asked.

"I mean the guys who ask special favors in exchange for allowing women to cross the border. And the ones who'll take cash, a bottle of fancy liquor, or sack full of jewelry and look the other way."

Rogers shifted nervously. After a too-long pause, he said, "There's bad apples in every barrel. But most of us are just protecting our neighbors."

"I know that." Lauren met the boy's eyes. "But if you want to make a difference, all of you? Go join the Wyoming National Guard."

Tolland said, "I second that."

"Can't," the boy said. "They have restrictions. I'm too young. I wouldn't make it. If I want to fight to protect my home, I have to be in the Militia."

"You could do what I'm doing, volunteer to help support the OPs. We need more line riders. This gets much worse and the four of us won't nearly be enough."

"But without Militia there's not enough eyes and boots on the ground to keep the raiders out!" a tall skinny guy in the rear called. He took two hostile steps toward Lauren. "We're working hard out here! You got a problem with the Militia, you better—"

"Hey! Shut your mouth," Tolland snapped. "Step back. She's Lauren Davis. She's paid her dues, Howie."

The man stalked off to the pickup, not saying another word. Climbing into the passenger seat, he slammed the door with extra effort.

"Don't mind him," Kyle Rogers said, as though embarrassed. "He's on edge because of the houses that have been burned by people coming across the line. They're raiding cupboards for food and killing livestock. Even shooting horses and dogs and eating 'em raw in people's yards. Can you imagine?"

Lauren nodded. "Don't have to. I've seen the butchered skeletons."

Tolland said, "Lot of hate building. Us against them. Hard to deal with sometimes. I've got family in Denver. Daughter and a son-in-law, four grandkids. For all I know, they're trying to get north, too. My little girl, the grandkids, Julie and Dave..." He took a deep breath, didn't finish.

Lauren stared off at the distance. Wyoming was beautiful and green, the hills sprinkled with brown dots of cattle and tan-and-white antelope. Even the constant brown haze had thinned, hopefully whatever was making it out West was burning itself out. "Hope they make it."

"I don't know if they are alive or dead. Then you hear about things like that massacre down at the Brown Palace Hotel. Forty-five people shot down for the loose change in their pockets. You think to yourself, please, God, let my family be okay."

Kyle scuffed his toe uneasily. "Government's gonna figure this thing out eventually. I mean, what's taking them so long? It's just pushing back the Chinese, ain't it? Where's the Marines?"

"Guess they're fighting out west," Tolland said, thankful to change the subject.

Lauren said, "The question is, fighting who? You sure it's the Chinese?"

"Hard to tell. Communications are still shut down. Even the news on the shortwave radio has dropped to nothing."

Kyle edged closer and lowered his voice to say, "Couple of guys on the line say it ain't Chinese. They claim the military has split in two, taking sides. Troops loyal to the western states are fighting the liberal pukes who've banded together to kill us. I told 'em they were full of shit."

Tolland didn't answer right away, as though he'd heard the same rumor. He raised a curious eyebrow as he glanced at Lauren. "You see Ragnovich every day. He tell you anything?"

"Not a word." She shook her head. "Even Warren Air Base is on lockdown. Security is tight. No news is getting out these days."

"That's a fact." Tolland lifted his hat and scratched his short-cropped hair. "My wife works on the base. Cafeteria. All I got was a note saying she'd be staying on base for the next couple of weeks. No explana…" Tolland stopped suddenly and his eyes fixed on the sky.

Lauren followed his gaze out across the rolling grasslands.

Against the brown-hazed sky, a distant spark of light flashed.

"What the hell?" Tolland whispered.

Lauren lifted a hand to shield her eyes. The spark became a thread of light. Brilliant, hot-white, it streaked up into the heavens trailing a thin white line.

"There's another," Kyle shouted and flung out an arm to point.

Miles to the north an even more distant flash lit the sky. And beyond that another. And another. A total of four, they raced upwards, tiny lances of fire rising above the horizon, piercing the high hazy overcast.

"What are those?" Kyle asked in amazement.

Tolland didn't seem to have the strength to reply. He stepped over to his cruiser and leaned unsteadily against his car door. "Jesus Christ."

In a stunned whisper, Lauren said, "Dear God. We're launching missiles."

The streaks of light were high now, arcing to the west with only wispy vapor trails to mark their paths. It had happened so quickly. Had she been looking the other way, Lauren would have missed it.

Neither Lauren nor Tolland spoke. Both were watching the sky. Were there enemy missiles inbound? Already dropping out of the stratosphere?

Lauren swung around to Tolland. "I can't believe it. We just launched an intercontinental ballistic missile strike!"

"Yep." Tolland swallowed hard. "F.E. Warren is a strategic missile base. Those are the big boys with megaton-yield payloads." His eyes were glued to the sky.

People in Wyoming had lived with the missiles for so long they'd become as much a part of the landscape as another bluff, drainage, or hill. Nobody even thought about the missile silos that scattered the sagebrush plains.

It took several moments before Tolland turned to Lauren. When he did, water glistened in his eyes. He softly said, "We just saw a nuclear launch."

CHAPTER THIRTY-FOUR

***

THE BEER BOTTLE IMPARTED A COOL RELIEF TO LAUREN'S PALMS AS SHE CLUTCHED IT WITH both trembling hands. Tough day out on the line. Scary day. She had to keep her shit together.

Could have been worse. Salina Valdez is dead.

She'd heard at the FOB that Salina was killed at dusk the night before. She'd been shot off her bike. The details had been worked out by a Guard team sent out to search for her. Salina had been riding down a ranch road on the way to Bravo Zulu with a replacement IFAK, or Individual First Aid Kit. She'd apparently been shot from ambush. Had no warning. The marks in the gravel road showed where she'd toppled from her Yamaha Tenere. The bike slid to a stop a couple of yards past where her body lay. A splay of blood marked the spot where she'd first hit the dirt, bounced and slid.

Her bike, the IFAK, and other supplies were missing.

But they'd left Salina's body where it stopped, a bullet hole blown through her chest.

That could just as easily have been me.

Shit. It damn near had been. Mere hours ago. Out on Goose Creek Road.

Lauren slouched in her customary booth in the Plains Hotel restaurant. Her M4 rested atop the table to her right. She kept pulling it close, then shoving it away, pulling it close. Her stomach and chest burned in nervous turmoil.

Trying to steady her breathing, she took another long drink of beer. Struggled to blank the continual replay of the afternoon's events. Turn her brain to other thoughts.

News of yesterday's missile launch had swept through the Guard like wildfire. No one had any information, so the rumors were wild. People were whispering crazy things out in the OPs. *Heard we hit Beijing... Naw, we erased San Francisco... No, we didn't, it was...*

But here in town, the news of the missile launch was still making the rounds, moving from house to house, mouth to mouth. Most people were skeptical, said it was all lies. Around her, men and women carried on soft conversations. Some actually sounded normal. A teasing hint that here, in this little sliver of existence, some semblance of that long-gone world still remained.

If she closed her eyes, the background patter of voices with the occasional laughter might have come from a now-vanished reality where the most pressing concerns were making the bills at the end of the month, whether the truck needed new tires, or if Billy should be playing video games with the Jones' kid.

Lauren briefly managed to still the tremors in her hands by gripping her bottle until her fingers ached. She willed herself to hear the idle chatter around her. Not the gunshots and screams. Not the terror in the voices of the soldiers at the OP.

Concentrate. Listen to the rising and falling of small talk.

Yes.

Relax. Her heartbeat slowed, her breath eased in and out of her lungs. Lurking right behind her eyes were scenes from that afternoon on Goose Creek Road. Images of a man spinning, brains and gore leaking from his exploded head as he tumbled to the ground.

She jerked, forced a swallow down her tight throat.

God, that was close. Too close.

A man in camo appeared in her peripheral vision as she forced herself to concentrate on her colorful beer label. Eased her fingers open one by one to release her death grip on the bottle.

"Captain," she greeted before he could speak. He must want to know what happened out there today. The last fucking thing on earth that she wanted to talk about.

Ragnovich seated himself on the opposite side of the booth. His white hair and uniform had not been washed in days. A rime of salt-stain traced an arc under each armpit, and smudges marred his jacket. The dark circles under his eyes, the deepening of the lines around his mouth, and the crow's feet at the corners of his eyes, reflected utter exhaustion.

"Heard you had a bad day out on Goose Creek Road. Want to tell me about it?" Ragnovich asked gently.

She blinked at him, acting as though she didn't quite understand the question. "Do you have any information about the missile launch?"

"That's not why I'm—"

"Dad was in charge of F.E. Warren for a while. All those missiles out in the silos? They're topped with nuclear warheads. What I saw? We launched a nuclear strike. Who did we hit? China? Russia? Was it retaliation, or did we shoot first?"

Ragnovich's sighed, "All I know for sure is that we're not dead."

He paused and stared for several moments at the black M4 lying across the table. It was intensely clean. She wiped it down constantly, almost obsessively.

Ragnovich leaned back slightly. "Okay, I did hear one thing…"

When his voice trailed away, she asked, "What?"

The Captain looked around the room with narrowed eyes. "Scuttlebutt is that it was retaliation."

"Retaliation for what? Against whom?"

Ragnovich almost tenderly ran his fingers over the M4's receiver. Given his continued silence, she figured he'd decided not to answer. Her voice came out hushed. "I heard we hit California."

Captain shook his head. "Somebody did. Not us. At least, I don't think it was us."

Lauren looked up at him through blurry eyes. "Heard a rumor. Tolland's wife works on the base. Not much gets out, but he said General Kyzer came to see Colonels Mackeson and Steadman, the major and you."

Ragnovich vented a sigh. "Yeah. Not a rumor. Day before yesterday, he came to debrief me. He hinted that the reason we haven't heard from Washington is because it's gone."

Every muscle in Lauren's body went taut. He'd dropped the news like it was nothing, just another tidbit of hearsay. "Nuked?"

Ragnovich shook his head. "Don't know. Kyzer says regional military is trying to piece together some sort of command and control. Maybe based in Cheyenne Mountain. But, hell, he doesn't know much, either, so take that little tidbit with a grain of salt."

She took another gulp of beer and added, "Not much to be cheery about, is there?"

"Actually, there is. My people love you. You're the hero who braves the back roads to keep them fed, watered, and supplied. You, Audra, and Breeze. After what happened to Salina, they're going to love you even more."

"Yeah, I think I'm up to twenty marriage proposals now. Wonder how many Breeze and Audra have gotten?" She made a face.

Ragnovich gave her a tight-lipped look. "Now, tell me what happened out there today?"

Lauren's face twitched. Despite her brain, her voice—of its own accord—was running on like a little brook. "Five guys were hiding in the ditch out near the Johnson Ranch. When I crested the rise, I saw the ranch house burning. Caught my attention. That's why I didn't see them scrambling out of the ditch. They had rifles and shotguns. I think they'd seen me ride past before, because they were waiting for me at the curve where I had to slow down. They ran out in front of me and started shooting, trying to knock me off the bike. Guess it was pure instinct. I flipped the M4 to fully automatic and strafed the whole lot." She took a breath.

"Heard you got three of them. Two got away?"

In my head, I'm on the road. Gripping the bars with my left hand, I let go of the bike's throttle. Swing the M4 around with my right and flip the fire control to auto. My aim is off, one-handed from a moving motorcycle. The burst stitches the three crowded on the left. But recoil throws the last rounds over the heads of the last two. Their expressions are frozen in my memory, panicked and terrified.

"Two. Yeah. As fast as they were running, I'll bet they passed antelope on the fly." She made an uncertain gesture. "Were they responsible for torching the Johnson place?"

Ragnovich nodded. "Looks like it. One of the ranch women escaped the fire. She's badly burned, but alive. She said the five raiders hung out there for a couple of days. Killed the men first. The women... Well, never mind. When they were done, they set the house ablaze to destroy any evidence."

A hollow sensation invaded her gut. "What about my two runners?"

"S.O.'s already on it. A guy from up on Harrison Road has hounds.

According to the survivor at the Johnson place, the raiders all worked at one of the upscale restaurants in Fort Collins before the collapse. Not the kind to be wise to the ways of the wild. They've got about as much chance of coming back alive as sheep-killing coyotes."

"Justice," she whispered, seeing it replay in her mind. "The only thing that saved me out there today was that they weren't expecting a full automatic. Sorry I missed the last two."

Ragnovich glanced down at the two bullet holes in her Ralley jacket. "They do that?"

"Yep." She reached up to tuck a finger into the larger hole in her sleeve. "But I'm not like Valerie who quit the first time it got scary. I'll be there tomorrow morning. Ready to go."

Ragnovich's lips worked, opening and closing, before his voice dropped. "Audra might be prickly, but she's riding out in a Humvee these days. Why are you and Breeze still using the bikes?"

Her beer bottle felt cool as she ran her fingertips down the glass. "Bike is more agile."

And my bike is Tyrell's. He's with me on every ride.

"Listen," Ragnovich propped a fist on the table, "you know as well as I do that it's getting worse out there. The people making it through the line are harder, meaner, more desperate. It's only a matter of time. Just like Salina, one of them is going to shoot you off that bike."

Lauren laughed. It just erupted from her throat.

He stared at her. "Did I say something funny?"

As her amusement drained away, the numbness returned to haunt her. She looked down at her hands where they clutched the beer bottle and slowly shook her head. "Captain, nuclear missiles flew over America. No one knows who we're fighting. Could be a foreign enemy, but half the men and women on the line are convinced the enemy is other Americans." She took a breath and let it out slowly. "The death of one person here in Wyoming just doesn't seem all that important. Even if it's me."

Ragnovich reached across the table and grabbed her sleeve. "Trust me. It will when you're lying out there alone with a bullet in your guts, and it takes you four days to die. There's nothing I can do about what's happening in the rest of America, but you are my responsibility. Got that? I don't want you dead."

Lauren studied his fist twined in her sleeve. "Thanks, Captain. Really."

He released her. "I'm serious. If you don't start taking more care, I'm pulling you off The Line. Luck isn't enough."

She glared at him. Almost maniacal. Maybe she was suffering a psychotic break after all.

"Captain, the only thing I've got going for me is luck. It's all I've ever had. It was luck that I had a job at a bank when it all came down. Luck that I could withdraw my cash before the run happened. Luckier than hell that my boyfriend was a Delta Force lieutenant, and that I have this thing for riding motorcycles. Luck that I had a father who taught me to shoot. Luck that I took the road west into the mountains instead of into Denver. Luck that I had a friend willing to sacrifice himself to save me. Luck that he had a wallet full of cash to add to my own."

Lauren leaned over the M4 to stare hard into Ragnovich's sad eyes. "But for any of those things—I mean, change just one—and I wouldn't be sitting here. I've totally beat the freaking odds, sir. And I'm the last person on earth who should have."

Ragnovich gave her a somber once-over. "But you are here, and I'm grateful for it, and so are a lot of other people. Could be destiny. Ever consider that? Maybe you're here because you're meant to be."

He stabbed a finger at her. "But don't think that gives you a reason to be careless, because maybe you're not. Get my meaning? There's more to life than this hell we're living. One of these days, we all may discover it."

She clamped her jaw against the sucking sense of despair and blinked, desperate to keep Ragnovich from seeing how close she was to breaking.

"Hope kills, sir. Don't need it. Don't want it."

"No? Well, it's the best I can do today. So use it if you're able."

She watched Ragnovich rise and walk across the restaurant for the door.

CHAPTER THIRTY-FIVE

***

LAUREN PARKED THE KTM IN THE CHEYENNE REGIONAL MEDICAL CENTER EAST HOSPITAL lot. Her fingers kept fumbling, still fighting the shakes as she unbuckled her helmet. Taking a deep breath, she forced herself to breathe. Slowed her heartbeat. Got the D rings unfastened and lifted the helmet from her head.

The sunset was another masterpiece of nightmarish orange in a smoke-filled western sky. Made her think of perdition—hell broken loose with its fires and burning souls consuming the western horizon. Tyrell was out there, somewhere. Wasn't he?

A shiver ran down her spine. Lauren stepped off the bike, unzipping her bulky riding jacket. In the heat, she shrugged it off. Taking a hard look at the dust and scuff marks. She'd gone down. Dropped the bike when two men leaped out on a gravel corner and tried to grab her off the KTM.

It had been on a dirt road north of OP Bravo India. Out by the Chalk Buttes. Rolling country filled with sandstone-capped mesas. Recent rains had left waving tall grass growing on either side of the barbwire fences. Meadowlark country, rich wildflowers, and lark buntings flitting after insects. Lonely and abandoned. Lauren had dropped off her load of emergency supplies, hung around for a cup of tea with the five men and two women, half Guard, half Militia. Then she'd lined the bike out, heading back to Cheyenne.

She'd slowed for the corner when the men leaped up from the ditch. Her impulse had been to twist the throttle, which—despite the traction control—spun the back wheel out. She'd low-sided, slid for about thirty feet. Her riding pants were torn over the knee armor. But the elbow, side, and back of the jacket, though abused, were still intact.

She'd stopped sliding, twisted around, and pulled her pistol from the large lower left pocket. Still on her side in the middle of the road, she'd braced her elbows and shot the first man.

A big dude, maybe thirty to thirty-five, in a filthy denim shirt, blue jeans and lace-up work boots. Her bullet had taken him through the left side of the chest. Dropped him like a pile of meat.

The second guy, maybe in his twenties, had come on like a freight train. He was shooting a small 9mm pocket pistol built by Glock. The crack of the bullets ripping past Lauren's head wouldn't be forgotten. If the guy had known how to shoot, it would have been over. Instead, he kept closing his eyes, jerking the pistol sideways with each yanking of the trigger.

Lauren had rushed her shot. Missed. Then she got the front sight fixed. Settled on his chest and put two rounds through the guy's rib cage. Watched him stop, a stupid look on his face, brown eyes gone wide.

He'd fallen over backwards, sort of like a toppling tree, to slam into the gravel, a puff of dust dancing out to be caught by the breeze and whipped away.

Lauren sucked air. Couldn't get enough of it. Wasn't sure when she'd stopped breathing. Had crawled to her feet, wobbling, unsteady. Tyrell's .45 was clutched in her right hand as she walked over to the bike.

"Damn it!" She hissed through gritted teeth as she stuffed the big pistol into her pocket.

Tyrell's gleaming KTM had never been over before. She reached down, grabbed the bars, and squeezed the front brake as she lifted. Had just muscled the bike up when a voice cried, "Dear God, you killed him!"

Lauren turned just as the pistol-shot sounded. Felt her jacket jump.

The woman was a disheveled brunette, twenty something, with short-cropped hair, thin nose, and lips twisted from either rage or grief. Tears were just starting down her smudged cheeks. The pistol was held out before her, straight-armed, trembling in a two-handed grip.

Lauren flinched when the brunette closed her eyes and shot. And again, and again. Lauren fumbled in the big pocket of her jacket for the .45. Clawed it out and jerked a shot.

Too rattled, she missed.

At that, the woman froze, eyes going wide. Then she clamped her eyes closed and fired yet again. Then the Glock was empty, slide locked back. The woman still impotently yanking on the trigger.

Lauren shot her through the sternum. Saw the breasts leap and judder under the flimsy shirt as the bullet punched through. Every nuance of the woman's expression, the shock in her wide eyes, the opening of her mouth. All frozen in Lauren's reeling mind.

And then the brunette collapsed in a loose-limbed sprawl beside the brown-eyed man.

Standing there, in the middle of nowhere, north of OP Bravo India, Lauren had to brace herself on the bike. She'd checked herself for wounds. Couldn't believe that they'd missed with all those shots.

The shakes were some of the worst. Like her bones had gone loose and begun to rattle down deep. Couldn't seem to get enough air. Gray formed around her vision, as if she were seeing down a long tunnel.

Must have been fifteen minutes she'd stood there, trying to get control of her body.

Only then, blinking, did she manage to inspect the bike. See where the slide on gravel had bent one of the turn signals, scuffed the handgrip on the left bar. The powder coat was scraped off the left side crash bar and the gleaming orange and black body work had been abraded. A bullet had punctured the seat, blown out foam padding.

She had turned, screaming, "See what you did! Damn you!" at the bleeding bodies.

In a haze, still shaking, she'd ridden here, to the hospital. God, she needed to just sit. To talk to Mike.

He'd help. He could make sense of all this.

She fingered the new bullet holes in her jacket as she headed for the door. Seemed like her legs were rubbery. Like one or the other might fold up on her without warning.

At the door, she handed her dust-streaked M4 to the guard, kept her hand from quaking as she signed for the weapon, and made her way up to Mike's room.

Walking down the hall toward his door, she noted the changes. The haggard looks in the faces of the nurses. The grim set to the mouths. And the rooms she passed used to be quiet. Now she was aware of the labored breathing, the slight groans from within.

At Mike's door, she paused, glanced in.

He was asleep. His breathing sounded labored. His chest rose and fell under the sheet.

The cannula that had once covered his nose was long gone. The hospital had been out of oxygen for a couple of days now. Word was that they were saving the bottles they had left for the operating room. Other than that, all they had were portable generators, and those went to patients in the ICU.

"Hey, Mike," she whispered, unwilling to touch him.

"Bad day," she told him softly as she settled into the visitor's chair.

Mike didn't react, no change of expression as he sucked for each breath. His eyes were flickering behind crusty lids.

"I killed three people. I don't feel anything. Not remorse. Not guilt. Not...anything." She paused, searching for words.

His slack features didn't change.

"If they had known anything about shooting? If they hadn't been scared and panicked? If they'd just taken a second. Steadied that Glock?"

After a pause, she added, "I heard they caught the guys that got away from the Johnson Ranch. Had to kill one, but the other was taken alive. Put him on trial. Just that fast, can you believe?"

Mike made a rasping down in his throat.

"Yeah, I agree." She hesitated. "I'm invited to the execution. Agar himself is supposed to be there."

A soft gurgle came from Mike's chest.

"What's that? Oh, sure. You can come if you want. Not that I think going to an execution's a great date."

At that, she reached out, took his hand. To her surprise, he didn't wake.

"Guess you'd rather talk about something more uplifting."

She thought his lips twitched.

"I remember our first date. Casper. The Rialto Theatre. Can't remember the movie. Just that we held hands. We did all right, you and me." A pause. "Best friends."

Running her fingers over the back of his hand, she traced the familiar lines. "Fun night. We always had good times. Right up to that night by the lake. You were only the second man I ever made love to. It was always so easy to be with each other." A smile. "Then Pam came along. And that was okay. We always made better friends than lovers."

Mike's sunken eyes were flickering harder. Must have been some intense REM sleep.

"But who'd have ever thought we'd end up here? Me, talking to a man who can't hear me. And you, lost in dreams while the world dies around us?"

CHAPTER THIRTY-SIX

***

BRIGHT NOON SUNLIGHT REFLECTED FROM THE BIKE'S CHROME AS LAUREN RODE HER KTM up Warren Avenue, past the Wyoming capitol building with its wide lawns and ancient trees. As she did, her thoughts returned to mulling over her dilemma: Since the day on Goose Creek Road, Lieutenant Barrow had been giving her milk runs. Making them sound important. Barrow kept dispatching Audra and her Humvee to the hot OPs, sending Lauren and Breeze on meaningless rides to quiet OPs in the Alpha district out east.

Damn it! Being a line rider was the only thing that gave her life meaning.

Tyrell would understand. It's what drove him to earn that Ranger patch in the first place, and then pushed him through the training and selection to win that Place in "The Unit" and then make the teams. He'd tell her to keep it up, to...

Stop it. Tyrell's gone. That future is over. Let it die.

Ragnovich had to be behind dispatching her on routes that didn't make sense. She'd been riding up and down the Fourth Quadrant long enough to know what the men and women manning The Line needed and when.

But what to do about it? If she made a stink, the captain could cut her off. She might be the famous Lauren Davis, hero of the Buffalo Camp, but she was also just a volunteer.

Enlist in the Guard?

"Bad idea," she told the chin bar of her helmet.

Any autonomy she had would vanish. Ragnovich, working with Colonel Steadman, could assign her anywhere. Put her back in the head shed, as the Guard offices downtown were called. Have her filling out paperwork—and there was still plenty of paperwork despite the new conditions in the world.

At Pershing Avenue, she slowed. All the traffic lights in Cheyenne blinked yellow. The miracle was that there was enough traffic to control. Governor Agar had concentrated on keeping a supply of crude flowing from the oil fields, which in turn kept the refinery east of town working. Fuel went first to the Guard and Militia, then to the farmers and ranchers, and then to the general populace. That, in turn, kept some of the gas stations open. Assuming a person could barter something for a tank of gas. Paper money was still in use. People were creatures of habit. But a cow would buy you a tank of fuel.

Lauren wasn't sure what sort of economy it was—corrupted free market or prehistoric trading society—but not only was it limping erratically along, it was keeping an entire segment of the population working.

She glanced out at Frontier Park, home of world famous rodeo called Cheyenne Frontier Days. Tents filled the grassy flats. They'd come from a house-to-house "tent drive" across the city. Every Wyoming citizen had camping equipment. The same with camp trailers, which now filled the parking lots around the grandstands at the rodeo ground. Even wall tents—normally used in elk hunting—had been set up for the hungry refugees who'd made it across the border despite the State's best efforts to stop them.

But feeding them was tough. This was July, the time of year when food stocks were at the lowest. Grain elevators in the wheat and barley country to the north and east were still empty. Harvests wouldn't come in for another couple of months. Ranchers refused to slaughter cows until the calves could be weaned.

The governor was walking a tightrope between slaughtering early to avoid famine, and giving the animals enough time to grow so that he could maximize meat production. He'd reluctantly started using fuel allotments as a means to increase the numbers of animals for slaughter. Everything hinged upon the coming harvests. How much wheat, barley, corn, sugar beets, and pinto beans could the farmers produce to fill human stomachs, and how much grass and alfalfa hay could they produce to feed livestock through the next winter?

Hundreds of people with signs lined the road in front of Frontier

Park. Too many to read, but one sign grabbed her attention. The woman's chunk of cardboard bore four letters: **WFFF.**

These days, everyone knew what that meant: Will fuck for food.

The woman—with three small children—sat on the curb, her feet in the gutter. She wasn't particularly attractive with her dirty brown hair in tangles and yellow cotton dress in need of washing. All of the children had filthy faces and snotty noses.

The woman gave Lauren a pleading look as she rode past.

Lauren blasted on down the street. For as tough as Lauren liked to believe herself, she couldn't bear the eyes of the kids.

If they survive and make it to adulthood, what kind of people are they going to be?

Not to worry. The chances of them growing up were slim to none.

Joseph Stalin's famous quote echoed from somewhere deep inside her: "A single human being's death is a tragedy, when a million die, it is merely a statistic."

The truth beat down upon her as she passed the hundreds waiting so patiently beside the road. All with a story to tell, and each one desperate, filled with hope, and fully aware of just how desolate the future really was.

For her, it was simply more human heartbreak than a single mind could assimilate.

Turning left at the north end of the Frontier Park, she continued until she found the line of parked police cars.

She shut down the bike, dropped the kickstand, and propped her helmet on the right mirror. Stepping off, she checked the bungee cords that strapped the MREs to the back of the bike, making sure they were still tight. By the time she got there around sunset, the soldiers out at OP Delta Alpha would be getting really hungry.

But this was something she had to do.

She walked over to where sheriff's deputies and Cheyenne police waited in a nervous knot.

Deputy Brad Tolland lifted a hand to her. A man and woman stood beside him. They looked hot in their sheriff's department uniforms. Sweat beaded foreheads and noses.

"Lauren," Tolland greeted, "haven't seen you lately."

"Yeah, well, the good captain is going out of his way to send me anyplace where there isn't a chance of getting shot."

"I approve. The captain just went up a couple of notches in my book," Tolland told her. "Let me introduce you to my friends. Deputy Tony Montoya and Deputy Valencia Simmons. Both have had my back a time or two."

"Lauren Davis," she said, shaking hands.

"My pleasure," Simmons told her, a slight squint to the thirty-year-old woman's eyes, as if unsure what to make of Lauren. "Glad you came. Lot of folks refused."

Lauren looked the deputy over. Hard hazel eyes. Deep lines around her mouth. "Are you the Deputy Simmons who caught Josh Newman?"

"That's me. I heard he tried to blast your head off with a shotgun."

Lauren nodded. "He did indeed."

Newman was one of the two men that got away that day out near Johnson Ranch. The story that was circulating through the ranks said that when Simmons caught up with them, the two men tried to make a fight of it, and Deputy Simmons obliged. One of the men died in the firefight. The other man—Josh Newman—threw himself on the ground and begged Simmons for mercy. She'd taken him into custody.

Simmons said, "Still not sure this is the way to handle it. Though God knows they deserve whatever they get."

"Justice is as justice does, Deputy," Lauren replied.

Simmons gave her a hard sidelong look.

Lauren turned her attention to the three men and one woman seated in chairs atop a raised platform. They wore orange prison jumpsuits. Their hands were manacled to the chair backs behind them, and their ankles to the chair legs.

The burned woman who escaped from Johnson Ranch had documented what she and her family endured before the raiders set their house on fire and left them to burn. She'd identified Josh Newman—the guy on the far left—as the leader.

Newman glared defiantly out at the crowd that had gathered on the other side of a yellow crime-scene-tape barrier. Mostly refugees from the park, the people waited on shifting feet, talking softly amongst themselves.

"Hard to think we've come to this," Montoya said, the corners of his eyes tightening. "Never thought I'd see the day."

Simmons slipped her thumbs into her duty belt, but she looked like she hated this as much as Montoya did. "We're on the edge, Tony. The ragged goddamn edge." She inclined her head toward the crowd. "Davis is right. They've got to know there's a price for murder and rape."

"Of course, but…" Montoya hesitated, "But it's like we've stepped back a hundred and fifty years in time."

"Not sure there's anything wrong with that." Tolland crossed his arms.

"I'm not either," Simmons said. "It was bad before the collapse. These days? People figure they've got a right to be animals."

"But why the hell can't we just send them off to prison in Rawlins?" Montoya asked. "I don't like making a spectacle of this."

Lauren barely glanced at him, instead focusing on the accused, but she said, "See that fellow, Newman? He and his friends killed the men, raped the women for a couple of days before he burned them to death. You really think we ought to give him a nice bed and feed him three squares a day in prison while we've got kids on the street starving to death?"

Montoya quietly replied, "Ooraw."

Lauren's lips pressed into a tight white line. She scanned the prisoners on the platform. "Who are the others up there?"

"All murderers," Montoya replied. "They're just as bad as Newman. I know it's good riddance, but I still hate the way this is coming down."

"Take it up with God," Lauren said. "The governor's right. We've got to send a message. Act like a savage? You'll get what's coming to you."

Montoya looked defeated.

"By the way." Tolland lowered his voice. "Most of the legislature is back in town. After the missiles went up, I guess folks scoured the mountains to find every elected official."

Lauren rubbed her forehead, thinking about Breeze's grandfather, Senator Bill Tappan. He had to be in his seventies now. Last time she'd seen him he was still hard as nails, but the roads through Wyoming were a nightmare. She prayed he'd made it past the raiders. "Hope the rest get here without problems."

"They should. Agar sent armed escorts to every part of the state to protect the last of the representatives on the trip to Cheyenne."

To everyone's surprise, the door of a police cruiser opened and Governor Peter Agar himself stepped out. Seeing him for the first time up close and in person, he was a smaller man than Lauren anticipated. Maybe five-feet-six-inches tall. He wore a dark gray suit with a blue tie. As the governor walked solemnly over to the knot of officers surrounding the prisoners, his short black hair blew in the wind.

Vincent Pachula, the duly elected sheriff of Laramie County, met the governor and extended a sheet of paper to the him. Off to the side, the Cheyenne police chief looked nervous, his face like a pale mask.

Agar read the paper, nodded, and folded it. Placing it in his pocket, he raised his voice to the crowd. "We all saw the missiles go up, and know our military is fighting back, but none of us really knows what's happening out there in the rest of the country. And that includes me."

The governor paused to take a breath, and the crowd went still and silent.

Agar continued, "But one thing I do know: The United States is currently governed by the articles of martial law. By order of the President of the United States, the Constitution has been suspended. Our civilization, all that we are as human beings and Americans, hangs by a thread. We cannot allow the current state of affairs to justify a descent into barbarity, cruelty and the lawlessness. It has to stop."

"Just get on with it, Governor!" a man yelled. "They got it coming!"

Agar paused, gaze taking in individuals in the crowd.

"I *know* you have all suffered. I *know* you and your families are hungry. That you are at the limits of despair. But you didn't descend to brutality, murder, rape, and torture." He extended one hand to the manacled people in the chairs. "These people committed unforgiveable acts of brutality."

A woman cried, "Do it!"

Governor Agar raised his hands as if pleading with the crowd. "Listen, people, the collapse has knocked us flat. Laid us out. Every man, woman, and child of us. But from this moment forward, we're starting the hard climb to get back on our feet."

Another shouted, "There's got to be law!"

Agar paused to listen to more shouts from the crowd. "Wyoming is literally rising from the dirt. I give you my solemn oath I will do everything in my power to protect the people in this state, but it's not going to be easy."

"We're starving! Where's the food?" a man cried out.

"Hear me! There isn't enough to go around. Not yet. I can't wave a magic wand and make food appear! I have to allocate resources where they will do the most good, and many of you are going to think it's unfair. It is unfair! I could loot the farms and ranches to feed a few people today. But if I did, we'd *all* die come winter. I have to make hard choices. I hope you will try to understand why. Starting now."

Agar turned, looking back at the prisoners. Then he addressed the crowd again. "The men and woman behind me were apprehended in the acts of murder and gang rape. Beyond the requirements established for martial law, they have been represented by counsel, allowed to offer a defense, and have been found guilty beyond any shadow of a doubt."

Agar paused again, took a breath. "Folks, everywhere I go people shout at me to do something."

"Then stop prattling on about it, Governor!" a man yelled at the top of his lungs. "Give the order so we can all go home!"

He stared out at the crowd. "You know the old saying, 'The Buck Stops Here?' I'm not shunting this responsibility off onto anyone else. I alone will carry out this first act of justice."

He took a deep breath, faced Sheriff Pachula, and said, "Please read out the sentence."

Lauren listened as the names, crimes, and death sentences were read out for each of the prisoners. But she could see no gallows, no wall for a firing squad. Just the prisoners, sitting in the chairs. They themselves looked slightly perplexed.

"The sentences will now be carried out," Pachula announced.

To Lauren's surprise, it was Agar himself who walked forward. Stepping around behind the prisoners, he pulled a small black pistol from his pocket. Stooping slightly, he placed the muzzle at the base of the woman's skull, and fired.

She jerked in the chair, flopped, and went limp. Blood began to stream from her nose and mouth, and Lauren could see her eyes had bugged out of her head.

The man sitting beside her screamed, "Goddamn you, you son of a bitch!" and tried to flip his head back and forth, but Agar caught the right angle and discharged his pistol with lethal effect.

"What's he shooting?" Lauren asked.

"That's a Kimber.380 Auto," Valencia Simmons said, voice devoid of all emotion. "I heard the governor practiced with a corpse to get the right angle to sever the spinal cord. A .380 has just enough energy to scramble the brain as the hollow point expands, but not enough to exit the other side of the skull."

The governor walked down the line, dispensing justice. When the last shot was fired, the crowd heaved a simultaneous sigh of relief that rang through the afternoon.

Lauren prayed the ghosts of the women who'd died in fire at Johnson Ranch could see through her eyes. It was for them that she watched until the very end, until Josh Newman stopped twitching.

Then she slowly let out the breath she'd been holding.

She should feel something. Horror. Disgust. Four bodies slumped in chairs.

But she just felt really tired.

Deputy Montoya hung his head and shook it. "God Almighty."

CHAPTER THIRTY-SEVEN

* * *

LAUREN NERVED HERSELF, SLUNG HER BOOGIE BAG OVER HER SHOULDER, AND WALKED through the Hilton lobby. No one gave her more than a glance as she crossed the polished-granite floor. As if young women in motorcycle gear—and armed with automatic weapons—were a common enough occurrence as they strolled through. Music—old Seventies hits—was playing softly through the speakers.

Lauren passed through the double glass doors that opened to the bar. Most of the tables were occupied by people in suits or up-scale dress. The backbar, like that at The Plains, was filled with bottles that sported hand-written labels as the originals had been emptied. Local "bathtub" whiskeys, vodkas, and other spirits were the norm these days.

In the far corner, out of most people's sight, stood a somewhat shadowed booth. An olive-green duffle, big, could just be seen in the seat.

Lauren's heart began to pound. She stopped short, mouth gone dry. Figured that if she could stand seeing people being shot in the back of the head—not to mention her own nightmares—she could deal with this, too.

Stepping up to the booth, she forced a smile.

Breeze Tappan—a half-empty glass of stout on the table before her—was curled in the booth, her back to the wall. She looked up, fixing Lauren with those unique tan eyes ringed in brown. The pinched look to Breeze's lips slowly relaxed into a wry smile. "What's gone wrong now?"

"Does the end of civilization ring any bells?"

Breeze exhaled wearily, relief softening her features. "Sorry. Thought you were here to collect me for another run. I'm still working through..." The smile went bitter. "Never mind."

"Got a minute?"

"Sure. Move the boogie bag. Take a seat."

Lauren did, propping Breeze's bag on the floor next to Lauren's and sliding into the seat.

Breeze indicated the bags, saying, "Hope you don't mind, but I've been putting together one of my own. Thought it was a pretty good idea. And two nights ago, what's in that bag saved my life."

"Yeah, mine's saved my ass a couple of times, too." Lauren looked up when the server stepped up to the table. The woman might have been in her early thirties, her hair up. The Hilton still dressed their staff in uniforms.

"Get you anything?"

"Whatever Breeze is drinking."

"My tab, Jenn," Breeze told the woman as she walked away.

"Hard day, huh?" Lauren asked into the lengthening silence. Breeze had that look—the tortured one so common to people on The Line.

"New trick," Breeze almost bit off the words. "On I-80 coming back from Delta sector. A way to highjack vehicles. They waited until I got close enough to see it was women and kids. Then they laid down. Head to toe, stretching across the highway. So, like, either I stopped, or I'd run over them, right?"

"Death wish?"

Breeze snorted derisively. "Trap. Premised on the hope that no one would run over women and kids. So, I clamp on the brakes, pull the bike to a stop. And that's when the four guys leap up from where they're hidden by the side of the road. Figure they're going to take me down."

Breeze rubbed her forehead as if to soothe a headache. Gave Lauren a knowing look. "Me or them, you know? They didn't back off when I whipped the carbine around. Didn't stop when I ordered them to."

Lauren asked, "Armed?"

"One had an old revolver. Said he'd shoot if I didn't get off the bike." A pause, Breeze's eyes going distant. "Thought he was going to bluff me. That I wouldn't shoot."

"Nothing you could have done," Lauren insisted.

Breeze frowned into the distance in her mind. "I see them, you know. Sometimes I want to beat my head against a wall. See if I can hammer all the people I've killed out of my memory."

"Doesn't work." Lauren leaned back as Jenn arrived to set a glass of stout in front of Lauren and a second full one beside Breeze's half-empty glass.

As she walked away, Lauren said, "Can't beat it out. Whiskey helps...for a while. Until you sober up."

A flicker of emotion crossed Breeze's face. "Whiskey always gets me into more trouble than it's worth." She rubbed her face. "Why are you here?"

"Because you're the Breeze Tappan who walked on water. You're the one who grew up shooting deer and elk, branding calves, living with life and death. You were the one who was always competent, tough, and tried. Like nothing in life could ever get to you." Lauren chuckled. "I was just the cream puff, the clumsy military brat. I was never good at anything."

"Oh, bullshit. You could always outride me on a motorcycle." Breeze's brow knit. "Well, maybe you were a little clumsy. And there was the time out at the ranch when you bawled for days after we shot that calf with the broken leg."

"So why don't I feel anything anymore?" Lauren gave Breeze a hostile look. "Where is that old me? And how do you hang on? I keep feeling like I'm going to fall into a thousand pieces."

Breeze pinched the bridge of her nose. "Yeah, well, Sister, if that's the case, I've got nothing to give you. Not one damned thing, 'cause I'm hanging on by the fingernails myself."

For long agonizing minutes, they sat there, staring vacantly at their drinks. The conversations in the background rose and fell. Occasional laughter—too loud and grating—sent tendrils of irritation winding through Lauren's gut.

In the end, Breeze, in a sotto voce, said, "Lauren, gotta tell you. I've been jealous."

"Huh?" Lauren craned her head around to stare.

Breeze gave a faint shake of the head. "You're Lauren Davis, the hero of Buffalo Camp. People on The Line idolize you. I keep wondering how you can be so strong, so together, when I'm always scared and shaken. I've been telling myself, 'If Lauren can do this, so can I,' and, 'If Lauren was here, she'd just suck it up and deal.' I ask myself, 'Why can't I be more like Lauren.' Things like that."

"Wow, Breeze. Is that fucked up, or what? Half the time out on The Line, I want to throw up."

Breeze shot her a sidelong glance. "So, not only do I not walk on water, I'm drowning in the bottom of the pond." A pause. "If it wasn't for you, I'd have given up long ago."

"You better find another role model."

Lauren took a swig of the stout, let it roll over her tongue, and sighed. There were only two local breweries still making stout. The good news was that both were outstanding, even if the IBUs were dropping as the hops ran out.

"You, too." A pause as Breeze sipped her beer. Hesitated, then added softly, "And, maybe...well, I've been avoiding you. Maybe I couldn't stand the thought that you'd find out how scared I really am."

"And that day down at the I-25 checkpoint?"

"Lauren, I was terrified. Just buying time. Figured I was going to die at any second."

"Me too, at Buffalo Camp." Lauren vented a weary sigh. "I was just doing whatever came next. But Breeze, the only way I can keep going? I'm no hero. It's because there's nothing else left. I don't have a ranch waiting for me. No family. Tyrell? Do you really think a Delta Force lieutenant has a chance of coming out of this alive?"

Breeze took another swig of beer. "He'd have the skills to survive, that's for sure."

"The mission won't let him." Lauren smiled bravely. "That's what's going to kill him in the end, Breeze. That's what got him from the 75th Ranger Regiment to the Delta Force Combat Applications Group and an assignment to The Unit. What they call Task Force Green." She paused. "He'll stick to the mission until his last breath. Compared to that, how could I do any different?"

Breeze studied Lauren thoughtfully.

To break the awkward silence, Lauren said, "Saw Mike. He's not doing well. Thought you should know."

"Thanks," Breeze acknowledged. "Drop by tomorrow. It's just..." She frowned, lines etching her brow. "Tough couple of days. Wasn't into company." She glanced up. "Heard that Agar shot that guy who got away from you out on Goose Creek Road."

"Yeah, I went to the execution." Lauren rolled the beer glass on its bottom, watching the black liquid leave foam on the sides.

"And then I drove back through Frontier Park."

"What happened there?"

"Nothing. Stopped and talked to some of the people out there. Just ordinary Americans. Families. Normal moms, dads, and kids. Individuals who were traveling on business, or who were moving, or headed cross-country on family business. Groups of friends who'd been on the road for the three-day weekend. They came from all over the country, most traveling on I-80 or I-25 when their credit cards were stopped cold that Friday."

"Yeah? Ordinary people?" Breeze chugged down the last of the stout and set the empty at the edge of the table. "Like the ones we're turning back on The Line. Somehow, I don't think anyone's ordinary any more, Lauren."

"That's what's bothering me. In the Frontier Park camp, I was talking to average Americans. Think about a cross section of your friends and neighbors. The people you work with. The ones you see at the store. Now drop them in a tent camp with nowhere to go."

"You ask me"—Breeze pulled the full glass her way—"they're the lucky ones. The citizenry of Cheyenne did their best for the folks who'd been stranded. To start with, the camp was supplied by donations. All those tents and travel trailers? The food drives? Until belts started to tighten, and even now, people are doing what they can to help. Beats being south of The Line."

"But the reality is that there's just not enough to go around. Lot of those people are hungry. There was a reason Agar executed those rapists and murderers out at Frontier Park. He was sending a message. And a pretty damn dark one, if you ask me."

Breeze's gaze had gone distant. "It's a society, like all others. Some of them have started business ventures. You heard about the three guys who are salvaging abandoned cars and trucks off the highway? They're parking them outside of town, stripping them for parts, tires, and the like. Another bunch are setting up kitchens; a couple of nurses opened a tent clinic; and they're putting together work teams who'll do odd jobs for food."

"See, that's just the thing." Lauren fingered her beer glass. "One of the guys I talked to, Bruce Saddler, was an internet marketing consultant from Ohio. His wife designs websites. They've got three kids and no clue about what comes next. No skills. Like head-struck chickens, they just keep blinking, waiting for it all to be over so they could go back to Chillicothe, back to their house and normal lives."

"News flash: There's no Chillicothe to go back to."

"That's just it," Lauren emphasized her point with an index finger. "How are they going to feed themselves? Or, as you found out today, are they going to be throwing those kids in front of traffic to get a handout?"

Breeze's expression had gone blank again. "Hope not. If those damn fools out on I-80 this afternoon are starting a new trend, it won't take long before people wise up and just run over the women and kids. Life's not what it was worth a couple of months ago."

"No, guess not."

Breeze looked up. "And that brings us right back to your original point: People with hearts and empathy, they can't do what we do. All of us down here on the Fourth Quadrant, we've killed our souls. We're the walking damned."

"So, what's left?"

"You said it. We're just doing whatever comes next." Breeze met her eyes. "It's just so much easier when you know it's short term. As soon as that bullet finds you, all the pain, the flashbacks and guilt, will be gone. No beating your head, no whiskey needed. You know when you and I finally get away from the Fourth Quadrant?"

"Yeah." Lauren took a healthy swig of beer. "When we're shot dead."

CHAPTER THIRTY-EIGHT

* * *

LAUREN QUIETLY TIPTOED TO THE DOOR OF MIKE'S HOSPITAL ROOM AND PEEKED IN. HE WAS lying flat in bed, sound asleep.

Leaning her shoulder against the door frame, she vacillated on whether she ought to go sit at his bedside. None of the nurses had told her she couldn't, but she was afraid of waking him when he needed his rest to heal.

An oxygen tank from a welding supply store stood beside his bed. The tank made her frown. Oxygen was saved for the critical cases.

A nurse swept by in the hallway. Lauren considered stopping her to ask, but the nurse was hurrying to another room down the hall, where she disappeared inside. Lauren could overhear terse voices. But then, that was the new normal for medicine in Wyoming.

Lauren padded into Mike's room and sat down in the chair at his bedside. If nothing else, she could watch him sleep for a time. She needed to. It comforted her to be close to him.

God, he looked thinner, his face even more sunken.

As she snuggled her back against the chair, she looked around at the white room. Someone had picked a bouquet of larkspur and brought it to Mike in a Mason jar; it sat on the bedside table, the flowers an unearthly blue. Lauren wondered who'd had the time to pick flowers? Didn't seem like something a man would do, but Mike had lots of female friends in the Guard. Breeze?

She'd said the night before that she'd be by. Something about sitting there, talking, had been like balm. Didn't matter that the nightmares had come. Somehow, she and Breeze had found a bridge through shared pain. And, knowing that whipcord-hard Breeze Tappan—the iron ranch woman and rodeo star—was just as haunted as Lauren?

Well, somehow it made it all easier to endure.

Sighing, she clasped her hands in her lap and let her thoughts drift to the executions. Not a bit of pity burdened her. But neither was there a shred of anger or vengeance. She'd seen too many burned-out houses, ranches, and dead livestock behind The Line. Too many victims' bodies left behind.

End of story. Move on.

Mike's soft voice startled her: "Breeze told me you and she had a heart-to-heart last night."

"Hey, you're awake. How are you feeling?"

"Lousy. Weak. Did you and Breeze talk about Jim?" His eyes were still closed, as if the light bothered him.

"Nope. Never got that far. It was more of a conversation about who we are now. Not what happened back then."

"Glad. This thing between you and Breeze. You don't know it, but you need each other." He smiled weakly. "Like fate dragging you both here."

"That was Tiffany. And you. Seems neither one of us can live without you."

"Did you really tell her she walked on water?"

"She was the tough one with all the answers, if you'll remember."

"Was. That was then. She told me she couldn't…have gone to the executions. Said you were there yesterday. That the governor himself did it. That it was…quick and clean."

To change the subject, she asked, "Did they have to give you oxygen today? I was looking at the tank."

He still didn't open his eyes, but a faint smile came to his bloodless lips. "Nothing major."

His hand crept across the blanket, as though trying to find hers. Lauren reached out and clasped it tight. "Want me to leave? You look tired. I can come back in the morn—"

"Stay. Tell about the missiles."

She hesitated, worried it might upset him. "Nobody knows anything. Not even Ragnovich—"

"Heard nurses whispering. Is it true? Both coasts are smoking rubble?"

She squeezed his hand. Gently, she said, "Even if it's true, there's not a thing you can do about it, so just sleep and heal."

He exhaled a shallow breath. When he opened his eyes, he gave her a weary look. "We still have missiles in silos. Eventually the Chinese are going to get around to hitting Cheyenne to keep us from launching more. I wish you'd get the hell out of here. You and Breeze, go find a place to hide before it's too late."

"Actually, I'm thinking about joining the Guard. They need every person, and when you are up and around, we could work together—"

"Bullshit, Lauren." His eyes fell closed. In a bare whisper, he said, "Stop it. Get enough of that from the nurses. If you're not going to tell me the truth, go away and leave me alone."

His desolate tone stunned her.

She squeezed his hand and released it. "I'll stop bullshitting you, if you'll stop bullshitting me. Why did they have to give you oxygen today? Did your heart stop?"

"Not for long." He faintly lifted his shoulders as though it was no big deal. "Are both coasts gone?"

Lauren looked at the floor for a moment, trying to decide what she should and should not say. "Ragnovich told me California is a war zone. If what General Kyzer says is true, Washington DC may be gone. Nuked, or at least taken out with an EMP. That's all I've heard, Mike."

Weakly, he nodded. "Thanks. Needed…to know."

His breathing deepened, and he drifted off in a matter of moments.

Lauren reached for his wrist to make sure he had a heartbeat. It was slow but regular.

When the nurse hurried into the room, she glared at Lauren and went straight to the readouts and triggered the blood pressure cuff. Without looking at Mike, she grabbed Lauren by the arm and hauled her out of the room into the corridor.

"For God's sake, Davis," she whispered. "Stay away for a few days, all right?"

Lauren fixed the woman with her deadliest glare. "He's not getting better, is he?"

The nurse started to say something, bit it off, and shook her head. "One day at a time, okay? At this stage? It's maybe fifty-fifty."

CHAPTER THIRTY-NINE

***

THAT MORNING, JUST AFTER SIX, LAUREN MOTORED UP ON THE KTM AND PULLED UP BESIDE Breeze's BMW 650 Dakar to join the collection of vehicles. Two armored Humvees—of course—an assortment of Militia pickups, and a line of pickups towing stock trailers with Colorado plates were parked in the grassy right-of-way along Carpenter Road immediately north of OP Bravo Alpha.

Lauren killed the engine, pulled off her gloves and unbuckled her helmet before hanging it on the Kaytoom's mirror. Just south, a knot of people had gathered, Guard, Militia, and representatives of the Colorado ranchers, all looking down the road at the approaching herd cattle.

Stepping off the bike, Lauren walked over to where Breeze was lounging, her hip braced against the right front fender of the OP's Humvee with its high-mounted turret. The long barrel of the M2 Browning machine gun was pointed south, as if the cows could ever be a threat.

Looking down the road, it was like a scene straight out of a Western movie: A solid river of cattle, a mostly black mass with occasional whites and browns thrown into the mix. The lowing, moos, and grunts carried on the still morning air. Dust rose in the distance where thousands of hooved feet had powdered the soil. Outriders, on horseback and ATVs, paralleled the flood of moving beef.

"Hey," Breeze greeted, saluting her with a cup of steaming tea. Obviously a gift from the OP's little camp stove. "You ready for this?"

"Guess we're cowgirls, huh?" Lauren unzipped her now-ragged jacket.

Breeze gave her that old familiar cocked-eyebrow look. The

skeptical one. And, if only for a moment, the last two years might have vanished. As if Jim were still alive. As if they were still the best of friends.

Wouldn't have happened but for that night at the Hilton. To Lauren, it was like a crack in glacial ice. A tiny flicker of relief in an endless night.

"Cowgirls?" Breeze asked. "Want me to remind you about your rodeo skills?"

"Hey, I can ride a horse."

"Just not fast," Breeze's teasing smile bent her lips. "And the idea was to go around the barrels, not over them."

Lauren shaded her eyes against the morning sun, staring south. "Yippee Kai Yay," Lauren said. "This time, we're on bikes. I was always a lot better on a motorcycle than a horse."

Breeze gestured with her cup. "Our job is to go through that gate, ride out in the pasture to the west, and scout our way south. We're the early warning if anything is going wrong. You get that briefing from Ragnovich?"

"Yeah. The governor wants all these cattle and the ranchers on our side of The Line. He's given them safe passage north. The stock growers can't hold their places, not against the kinds of raids rolling out of Fort Collins and Greeley these days."

Breeze's expression pinched, her thoughtful Tappan eyes on the approaching herd. "Hard to believe. Some of these families are fifth and sixth generation. Tough enough folks, but the raiders are using high-powered rifles with those twenty-power long distance scopes. Shooting them from ambush. I mean, how do you cope? You stop, get out of your truck to fix a couple of broken wires in the fence, and *pop*! Someone shoots you from a distant hilltop."

"Yeah, and then they drive in, shoot a bunch of your cattle, winch them into the back of a truck, and fog it back to the city." Lauren shook her head. "If I was a rancher out here, I'd broker a deal with Agar, too."

Over the sound of approaching beef, the distant pop, pop, of gunfire carried on the morning air. The cluster of watching ranchers and Guard stopped, heads cocked.

"How many cattle do you figure?" Lauren dared to lean close and prop her own hip.

Breeze gestured with her cup. "Word is over ten thousand. That's almost all the cattle that are left in the drylands east of Greeley and north of Highway 14. Most of the families crossed last night. A whole caravan of trucks pulling stock trailers and flatbeds loaded with whatever was too valuable to leave behind. They're up north of the Interstate."

More faint popping could be heard in the south.

Sergeant Mathers stopped talking to one of the ranchers and walked over.

"Morning, Sergeant," Breeze greeted.

Mathers was in his thirties. He'd done a couple of tours in Afghanistan before the withdrawal and hadn't bothered to re-up after the shambles of America's retreat from Kabul. He'd been selling real estate in Sheridan and serving in the Guard when the collapse came. He gave Breeze and Lauren a gray-eyed evaluation and nodded toward the south. "Think you two could run a scout for us? That's more shooting than we hoped to hear this morning. Nothing's come in on the walkie talkies, but a line of folks are working the tail end of the cattle herd."

"What we call the drag," the rancher added. "Listen, this bunch out of Greeley, they've been watching us gather. They know that something's up, that we've been moving the cattle north, trying to keep them out of reach. By this morning, they've probably figured out what we're doing. Wouldn't put it past 'em to make a hail Mary. Hit us hard. Try and stampede as many head as they can."

"But your riders back there are armed, right?" Breeze asked.

"Hell, yes," the rancher told her, rocking his jaw as he gazed off to the south. "But you've got to understand. We're taking their source of power and wealth right out from under their noses. It's one thing to drive thirty minutes from town, hit one of our places, and kill a half dozen head. They can have them loaded and be headed back to town in twenty minutes." His lips twitched. "It's whole 'nuther thing if they have to drive a couple of hours out past Buckingham and nigh onto Sterling. Stretches 'em too thin. Makes 'em vulnerable to other raiders."

Mathers added, "You're on bikes. Here's a radio. Go check out the south end of the drive. See what that gunfire was about."

"Roger that," Breeze told him taking the radio. She clipped it onto her belt and led the way to the bikes. At her BMW, Breeze slung her own M4, squinting into the distance in the south. Past where the line of cattle was moving inexorably down the road. "That's down beyond those sandstone-capped bluffs."

"Hope we don't get into shooting," Lauren said as she pulled on her helmet and then stuffed her gloves into the tank bag to leave her hands unencumbered.

"It's just a scout," Breeze reminded. "Soon as we know what's what, we can boogie." A pause. "No heroics."

"Amen." Lauren smiled inside her helmet.

She thumbed the starter, settled into the seat, and snicked the KTM into first as Breeze pulled out. Watched by the knot of Guard, Militia, and ranchers, Breeze led the way to the gate in the right-of-way fence. Mathers opened it, giving them a nod as Breeze rode out into the pasture on the west side of the road.

Lauren immediately rose, standing on the pegs. The KTM's supple suspension absorbed the bumps as she thundered across the gramma and bunch grasses. Using her weight, Lauren wove her way around the clumps of yucca, and tried to dodge the bigger patches of prickly pear.

Paralleling the right-of-way fence, they headed south past the endless line of cattle, attention on what the undulating grasses might be hiding and dodging occasional outcrops of weathered sandstone.

Dropping into a drainage, Breeze took an old cow trail, crossed the dry bottom, and thundered up the other side.

Lauren followed. Wishing for the first time that she were on her 350 instead of the big 790. Not that the KTM wasn't outstanding off road, but it was still a four-hundred-and-forty pound machine the way it was set up and loaded. Nevertheless she made it, cresting the top of the drainage and riding out the wheelie.

She and Breeze rode south, passing an amazing four miles of moving cattle before crossing the bluffs. There they encountered a lone rider on a palomino gelding. The woman, wearing a ball cap, her hair in a pony tail, a jean jacket on her shoulders, was squinting off to the south. She held a scoped hunting rifle across the saddle.

As they approached, the woman gave them a wary appraisal, waving with her hand in a gesture to slow down.

Breeze kept a respectful distance from the gelding, stopped and killed the engine.

As Lauren followed suit, Breeze flipped up her helmet calling, "We're with the Guard. They heard shooting. But nothing came in on the walkie talkies."

The woman might have been in her forties, lithe, sitting the horse like she'd spent her life in the saddle. Her face was tanned, thin, with hardened lines around her mouth and deeply etched crow's feet at the corners of her faded blue eyes.

With a tip of her chin, she indicated the line of low sandstone-capped bluffs maybe four hundred yards beyond the next swale. "See that four-wheeler? He's not one of ours. The Kapshaws were riding last in line. We've been shadowed since last night. Those shots came from the other side of that caprock. Then that guy showed up."

Lauren pulled up her visor, staring across the distance. The guy on the ATV was watching them with binoculars.

"Long shot for the M4s," Breeze noted.

"Not for my .270," the woman told her. "Problem is if I get off to shoot, Old Firecracker, here, will be headed north faster than my bullet heads south. He doesn't like gunshots."

Lauren glanced at the last of the cattle, now passing. A clump of ATVs and a handful of riders were tight behind them. Pushing the stragglers. The drag riders kept throwing anxious glances over their shoulders. Must have had a bad feeling about the shooting, too.

"What do you think?" Breeze asked her.

Lauren took a hard look around. "That guy's just sitting there. No, wait. He's looking off to the west. That's like the third time just since we've been here."

"Makes you wonder what's on the other side of that butte over yonder, doesn't it?" the woman asked. Lifting her rifle, she used the scope to study the elevated sandstone rim maybe a quarter mile to the west.

"We're on bikes," Lauren told her. "What do you think, Breeze? Slope's not too steep. And there's a gap in that rimrock. We can check. Be there in five minutes. And from that elevation, we'll know what's south of those bluffs where that guy's watching us. See if there's any sign of the Kapshaws."

To the woman, Breeze said, "Go on. Keep up with the cattle. We've got this."

The woman gave them an evaluative look. "You two remind me of my daughter. You be double-damned careful. And I hope you know how to use those guns."

"Must be a hell of a daughter you've got," Breeze told her.

"She was. Buried her last week. She caught a crew cutting up one of our heifers, and some son of a bitch shot her."

With that, the woman reined her horse around; the big palomino left at a trot.

"Me and my fucking big mouth," Breeze muttered. "Come on. Let's see what the hell's happening."

As Breeze turned the BMW west, she wrung the bike out, flying across the grass and yucca. Against her better judgment, Lauren twisted the KTM's throttle wide, heart hammering as she matched the flying BMW's speed.

If she'd had time to think about it, she'd have never made that ascent up the side of the butte. Too many rocks, loose soil, and scrubby stands of currants. Instead, hot on Breeze's heels, she just blasted her way to the top, through the gap, and pulled up next to where Breeze had braked to a stop, sliding the back of the BMW sideways.

The butte was flat-topped, rising slightly to the west for another half mile or so. From this elevation, the Chalk Buttes were visible in the distance. Scrubby bunch grasses, exposed sandstone bedrock, patches of prickly pear cactus, and rabbitbrush dotted the ground.

And, not more than two-hundred-and-fifty yards away, was a collection of pickups. Maybe ten of them. The kind of off-road four-wheel-drives that hunters and back-country travelers fawned over. Men stood in the backs, rifles at the ready, most of them braced on roll bars to which winches had been affixed—an arrangement that would allow them to hoist freshly killed cattle into the truck beds. Just below the noses of the trucks, the caprock sloped off to the north, down a low ridge to the drainage below.

All they'd have to do was barrel down, through the right-of-way fence, and into the middle of the cattle drive.

"Breeze!" Lauren screamed. "Go! Now! Get off this crest! Radio for help. We need the Humvee and Ma Deuce. Go! Go! Go!"

Even as she screamed, Lauren let the clutch out. Killed the KTM's engine. She wrestled her M4 around as Breeze flipped her BMW sideways and gunned the bike, flying back through the gap and headed down.

Lauren tugged the M4 straight, flipped the fire control to automatic. As she brought the weapon up, found the red dot, it was to see the guys in the back of the pickups pointing, scrambling for position as they raised their rifles.

The M4 chattered, vibrating in her arms as it spit a stream of brass off to the right.

Lauren kept her control, lacing a stream of fire across the trucks. And then the bolt locked open.

With frantic fingers, she hit the bolt release. Clawed for her second magazine and slapped it home. Lifting the M4, she threaded rounds across the trucks, saw window glass webbing with strikes, paint leaping from the cabs and boxes. Could hear the 5.56 bullets pattering on metal. The guys in the truck beds were dropping, some bailing out the other side. One, hands to his chest, staggered backwards, lost his balance, and tumbled over the tailgate to hit the rocky ground face first.

Where men crawled beneath the closest truck, trying to get into position, she unleashed a burst into the dirt and rock. Screams came in return as the riflemen dropped their weapons, clawing at their faces.

The bolt locked open again.

Lauren tossed the M4 over her shoulder, felt it jerk on its sling. Grabbing the bars, she pulled the clutch. Stabbed the starter and threw the big KTM in a tight circle. Never, in her wildest dreams, would she have dared to cut a donut with Tyrell's big bike.

But she did.

Then she was flying through the gap and down the rocky slope in Breeze's wake as the first high-velocity rounds cracked and snapped over her head.

Fifty was too fast. But with bullets kicking up dirt to either side, Lauren figured she was dead anyway. And a zigging and zagging bike, racing away at that speed was a damned hard target.

She credited the KTM's remarkable suspension. More than once she should have "endoed" on a rock outcrop or done a flying W over the bars when she hit a hole. Or lost it when she hit a pucker bush. Instead she worshipped at the altar of WP's best long-stroke suspension.

By the time she slowed, dropped down through the drainage on the cow trail and up the other side, parallel the cattle drive, only the occasional bullet whizzed past.

Breeze had found a place to radio, all right.

And when the raiders finally picked up their dead and wounded, reorganized their assault on the cattle drive, they came charging down the ridge in their shot-up trucks. They had guns at the ready, all set to blow through the fence and scatter as many cattle as they could.

Except that—as a measure of Agar's commitment to the ranchers—one of the Guard's precious Blackhawk helicopters came thundering down from the north. Call it a real "come to Jesus" moment; Lauren watched as the minigun shredded the collection of pickups and SUVs.

"My God, is that hell broke loose or what?"

As the Blackhawk wheeled, turned, and hammered its way back toward Cheyenne, only smoking plastic, torn steel, and ruptured and exploded bodies remained as a marker of the raiders' last stand.

CHAPTER FORTY

***

THE ONLY DOWN SIDE TO THE DAY WAS THAT AFTER THE LAST OF THE CATTLE WERE NORTH of The Line, when the Guard went looking, they found the Kapshaws. Two brothers and a sister. Dead where they'd been shot. Their saddles and tack had been left lying in the grass beside their bullet-riddled bodies. Their horses and weapons, however, were missing. Tracks showed where the horses had been shot and then winched into trucks and driven off.

A common pattern. It illustrated that compared to a horse carcass, human life was worthless.

The sun was just setting in the July sky as Breeze and Lauren pulled up onto the sidewalk by the Cheyenne Hilton's front door; together they backed the bikes against the hotel wall, where Breeze chained them to the polished brass fire hydrant.

As she unstrapped her boogie bag, Lauren asked, "So, what do you think the big deal is? Ragnovich ordered us to be in the Hilton restaurant by seven." She glanced at her watch. "It's almost eight. Think we're screwed?"

"Whatever," Breeze told her as she clipped the lock and straightened. "We just spent close to fourteen hours straight scouting, getting shot at, and helping to move over eleven thousand head of cattle north of The Line. I'm thirsty, hungry enough to eat roadkill, and exhausted." She pointed at the green-brown smears on her BMW. "And my bike's covered in cow shit. If Cap wants to chew on my butt for being late, he'd better sharpen his molars."

Lauren gave her KTM a pained look; it, too, bore its own dried coating of spattered manure thrown up by the tires. Not to mention that keeping the bikes upright in the stuff had been like riding on marbles.

Wet manure was slicker than snot, and eleven thousand beef left a lot of crap behind.

Dewey, the doorman, saluted, calling, "I'll keep an eye on the bikes." The guy watched with adoring eyes as Breeze passed. Lauren just got a slight nod.

"Thanks, Dewey," Breeze—her boogie bag over her shoulder—told the young man as she led the way inside.

"Looks to me like he's got a crush on you," Lauren noted as they walked across the lobby in their manure-spattered boots.

"Yeah," Breeze shot her a knowing look. "But I think if he ever really got to know me, he'd be running for the high country."

"Don't be so hard on yourself. Lots of guys are into being dominated by strong women."

"Strong, huh? The point I was so poorly trying to get across is that he'd run the first time I jerked awake, screaming, drenched with night-sweat and clawing for a pistol."

"For some it's a tic, for others a fear of clowns. Maybe some phobia over spiders or a sexual anxiety. Nobody's perfect. For you, it's screaming night sweats. See? Makes you just like the rest of us."

A crooked smile bent Breeze's lips. "I'd forgotten how twisted that sense of humor of yours is."

At the restaurant, Jillian Nelson, the night hostess, met them with a smile. "You made it! This way."

She led the way back to one of the tables in the rear. Not only had it been set up with a white tablecloth, but it sported a wax candle, a prominent bottle of McNab Ridge Largo, and roses in a glass for a centerpiece.

"What the hell?" Breeze asked.

Jillian's smile expanded. "Compliments of what's left of the Weld and Morgan County stock growers' associations. A special courier delivered fresh fillets from a yearling heifer they had to butcher. And that bottle of wine was being saved by one of the families for a special occasion. Apparently the two of you broke up an attack that would have ruined everything. They want to show their gratitude." Her smile widened. "Oh, and the governor sends his appreciation as well. Calls you both heroes."

Lauren arched her eyebrows as she shrugged out of her heavy riding

coat and took a seat, Breeze across from her. She tried to ignore the
odor of stale sweat and dusty cow that clung to her clothing.

Jillian paused only long enough to light the candle and then
retreated. All around the restaurant, people were watching, clearly
curious. Wasn't another table in the place set up like theirs.

Breeze burst into laughter. "Wow. Can you believe this? Candlelight,
special bottle of wine? And here we are, spattered with cow shit,
dressed in riding gear, covered in dust, and smelling like a feedlot."

Lauren was glancing around; as her eyes met those of the other
diners, most smiled and nodded as if in pleased salutation. "Hope they
don't think it's a special occasion, like we're engaged or something."

Breeze considered it, frowned and shook her head. "Naw. If it was
an engagement dinner, we'd have taken a shower first."

Jenn came hustling up to announce, "Chef Williams has the fillets
on. How do you want them cooked?"

As Breeze and Lauren put in their orders, Jenn poured the wine.
Then she vanished into the kitchen.

"Governor sent his regards?" Breeze wondered as she unfolded the
napkin and dropped it onto her lap.

"We did good work today." Lauren leaned forward. "That's eleven
thousand head for us, nothing for the raiders." She shook her head,
"But it's going to be a while before I get the memory out of my head.
I still can't believe that Blackhawk shooting the living shit out of those
trucks and SUVs. Saw one of the rounds splatter a guy wide open. Tore
up those trucks like they were tin foil. Never seen anything like it."

Breeze's smile died. "Yeah. Some of the guys on The Line were
talking about it. Memorized the name. That's the Mk44 30 mm
Bushmaster chain gun. They had one for training purposes up at the
National Guard training center in Guernsey. Agar had it brought down
and mounted on one of the Blackhawks. It's a measure of how serious
he took this cattle drive. Word is that once the helicopters break, that's
it. They'll only last as long as their spare parts do. So it's kind of a
balance between flying them or letting them sit. Either way, they aren't
going to last forever."

"Same with the ammo, I'll bet. I mean, how many rounds of 30
millimeter do we have for that chain gun? It had to chew through a
couple hundred rounds shooting up those trucks today, and I'll bet you

don't just buy them at the sporting goods store."

"You don't buy anything at any sporting goods store. At least, nothing that isn't locally made."

Breeze sipped her wine, made her "that's really good" face, and said, "I saw a bunch of Militia out in the sagebrush picking up thirty millimeter brass below where the fight came off. Hey, you dated Brandon. My brother had you reloading cartridges as I recall. And brass can be machined. So can bullets. It's the primers and powder that are the problem. Double-base nitro-cellulose powder is not something you just cook up in the kitchen late at night."

"Guess not." Lauren tried her own wine. Picked up the bottle to read the label. California. She'd never been much of a wine person. Maybe her four-and-five-dollar a bottle on-sale vintages hadn't been a true representation of the drink.

Breeze had that look of satisfaction. "Today we broke up a major ring of raiders. Saved a lot of cattle." She lifted her glass. "To us."

"To us," Lauren agreed, clinking her glass to Breeze's.

When Jenn brought the steaks, they were cooked to perfection. And to top it all off, a slice of honest-to-God real dark-chocolate cake was offered for dessert. Maybe the last either of them would ever taste.

Lauren let the pain go, shut off the memories. For three wonderful hours, she and Breeze talked, laughed, and made believe that they weren't wounded-and-haunted souls racing toward early graves. That tomorrow morning wouldn't come.

CHAPTER FORTY-ONE

* * *

THE NEXT DAY, LAUREN LEANED THROUGH THE CURVES, HEADING OUT TO OP DELTA ALPHA.
Turning off at Harriman junction, she could see where the OP perched
on the hilltop off to the west. Dusk was coming fast. The sun hung
like a fiery red orb just above the smoke-brown western horizon. By
the time she got back to Cheyenne tonight, it would be pitch black.

With her helmet visor up, wind whipped hair in front of her eyes;
she brushed it away with a gloved hand. She had to keep her vision
clear. On this lonely stretch of dirt road so far west of Cheyenne, rock
outcrops and patches of brush made perfect hiding places. Most of this
land out here was public, meaning it used to be managed by the federal
government. The private sections still had the occasional ranch house,
but mostly the pre-collapse population had been on five to ten-acre lots.
Fancy houses. What they called "horse properties" in real estate. All
upper class homes. Abandoned as indefensible. Most had been looted.
A lot of them were nothing more than burned-out shells.

No man's land. Just empty miles of weathered hills, barbed wire
fences, pine groves, lurking raiders, and outcrops of exfoliated granite.
In the old days, riding this stretch had been beautiful and fun.

Now it was nerve-wracking.

As she crested a hill and plunged down the other side, she saw the
armored Humvees—mounting big guns—that marked the location of
the OP on the opposite ridge. Relief filled her. She was late, but they'd
forgive her. They always did. God, she loved these people. Each and
every one of them.

When Sergeant Sam Hughes heard the distinctive purr of her
Kaytoom, he climbed out of his foxhole to wave to her. She waved
back, turned onto the two-track that led up the slope to the OP. Doing

so, she wobbled her way around the potholes and washboard to pull up beside one of the Humvees. The air smelled sweetly of the blooming locoweed and goat's head that covered the countryside.

"Hey, Lauren," Hughes called. "We're starving up here. You weren't down eating a steak at the Plains and forgot us, were you?"

"Naw! It was a four-pound Maine lobster with an escargot garnish washed down with a bottle of Dom Pérignon," she yelled back. "But to cover my sorry ass, the story I made up is that I just finished a delivery to Charlie X-Ray. More fricking batteries for their night-vision gear. Sorry I'm late."

"No problem. We're just relieved to see you."

As she put down the kickstand, two smiling privates in camo rose from folding chairs beside their foxhole and trotted over to help her offload supplies.

Lauren walked to the back of the bike and unhooked the bungee cords. When she reached to lift the case of bottled water, Private Lewis said, "Let me do that, okay?"

"Be my guest." She stepped back, watching as the privates lifted everything she'd brought, in muscular arms and carried it back to their foxhole.

"If you weren't full of lobster and champagne," Sergeant Hughes said, "we'd invite you to come eat with us. We saved the turkey and gravy MRE for you, but after all that feast—"

"Mine!" she cried. "Wouldn't want to insult my hosts. Somehow, I'll manage to choke it down!"

Everybody laughed. They all knew it was her favorite.

"You're a saint, Sam."

Lauren smiled, headed for the foxhole, watching her footing so she didn't trip on a rock in the growing dusk.

The sound of the jets didn't register at first, but when they did, Lauren glanced up to scan the sky. A few clouds drifted lazily through the haze, their edges glowing brilliant orange.

Though the roar was getting louder in the west, a flicker of sunlight to the north caught her attention. Light on a silver wing.

"There!" She pointed. "See it?"

Sam trotted over to stand beside her. "I see it."

A con trail corkscrewed through the sky. From the west came a second jet. Tiny lances of light streaked out from the pursuing aircraft, and curving threads of fire wove their way toward the pitching and weaving dot at the tip of the con trail.

When the fiery threads reached their quarry, they converged on the evading airplane. An explosion lit the sky, flaring in a widening arc.

"Dear God," Sam said as they watched pieces of burning plane tumble down.

Faint booms carried down from on high. The attacking plane banked, and soared off.

"Hey!" Lewis yelled. "Look over there."

Fiery wreckage hit the high peak barely a mile to the west, landing amid the granite outcrops. The sound of the impact carried, and several of the pines at the site caught fire.

"There's more!" Lauren called when a section of wing spiraled down and crashed in the trees just north of the OP.

"Holy shit." Sam refocused on the heavens. "Is that what I think it is?"

Lauren glimpsed the single parachute with a limp figure hanging from the shrouds. "Think that's one of ours?"

"I wager it is," Sam cried. "From the way he's hanging, he's injured."

The wind was carrying the pilot toward the high ground maybe a mile north of the OP. The parachute disappeared behind a line of pines, then it reappeared, dragging the pilot across the ground toward the head of Deadman Creek.

Lauren shouted, "I can get there faster on my bike!"

"Go! I'll follow in the Humvee," Sam said, and turned to order, "Rest of you stay at your positions!"

Lauren ran for the KTM, and took off like a shot, headed along the ridgetop on an old two-track. Fortunately, the gate was open in the rusty barbwire fence, and she followed the old trail as it wound through the scattered Ponderosa pines.

When she neared the place they'd seen the parachute dragging, she veered off the road and humped her way out across the grass, sagebrush, and mountain mahogany. Rising on the pegs, she stood, zig-sagging the bike in a search pattern through the hollows and around the boulders.

The roar of the Humvee's engine rose above the KTM's puttering exhaust.

The sun was now a glowing red disk, shooting black shadows that made inky pools behind the pines, tall sagebrush, and clumps of mountain mahogany. Made seeing anything in the chiaroscuro difficult, and the terrain was full of dips and outcrops.

The Humvee came bouncing over the sage, headlights on. Out his window, Sam shouted, "Ought to be a couple of hundred yards to the north of here!"

She waved in agreement, curved around a stand of stunted pines, and headed across the rolling hills. The stench of burning fuel and plastic filled the wind.

As Lauren swung right away from Sam's path, he cried. "There he is, just down the slope! Can you get to him? There's a lot of rocks out there. I don't think I have the clearance."

"I got him, Sam!"

She angled away and headed in the direction Sam was pointing.

The pilot's white chute billowed where it had caught in the brush. But she didn't see a human near it.

Glancing over her shoulder, she saw Sam throw the Humvee's door open and emerge with his rifle. He was coming at a trot as he wound through the sagebrush.

Lauren rode to within twenty paces of the chute, stopped and put the kickstand down. Warily, she got off the bike and scanned the hills and rocks. She didn't see anyone, but she pulled her M4 from the rear of the bike and cautiously moved toward the wind-whipped chute.

When she got to within ten paces, a man stood up. Wavered on his feet. Seemed to be having problems with his balance, especially the way his left arm flopped.

"Hey," she called, "You okay?"

He didn't answer. He wore a G-suit, had a helmet on, and was frantically trying to get out of his harness with his good hand.

Sam ran up behind her, breathing hard. "Is he one of ours?"

"I can't tell from here."

"Don't see an American flag anywhere, do you?"

"No." But silhouetted as he was by the dying sun, the pilot was nothing more than a dark figurine. Lauren shouted, "Hey! You American?"

The pilot staggered. Barely caught himself. He lifted his right hand and he flipped up the visor. The way he stood, Lauren couldn't see his face. She approached warily; downed pilots carried pistols. Whatever side he was on, the guy could be addled or wounded. He might not be able to identify them as friendlies.

From a better angle, she saw that the flier's left arm was definitely broken. The way it dangled, had to be a snap-fractured humerus.

"Hey!" Sam lifted his rifle to cover the aviator. "Are you American? Answer me!"

The guy finally caught sight of them. Almost toppled over as he tried to turn their way. Silhouetted by the sunset, his face remained in the helmet's dark shadow. He shook his head and pounded on his helmet as though he'd lost his hearing in the explosion.

Lauren's breathing went shallow. "Sam, that's a red star on his helmet, and I think that's Chinese writing on his flight suit."

"Yeah," he replied with narrowed eyes. "I see 'em."

The pilot was young, maybe mid-twenties. He shook his head again and seemed like he was trying to focus his eyes.

Lauren aimed her M4 at the pilot. "Why isn't he running?"

"Don't know. Doesn't make any sense."

Instead, the pilot lifted his good hand over his head, and in badly accented English shouted, "Chinese! Do not kill! Free America, yes?"

Lauren and Sam both stopped dead in their tracks and exchanged a glance.

"Free America?" Lauren asked.

"Do not kill!" the pilot pleaded. "Chinese! Free America, yes?"

Apparently that was the only English the guy had been taught.

Sam said, "I don't get it? Does he mean he's here to help free America?"

The pilot had started to get nervous. After all, they were pointing guns at him. He was manically licking his lips and swallowing, like he expected a bullet at any instant.

"I don't know, but... I took a history course last semester. You remember the Doolittle Raid in World War II?"

"Sure. You thinking how China and America were allies, fighting against Japan? How our bomber crews were taught four Chinese words, which translated '*I am an American*'?"

The pilot lifted his hand higher, and called in a loud voice, *"Do not kill. Free America!"*

Lauren studied the man's terrified face. "What do you think we should do?"

Sam's jaw moved with grinding teeth. "Hell. Capture him and turn him over to Ragnovich."

CHAPTER FORTY-TWO

* * *

LAUREN PROPPED HER ELBOW ON THE ARMREST IN RAGNOVICH'S TRUCK, WATCHING THEIR Highway Patrol escort lead them to a spot in the capitol parking lot that was surrounded by armed guards. Darkness cloaked most of the capitol grounds, but she could see the giant old cottonwoods swaying in the night wind.

"I ever tell you I hate meeting with the legislature?" Ragnovich asked.

"No. Why?"

"Politicians. They all think they know my job better than I do."

Captain Ragnovich shifted into park, and Lauren got out the passenger door. The air smelled like freshly mown alfalfa hay, which must be wafting in from the fields outside of town. After the eternal stench from the brown cloud, it was a relief.

"Straight through the front door," the Highway Patrol trooper told them. "Do not veer left or right. Have a good night."

"Thanks," Ragnovich called. "I know the drill."

Lauren tilted her head back to look up at the golden dome; it had turned bluish silver in the moonlight. The capitol was imposing. A fortress mix of grayish-tan stone, classical columns, arch-topped windows.

"Come on. Let's get this over with." Ragnovich stalked for the capitol steps.

"The entire legislature is here at this time of night?" she asked with so much hope in her voice, it was difficult to listen to, even for her. Senator Bill Tappan would be here.

"I'm sure they rounded up as many as they could. Guess we'll see how many."

They walked up the steps to the main entrance, where a soldier in fatigues with a clipboard, saluted, and said, "Good evening, sir. State your names."

"Good Lord, Jamie." Ragnovich saluted back. "You know exactly who I am, and this is Lauren Davis. Yeah, from the Buffalo Camp. She captured the prisoner. The governor requested her presence for a debriefing tonight."

The soldier checked his clipboard, and said, "Third floor conference room, Captain Ragnovich. Didn't mean to annoy you. Just following orders."

"Sorry I snapped at you. Carry on."

"Yes, sir. Private Logan will meet you at the elevator and escort you to the conference room."

"Understood."

When they reached the elevator, the private saluted, and said, "Follow me, sir. The governor's been waiting for you."

"Lead on, Private."

Lauren stepped into the elevator behind the men and watched the numbers flash as they went up. Another soldier met them when the doors opened.

"Captain Ragnovich, sir, the meeting is in the conference room E303 just down the hall, on the left."

Ragnovich returned the man's salute, said, "Thanks," and marched down the hall like a man on a mission.

When he shoved open the conference room door, he startled the young man who was placing notepads before chairs around a central table.

"Evening, Captain," the man said. "The governor and a few of the legislators are down the hall in the Senate Gallery. I'll go tell them you're here."

"Thanks." Ragnovich extended a hand to Lauren. "Ryan Monroe, this is Lauren Davis. Took our first prisoner of war."

"Honored to meet you, ma'am." The way Monroe said it—filled with reverence—just added to Lauren's unease.

"Don't make more of it than it was. Just at the right place at the right time."

As he backed away, Monroe asked, "The governor has authorized coffee. How many cups?"

"I'm in."

"Me, too, please," Lauren said.

Monroe hurried out of the conference room, and Ragnovich heaved a sigh. "Well, at least the coffee is a perk."

Ragnovich pulled a chair out from the table. Lauren took the seat beside him. She rubbed her hands together and looked around nervously. "Cap, I'm meeting the governor in my bullet-riddled touring jacket, my dusty armored pants, and clunky motorcycle boots. Do you have any idea how humiliating this is?"

Ragnovich's crooked smile went even more crooked. "Lauren, you couldn't be more perfectly dressed if I was introducing you to the president herself."

A few minutes later, Senators Merlin Smith and Sally Hanson entered. They shook hands all around. It was the first time Lauren had met the movers and shakers from Big Horn county. Sally Hanson had a deeply wrinkled face and white hair that had blue highlights in the fluorescent gleam.

The next two men were older. The first, a tall, elegant-looking fellow with silver hair, was introduced as Terry Tanksley, or "Tank", from Park County. He wore a Western-cut suit, gleaming black pointed Western boots, and turquoise-inlaid bolo tie. The man had thick, bushy, black brows. His companion—short but built like a stout tree stump— was ex-state senator Barry Klyde.

While they pulled out chairs, Ryan Monroe entered carrying a tray of coffee cups, followed by a young woman with a large pot that she plugged into the wall. One by one, Ryan poured, and the young woman handed the cups around.

"Drink it up, folks," Ryan called. "Governor splurged for a whole pot given the special circumstances."

"Looks like the sacred cabal is here." Sally glanced around the room.

"When did you get to Cheyenne, Senator?" Ragnovich asked.

"Two weeks ago. I was one of the first to arrive. Had my nose to the grindstone ever since. Got trouble brewing in the Basin with that snake-in-the-grass Edgewater. Agar is as serious as a heart attack when it comes to holding this state together."

Tank said, "So, what's the big dire news that made him call a meeting at this time of night?"

When the other senators shook their heads, Ragnovich leaned sideways to whisper to Lauren. "That's why you're here. Nobody 'cept the governor knows yet."

"Roger that," she said.

Voices sounded out in the hallway, and Governor Agar stepped into the room.

Lauren sat up straighter.

Five more senators filed through the door after the governor and took seats around the table. Introductions were made.

"Thanks for coming," Agar began as he walked to the head of the table. "We don't have much time, so let's cut to the red meat: We captured a prisoner. A pilot whose plane was shot out of the sky about twenty miles west of here. He drifted down in a parachute and two of our people found him, including Ms. Davis." He gestured to Lauren. "The pilot is Chinese. A fact corroborated by wreckage of what appears to be a Chengdu J-20 combat aircraft."

Sally slapped a hand to the table, muttering, "Then it's true? The Chinese attacked us?"

Agar spread his arms. "From the few words of English that he kept repeating, he says no."

Tank made a face. "I don't understand. Who shot him down?"

Agar sank into the chair at the head of the table and loosened his blue tie. "Ms. Davis, you saw it happen."

She looked around the room. "It was about sunset. I'd just delivered supplies to OP Delta Alpha, when we saw two jets approaching from the west. They were flying too high for us to make out what kind of jets they were. The plane in back shot down the lead plane with a missile. We watched the pieces fall across the hills. Then we saw a parachute drifting down. Sergeant Sam Hughes and I rode out to see if the person was alive. When we got there, we saw the red Chinese Star on his helmet and Chinese writing on his flight suit. He's got a broken left arm, and while he had a pistol in his flight suit, he offered no resistance. Just kept repeating, 'Do not kill,' and, 'Chinese! Free America, yes?'"

Eyes narrowed around the table.

The governor said, "I've spoken to the prisoner, or tried to. The guy seems earnest. Doesn't act scared. And, not that I've had any experience with POWs, but he hasn't brought up the Geneva Conventions, offered his name, rank, or serial number."

The Campbell County senator, Bill von Gaur propped his chin, wondering, "He said, 'Chinese. Do not kill. Free America, yes?'"

Sally leaned back in her chair. After a few thoughtful moments, she turned to Agar. "What did he mean? Was he asking if Wyoming was part of Free America or saying he'd come to free America?"

The governor lifted a shoulder. "We're not sure. General Kyzer sent a detail of MPs, snatched the guy up, and hustled his butt off to F.E. Warren. I am assured that the general will share any information as soon as he can get it."

Merlin Smith said, "We sent two carrier groups into the South China Sea just before the collapse. It wasn't like the US and China were all warm and fuzzy. And something's got to be behind these rumors of fighting around San Francisco and Seattle. Damn it! If we just knew what was going on."

"Don't forget that air wing that flew west a week ago." Tank reminded. "They didn't relocate that kind of power to prop up the banks."

Barry Clyde added, "Last Express Rider out of Sacramento said it was North Korea."

Sally threw up her hands. Her age-lined face contorted. "I've heard that rumor, but it doesn't make sense. North Korea would be insane to launch an assault against America unless China and Russia were backing their play. Not to mention that they don't have the logistical capacity to transport an army, let alone land it without our intelligence agencies knowing."

Agar blinked and seemed to be staring at the table top. "I agree."

"Then what about all these stories that the attack force was unloaded from one of those monster container ships?" Tank asked. "One of those giant container ships could transport an entire army, its weapons, and support. When it pulled into port, we'd have no clue. Our own longshoremen would unload the containers."

Von Gaur snorted, said, "Bullshit. That many troops would suffocate inside a container."

"Depends on how you design and engineer the containers."
Agar took a drink of his coffee. "Stack them right—with hatches
interconnecting, ventilation and air conditioning—you create a multi-
layered city. Complete with plumbing, cafeterias, hospital, everything."

Ragnovich sat forward, his mouth tightened into a hard white line.
"The pilot's lying. China is not our ally."

"So you think the man is just trying to save his own skin?"

"Wouldn't you?"

Agar rose and walked to the big window to stare out across the
moonlit capitol grounds. On the pole outside, the American flag shone.
The white stripes seemed to glow. When the governor looked back at
the table, longing filled his eyes.

No one said a word.

"Senators," he finally said, "we have to make some tough decisions."

Tank's thick black brows drew together over his long, hooked nose.
"I heard you're thinking about creating a Wyoming dollar."

Agar folded his arms across his chest. "Let's discuss more pressing
issues first. And everything you hear next is absolutely confidential.
If you repeat a word of it, I'll have you shot." He stabbed a finger in
the general direction of the senators.

Sally said, "Didn't think you were joking, Pete."

The governor's eyes glittered. "With the exception of shortwave
radio, communications are down across the country. And we're not
sure what to make of the shortwave radio we're receiving. Lots of
contradictory stuff. Not always in what you'd call the best English.
We think a lot of it is propaganda and misinformation."

"What about the military?" Tank asked.

"They've been flying reconnaissance missions and relaying the
information from one base to another. But that's tenuous, as fuel, parts,
and hours between maintenance runs out."

"Kind of like Express Riders in the air?" Sally asked.

"Exactly."

Agar swayed on his feet and had to prop a hand against the wall
to steady his legs. Two senators shoved back their chairs to rise, but
Agar stopped them. "No, I'm all right. Just tired. Haven't been getting
much sleep."

The governor walked to the table with his fists clenched. "I can now confirm that Washington, DC is gone. That comes straight from General Kyzer at Warren Air Base. I've been withholding this information. Didn't want to fuel a panic. Things are bad enough as it is. I thought if I could get some sort of structure established in Wyoming first, maybe we could survive the loss of the national government."

Images of Tyrell came to haunt Lauren. If he was alive, where was he? Fighting on the west coast? God, she prayed he hadn't been sent to DC.

Ragnovich said, "Nuked?"

Agar lifted his hands uncertainly. "That's the best guess. The pilots in the air at the time—those who survived—saw blinding flashes, but no mushroom clouds. Could be some new weapon."

Tank asked, "Are you telling me for certain that the president is dead?"

Agar bowed his head. "No. She could be in a bunker somewhere, I suppose. If so, command and control are so compromised that General Kyzer and the surviving military aren't aware of it. It's like everything east of Omaha just went silent."

When his voice faded, a din of conversation erupted, people talking over each other, but Lauren heard phrases like "neutron bomb" and "electromagnetic pulse" and "probably exploded nukes in the atmosphere".

Agar held up a hand to get everyone's attention. "We do know for certain that enemy troops landed in Seattle and San Francisco. General Kyzer's information is that the invasion has been stopped in the Cascades in the north and Sierras in central California."

"Then why don't we know who we're fighting?" Ragnovich asked, sounding angry.

Agar said, "They wear camo uniforms with no national insignia. Kyzer suspects this is like when Russia took Crimea. Putin sent in soldiers wearing no Russian insignia to delay the world long enough that by the time we could verify the troops were in fact Russian, Putin had already taken Crimea, and wasn't going to let it go without a fight."

"Are they Asian?" Sally's eyes narrowed.

"Conflicting reports," the governor replied. "Some are. Others, apparently, are not."

Lauren picked up her coffee and took a drink; she studied the frozen faces in the room. Ragnovich looked like he was about to tear someone apart with his bare hands.

"Then it's an international coalition?" Sally asked.

Agar rubbed his eyes. "No one knows the identity or exact strength of the forces." He paused to look around the table, meeting the eyes of each person present. "But we're on our own out here. Nobody's coming to help us."

"What about Warren Air Base?" Tank asked. "Why isn't General Kyzer—"

"Every asset he has is dedicated to the protection of F.E. Warren Air Force base and its nuclear missiles. He has skeleton crews scattered elsewhere in the state, at the missile silos, the base, the secret communication centers. He's just as isolated and understaffed as we are."

"All right." Ragnovich gave the governor a stern nod. "What's next?"

Agar, teetering on his feet, said, "Things are deteriorating up in the Bighorn Basin. That son of a bitch, Edgewater is in the process of carving out a little kingdom for himself. Time's come to deal with him. Captain Ragnovich, before you go, if I need to pull some of the Guard off The Line, how many companies can you spare from the Fourth Quadrant?"

Ragnovich stared down into his coffee, slowly shook his head. "None, sir. The pressure is building. We're getting pushed harder with each day. Used to be just occasional refugees, but the Front Range has pretty much eaten itself out of food. People who followed directions to shelter in place are figuring out that no one's coming to the rescue. The power and water aren't coming back on. Lots of them, who banded together as armed neighborhood block-defense committees, are starting to move out as organized units. They've discovered that in strength, they can take on the gangs. Other bands, not as powerful, just let them pass."

"So, where are they going?" von Gaur asked.

"Anyplace they can find food," Lauren muttered. "In the beginning, individuals in vehicles would drive out, shoot someone's cow, cut it up, and take it back to Fort Collins or Greeley, and trade it for whatever they needed."

"But the fuel is running out," Ragnovich told them. "So now these groups of armed people are fanning out to where the livestock can still be found. They're getting pretty good at killing the folks trying to protect their stock. Once that's done, they'll set up shop and live off what they've killed."

Lauren added, "Until someone comes along behind them and is a little trickier, or stronger, or better armed, and either drives them off or kills them. When the last of the beef, horses, pigs, or whatever are eaten, they move on to the next ranch."

Ragnovich said, "Lot of fighting out by Sterling down in Colorado. Hit and run stuff. Nebraska militia is sending reinforcements."

Agar told the others. "I've been in contact with stock raisers and producers all across northern Colorado. We've been letting them bring their herds north of The Line. We've got miles and miles of highway right-of-way for them to graze their way north until we figure out where to put them."

"Good policy." Tank nodded. "That's free beef—and the people to care for them. Not to mention food and support denied to the raiders down south."

"So," Agar said, "getting back to the point: I can't look to the Guard to spare people for an assault on Edgewater up in the Bighorn Basin?"

"Not without losing the Fourth Quadrant, Governor." Ragnovich glanced at Lauren. "You know my people better than anyone, Lauren. How are they doing?"

"Worn out, sir. Heartbroken and depressed." Lauren frowned. "But beyond that, the ones who've stuck to the OPs understand the mission. They know what they're doing, and why."

"We've heard of suicides," Tank noted. "That true?"

"It is." Ragnovich met the senator's eyes, held them. "How'd you like to find out that you'd just shot a kid? Maybe turned back a child who then got picked up by raiders, sexually abused, and left with a slit throat? The body rotting in the sun and drawing flies."

"Everything comes at a price," Sally added, eyes downcast.

Lauren glanced at the others. "As the soldiers in the OP foxholes see it, they know the country's collapsed and they're, excuse my language, 'in the shit'. By denying entry to Wyoming they condemn fellow Americans to be murdered or die of starvation. Or worse. They can hold The Line because they know that by protecting Wyoming, they're fighting to save their homes and families."

Agar took a deep breath. Shot a look at the senators. "We need to remember this while we're working to keep the power plants producing, the refineries working, and food distribution and communications functional. We can't do it without those people on The Line. They're buying us time. And we damned well don't want to squander a single second of it."

He got several grunts of assent from around the table.

"Need us for anything else?" Ragnovich asked.

Agar shook his head. "Captain Ragnovich, Ms. Davis, thank you for your help. I'm invoking a closed session now."

Lauren got to her feet. "Governor, sir, if you don't mind, can you tell me what's going to happen to the Chinese pilot?"

Agar shook his head. "Nothing's going to happen to him. General Kyzer's a by-the-book kind of guy. Your pilot's a POW, and he'll be treated as such."

"Thank you, sir." Lauren followed Ragnovich out into the hallway with its polished floors and high ceilings. Barry Klyde exited behind them, nodded, and headed in the opposite direction.

When the doors closed, locking them out, Ragnovich turned to stare hard at Lauren. "Wonder what else Agar is telling 'em? Must be far worse than what we were allowed to hear."

"Yeah. Looking forward to another night of happy dreams, huh?"

CHAPTER FORTY-THREE

★★★

10 AM OBSERVATION POST ALPHA ALPHA

LAUREN SHIFTED TO FOURTH GEAR AS SHE TOPPED THE HILL AND HAD A CLEAR VIEW OF THE narrow strip of asphalt ahead. A golden eagle circled overhead. Instead of stench from the brown haze, the world smelled like rain from the morning shower and, for as far as she could see, the green grass shimmered wetly. It was a cool morning, and—given her whiskey head from the night before—that was a relief. Gray skies were easier on her aching eyes. By the time she turned onto the dirt road that led to the OP, she was chilled to the bone.

Pulling up beside the Humvee with its shrouded machine gun, Lauren used her heel to put the kickstand down and stepped off her bike. Alpha Bravo, the associated OP, had been dug into the hilltop about fifty feet away, and Alpha Charlie was a little over one hundred feet down the slope. As the eastern terminus of The Line's Fourth Quadrant, the three OPs had been situated to cover all approaches. A fortified position that would be harder to flank, and self-reinforcing.

Since the ranches had been abandoned down south, what used to be the safest and dullest part of The Line was now one of the hottest. With the help of the Nebraska Militia, the population around Sterling had been able to stop depredations at the Logan County line down in Colorado. That left raiders desperate to turn north, see if they could find a weak spot.

Lauren could see heads moving over the rims of the foxholes. Soft voices carried on the wind.

"Hey, Davis, you bring me a Guinness?" Private Mack Jonesborough called from the closest foxhole. He was eighteen and freckle-faced, with coal black hair. He'd graduated high school at the top of his class, and planned to attend the University of Wyoming to study archaeology this fall.

She wondered if Mack felt as lost as she did, trying to figure out what to do with his life now that the invasion of America had killed his dreams.

Does every teenager feel this way when their country goes to war? Throughout history, and in most of the world today, armies are largely made up of teenagers, some as young as twelve or thirteen.

Lauren called back, "You're on duty, Mack. You forget that?"

"Does that count these days?"

She pulled off her gloves and unbuckled her helmet. "I brought you MREs and bottled water. Word was that you were good to go on ammo and prophylactics."

"Who said we were good on prophylactics?" Corporal Potts, nineteen, replied. He had a baby face with round pink cheeks.

Down in the foxhole, Stacy stuck up a middle finger, announcing, "Don't you wish?"

Potts chuckled. Said, "Mack, go help Lauren."

"Yes, sir."

Mack climbed out of the foxhole and trotted over to Lauren. While she unstrapped the case of bottled water from the back of the KTM, he grinned at her. The other two soldiers in the hole were women, both privates, Stacy Kallahan and Anna Jones. They'd be seniors at Cheyenne High next year. If schools were open. If they weren't all Chinese re-education centers or forced labor camps. She could just see the backs of Kallahan's and Jones's helmets where they rested their rifles over the top of the berm and scanned the hinterlands.

"You want to go out with me, Davis?" Mack asked for the tenth time.

"Hell, no." Lauren lifted the case of water and shoved it into his arms. "How many times do I have to tell you? I'm engaged."

"Yeah, but Ramirez ain't here and I am."

"Really? Didn't notice."

"You mean I turned invisible?"

"Pretty much."

Mack grinned, gave Lauren a pining look, and carried the case of water away.

Potts took the water from Mack and handed it to Anna Jones, who used her knife to cut the shrink-wrap, then Potts stood up to watch Lauren unlock her saddlebag and draw out a big plastic sack stuffed with small bags of potato chips.

"Holy Mother of God!" Potts cried. "Those have to be the last bags of chips on earth. Where'd you get them?"

"Lucy, at The Plains, likes you guys," she said and tossed him the bag. "She's been hoarding these like gold nuggets."

"My God," Anna cried, "I almost feel normal!"

Delighted laughs went round as they handed out bags and tore into them, stuffing chips into their mouths as fast as they could.

In the meantime, Private Jones tossed bottles of water to each soldier.

"What kind of MREs did you bring us today?" Potts called.

"Chicken, corned beef, and something that says it's prime rib, but I'd be suspicious if I were you. Saw a guy open one of these, and it looked like gray mush."

"No turkey and gravy?"

"No, and I'm brokenhearted. I'm eating with you guys today."

"You can have my chicken," Mack called.

"Hallelujah, I'll take you up on that." Lauren smiled.

As she started walking for his foxhole, she glimpsed movement down the hill in the tall grass. Probably nothing, but she stopped and squinted. The blades were bending sideways, like something was slithering through the…

An arm flashed in the grass, something that looked like a tube went cartwheeling through the air.

The explosion rocked the hill, throwing Lauren backward, where she landed hard on her back. It knocked the wind out of her. Panic seared her veins as she rolled to her side, and fought for enough breath to scramble on all fours into the foxhole. Jones and Kallahan opened up with their M4s, strafing the hillside.

When the barrage halted, Potts yelled, "What the hell happened?"

Mack's eyes had gone huge. "Bomb. Saw it whirling in the air. Landed right in Alpha Charlie's foxhole! Then I saw four people come charging up the hill!"

"I saw it, too. Homemade pipe bomb, I think," Kallahan called. Locks of dirt-coated blonde hair blew around the base of her helmet.

Mack lifted his binoculars and glassed the OP. "Oh…Christ. Jamison's alive. I can see her moving. She's waving one hand."

Lauren crawled to the lip of the foxhole and tried to see what Mack was looking at. Down the slope, Alpha Charlie was little more than a crater in the earth, but a human hand was visible.

"You're crazy as hell," Corporal Potts said. "Nobody could live through that. Give me those glasses."

The eighteen-year-old private handed over the glasses. Potts adjusted the focus, stared, and slowly lowered them to swallow hard.

Mack's voice turned tortured. "Do you see her? She alive, isn't she?"

"Yeah."

"How are we going to get to her? We don't know how many hostiles are still out there hiding in the grass."

"Get to the Humvee. And we need Alpha Alpha's, too. The slope down there is steep, but we're going to split. Anna, you're driving. Mack on the M240. Anna, curve in from the west. The team from Alpha hits 'em from the east. Pincher movement to catch them in a crossfire, right? And we blow the mother fuckers away."

"Roger that," Anna called. "Covering fire."

Potts and Stacy braced their M4s on the dirt and began firing bursts into the grass below Alpha Charlie. As they did, Anna and Mack beat feet for the Humvee camouflaged behind the crest of the hill.

"They're out of sight!" Lauren yelled. "They made it."

Without looking at Lauren, Potts said, "Davis, in about two minutes, this whole ridge is going to sound like the beaches of Iwo Jima. You're a civilian. Get out of here. Move! We'll cover your retreat."

"Fuck that! Who do you think you're talking to?" She pulled her M4 around on its sling. Brought it up on the dirt berm and started searching for targets. There. Farther out. Two people rose, charged forward a couple of steps and threw themselves flat. God, how many were out there?

"What the hell do they want?" Potts wondered.

"Hey, buddy," Lauren told him as she waited for her two hiders to rise and rush again. "This is the Fourth Quadrant, they could want anything. But hitting the end of The Line like this? It's not like they're trying to sneak past."

She had her eye on the red dot when her two attackers rose. As they did her finger eased the trigger back. The M4 blasted her hungover eardrums, and brass flew; the attackers dropped. Not the pitched forward of a dive, but the loose flop she'd come to associate with being shot.

A combined rhythmic thumping from the thirty calibers on the Humvees was accented by the snapping chatter of the M4s. Other gunfire, cracking like high-velocity rounds from hunting rifles, meant the raiders were shooting back.

The explosion came as a shock. Shaking the ground, convulsing the air. Dirt jumped on the berm. Lauren felt it through her bones and body.

Tell me that's not Mack and Anna. That this whole thing wasn't a trap to lure them down in the Humvees and blow them all to hell.

When Lauren dared to lift her head, it was to see the west-flanking Humvee, shattered and leaning at an impossible angle. Smoke and dust rose from the turret and around the blown-out doors.

In the sudden silence, as the boom rolled away over the grasslands, the attackers screamed. Maybe ten of them rushed forward up the slope.

Everything would have been different, but the attackers hadn't counted on *two* Humvees at Alpha Alpha.

CHAPTER FORTY-FOUR

***

IT IS LIKE LIVING IN A DREAM: THE FIGHT IS OVER. AS QUICKLY AS IT BEGAN. LAUREN CLIMBS
out of the foxhole at Alpha Alpha. Her head still rings from the muzzle
blast of her weapon and Potts's. Ears still numb from the explosion.
She has oddly disjointed memories of the second Humvee rounding the
slope. How the turret-mounted M240 opened up. How the thirty-caliber
slugs ripped the remaining attackers apart.

Then the silence.

The hazy-dark sky is a heavy weight pressing down, driving light
and joy from the planet. The faint tang of burned gunpowder—fades
as the breeze slips in from the west.

She doesn't feel her feet as she walks through the trampled grass,
down past Alpha Charlie. A glance into the foxhole sends a flutter
through her already-roiled stomach.

She imagines what a giant pestle would do to human beings if
dropped down from the sky and ground four people into smeared and
bloody pulp. Meat, splintered bone, torn cloth, and pressure-crushed
entrails all mashed into the chalky soil. Even the guns are bent and
impressed into the mess.

These are people I know.

She searches for names, knows she knows them. But can find
nothing in the ringing that fills her skull. Like the whole world is on
heterodyne.

Walk past.

The others.

Potts, Stacy, are ghosts. They stumble down the hill, weapons up.
Expressions on their faces are wide-eyed with horror. Seem to shimmer
in Lauren's vision as she stops short. Sees what lies at her feet.

Two bodies. Face down in the grass.

A man, maybe thirty? She can't tell from the back of his head. His face is buried in the grass. Two of her rounds blew through the camo jacket he wears. Both exited to the right of the spine. Bubbly blood seeping into the Mossy Oak fabric around the exit wounds tells her they were lung shots. Looks uncomfortable the way he's bleeding onto a short-barreled AR with a trick laser and flashlight attached to the tubular accessory rail.

The woman appears to be in her twenties. From the way she's posed, she might be asleep. Lies on her stomach. Left cheek pressed into the grass.

Bucolic.

But for her long ash-blonde hair; it is matted with gore. Lauren's bullet has torn some of her hair out of the ponytail. The breeze plays with strands. An AR15 lies by the woman's outstretched right hand. She wears tight-fitting Levi's that are grass stained, and hiking boots. A small semiauto pistol in her back pocket where the jeans conform.

Lauren stands over them, the reassuring weight of the M4 in her hands. Wonders who they were before the collapse. Why they came here. On this particular morning. To have Lauren shoot them down.

A scream—as if from a thousand yards away—eats its way into Lauren's hearing. Pierces that ringing inside her head.

She turns, sees Potts where he stands down the slope by the tipped Humvee. Threads of smoke still rise from the blasted vehicle. The right front wheel has been blown off, the passenger door gaping.

Lauren watches Potts climb into the ruined vehicle; he is pulling out what's left of Anna. Her remains come out like an elongated and sagging string. Like all the bones have been pulverized. The woman's face is missing. Just a red skinless mass, holes where the eyes once were.

Lauren blinks.

Her heart pounds so hard it hurts.

She slowly sinks into the grass.

The inside of her head is blank. Thoughtless. Opaque.

She sees only the waving blades of grass; they bob slightly on the breeze. A grasshopper clings to one. He is yellow and green, eyes translucent, rising and falling on his blade of grass.

CHAPTER FORTY-FIVE

***

2 PM

THE FIGHT AT ALPHA ALPHA KEPT REPLAYING IN LAUREN'S HEAD AS SPED ALONG, HEADED
back to Cheyenne. A huge flock of crows and magpies exploded from
the drainage bottom in a flurry of wings. She had to swerve the bike
as the birds careened and squawked in front of her. Came close to
crashing the bike, startled as she was.

"Goddamn it."

She managed to miss them and watched the birds circle above the
road. They must have dinner somewhere just off the shoulder. Lauren
rode up the hill and down the other side, searching for the carcass that
must be out there. Lauren was twenty-four miles east of Cheyenne.
Wasn't her usual route, it was Breeze's, but Alpha X-Ray, off Thunder
Basin Road, had been hit hard. Had to rely on Ma Deuce to save their
asses. They'd needed a couple of boxes of fifty-caliber ammo. ASAP.

A quarter mile ahead, another motorcycle leaned on its side stand.

With a click, Lauren toed the transmission into neutral and let the
bike roll to a stop. Checked out the dusty BMW 650. Breeze's bike.

Shifting the M4 to her right hand, she scanned the surroundings
for any sign of trouble.

Where's Breeze?

OP Bravo Alpha sat astraddle Thunder Basin Road, maybe three
miles south and east. OP Bravo Charlie stood on a low bluff just
back from the state line, about three miles south southwest. From
its sandstone-capped top it had a total view of Porter Creek valley.
Maybe Breeze had run out of gas or broke down and decided to walk
to one of the OPs?

God, let it be that. Tell me she wasn't flagged down. Taken at gun point.

Lauren stayed on her bike as she cradled her M4. Heart beating slowly, she thumbed the fire control to burst and searched the landscape for an ambush.

Meadowlarks perched and trilled on the spiky clumps of yucca; green, pod-like flowers were on the verge of blossoming.

The sky overhead burned reddish-orange where the mid-afternoon sun penetrated the brown haze.

She shut off her engine and listened.

When the wind shifted, the buzz of flies reached Lauren, and she thought she heard someone gasp for breath.

"Breeze?" she called. "You down there?"

Lauren flipped the kickstand down, leaned the bike, and cradled the M4 in her arms as she threw her leg over and stepped off.

"Breeze?"

With her skin crawling, Lauren eased to the edge of the gravel road. The road bed was elevated here where drainage ran down toward Crow Creek; when it rained, water ran through a culvert buried in the embankment. More crows burst from the grass and wings filled the air. Dead bodies scattered the border. That's what she expected to find.

Another gasp, like someone vomiting.

"Breeze?" Lauren shouted. M4 at hand, she stepped to the drop-off and looked over. "Are you hurt?

The bright yellow tent was completely hidden from view of the road. It had been pitched just across the barbed wire fence in the bottom of the dry creek bed and no more than four feet from the culvert.

A cobalt-blue backpack lay to one side of the tent, its pockets unzipped. Occasional articles of clothing were scattered here and there.

Lauren scaled the fence and jumped off the other side. Her M4 at the ready, she studied every dip and cranny that might hide a potential enemy.

A short distance from the tent, the dead woman lay on her side. The wind played with the mouse-brown strands around the bullet hole in her skull. Her eyes had been plucked out by the crows, her mouth agape and swarming with flies. She wore a flower-patterned blouse that hadn't been washed in days. Filth covered her red pants.

The little boy lay face-down in the grass next to her. Lauren's heart pounded as she walked closer. The kid's hair had been blown away by the discharge of a firearm, and the star-shaped entrance wound in the back of his skull couldn't be missed. She didn't bother to turn him over. Gore puddled beneath what was left of his ruined face.

Beyond them, the man lay on his back, left arm flung out to the side. His right index finger remained inside the trigger guard of an old Model 10 Smith & Wesson .38 pistol.

Not hard to figure out how it had gone down. He'd killed his family, then himself.

Down the drainage, just out of sight where a creek bottom turned: Sobbing.

Lauren's alert gaze scanned the grass as she walked toward the agonizing sounds. She saw the familiar motorcycle touring jacket. Hunched, head down, in the lee of a bunch of squaw currant.

"Breeze, are you hurt?" Lauren pulled up, still wary. "Answer me!"

Breeze straightened, stared sidelong at Lauren through glittering eyes, and seemed to come to her senses.

Swallowing hard, she leaned her head back to the gaudy sunlight and took a deep breath. "I'm all right," she answered as she brushed off her sleeves and pants.

"You hurt? Let me look you over."

"Not necessary."

All emotion had vanished. In a matter of heartbeats Breeze became the same tough woman Lauren had come to rely on. Dressed in camo and wearing scuffed Lucchese boots, Breeze once again looked tough and lean. Only when close could Lauren see the tangled brown hair was matted wetly to Breeze's cheeks, her eyes swollen.

Breeze squared her shoulders. Halting one pace short, she adjusted her gun belt. "Lauren, just get on your bike and ride away. Stay away from the tent. You hear me?"

"Yeah. Sure." Lauren made a face. "That bad, huh?"

Without another word, Breeze stalked off, scaled the fence and climbed the hill. Lauren heard her BMW putter to life. The click when Breeze toed it into gear, and then the roar as she flogged it away. The big single rapped out every gear change until it vanished over the distant hill.

Lauren turned to frown at the yellow tent.

What's in there?

At the sound of a truck engine, Lauren trotted back, scrambled over the fence, and got a look at the pickup heading her way in a dust cloud.

The truck approached slowly from the south. The Militia sign on the front bumper was prominently displayed. Three people were visible through the windshield. One of Agar's behind-the-lines patrols.

When the truck stopped, the doors flew open, rifles leveled and steadied in the gap. Three people were in the Ford F-250's cab.

"Who are you?" a man wearing a cowboy hat called as he popped up from the driver's seat.

"Lauren Davis." She slung her rifle and held up her hands. "Working for Captain Ragnovich in the Guard. I deliver supplies to the OPs."

"Are you *that* Lauren Davis? From Buffalo Camp?"

Lowering her hands, she answered woodenly. "Yeah." And then, "I'm her."

"Where's your pass?"

"On my bike." She tilted her head toward the KTM. "Who are you?"

"Corporal Toby Eppson. Charley Company, Border Battalion, Wyoming Militia." He stepped out from behind the driver's door, his AR15 rifle at rest in the crook of his arm. To the others, he said, "You guys stay with the truck. Keep an eye out."

As he walked up, Eppson said, "I've heard of you, Davis. Heard good things. What are you doing stopped out here? Isn't this Tappan's route?"

"Emergency run. Alpha X-Ray ran out of rounds for Ma Deuce. Too many bullets flying around today."

Eppson walked toward her and glanced down at the bodies sprawled in the grass just past the yellow tent. "What happened here?"

"Looks like a murder-suicide to me. Got to be. No one would leave a gun behind. Come on, let me show you."

In the lead, Lauren slid her way back down the embankment, scaled the barbed wire fence, and headed for the yellow tent. Eppson followed her.

When they reached the bodies, Eppson wiped his mouth with the back of his hand. "Mom, Dad and son? How long ago did this happen?"

"From the condition of the wounds, yesterday, late. Maybe last night."

"What were they doing way out here?" Eppson frowned out at the hills. "It's miles from anywhere."

Lauren watched the crows and magpies who flapped down to roost on the fence posts and squawk to one another, waiting to return to their dinners. "They may have thought they could walk from ranch to ranch, begging food along the way. Others have."

"But all the places around here are either abandoned or burned," Eppson said.

"Doubt they knew that."

Distastefully, Eppson said, "Man, I never saw a dead person outside of a funeral home until all this happened."

Lauren frowned at the yellow tent.

"Davis, can you help me document this site, so I can speculate on what happened here in my report? Can you believe? Civilization's cratered, and the Guv's already got us doing paperwork."

"Yeah. Okay."

A recent scatter of trash lay in the grass around the yellow tent; Lauren found a piece of paper rolled and stuffed in the top of an empty water bottle. She pulled it out and unrolled it.

"What's that?" Eppson asked.

"Note. Written in blue ink, says, 'Lost. No water in three days.'"

Lauren handed the note to Eppson and squinted at the tent. She wondered if Breeze had ridden past yesterday and seen this family waving, desperate to get her to stop. If she had, she would have assumed the same thing Lauren would have: *The family's a distraction for an ambush. Pin the throttle and get past them fast, before the guns come out.*

What would it have taken to save them? A couple of bottles of water? Couple of MREs?

Eppson glared at the bodies. "The pistol is still in the man's hand."

Lauren adjusted her slung M4, and took in the sprawled bodies, idly wondering what the man felt when he shot his wife and son. What thoughts were going through his head? Did he shoot the wife first, so she couldn't object to him killing the boy? Or did Mom hold the child for as long as she could, telling her son everything was going to be okay, before she stepped away to make room for Dad to blow the boy's brains out?

Lauren spread her feet. "Looks like he couldn't stand to see his family suffer any longer."

"Yeah. Ground's not torn up. No sign of struggle. Contact wound on the side of the woman's head. No, I'd say she was in on it. Boy died first. Then the woman."

Death was now regarded with a whole new, and totally callous ambivalence. After all, the number of human corpses south of the line so overwhelmed the senses that it was like seeing a foregone conclusion. You just swerved to miss the carcass and drove on by.

Eppson walked over and used the toe of his boot to roll the man over, then he pulled the billfold from the guy's back pocket and flipped it open. "Matthew Hammond Grant, date of birth, June 12, 1990, lived at 4467 Smith Street, Boulder, Colorado. And here's his business card. Senior technician, diagnostic repair, L & M Computer Solutions on 28th Street, Boulder. No cash, of course. Just useless credit cards."

Lauren waved away the swarming flies and knelt to examine the blue backpack. She dug through every pocket, pulled out a red toy car and a tiny plastic doll. "Nothing in the backpack but kids' toys."

"Okay." Eppson tucked the wallet into his coat pocket. "Have you checked inside the tent?"

When she rose to her feet, Lauren suddenly shivered. Breeze wouldn't have told her to stay away unless...

"No."

"I doubt that little boy was playing with that doll."

It was as though Lauren's soul heard a voice that her ears did not. She squinted at the yellow tent. The front was zipped closed. Trying to keep something in? Or something out?

Eppson extended a hand to the tent. "Could you check it out while I roll over the woman to see if she has any ID?"

"I...I've got to get back to Cheyenne, Corporal."

Irritated, he said, "Yeah? You think I might have other things to do, too?"

Lauren clenched her jaw, thought about Breeze. "Sorry, you're right. I got it."

Lauren walked over, knelt. The tent had been zipped all the way to the top. As she pulled the zipper down, an angry swarm of flies burst out right into her face.

CHAPTER FORTY-SIX

***

SILVERWARE CLINKED. LAUREN BARELY HEARD IT WHERE SHE HUNCHED OVER A GLASS OF stout in the Plains Hotel bar.

Like flipping a light switch, she was just suddenly there. Had no clue how she'd gotten there. What she'd been doing.

"Was I out on The Line?" Flashes of memory, like some disjointed druggie's action film flickering in her head. Shooting. A detonation, as the Alpha Alpha Humvee was blown up. People dying behind the MTV as they tried to overwhelm her and Mike. Potts, laughing. Corporal Eppson, of the Guard...

Eppson. Staring into her eyes.

Saying...? What?

It was as if the memory faded.

I'm all right. I'm in the bar.

Things were normal. She had a full glass of stout clasped in her hands. Felt warm. She lifted it, savored the taste.

All around her, normal-looking people chatted and ate sandwiches, while Lucy took orders and delivered food. Most of the patrons were military, wearing National Guard camo or the dark gray shirts of the Militia. The civilians must be state employees.

What the hell happened to me?

"Lucy? Can I order?" she called as the waitress walked by carrying plates to another table. The tight high voice didn't sound like hers. "I'll have the bison chili, please."

"Got it!" Lucy called back. The woman spared Lauren a worried glance as she delivered her plates.

A corporal at the table across from hers smiled when her gaze drifted across him, then he let it fade at the hateful look she gave him.

Lauren propped elbows on the table and dropped her head into her hands. Exhaustion and defeat weighted her shoulders. More images replayed in her head. She'd seen plenty of awful things: Shrieking infants crawling alone through the grass. Huge pile of bodies covered with black fluttering wings. Growling dogs pulling out intestines. What the hell was the matter with her?

She needed to get her head screwed on straight.

In the near future, she and everyone else in Wyoming would be in a fight for the life of their country. That's what she needed to think about. For all they knew the west coast wouldn't hold, and the Chinese would be moving across Idaho.

Yellow tent. There it was, an image, like an orphan in her mind.

She sipped carefully, slowly. The tortured knot in her gut began to unwind. She should know that yellow tent. Something horrible. If she could just place where.

Closing her eyes, images formed. The ones from her nightmares. The ones that not even an ocean of alcohol could drown.

Little girl in a tent. Arms stick-thin from starvation.

Just a drink, please. I'm so thirsty.

"Davis?"

The captain's voice startled her. She glanced up when Ragnovich came striding toward her with his cover tucked under his left arm.

He tramped across the restaurant and slid in opposite her. "Corporal Eppson said he gave you a ride to town. That something had happened to you. Maybe a concussion. Said you were just out of it. Almost like a zombie."

Lauren gave him a hollow stare, frowned. I was?

He removed his cover from under his arm and placed it on the table beside her M4. "Breeze said she was worried. Asked me to check and make sure you made it home."

She leaned back in the booth. Struggled to find something to say. Anything. And then the words came from somewhere. "Heard the people at Charlie Echo had trouble last night. Shot up an armored dump truck."

Yes. She knew that. That was real, wasn't it?

"Understatement," Ragnovich ran a hand through his stringy hair. "Figured they could smash the Humvees out of the road. Maybe they forgot to scout it out. We've got two Brownings out there."

"Guess even armored dump trucks can't stand up to Ma Deuce, huh?"

I took fifty caliber ammo boxes out to Alpha X-Ray. I remember that.

She could see their relieved faces as she unstrapped the ammo cans from the KTM's luggage rack.

"We lose anyone?" she asked, surprised by the fear in her voice. In addition to the guys, Charlie Echo was manned by four sixteen-year-old women who had a special place in her heart. They were all too brave, too grownup.

"Two wounded. They'll be off The Line for a couple of weeks."

Lauren shook her head at the news. "We can't afford to lose them."

"Don't have to tell me that. And we're losing Tappan, too. Her dad and grandfather are in town. Unless I miss my guess, she's heading back to the family ranch tomorrow."

A sense of panic, as if she were drowning, rose in Lauren's chest. *Breeze? Leaving?* She couldn't breathe.

Ragnovich ran fingers through his hair again. "They've got their own trouble up in the Bighorn Basin. There's going to be a showdown with Edgewater."

Lauren took a swig of beer, managed to get a breath. Struggling, she tried to understand what that meant. "You going to let me ride Charlie sector?"

The captain arched a knowing brow. "Come on, you know how the whole Line feels about you. Every man and woman along the Fourth Quadrant would die for you. They think you walk on water, but you're not a god-damned god. What happened today? Was it the yellow tent?"

Lauren engaged in a steely eyed staring match with Ragnovich.

Her heart began to pound, sweat rising on her back and sides. She knotted her hands around the stout glass, as if she could crush it.

God, it all came back.

Finally, she said, "Yellow tent in a gully. There was a little girl. If you've had this conversation with Breeze and Eppson, you know about dad, mom, and the brother. Son of a bitch took out his whole family and left the little girl to die. Alone."

"Breeze thinks maybe she died first. That that's why the father—"

"Locked in a tent, cuddling her favorite toy. A filthy s-stuffed sheep.

She was h-holding it." A mixture of rage and repressed tears strained Lauren's voice. "Hugging it."

The panic rose. "Goddamn him! *Why didn't he kill his daughter?*" She half-shouted. The restaurant went quiet.

A little, delicate, broken doll of a girl. Her parents and brother dead. Her only remaining companion: the stuffed sheep she had loved enough to carry across Colorado to that lonely drainage. She had the sheep clutched to her chest as if to mash it through her skin and bone and into her very heart. Did she hear her brother crying? Her mother? Had she buried her face in the fuzzy sheep to hide when she heard the final shot, and Dad's body hit the ground?

Something monstrous was shredding Lauren's insides. She felt the liquid warmth as tears slipped past her lids.

"I don't... I can't... Explain it." She fought for control. "No food. Empty water bottles. Nothing in their packs. The goddamned father! Cowardly son-of-a..."

When she choked on the words, the silence stretched.

Lauren wiped at the tears. Tried to block the images. The little girl would have been sitting alone in the tent when she heard the gunshots outside. Then, when no one came back for her, she probably tried to unzip the tent, but the zipper would have been way over her head. She couldn't reach it, so she went back to hug her toy.

"You need a break, Lauren. There's no law that says you have to be out there twenty-four seven."

"I'm not doing anything any of the Guard wouldn't do without a second thought."

"You were in the thick of the fighting at Alpha Alpha. You were damned lucky. But luck don't hold, and you know it. Take some goddamned time off!"

She shook her head. "No. You need me."

The captain pointed a hard finger. "It's not just families running from the hell in the cities. Just like at Alpha Alpha, and Charlie Echo, it's gangs with guns. They've killed all the livestock left south of The Line, and too God damned many on our side. Hell, if you believe the stories, they're *eating* people. They've burned and looted everything lootable. These new raiders are the worst sort of human filth we've seen."

"All the more reason, like with Alpha X-Ray, today, you need me to keep the OPs stocked when the shit comes down."

"I'm calling it," the captain said softly. "You've got a choice: enlist in the Guard where you are subject to my orders or take a month's leave."

Hoarsely, she said, "My people out there—"

"*Your* people?" Ragnovich glanced around at the other patrons pretending not to watch. The room was silent as a tomb. "Lauren, you're teetering on the edge. I'm not going to let you get yourself killed because you're too raw inside to see the hit coming."

She sat there, muscles tense, feeling brittle.

The captain pushed his chair back and stood. "You're relieved, and I've given orders at the quartermaster's."

Her voice might have been an overstretched wire, when she said, "Understood."

CHAPTER FORTY-SEVEN

***

IT'S MORNING, SHE THINKS.

Where she lies on her back atop the still-made bed, fully dressed, Lauren looks up at the paint on the ceiling. Her heart thumps a slow martial drumbeat. All night long snippets of college lessons drifted through her mind. Especially the words of the great Catholic scholar, Thomas Aquinas: *Evil cannot exist but in good; sheer evil is impossible.*

She rolls to her side.

…isn't true.

Sheer evil is a little girl dying alone with a filthy stuffed sheep in her arms.

The ceiling rolls like waves headed for a distant shore. The walls bend inward. Her fingers clench into fists that she cannot unclench. Adrift. Angels don't come to the prayers of soldiers.

She waits…

Finally, Lauren forces herself to rise and walk to the bathroom. Turning on the faucet, she sticks her head under the cool water and leaves it there for long minutes. Except for the sound of running water, the hotel room is silent. No chatter of tires on gravel outside. No gunshots. Oh, there's a whiff of nervous laughter, an echo in her brain from the friends still out there in the misery. Whispers from Tyrell. *Get moving.*

She focuses on the feel of water. Every soul manning The Line gives way to gravity and falls into the dark monstrous center of the earth. You know it's coming. Each day you fear the fall. When it happens, you drag yourself up and carry on.

It occurs to her that she's counting breaths, four, five, six…

Time has become a kaleidoscope. Prisms seen through hot stinging eyes. Sometimes she's here in the now, other times locked in the past. Past? A ridiculous word. It's never past, she's there. Flashbacks. Never flash forwards, because there is no forward. No future.

Finally, on wobbly legs, she walks out of the hotel room with Tyrell's boogie bag over her shoulder. The bag never leaves her sight these days. Packed with the M4, ammunition and magazines, and the rest of Tyrell's precious kit, it's her last link to a vanished happiness.

CHAPTER FORTY-EIGHT

***

LAUREN MADE HER WAY CAREFULLY DOWN THE STAIRS, NOT QUITE TRUSTING HER BALANCE with the boogie bag over one shoulder and the M4 slung over the other. Glancing out the front doors of the hotel, she was reassured to see her bike waiting faithfully in the sunlight at the curb. What didn't reassure her was the Guard private who obviously stood sentry over it. Did Ragnovich think she'd try to flank the quartermaster's warehouse, steal a load, and deliver it helter-skelter to whichever Observation posts needed it?

He knew her too well.

She veered left and entered the restaurant. Lucy, bless her heart, had placed a card that said "Reserved" on Lauren's booth. Seeing it brought tears to her eyes.

She walked over, slung her bag down on the floor, and gently rested her M4 on the table, then Lauren slid wearily into the booth. Lucy immediately placed a steaming mug of black coffee on the table before her. Coffee? From where?

"I've been holding a little back," Lucy said. "After your argument with the captain last night, figured you could use a cup."

"I can. Thanks."

Lucy looked at her with a serious expression. "You had me worried. I thought you'd gone catatonic, just sitting there for two hours staring at nothing after Ragnovich left."

"Two hours? I did?"

"Couple of guys from the Guard came in. Tried to talk to you, and you didn't say a word back. They thought you just wanted to be alone, so they left." She paused. "I'm right here, you know that, right? You ever to—"

"I'll have the buffalo sausage special." Lauren lifted her coffee cup to cut the conversation short and drank it. The last thing she needed was sympathy. Sympathy dissolved courage. Sympathy was Satan. Made you weak.

Lucy said softly, "I understand. On it."

Lauren savored the flavor of the coffee. Two semis that had been stranded at the Love's Truck stop when credit went away had been full of coffee. The governor had confiscated both. Soldiers and support crews got preference. Now that was gone.

Lauren wondered what they'd drink when the black tea ran out? Or if she'd ever taste pineapples, oranges, or chocolate again. The other "hot" item was alfalfa tea. She hoped that when the coffee ran out, that she'd actually come to like it.

"So what's left?" she whispered aloud as she tried to fathom the reality that she wasn't eating breakfast in a rush. That she wasn't hurrying out to the bike to ride over to the Guard quartermaster's to pick up supplies, so she could keep the sentries' bellies full to ease their fear just a little. That even if she managed to get to the quartermaster, the people there would tell her to go away.

She forced herself to calm down. What surprised her was the length of the moment. Each second stretched into an eternal nightmare. Patience, she told herself. Hold on. Let it pass.

Her brain was firing furiously, but no information seemed to be getting through. Like puzzle pieces flying about, her thoughts were shattered, spinning out of control. Vague shapes flashed by. Glimpses of faces. Eyes. The world had let go of her, not just the Guard. Her fingers moved. Clutched her cup.

Lucy slid a plate of eggs and buffalo sausage under her nose, saying, "Enjoy the hash browns. That's the last of them. We're not getting more until the potato harvest comes in, or one of the local people with a backyard garden takes pity on us."

Lauren realizes she's shaking. Hides her hands under the table.

Lucy says, "Take your time, okay? The rush hour is going to start soon, but I don't care. You stay in that booth as long as you want to."

Then she bustles away.

Lauren eats carefully, slowly, taking small bites and washing them down with strong black coffee. Her gut slowly unwinds from the tortured knot into which it has tied itself.

When she is done, she pushes her plate to the side, and closes her eyes while she drinks coffee with both hands.

The staccato of her M4 fills her ears.

In Lauren's vision, a little girl tries to unzip a yellow tent. Can't. Crying, she calls for her mother and father, her brother...

It takes all of Lauren's strength to fight the tide of emotion...

"Lauren?"

"Yeah." She blinked her eyes open. Realized she was back in the restaurant. That she'd been...away...

Lucy looked down in concern. "You okay?"

"Case of the shakes." Lauren tried to muster a reassuring smile. "It'll pass."

Lucy turned when a group of people came in and started to take chairs on the far side of the room. "Call me if you need anything. You got that? *Anything.*"

"Yeah, Lucy."

She stared down into her coffee. Her reflection stared back. Dark. Everything was so dark. Dark sun-bronzed skin. Dark soul leaking out of her eyes. Some vague part of her brain registered the woman as she clumped across the floor on combat boots. Lauren was still staring into her coffee, desperately trying to see light somewhere, when the woman stopped beside her booth and shifted her feet uncertainly.

"Lauren," she said softly.

It took several moments for recognition to sink in.

Lauren looked up at Breeze. Her friend's face could have been a frozen mask.

Breeze asked, "You all right?"

Lauren lurched out of the booth and wrapped her arms tightly around Breeze's chest, hugging for all she's worth. Breeze briefly staggered under the weight, then her arms tightened around Lauren like a vice. They stood there, clinging to the other.

"Got something to say to you," Breeze said against her ear. "Sorry, Breeze. I'm so sorry about Jim."

Breeze seemed to realize the apology had nothing to do with the yellow tent. She replied, "Wasn't your fault, Lauren. Jim asked you to drive home because he was too damned drunk to do it himself. His fault. Not yours. I never should have said the things I did."

Tears burned Lauren's eyes. She pushed away and gave Breeze a long look. The restaurant suddenly smelled like burning coffee, and Lucy hustled back for the kitchen.

Lauren said, "Heard your Dad and Grandad were in town. Ragnovich said you might go home."

"Yeah. Mom's been shot."

"What?"

Breeze clenched her fists and glanced at the Highway Patrol officer standing by the door. The patrolwoman kept shifting nervously, as though anxious to be on her way. "We just got word that Edgewater's people attacked the ranch last night. Mom's in the Hot Springs hospital. Another woman was killed." Breeze exhaled hard. "Tappans aren't going to stand for this."

"Is Pam all right?"

"Don't know." Breeze shook her head. "You could come? We could use another gun."

"No. No, I…" Lauren shook her head and slid back into the booth. "Can't. Got things to do here. Mike…"

Mike, what? She wondered.

"Bring him, too," Breeze said. "Hey, I'm out of time." A pause, and a smile. "I love you, little sister."

Breeze turned and hurried through the door and into the overcast morning.

The words—unspoken since Jim's death—brought tears to Lauren's eyes. The joke was that Breeze was marrying Lauren's older brother. That it would make Breeze her older sister.

Lauren peered unblinking at the restaurant door. Men and women in uniform came and went. Most had empty eyes and kept one hand on their belted pistols. They'd all been pushed way beyond their limits by the constant terror and horror that went with holding The Line.

I could leave.

Her bike was out there on the curb. It wasn't like she was trapped here. She didn't have to wait for the Highway Patrol. She had the cash—and nothing but nightmares tied her to Cheyenne. Nightmares and Mike Vinich.

She could make it to Tappan ranch. She already had a pass, and she was a Line rider. More than capable of dealing with any raiders or thugs along the road.

Edgewater's people shot Pam?

Back in the days when she could feel something, Pam Tappan had been like a second mother to her, and now she might be dying from a raider's bullet. The Tappans were old-time Wyoming ranchers. Nobody, ever, would hurt a member of the family and get away with it.

Reaching for her coffee cup, Lauren stared down at the black liquid as though maybe, if she looked hard enough, she'd see the answer there.

CHAPTER FORTY-NINE

***

LAUREN'S SLUGGISH STEPS POUNDED THE FLOOR AS SHE MADE HER WAY DOWN THE WHITE corridor toward Room 242. The soldiers who stood at ease around the hospital nodded to her as she passed. A deferential nod, telling her she was one of them, and they understood what she was going through. She nodded back as she continued on her way. It was heartening to look in their eyes and see herself reflected there. Meant that her suffering was not hers alone but shared with countless men and women along the Fourth Quadrant. Each had witnessed an act that shattered the soul. If they were lucky—if she were lucky—that purgatory would, at some point, turn to numbness.

"Please, God," she whispered.

A nurse trotted by her carrying a chart, and Lauren noticed that one of the fluorescent lights was flickering badly. Once it burned out there would be no more replacement bulbs. Not in Wyoming.

She slowed down when she approached Mike Vinich's door. A doctor leaned against the doorframe, dressed in blue scrubs, saying some final words to another nurse before he turned and swiftly strode down the corridor past Lauren without even a glance.

She leaned her head in the doorway, studied Mike. His bed was partially raised, pillows under his head. Damn, he looked thin. His chest rose and fell under the sheet. The monitors glowed, showing a heartbeat on the screen.

"You up to visitors?"

Mike didn't react as she walked in, squinted at the squiggly line that recorded his heartbeat. She wasn't sure what the peaks and dips meant. Hadn't a clue, actually. But, was it her imagination, or were they smaller now, farther apart than last time she'd been here?

She settled into the chair, studied his thin face. Mike's eyes flickered under the lids.

"Big news! Breeze is on the way home with Frank and old Bill. Seems that Director Edgewater raided the Tappan ranch. Bad news. Pam's been shot. She's in the hospital in Hot Springs."

Mike showed no reaction.

"So, there it is. You and Pam. Both healing from gunshot wounds." Lauren rocked her jaw. "On her way out of town, Breeze called me 'Little sister'. Remember? Back when she and Jimmy were going to get married? That was the joke we shared."

Mike's throat made a clicking sound.

"Thought you'd like hearing that. Also, here's the thing: We can go. You and me. Breeze said that they had room for the two of us at the ranch."

She leaned forward, taking his hand. "So, old friend of mine, I need you to get this heart of yours back to normal, so we can beat feet and get the hell out of Cheyenne."

Mike's hand remained limp in hers, and she thought it was a little too chilly.

"As for me, I've been working," she announced simply, preferring not to reveal that the nurse had ordered her to stay away for a few days. "Had a hot time of it out at Alpha Alpha. Don't know what possessed them to hit the OP that hard. They had explosives. Blew up a Humvee, killed some good people."

She frowned down at his hand. "Guess we'll never know what they were after. None of us were in what you'd call a forgiving mood afterward. Wasn't anyone left alive to interrogate."

Looking at his face, she wasn't sure, but thought that they'd been in to shave him. The beard wasn't even five-o'clock shadow.

"You clean up pretty good," she said with a smile. "If you'd get your lazy butt out of this bed, I'd take you for buffalo steaks at The Plains. Looks like I'm going to have more time to come visit."

She didn't have the strength to tell him about the yellow tent. "I'm off The Line. Ragnovich relieved me of duty. Told me to get out of town for a month. I...I think I might do that."

Part of her wanted to unfeel the things she felt for him. She kept telling herself that when Tyrell came back, none of this would matter...

Except that it did.

She looked away, out the window to where the waving grass seemed to roll on forever to the east. Thunderheads drifted across the blue-hazed sky, trailing streamers of rain beneath them.

Two nurses stopped in the corridor outside the door, speaking softly to one another while they studied what looked like a vial of blood.

Ravens squawked, and Lauren saw the black birds flap past the window with their wings shining in the sunlight. They looked fat and sleek. It sent an unexpected chill through her.

Rising, she walked to the door, asking, "Excuse me. But could you give me an update on Mike Vinich. I mean, I've been holding his hand. He's sort of... Well, not responding."

The older nurse shot Lauren an appraising glance. "Sorry, but you are?"

"Lauren Davis. Mike and I—"

"Ah, yes. From Buffalo Camp where Mike was wounded." The nurse looked past her at Mike where he lay more like a log than a man. "Ms. Davis, for the time being, Mr. Vinich is in a chemically induced coma."

"Excuse me?"

"We're trying to lower the stress on his heart. See if it will strengthen on its own."

"Coma?" she whispered, sinking back against the door frame.

The younger nurse said, "Ms. Davis, this is a last resort. The guy's a hero, you know?"

But Lauren didn't hear the rest. The room seemed to sway, and she was falling. Like the entire world was dropping away into a gray haze.

CHAPTER FIFTY

***

A DAZED FEELING KEPT SPINNING THROUGH LAUREN'S HEAD AS SHE TOSSED HER BOOGIE bag into the corner of the booth in The Plains' bar. Perhaps half the tables and booths were occupied. Most with men and women wearing uniforms.

Mike's in a medically induced coma?

What the hell? His heart should have been healing. What was it? More than a month since he'd been wounded at Buffalo Camp?

But then, these days the doctors didn't have the medicines they'd been used to using: anticoagulants, antiplatelet agents, ACE inhibitors, angiotensin blockers, Beta blockers, calcium channel blockers, diuretics. All of it the miracle of a vanished world. There were no more. Would never be.

The hard, sobering fact was that had Mike not been a Guard hero, they probably wouldn't still be wasting a room on him.

Lauren signaled Lucy for a beer and pursed her lips, staring emptily at her M4 where she had laid it on the wooden table top. Mike still had a chance. By lowering the strain on his heart, it might be able to recover. But how was he going to eat? Drink? She hadn't seen an IV bag.

A cold shiver ran through her as she faced the reality: Mike really might die.

And then what? What did that mean for her? He was her best male friend. Someone she'd loved enough to have slept with. And had hoped...hoped...

What, Lauren?

God, she felt so confused. Adrift. Like a bit of flotsam washed back and forth by the waves. She'd been so distracted by the needs of The Line that she'd never taken the time to think about herself. About where she was going, what she'd do if she weren't putting her butt out to get shot at all the time.

So, what does Mike mean to you? And why?

She ran her fingers over the M4. Tyrell's M4. She glanced at his boogie bag. Thought about the KTM chained to the light pole outside.

If she loved the guy enough to have said she'd marry him, why the hell had she been thinking so much about a future with Mike? Like there was some sort of disconnect. She was back in Cheyenne. As if that old life and its patterns had reestablished themselves.

Tyrell Ramirez was from the world she'd known in Colorado Springs. Like he'd ceased to be part of her plans the moment she'd left the Springs behind. Part of a now-dead world.

Using anxious fingers, she rubbed her forehead. Trying to put it all into perspective. What if Tyrell walked through that door, strode in and swept her up in his arms? Gave her that mocking and charming smile, his black eyes twinkling.

What if you're not dead, Ty?

In her subconscious, she'd come to believe he was. In her own way she'd mourned him and needed to move on.

"Hey? Lauren? How you doing?" The words caught her by surprise.

Lauren glanced up to see Lieutenant Virginia Barrow. The tall woman looked like she'd just come off duty at the FOB.

"I just learned that Mike Vinich is in a chemically induced coma. You?"

Barrow indicated at the seat across from Lauren, arching an inquisitive eyebrow.

"Yeah, sit," Lauren told her. "Beer's on me. By now you've heard that Ragnovich canned my ass, so let's lift one in celebration of my inglorious departure."

Barrow slid in opposite her, shoved the M4 off to the side, and laced her fingers together on the table. "Audra Barkley had her bike shot out from under her today just north of OP Charlie Hotel. Bullet hit the motor in front of her leg, another went through her saddle bags and took out a shock absorber. Miracle was that she could limp the bike back to the OP. Guess she's got a bad burn on her leg from the hot oil the engine was blowing out."

"Shit."

Barrow was giving her that hard-eyed stare. "Gasoline production is up at the refinery. We're going to start using Militia trucks to run supplies out to the OPs. They're just about as fast as the bikes, and when someone takes a pot shot, they can shoot back, drop skirmishers off, and hunt the motherfuckers down."

"I see." Lauren stared down at her beer while Barrow asked Lucy for one of the local IPAs. Word was that the IBUs were going to drop as the supply of hops ran out. Something else that was on the growing list of "remember whens". At least hops could be grown.

Unlike heart meds.

"So," Barrow asked, "you going to take some time and decompress?"

"Do I have a choice?" Lauren ran fingers down her glass. "If you could have a word with the captain. Maybe tell him—"

"Not a chance, Davis. I'm on his side in all this." Barrow's gaze had hardened. "You did your share. Only way I'll take your side is if you enlist. Otherwise, you're wired too tight. When that happens, you're just as likely to get someone killed as you're likely to die yourself."

"So, what the hell am I supposed to do with myself? Take up some bullshit like knitting?"

Barrow chuckled and leaned back as Lucy set her beer before her. "I heard that Breeze went back to her ranch."

Lauren saw the Militia officer as he hurried in from the street. The guy had a neatly trimmed beard, was dressed in canvas jacket, Carhartts, and work boots. The Militia patch on his shoulder proclaimed him a corporal.

The young militiaman spotted Barrow—a sudden look of relief on his face. Hurrying up to the table, he remembered to pull the Stetson off his head. "Sorry to disturb you, Lieutenant."

"That's all right, um, Corporal...?" Barrow replied, looking up.

"Gastrop, ma'am. Bill Gastrop. Um, from over at Elk Mountain. Company A, Border Battalion, Third Quadrant." He remembered then to salute.

"What can we do for you?" Barrow was looking amused.

Hesitantly, he said, "Got a flash traffic alert. Captain asked me to find you. We just heard that the checkpoint down on Highway 287 at The Forks was overrun. Some kind of military armored vehicles." He squinted. "JTV something? That sound right to you? Anyway, it's an armored truck. Two of them, if the reports are right. Used heavy machine guns to blast their way through the checkpoint at The Forks on highway 287. And they had a bunch of regular pickups behind them."

"JLTVs?" Barrow asked, stiffening.

"Yeah! That's them. Two JLTVs. What the hell are they, anyway?"

"Stands for Joint Light Tactical Vehicles. Replaced the MRAPs. They're like heavily armored trucks. Shit! And you say two of them?"

"Yeah, and I guess that our defensive fire didn't even faze them. Made a chowder out of the checkpoint." The corporal scuffed his boots, aware that the entire bar had gone zombie quiet. Every uniform in the place straining to hear.

"Thirty millimeter chain guns, or Ma Deuce?" Barrow asked.

"Hell, I don't know. Just that they blew through the checkpoint and headed off to Laramie. Last I heard, they were passing the cement plant south of town. That's when I was sent after you. Captain Ragnovich wants you at the FOB, as he said, 'Fucking fast.'"

The corporal barely had time to get out of Barrow's way. She left a run, barreling through the tables. Most of the other Guard and Militia were hot on her tail.

Lauren's world tilted.

Breathe.

Each finger froze, clutching her knees, hooking her jeans in holds that she knew would crumble. It's a full press raid on Laramie!

"You know Trevor Phillips?" Lauren asked, getting to her feet.

"Sure. He's with a unit down on The Line. Hell, he's probably in the thick of this thing."

"How you getting there?"

The corporal shrugged. "Got an old beet truck waiting. We're headed that way now. Reinforcements. 'Cause, if they're hitting Laramie like this, it's gonna be bad."

The serpent loops in Lauren's soul begin to coil into a painful knot. Colors drain from the room. Fading. Until all that remains are shades of gray. Some light. Some dark. Somewhere in the last hour, she has lost the ability to feel rage or terror. She focuses on the corporal's hat, flipping nervously in one hand.

"Gotta go now. Militia truck's waiting. Got any message for Trevor?"

Clarity. Crystalline. Like the inside of a diamond glitters to life inside her.

"I'm going with you." She is on her feet, has the boogie bag by its strap. The M4 on its sling.

Without even realizing it, she's marched past the corporal and out into the afternoon that burns crimson in the smoke-hazed sky, where the air shimmers with splinters of light.

CHAPTER FIFTY-ONE

★★★

THE MILITIA TRUCK DROVE INTO LARAMIE A LITTLE BEFORE SIX THAT AFTERNOON. FROM where Lauren rode in the back with twelve other young Militia men and women, it was like a ride into an armed camp. Roadblocks consisting of cement and dump trucks were set up on the I-80 exits.

Despite the Militia emblem and Wyoming state flag flying from the left front fender, the big Ford beet truck was waved to a stop at the Highway 287 checkpoint.

Leveled rifles were pointed their way as a bearded guy in his forties stepped warily out, calling, "State your rank and business!"

"Corporal Gastrop!" The militia man leaned out the passenger window. "Francis Monaghini, you know better. What's happening? All I get on the radio is conflicting information."

"Bad shit, Cal. These guys hit us hard. You heard about The Forks?"

"Something, yeah. Some kind of army armored vehicles shot the hell out of us and headed north."

Jim Dowdy, a young guy in Wranglers and Scully shirt demanded, "What's with all the fires downtown?" He pointed to the three big plumes of black smoke rising from the center of town."

"Raiders did that." Monaghini's expression soured. "You might say things got a little Western. Quite a fight. We'd have stopped them cold but for them damned armored trucks. Lot of people dead, boy. More wounded. And a couple of the raiders are swinging from ropes out at the lumber yard."

"So, you got them cornered?" Gastrop asked.

"Hell, no. Sons of bitches tried to break back south when it all went to pieces. By then we'd blocked the south-bound with cement mixers, and not even the military armor could get by. So they managed to shoot their way through the checkpoint on 130, headed out Snowy Range Road. Half the Guard and most of the Militia are on their tail."

"Then, that's where we're headed," Gastrop told him. "Who the hell are these people?"

"Before they got strung up, one of the raiders talked. The JLTVs were 'liberated' from Fort Carson. The guys who took them were disaffected Colorado National Guard soldiers. They'd intimidated their way up the Front Range, taking what they wanted from outlying communities."

Monaghini shifted, pulled a can of Copenhagen from his back pocket, and shifting his rifle, took a pinch. "When they reached Wellington, of course, they heard about The Line. That the electricity was still on in Wyoming, that life was golden. People had full bellies, and gas, medicine, and drugs could be had."

Monaghini replaced his can. "So they put together a strike force. Figured that with the armored JLTVs up front, they could blast their way up 287, loot the pharmacies and hospital for their precious drugs and supplies, gas up, and be headed back south before the Militia could get its hick-stupid head out of its ass to respond."

"Guess that didn't work so well?"

Monaghini grinned with tobacco-spotted teeth. "History wasn't their strong point. Maybe they should have read up on the famous Northfield, Minnesota raid."

"What? Never heard of it," Gastrop replied.

Monaghini chuckled, looked off to the west. "Might want to look it up before you plan a raid on a Wyoming border town. Now, you take the Snowy Range Road. Last thing we've heard, they're still fleeing west. But somewhere out there, there's going to be one hell of a fight."

The Militia man paused. "Oh, and one last thing, Bill. They took hostages. Hit the elementary school. You know that summer program they put together for the kids? Well, the bastards scooped up a bunch of kids and some of the adults. Otherwise, we'd have shot the shit out of the pickups and SUVs."

"Snowy Range Road. Got it!" Gastrop called as the driver put the beet truck in gear and accelerated past the hard-eyed men and women watching from the dump truck bed.

As they did, all eyes were on the big fires that burned in the center of the historic downtown area.

"If those sons of bitches set fire to either the Elkhorn or Cowboy Bars," Jim Dowdy, the twenty-three-year-old from Tie Siding, said with slitted eyes, "I'm going to shoot each one of those mother fuckers."

"They took little kids?" Janeen Baker asked. "If one of them is my niece Becky, I'll make them wish they'd never been born."

The old beet truck growled its way to the Wyo 130 exit, took the ramp to the bottom, where they were waved past a roadblock, and west past the truck stop and restaurant.

Climbing partway up the rack, Lauren leaned over the cab, calling, "Where are we going?"

Corporal Gastrop called up from the open cab window. "Just came in over the radio. Kind of a running gunfight all the way out to Albany. Then the raiders forted up in a valley somewhere in the forest. Took over a ranch."

"So, they're trapped?"

"Complicated," Gastrop shouted over the whine of the truck. "They've got hostages. Those little kids from the elementary school."

Lauren grabbed for a hold as the beet truck downshifted, howling louder, and took the Highway 130 exit way faster than it should.

"What kind of sons of bitches take little kids hostage?" Dowdy asked warily as the truck shifted into high, roaring its way west past the last of the houses and into open grasslands. "I'm gonna kill the fuckers twice!"

Lauren ducked down, out of the wind, staring at the rest of her associates. These were all Militia. Mostly men and women in their late teens to early thirties. They'd been working in food service, hospitality, construction, sales, plumbing, HVAC, and, well...you name it. When the collapse shut down the economy, the Militia was not only something to do, it offered a paycheck at the end of the week and three meals a day.

The weapons they carried were as varied as they were. Lots of AR variants, of course. A couple of Mini-14s, an assortment of bolt-action hunting rifles, and even a smattering of lever-actions. The only thing that identified them as Militia were the arm patches of varying quality and size. The only uniform article of apparel seemed to be heavy Vibram-soled boots, but each was dressed for the outdoors. Heavy pants, long-sleeved shirts, hats varying from ballcaps, to western, to boonie, and even a porkpie worn by a petite blonde from Wheatland. Go figure.

The most uncomfortable part of the trip for Lauren continued to be the awe in which they held her. As if she were some sort of oracle of war descended from Olympus to grace their mission. It was in the way they looked at her, the almost worship in their eyes. How they shut up the second she spoke, as if in fear of disrespect or that they were treading on insubordination.

Damn it, half of them were older, meaner, and tougher than she was. And a hell of a lot more experienced, given their time in the Fourth Quadrant.

The truck was waved on west again at the airport, the old Ford 550 back to howling down the road at a full-out sixty-five.

This was the Laramie Basin, where, at over seven-thousand feet, the high Upper Sonoran environment edged into Montane. Flats of greasewood gave way to rabbitbrush and sage in the uplands; the low valleys were filled with lush wide grasslands fed by tightly meandering loops of the Little Laramie River. The ranches here were dotted with fat black cattle wading in hock-high meadows.

The sun was a burning red ball by the time they turned off on County 11 and bounced their way south to Albany. As they rolled through the little community, the sun had sunk below the forested bulk of Muddy Mountain. The sky overhead, burned in an evil crimson, as if it were Judgment Day.

With the climb in elevation and the coming darkness, the temperature was dropping. Lauren dug into her boogie bag for her Ralley jacket as the five-ton truck bounced over the potholed forest service road. The smell of conifers, grass, and water seemed to intensify with the night.

At last, the truck pulled up at a final checkpoint, hailed by a Guard soldier. "Who comes?"

"Militia. Border Battalion, Cheyenne. I'm Corporal Gastrop. Company A. And in the back is Lauren Davis. She's come from the Fourth Quadrant to lend a hand."

Where Lauren stood in the bed, she winced. Ground her teeth. *Give it a rest, Corporal. It's not like I fucking walk on water.*

The Guard soldier raised his flash to illuminate her, saying, "Hey,

Lauren. Catch any Chinese pilots lately?"

"Lewis?" She called. "That you? Last time I saw you, we were eating supper at OP Delta Alpha."

"Yeah. You heard what happened three days after?"

"Heard you guys got the shit shot out of you. That Hughes was killed. What's up?"

"They're planning the attack," Lewis said as the rack was lifted in the back. "Hop on down from there. I'll take you to the big wigs."

"Hey, I'm just here—"

"Lauren," Lewis told her. "It's already the talk of the Guard. Best you hear it from me. You know Trevor Phillips? You know his fiancée?"

Lauren's heart skipped, turned crystalline, as if she were in a bottle, hearing through the thick glass.

"Tiffany?" her voice asked from across an incredible distance.

"The raiders took her," Lewis said as the rest of her Militia companions crowded around. "Raided the school she was working at. Grabbed up a bunch of kids, Tiffany, and couple of teachers. Got them down in a barn at the ranch. Said we have to give them ammo and fuel for the JLTVs and trucks and let them have safe passage back down south of The Line. That they've got nothing to lose. To prove it, they killed the two teachers. Left their bodies in the road. We've got 'til dawn, then they're killing everyone."

CHAPTER FIFTY-TWO

***

THE NIGHT WAS UNEARTHLY BLACK AND FILLED WITH THE SWEET FRAGRANCE OF CONIFERS.

Lauren drew it into her lungs as she walked toward her assigned horse. They'd trucked the animals in from one of the dude ranches down on the Laramie River. The idea was that on horses, Lauren's party could circle around by following the ridgetop, and then filter down through the trees. The outfitter who'd supplied the animals, assured the Militia that this particular string were used for elk hunting, that they were used to rifles and working in timber.

His name was Book: a black and white gelding who was in the process of eating hay. The big horse jerked his head up to eye Lauren severely as she got closer. Book had a reputation for being fractious on the trail, so they'd assigned Lauren to him. Trevor had said that she used to rodeo. Either Trevor didn't know how bad she'd been, or he forgot to relay that fact.

Book was already saddled, one of the outfitters standing by in case she needed anything.

As she got closer, she softly said, "Whoa, boy. Everything's all right."

Lauren ran her hand down his neck and rubbed behind the halter. Book watched her suspiciously from the corner of his eye.

Using the saddle strings, she tied her M4 onto the skirts and checked the cinches, making sure they were tight. She adjusted the stirrups before sorting through her boogie bag for the gear she'd need, and loaded her pack with the AN/PSQ-20 night vision goggles, an IFAK medical kit, extra magazines for the M4—and, at the last instant—stuffed her two grenades into her coat pockets.

As the men around her saw to their own horses, she looked around.

On the forested mountain slopes, tall lodgepole pines stood silhouetted against the few stars and gibbous moon that tried to penetrate the haze.

The ridge where the Militia had set up camp overlooked the Marsy ranch where it nestled in the valley below. They could see no lights, not even a campfire gleaming. The dark pole barn was little more than a shadow in the faint moonlight that made it through the smoky haze.

As Lauren put her foot in the stirrup and swung up into the saddle, she heard one of the militiamen rack a shell into the chamber of his shotgun. He came forward in a wary walk, as if feeling his way. His eyes focused, laser-like, on Lauren. Book took one look at the gun in his hands, whickered and sidestepped. Lauren reined him back around.

"Trevor? That you?"

His rectangular eyeglasses reflected the gleam of the quarter moon. "Lauren? You got any last suggestions?"

Book glared at the shotgun and anxiously mouthed his bit. The horse kept tossing his head, eager to be away from the gun and on the trail. Book could probably feel the tension in the air, too. All the horses on this ridge top were fidgeting and stamping.

Lauren stroked the horse's muscular neck, trying to get him to settle down. "No, sounds like a good plan. Where do you want me?"

He frowned up at her. "You've got night vision. Captain Manford wants you up there in the lead with him."

"Got it."

Lauren walked Book up alongside the grizzled leader, Steve Manford. Grey-headed and hard-eyed, the man looked her over carefully. He wore a navy-blue down coat.

"Glad to have you here, Davis," he said. "Seeing you out front gives my people hope. But follow orders, all right? I don't need anyone going off half-cocked, trying to be a hero."

"I'm no damned hero, sir. Just tell me what to do."

"Awright, then." He lifted a hand to the thirty other riders, waved them forward, and when they circled him, he said, "Listen up! We're going to take it slow. We're more than ten thousand feet above sea level here. Nobody with sense pushes themselves or their horses in the high country. Not unless they're idiots. Hurrying is a fast way to get yourself killed. Am I clear?"

Nods and calls went around.

"Okay, let's go free those kids."

Manford walked his horse for the elk trail where it snaked across the slope through the pines and firs.

As they entered the trees, the smell of the evergreens was stronger, the sounds louder: metal clinked; shod hooves clacked on rocks; horses snuffled. Quiet night like this? They couldn't have missed it down in the valley.

In the pale moonlight, every pine needle shone as though it had been dipped in liquid silver. The heart-stopping vistas of angular basalt peaks, dramatic valleys dropping away into stunning depths, and remnants of glaciers in their high cirques, were stunning. Lauren had forgotten the adrenaline buzz of riding on horseback along some of the most beautiful and perilous trails in the Rockies.

That peculiar sense of clarity fell over her again when they broke out of the trees and started across the talus slope.

"Are you crazy?" one of the men called. "We're riding across all this loose rock?"

The broken and cracked slope shimmered in the moonlight, and the trail led straight across it like a thin gray line.

"Trust your horses," Manford called. "You may not be able to see, but they can. Just relax and don't do anything stupid."

Lauren glanced back, seeing a gap between the last horse and the trees. Trevor rode in the rear.

She found a macabre amusement in the curses that laced the air every time a horse slipped and had to right itself. They were heading across miles of mountainous wilderness to try to tangle with a private army; what was a talus slope compared to that?

When they were past the talus, they followed game trails that cut west along the base of the high peak and skirted a meadow before dropping into the black timber. With no sign of human hand, Lauren could well have believed that she was the first human to pass this way.

Keeping busy, minding her horse, and enduring the labor of walking Book up and down steep slopes, kept the flashbacks at bay.

Kept her from thinking of Mike Vinich, lying comatose in a hospital bed, each beat of his heart one step closer to either recovery or death.

She couldn't stop thinking about death. Hutch's, the people she'd shot down, the bodies along the road…a little girl in a yellow tent, clutching a filthy stuffed sheep.

It was as though she had moved everything that was precious outside her body. Everyone she loved. Even her own soul dangled high above in the star-filled sky, watching her ride across the extreme vastness of the mountains like something mechanical, moving, breathing, praying. But dead nonetheless. Memory was in exile. Had to be, or she couldn't bear to do what had to be done.

Three hours later, after a couple of dead-ends, Manford ordered them to take a break and eat something. Lauren took the opportunity to lead Book to a trickle of spring water and let him drink.

Trevor rode up beside her and stepped off his horse.

"We're not making very good time," Trevor said. Beneath his battered-looking cowboy hat, his blond hair shone in the starlight.

"No, we're not. At this rate, we're not going to get there until dawn, which means we won't have the cover of darkness."

"I know. Manford's on the radio. Calling a delay. The Militia is waiting on the road just over the divide. Those two platoons should be feeling their way down through the timber."

Trevor hesitated, led his horse closer to her. "Lauren, when the time comes, can you do something for me?"

She could hear the sympathy in his voice. Each word was like a bright shining blade cutting her apart.

"Such as?"

Trevor continued, "We're going to need someone to take care of the horses. I was thinking that you—"

"No."

"Oh, come on, Lauren. You—"

"Jeremiah's a good choice. He's barely fifteen."

Trevor shot back, "If we lose this fight, and you're captured, you're going to find yourself tied up in a horse stall being gang-raped. Do you understand that?" He gestured wildly in the direction of the pole barn where the person they both loved was being held, and Lauren suddenly understood his deepest fears.

That's what he thinks is happening to Tiffany.

Lauren narrowed her eyes. Trevor wore guilt like a contorted mask.

She said, "Tiffany would still be down there in that fucking hole, Trev, even if you'd been there when the raiders hit. The only difference is that you'd be dead right now, instead of riding down to save her."

Trevor heaved a breath that formed a white cloud in front of him. "All right. I did my best."

"Appreciate it."

He walked around his horse, put his foot in the stirrup, and swung into the saddle. Without another word, he reined his horse around and trotted back to the end of the line to take up his former position.

All she saw, when she looked up, was a few stars strangling in a blanket of smoke. It even seemed to pollute the half-choked moon.

CHAPTER FIFTY-THREE

***

IT WAS TOUGH GOING. NOT ONLY DID DEADFALL HAVE TO BE CUT WHERE IT BLOCKED THE path, some sections of trail had literally been washed away down the mountainside. In those places, finding footing for the horses wasn't easy. They were running way behind.

By the time they finally stopped to rest on a rocky ridge overlooking the Marsy Ranch, they were all exhausted and edgy. Hushed and anxious voices could be heard in the cold night air; tired horses stamped their feet.

Lauren dismounted on stiff and sore legs. Been too long since she been on horseback. With mincing steps she led Book to an exposed patch of grass. In the darkness, she tried to get her bearings.

This high point would be their last refuge. The old ranch house and outbuildings could barely be seen in the night-dark meadow. The structures appeared as squares at the edge of the trees. She could see pickups and SUVs parked in a ring like an old-time wagon train. The light colored trucks stood out in the feeble moon glow.

"All right, gather round. Let's talk," Manford said as he led his horse to the rim and looked down at the ranch. He picked up a stick, using it like a pointer. "Okay, here's the layout: The old ranch house is a frame structure. Probably two-by-four construction with one-inch plank. You should be able to shoot right through it. They've got the pickups and SUVs in a circle, so that's probably their fallback position. The JLTVs are those two honking big armored trucks up at the head of the valley. They're positioned to take out anything coming down the ranch road. We know from what they shot up already that they're fifty-caliber Brownings.

"Nothing we have is big enough to penetrate that armor, so if they head your way, run!"

"What about fuel. Heard that they're low on it."

"Hey, that's what they're demanding. Fuel for the trucks, food, and safe passage south to Jackson County and the Colorado line."

"What about ammo?" Lauren asked. "Even on The Line, we're running low on fifty caliber."

"Can't say. Those LTVs had to come up from either Fort Carson or Piñon Canyon. Who knows how much shooting they've had to do to get here? And they expended a lot of rounds getting out of town. The fact that they hit pharmacy after pharmacy in town took them longer than they'd planned. Had them using up ammo to keep us at bay."

"Yeah," Jillian Hanson muttered, "Good thing all the drugs and meds were relocated to the Sheriff's Office for security, huh? Every pharmacy in town was down to bare shelves. They got jack shit."

"They got Tiffany and the kids," Trevor said bitterly. "And killed a lot of good people."

Manford pointed his stick toward the little valley that cut the slope just to the west. "Phillips and Davis, I want you to follow that ravine down and scout ahead for the rest of us. It'll give you cover, and Davis' night vision should let you do it quietly. There's bound to be at least ten or twelve guards posted around the corrals, the horse paddock, and pole barn. A bunch of them are probably sleeping in the ramshackle ranch house, and maybe in the trucks. Expect that."

"Where will you be?" Lauren asked.

"We'll filter down through the trees, flank them, and come up the two-track from the hayfield on the east. We estimate there are around forty to fifty raiders down there. The guys in the JLTVs are military, so watch for traps along the trail. Maybe trip wires or who knows what? Take your time. You both have walkie talkies, but don't use them until you're ready to call me and tell me the lay of the land. Do not make a play for the kids in the pole barn until you hear back from me. Understand?"

"Yes, sir," Trevor called.

Manford continued, "In case of emergency, fire three shots. We'll know that something's gone really wrong and come running."

Lauren surveyed the ranch below. The paddock, corrals, pole barn, and a haystack stood just to the left of the mouth of the ravine. It would be the first thing they saw.

Her gaze moved across the meadow that sloped down toward the old ramshackle ranch house. Built in the early twentieth century, it was little more than a clapboard-sided bungalow with small windows. It didn't even look habitable, but they could still be in there.

After they rescued the kids, anyone standing at those dark windows, or around the ring of vehicles, would see them.

Have to lead the children back up the ravine into the forest.

"Awright, get started," Manford ordered. "We'll be waiting to hear from you."

Lauren nodded, donned her night vision goggles and led the way. Book, like all good horses, could sense the fear in the air. He kept working his bit and tossing his head.

In the goggles' eerie green light, she scanned the trees and enormous granite boulders that choked the ravine. Each shone whitely.

The familiar paralysis filtered through her muscles. It was probably some sort of "rigor", like the stiffness that possessed a dead body, or maybe it was just a cocktail of fear mixed with focus. *Shaken not stirred.*

Her body had already locked on target. Her breathing had slowed. She had a mild form of tunnel-vision. Despite Tyrell's state-of-the-art night vision, the size of the world narrowed to the sight-picture visible through a rifle scope. Nothing else would exist now.

As they descended in single file, the trees closed in around them and they were constantly ducking branches. The ravine ran with water. On either side, lodgepole pine and firs rose high over their heads, and gravel and twigs crunched under their horses' hooves.

They moved as slowly and quietly as they could, but their horses kept slipping on the debris. There were probably deer or elk hidden along the trail. Going slow allowed the animals to drift out of the way instead of sending them crashing away in a panic that would alert any sentry.

At a particularly steep section of the ravine, Trevor pulled back on his reins, and stopped to wait for Lauren.

As she worked Book down the incline, she listened, *really listened.* Great horned owls hooted across the mountains, accompanied by a distant chorus of coyotes. Down in the valley bottom, near the ranch, a stream burbled over rocks.

"I think it's time to walk," she told Trevor as the valley narrowed, exfoliated granite rising steeply on either side. The game trail they followed stopped at a fallen fir tree that effectively blocked the way.

"All right," Trevor whispered as he stepped off his horse.

Walking Book over to a tree, Lauren tied the lead rope to a limb, then watched Trevor tying off his horse. Like her, he'd secured not only the reins, but clipped the lead rope to the halter and double-knotted it. Lauren had a fleeting worry. Who'd free the horses if they were both killed?

Hell, Lauren, for all you know, there's a radioactive cloud headed your way and everything breathing will be dead in a week.

"Ready?" she asked.

"Let's roll."

CHAPTER FIFTY-FOUR

***

ONE NIGHT IN THE PLAINS BAR, BEFORE THE WHISKEY REALLY DEADENED LAUREN'S SENSES, a grizzled old Vietnam vet was pontificating at a nearby table. The subject he was expounding on to his fellows—all older Guard—was how the "kids" holding the OPs could keep doing what they were doing.

"Just like Nam," he said. "See, the thing about a nineteen-year-old kid is that you can ask them to do anything. And they'll just bulldog down and do it. Doesn't matter if it was going on patrol outside Dak To or climbing into a B-17 to go bomb Berlin in World War II. They just shut off that part of the brain that says they're going to die, and with the belief that they're immortal, they do what they gotta do."

Lauren wondered if he might have been describing Trevor and her that night as she led the way, her night vision turning the blackness into a green wonderland; she directed the stumbling, night-blind Trevor down along the drainage.

Holding his hand, she got him over deadfall, and hunched beneath low-hanging branches. She could hear Trevor breathing hard behind her, his boots raking gravel. Occasionally, the butt of his rifle struck a hidden rock and he cursed; he loved that Savage 110 Precision in 6.5mm Creedmoor.

When the ravine opened up, Lauren could see the circular arrangement of pickup trucks and SUVs between the paddock and ranch house; she waited for Trevor to ease up beside her.

"There's a guard perched on a roll bar of that truck on the far right," she whispered. "See him?"

"Not really. It's fucking dark, remember. You've got the night goggles. See any other people?"

"Four men off to the left in front of the old ranch house. Could be more inside the pickups though."

"Looks like a one hundred yard shot. Think we can we pick 'em off from here? Or should we crawl closer?"

"There's nothing between us and them. The instant we fire our first shot, we're going to be chowder." A pause. "And that's without the LTVs and their big fifties."

He frowned. "What do you suggest?"

"Crawl closer so we can make a better assessment."

Lauren cradled the M4 in her arms, stretched out on her belly, and combat-crawled down through the scruffy sagebrush to where she had a clear view of the ranch and the trucks. She didn't need the night vision to tell the eastern horizon was now a light gray.

Trevor inched up beside her and examined the line of pickups. "Don't think we're getting past that, Lauren. Wait. What the hell? Check that Toyota on the end. What's on that roll bar?"

She turned, studying the Tacoma's outline. A guy in the back, seated in a chair, had obscured the gun's outline. "Yeah, shit. Trevor, if I'm not mistaken, that's one of the new generation squad automatic weapons. Tyrell was gassing about it one night. Shoots the new 6.8 millimeter." She studied the gun's profile, considered how it was situated.

After all that time in the OPs, she understood what "field of fire" meant.

She told him. "It's on that end to provide covering fire against anyone trying to rush them from the east. And that's Manford and his riders."

"Yeah, and as light as it's getting, that machine gunner couldn't miss us. Can we make it back up the ravine and around the bend before he sees us and shoots us in the backs?"

"Maybe. Call Manford. Tell him the situation."

Trevor nodded, pulled his walkie talkie from his pocket, and in a whisper-voice said, "High Yankee, got a line of pickups covering our approach to the pole barn. One has a machine gun mounted on the roll bar. We can see four guys. Over."

Manford's tinny voice came back. "Almost there. Give us ten to get into position. Take out that machine gun, then make a play for the pole barn. Understood?"

"Roger that."

Take out the machine gun, huh? Just like that?

Trevor shoved the walkie talkie back into his pocket and edged closer to Lauren. "Think the two of us can shoot all four guys before one of 'em opens up with the SAW?"

"No."

She slipped a hand inside the front of her coat and pulled a grenade from the interior pocket; she handed it to Trevor. He wouldn't have been as wide-eyed if she'd dropped a rattlesnake in his hand.

The remaining grenade from Tyrell's boogie bag remained stuffed in her other coat pocket. "You were a baseball star in high school. You can throw farther than I can."

Trevor glanced at the grenade, then back at her. "Never thrown a hand grenade before."

"Well, we can't all live happily as virgins forever. Pin won't release until you squeeze the lever. Once you pull the pin and throw, the lever will snap out to light the fuse. After that, you've got three seconds."

He swallowed. "All right. What's the plan?"

"We're going to crawl down to within throwing range, then, when I give the word, you're going to lob the grenade into the bed of that Toyota. While the dust is clearing, I'll run for the pole barn and free Tiff and the kids."

She jabbed a finger into his chest. "You hightail it back to an elevated position and use that fancy long-distance Savage with its high-powered scope to cover us."

Trevor sucked in a breath. "The explosion is going to wake the dead. In a matter of seconds, every man sleeping in the ranch house or trucks is going to come boiling out. They'll be crawling all over us."

"Manford's troops should be here by then."

"I know, but what if—"

"You've been working the Third Quadrant for a while, Trev. You know how this works. Toss the grenade. Find a high spot and hunker down. Breathe. Aim. Fire. That's all you have to do."

He had his jaw clamped tight.

"Yeah. That's all," he said. "Except that Tiff is in that pole barn."

"Don't think about that. Make each shot count. Once Tiff and I lead the kids out, you're going to have to kill anyone coming after us. Let Manford and his people handle the rest."

"I will, Lauren." Sounded like he was making a promise to himself.

As she belly-crawled toward the corrals bordering the sheet-steel-sided pole barn, her nerves were on fire. She heard male voices, smelled cigarette smoke wafting on the pre-dawn air.

Trevor crawled to her right.

One of the men walked out from the line of pickups. She and Trevor froze. The guy stopped, unzipped his fly. As he let go with a stream of urine, he stared straight at them.

"Hey!" he yelled. "Who's there?"

"Trevor, now!"

Trevor leaped to his feet, rifle slapping on his back as he pulled the pin. Just like in the movies, he stepped forward. His right arm whipped the grenade high. It made a beautiful arc, tumbling through the air, and landed with a clang in the back of the Toyota's bed.

Lauren had a glimpse of the guy in the back of the pickup. He danced to one side as the hand grenade clattered around the bed. His eyes almost popped from disbelief.

Then she and Trevor both flattened out and threw their arms over their heads.

The explosion came like a lightning bolt, blasting bits of metal into the air, leaving her ears ringing.

She looked up to see the Toyota, still rocking on its suspension. The pickup was now a flat bed, the sidewalls peeled away. The SAW was missing from the roll bar. The gunner's body was bleeding where it had been tossed onto the hood.

The guy who was taking a leak had been thrown face-forward onto the grass and wasn't moving.

"Cover me!" she ordered.

Lauren was on her feet, running hard. She vaulted the heap of broken debris that had been the Toyota's tailgate, and pounded for the corrals. Charged through an open gate and rounded the front of the pole barn. Two men dashed around the haystack with rifles in hand. A rifle shot popped; the *ka-pok* of a bullet hitting flesh was simultaneous. One man fell. The other turned and ran.

Good work, Trevor.

A big man wearing filthy chinos and a T-shirt proclaiming MICHIGAN STATE burst from the pole barn's side door. He had a pistol in his right hand.

No more than ten feet away, Lauren shouldered the M4. Cheek pressed against the gun, looking through the red dot, she was eye-to-eye with evil. Deep ragged breath. Squeeze the trigger, don't jerk it.

Her three-round burst took the guy full in the chest just as he was turning to run.

Ragdoll. Arms flailing, he hit the ground.

Lauren launched herself forward again, running for the open side door. She glimpsed someone in the trees next to the horse paddock. Saw a rifle glint.

Shouts rang out, and men poured out of the dark ranch house with weapons in their hands.

The walkie talkie on her belt crackled. "...*coming up from the drainage north of the main house.*"

Trevor responded, "*I see you.*"

The pole barn was a long rectangular building with a silver-tin roof. The big garage door in front was closed. In the faint orange-red reflections of morning light, it looked like it had been washed in blood. Pray that was just an illusion.

At the door, Lauren paused, screamed, "Tiffany?"

When she charged in, she barely had time to catalog what she saw. Illuminated by a glowing Coleman lantern, the barn had a pressed-steel ceiling; big sun-faded Massey-Ferguson tractor with star-patterned glass in the cab; work bench with tools on the far side; large half-ton square bales of hay stacked three high. And in the rear...

Her attention went to the man who leaned out from behind one of the large square bales, a pistol pointed her way.

The bang was accompanied by the pistol rocking back in the man's hand. The bullet cut air beside Lauren's left ear.

The M4's report deafened in the confines of the building.

The gunman dropped like he'd been poleaxed. Lauren cried out, "Tiffany? Tiffany Bishop, are you here?"

There was an agonizing pause, then, "Back here! We're back here in the feed room!"

In the shadowed back Lauren could make out the poured concrete room. A metal door was blocked by a crate. Such rooms were often found in barns. Rodent-proof, they provided dry and safe storage for sacks of cake, pellets, and grain.

Lauren raced to the crate, threw her weight against it, and wrestled it away from the door.

Outside, horses thundered across the ground, accompanied by the staccatos of automatic weapons firing and the slower cracking of high-velocity rifle shots. Men screamed and shouted.

A fifty-caliber machine gun chattered, and she prayed it was covering the ranch road in. If not, this was going south in a hurry.

Manford's voice crackled on her belt: "...*My God, there's more of them! See 'em fogging up out of the creek drainage?*"

"*Roger that. Looks like another twenty or so.*"

Tiffany screamed, "In here! We're locked in here, Lauren!"

"Please," a little girl called, "help us!"

"Help us!" It was a chorus of many childish voices now.

The door to the feed room was old and gray, spotted with rust on the bottom from years of neglect. Fists pounded the metal.

Lauren grabbed the knob, twisted, and flung the door wide. Illuminated by the lantern's light, the terrified filthy faces of twenty or more children stared back. They'd been packed in, crammed together in the small space. It now reeked of urine, of mold, and human fear.

A desperate crowd of children—some no older than four or five—lunged forward, pushing their way past as they headed for the way out.

"Wait! *They'll kill you!* Stay inside!"

Last out of the feed room was Tiffany. With tears streaming down her face, she grabbed Lauren in a hard hug and said, "Thank God you came for us! I don't know what—"

"Later, Tiff." Lauren shoved her best friend back and took her hand in a wrenching grip. "Listen to me! Trevor is out there. He'll cover you as you run for the ravine to the west. You have to lead the kids up the ravine to the ridge top."

"But, Lauren, they're weak—"

"Do it! There are men dying out there! Move!"

Tiffany turned and more stumbled than ran for the side door. At sight of the dead man, she uttered a wavering moan. Backed into the tractor tire, then she fled to where the kids huddled, crying against the barn wall. They were afraid to step outside into the growing daylight and popping gunfire. A horse screamed in agony as another fusillade of shots broke out.

Tiffany shouted, "Come on. We're going to run. Just follow me, okay?"

Lauren—watching from the rear—saw most of the children gather around Tiffany, but two or three shrank back against the hay bales, sobbing, too terrified to move.

"Goddamn it! Go!" Lauren bellowed. "Keep running, or they'll kill you!"

Tiffany shoved the door wide and ran. All but two of the children charged after her, a boy and a girl. Maybe seven or eight. Brother and sister? Shrieking, faces contorted and tear-drenched, they huddled down behind a hay bale.

Through the door, Lauren glimpsed muzzle flashes, horses rearing and charging past, men on the ground, reaching out for help.

She lunged for the kids. "Come on! We have to get out of here."

She grabbed the little boy's collar and tried to pull him to his feet, but he fought her, yelling, "No! No! Leave us alone!"

As she jerked him to his feet, his bladder let loose. Screaming his fear, urine soaked his pants. The smell of it rose in the musty air.

The little girl broke and ran back for the safety of the feed room.

When a bullet pocked through the wall, tore past Lauren's ear, and cracked into the tractor's engine block, Lauren dove for the floor. As the side door swung slowly closed, her last glimpse was of Tiffany leading her herd of children away. Trevor's rifle kept banging, dropping anyone who chased after them.

Staying low, Lauren crept to the door and pushed it open a crack. Down at the main house, it sounded like D-Day. Men hunched behind the cover provided by the pickups. They kept popping up to shoot at the Militia.

"*Lauren, what are you doing?*" Trevor's voice sounded on her radio. Almost drowned out by the staccato of rifle fire. "*Come on! Come on!*"

She heard the *pock* as a bullet blasted through the door just over her head.

Manford's voice crackled over the walkie talkie: "*Time to get the hell out of here. LTVs are coming down the road. Move it!*"

More bullets pattered on the steel siding. Knocking out holes and rattling around the barn, the sound reminded her of hail on tin.

Lauren scrambled over and threw herself on top of the sobbing boy, protecting him as best she could. "Stay down!"

The unmistakable rhythmic banging of the LTV-mounted big fifty rose over the melee.

Manford: *"We're out-gunned! Everyone! Get out any way you can!"*

Trevor yelled again, *"Come on, Lauren! Lauren!"*

She jumped to her feet, grabbed the little boy by the coat sleeve and dragged him up, then…

The explosion sucked the air from the room and shook the walls like an earthquake. Through the rents in the big shop door, Lauren saw the huge ball of fire engulf the old ranch house. Sprays of glass shot from every window like bursts of diamonds. The force flattened everything in range. Chunks of wreckage, pieces of house and truck, cartwheeled across the yard and into the closest pickups, pounding them like hurled rocks. Debris hammered and banged on the sheet steel siding and roof to leave the paneling dented and pocked.

"Mommie! I want Ma-Ma," the boy shrieked.

Hooves pounded outside.

"Horses headed our way. We have to…"

To her surprise, someone outside hoisted the big barn door up. As it opened high enough, seven riders thundered inside, crowding their horses between the tractor and workbench. When they headed her way, caused Lauren to sweep the kid up and leap onto one of the big hay bales. Manford was in the lead, carrying a wounded man over his saddle.

"Get those doors closed!" he ordered.

The man on the door threw his weight against it. The door came crashing down accompanied by a barrage of flying bullets; the fellow, jerked, fell limply outside. The heavy steel slammed shut with finality.

Manford handed his reins to the rider crammed in beside him. The horses were wedged in around the tractor's tires, stomping and blowing in their panic. "Get the wounded off these saddles, then secure the horses. Put 'em in the back where they'll be safe."

"Yes, sir."

Three men dismounted and tried to maneuver the wounded between the panicked horses; the others struggled to lead the horses to the stalls in the rear of the barn.

In the brief lull outside, a man shouted, "She took the kids up that ravine. Go get 'em!"

Lauren got a good look at Manford's wild eyes. Sweat beaded on his face, trickled down his neck. One sleeve was soaked with blood. Whether it was his or the wounded man's he'd saved, she could not tell.

"What happened?"

"Got cut off," Manford said. "Those damn machine guns."

He turned and ordered, "I said, get these horses back. Pile those hay bales in front of the doors! Right now! Maybe we can hold them off for a few hours."

Really? Lauren thought. A few hours? With those big fifties out there on the LTVs?

But then everyone loved an optimist.

CHAPTER FIFTY-FIVE

***

8 PM

MOANS CAME FROM THE WOUNDED MEN BACK IN THE FEED ROOM. THE AIR LAY HEAVY WITH the scents of hot horse manure and urine, burned gunpowder, stale sweat, and fresh blood mixed with the sweet smell from the hay bales.

Lauren crawled forward, maneuvered between the stacked hay. On her belly, she peered through a grapefruit-sized rip in the bottom of the big shop door. Her hair dangled around her face in filthy strands. Leveling her M4, she aimed at the shadowed shape that foolishly moved between the remaining pickups.

Most were damaged now, either from Trevor's grenade, bullet strikes, or the explosion that had taken out the ranch house and tossed the closest trucks as if they'd been toys.

Just one more good shot.

Red dot on target, hold, pull slow and easy on the trigger, weather the kick.

At her M4's report, the black shadow spun and hit the ground. Shouts of anger came from behind the wrecked trucks. Three bullets slammed the bullet-riddled steel door over her head. Lauren scuttled backward into the hay bales.

"You get him?" Manford called.

"Got him."

Lauren realized the M4's slide was locked back. She had fired her last bullet. Damn it! When had she lost count? Checked her magazine?

She tried pulling herself up by grabbing hold of the stacked hay bales to her left. Gave it up. Screw it. Her strength was gone, muscles too weak to hold her. So she settled back to the floor to wait. The sweet scent of baled hay surrounded her.

"Can't stand it," a man softly groaned.

His friend whispered, "Won't be long now, Joe. They're coming."

Off and on throughout the long day, they'd heard distant firing. They'd watched through the bullet holes as the LTVs had roared across the yard, heading for the shooting. Militia were still out in the trees, infiltrating close enough to take a shot or two. Then the raiders would regroup, firing back.

God bless the Militia.

Somewhere behind Lauren, a child cried. Probably the girl. It was high-pitched. A man shushed her, spoke gently, and the crying dropped to a whimper.

If only she'd made it outside…

Out in the open, she could have died looking at the snow-capped mountains, smelling the pines. In exchange for two children—who were going to die anyway—she had gotten a lot of men killed.

Her fault. All her fault.

If the Militia hadn't been waiting for her, they'd have been long gone, riding like hell for the high country. Instead—surrounded and outnumbered—the last of the Militiamen had taken refuge in the barn. Become hostages themselves.

It was the only explanation. The fifty-caliber Brownings could have riddled the barn, chewed through the concrete walls, and blasted the tractor into scrap and ricocheting hot metal.

People shifted in the pitch blackness, moaning and panting as though they'd just run marathons. Unhappy horses snuffled, stamped, and pawed at the concrete floor. Most of the sounds came from far back in the feed room where the wounded had been taken. Three women and seven men, four of them wounded, one of them a fourteen-year-old on his first Militia ride—that's how many they had to defend the barn.

Someone in the darkness whispered, "Davis? What did you see out there?"

Lauren didn't recognize the voice. She didn't know most of the people here. But they knew her. Even in the Third Quadrant west of Laramie. Larger than life. Fearless. False. All a masquerade, and she couldn't remove the mask. Not here. Not now.

"Well," she said as she wiggled her way under the tractor and squinted one eye to look through a bullet hole in the door. "Most of the wreckage from the ranch house explosion has burned out. Means we can't see them coming anymore."

"What about the JLTVs?" a man called. "They still got a fifty-cal aimed at us?"

"Yep." The question was ludicrous, of course, but everyone longed for deliverance.

"'Course, they do, you idiot," someone responded. "Think they all went home?"

"Hold on. Something's happening." Lauren concentrated on the sound. "Truck's coming. The second JLTV."

Lauren pressed her eye to the bullet hole, watching the armored truck roll into the ranch yard, circle the burned-down ranch house, and pull up next to the first. The men who climbed out wore fatigues and had military swaggers. She tilted her head, clapping her ear to the bullet hole.

"...the last of the M2 ball. Leaves us ten rounds per gun. So don't..." and then the voice was too faint.

She said, "These guys are from the LTVs. Wearing ACUs. They're down to ten rounds per gun on the Brownings."

"You sure?" Manford asked.

"That's what I just overheard."

"Where'd they come from?" someone in back asked.

Manford sounded weary. "Maybe a rogue unit from Fort Carson? Piñon Canyon? Or maybe a bunch of civilians that raided a military warehouse and like the feel of clean fatigues."

"Goddamn traitors," a man cursed.

Lauren exhaled a slow breath and let her gaze rove beyond them to the blood-red heavens. Would the skies ever be blue and crystal clear again? Or had world-wide war filled them with so much haze, smoke, dust, and pollution that it would choke the earth to death. Out in the trees, the shadows of riderless horses drifted through the darkness. Magical creatures slipping along the high wire between life and death.

Sporadic gunfire erupted up in the timber, echoing through the narrow valley, and seemed to come from every direction at once. The Militia, the men and women who'd escaped, still fighting.

Had to be sobering for the raiders. Half of their trucks destroyed, low on ammo, and a ring of pissed off Wyoming Militia creeping down through the trees with scoped high-power rifles looking to pick off raiders one by one.

But for them, the raiders could have peeled Manford's small force out of the pole barn any time they wanted. But with the coming of full dark, hidden marksmen with twenty-power scopes would be blind. Unable to pick their targets.

Lauren pulled away from the gap, turned around, and leaned against the tractor tire with the M4 across her lap. A round had punctured the rubber earlier in the afternoon. But, as the old saying went, it was only flat on the bottom.

She ran fingers down Tyrell's use-battered M4. Wasn't much good for anything now, except to be used as a club. When it became relevant she'd see if anyone had an extra magazine. But for now. Try to rest.

Fingers slid along Lauren's arm, fumbling until they found her hand and took it in a desperate grip. Lauren squeezed it back. A big hand, slippery with warm blood, she continued holding it tightly, though she had no idea who the hand belonged to.

Bullets pattered across the roof, falling like hailstones.

"Are they coming?" her companion asked in a voice as weak as a kitten's.

"No," she answered. "No reason to risk more of their men. They've got us, and they know it. They'll just wait us out."

"What about our reinforcements? They're coming, right?"

"'Course, they are," she lied. As long as there were rounds for the Browning M2s, there was no rescue coming.

"Thanks," the man murmured. "For saying that."

Lauren leaned her head back against the thick rubber and stared blindly at the roof where the darkness seemed to ripple.

Make believe, she wanted to tell him, make believe we're up in Yellowstone National Park and wildflowers cover the hills.

Images flared and faded behind her eyes: Buffalo calves frolicking in green meadows. Lovers sitting with their heads together on park benches.

The hand in her grip slowly relaxed. Went dead. Gently, she moved it aside.

More vehicles roared into the yard outside, and Lauren jerked awake. Wondered when she'd fallen asleep.

"What's happening?" one of the women cried from the back. Might have been Tana, a twenty-two-year-old from up at Bosler.

As people shifted positions, the darkness congealed into swaying black shapes.

"Get down!" Manford cried where he was looking out where the side door was opened to a slit.

A loud barrage of gunfire clattered on the walls, ripping the air, spurring an eruption of goddamns and cries of terror. They were followed by the sounds of hands and knees hitting the floor as people scrambled away.

A horse uttered a half-choked rasp, breathing labored, and gurgling, before it struggled for footing on the concrete, then came the sound of it collapsing. The big body hit the floor with a wet-sounding thump. Then came the beast's death rattle.

Lauren belly-crawled to the bullet-riddled shop door and pressed an eye to one of the holes.

Despite the blinding lights illuminating the pole barn, she could see the JLTVs, parked side-by-side with the barrels of their Brownings shining in the glow cast by pickup headlights.

"Guess I was wrong about them waiting us out," she said to no one in particular.

"Davis? Sit rep?" Manford, again.

"Both LTVs they're... Holy shit! Get down!"

The right-hand LTV's fifty opened up, the muzzle flash like flickering lightning atop the armored cab. Five rounds. Lauren had flattened herself on the concrete floor as the seven-hundred-grain bullets ripped through the barn. One blasted its way through the Massey Ferguson's cab, another blew hay out of one of the big bales.

In the back, another horse screamed and fell, kicking and snorting.

Yet another fifty-caliber slug tore its way down the work bench, scattering tools and exploding the vise into two pieces as hot metal pattered around.

Someone behind Lauren began panting in rapid bursts, like a woman giving birth. Someone else whimpered. She wished she could plug her ears against the rasping wheeze that came with each of the horse's dying breaths.

"Moments now," she called to the darkness. "They're going to open up. Get behind anything you can."

Faint words drifted around the cold air. "Holy Mary, Mother of God, pray for us…"

Manford commanded, "All of you! Get into position! Once they blast those doors apart, they're coming in! We're going to take as many of these bastards with us as we can."

Lauren smoothed her fingers down the cold barrel of the M4, and wondered if the matter had become relevant, or if resistance had lost all profit? "Anyone got an extra magazine?"

"That an M4?"

"Yes."

"Here. I'm passing up my last extra for my AR. Magpul, you know? Ought to work in your gun."

Moving along the floor from hand to hand, it arrived. Lauren took the magazine and slapped it into the M4.

"…hallowed be thy name."

"You in the barn!" a voice called from outside. "Get real. Our guns can tear that tractor to pieces. And that cement wall in there can't stop fifty caliber armor piercing rounds. Hey, it's hopeless, and you're fucked. Give up!"

"Manford? This is stupid," someone in back called. "Can't we just surrender?"

A woman half-screamed, "I'm not surrendering. You don't know what they'll do to a woman. They're animals!"

"Better than dying! Let's give up. Give them the fuel they want and free passage. Maybe they'll just let us go!"

Another voice in the darkness said, "You're going to die no matter, Jimmy. In here or out there. May as well make it look like we were brave about it."

"How can you say that? You don't know that!"

Lauren crawled to a better position, but when she edged forward, her hand landed in the middle of a dead man's face. Her companion. The who'd held her hand. She jerked her fingers away.

Sliding back to her former position, she wiggled forward under the tractor. Through a rip in the bottom of the door left by a ricochet, she could see a man's head and torso sticking up from the hatch above the passenger's seat in the JLTV.

"This is your last chance," the man shouts through cupped hands.

Lauren can feel the rising tension. What are they down to? Fifteen rounds?

Still enough to gut the barn and everything in it.

This is strange. This feeling.

She grips the M4 with all her strength and wills time to stop, to rewind, to take her back to the beautiful summer morning before the world ended. But that's impossible, and she knows it.

More headlights flare to life outside, and the interior of the barn transforms into white shafts of light, pouring through the holes in the roof, doors, and walls.

The air warms instantly. She starts to perspire. The darkness takes on a shimmer. Her soul has dropped into the zone.

Let others waste their time praying.

The rifle is her lord and savior.

CHAPTER FIFTY-SIX

***

THE VOICE ON THE MEGAPHONE SOUNDS SO REASONABLE: *"WE'RE NOT GOING TO KILL YOU. We want hostages to trade for supplies, not corpses."*

"Go fuck yourself!" Manford cries.

"Last chance! You have thirty seconds!"

Nervous laughter moves through the dark paddock.

Lauren is so tired, but there's a flash flood rushing inside her. Faces, smiling people, counting stars on summer evenings, the feel of his calloused fingers slowly trailing across her skin, all tumble through her mind. She remembers the taste of mesquite-smoked chicken, the rough texture of a buffalo calf's tongue licking her cheek, the scent of wet junipers after a rainstorm.

The soldiers in Airborne talk about this. The point in the dive where the rip cord won't pull. The chute won't open. You finally stop falling faster because your body has reached "terminal velocity", one-hundred-twenty miles per hour. That's when it hits. Your whole life, everything that has ever been important to you, is right there. Right behind your eyes, staring you in the face one last time.

Then the chute does open, and you realize that the sum of all your fears was simply the price of truth. You had to pay for one blinding moment of illumination before you could see the vault of heaven open in your soul.

…Isaac lying bound upon the altar, watching his father Abraham lift the knife.

God is such a son of a bitch.

Lauren bowed her head and softly laughed. Terminal velocity. That's where she was.

The voice outside calls, "…Five, Four, Three…"

Lauren stood up and shouldered through the hay bales to get to the side door. "Hey!" she called to the men outside. "Hold your fire. I'm coming out!"

"What?" Manford cried. "The hell you are!"

"Wait a minute!" Jimmy pleaded. "Let's at least discuss it, okay. How do we do it?"

"I've never quit before, and I'm not doing it now!" Manford growled. "Davis, get your ass down!"

Another man yelled, "You'd better not do it, girl, or I'm going to shoot through the middle of you!"

The voice on the megaphone: *"Hurry it up, or else!"*

Another voice from the abyss outside, deeper: "*Where the hell are the choppers they're supposed to be sending us?*"

"Dear God," Manford said. "They have choppers?"

"Lot of military down in Colorado," another growled.

Lauren turned around, tried to see Manford in the slanting rays of white light that stabbed through the bullet holes. His breath steamed in the cold night air.

Reluctantly, she leaned her M4 against the wall and pulled her last grenade from inside her filthy touring jacket, holding it up so Manford could see it.

"What the hell are you doing?" he cried, stepping forward.

Lauren might have been dry wood inside for all the emotion she felt. "I'll have to get close to the LTVs to take out the big guns. I'll only be able to take one. And that's if I get the hand grenade to fall just right. But they won't be expecting it. You're going to have one chance to run. Do you understand?"

Gasps and murmurs went around the barn.

Manford's face slackened. He took a deep breath and held it for a few seconds. "We really down to this?"

"They unleash both of those fifties, we're all dead. You know it as well as I do."

"Yeah, I know." He hung his gray head for a few moments, before he exhaled hard. "Tom. Jimmy. Move those bales away from the doors. The rest of you, get back there and mount up. We got five horses. There's eight of you. Three are going to have to double up, and somebody has to carry the kids. Don't make your break 'til I call you. When I yell, you come boiling out and ride hell-for-leather for the high country."

"But what about you, sir?" Jimmy asked.

A grim smile turned Manford's lips. He turned to stare into Lauren's eyes.

"I'm staying behind to cover your escape."

CHAPTER FIFTY-SEVEN

***

LAUREN BENT, GOT HOLD OF THE DOOR AND LIFTED. THIS TIME, SHOT-UP AS IT WAS, IT groaned going up only half way before it jammed. That was all right. The horses could still clear it if the riders ducked.

Floodlights hit her, blinding her for a several seconds. Behind the hulking Massey Ferguson, people where mounting, getting ready to make their try. Then, through the smoke and dust, Lauren glimpsed the faint image of the man with a megaphone. Big man. Muscular and tall. He had to be standing on the LTV's seat, his torso sticking up through the hatch next to the Browning's barrel.

He ordered, *"Come on out! All of you. Be quick about it. We don't have all night!"*

Lauren lifted her hands over her head. Wouldn't be long now. In the rear of the barn, she heard horses snuffling, metal jingling, and the quiet, quiet voices of riders trying to calm animals that were charged with the smell of blood, death, and human fear.

Manford knelt in the shadows to the right of the door with his rifle braced on two hay bales, his eyes glued to the red-dot sight.

Far out in the forest, gunfire broke out, followed by ragged screams. So, don't count the Militia out yet.

Lauren shook herself and emerged from the gaping door. Fixed her gaze on the burly man with the megaphone where he stuck out the LTV's roof hatch. If she had any wits, she'd get religion at this point—not that she expected to see avenging angels soar down from the clouds to save her. It might even make the enemy laugh.

And laughter was moments. Precious moments for the people behind her.

She kept walking, slowly, hands high over her head. Had to look perfectly natural. Eyes wide open, she expected a bullet at any instant. Men with guns shifted behind the protection of the pickups. Every barrel aimed at her or at the doors behind her. Pale blue smoke braided the moonlight.

Suddenly, she couldn't feel her feet. She might have been hovering—sailing forward like a balloon cut loose from its tethers. Brain must be starving for oxygen. That explained the curious sensation that she'd been divinely anointed. Chosen for this.

"Where's the others?" A ghostly shape rose from behind a truck to her right. His face and red hair gleamed in the hoarfrost of moon and headlights. "Why aren't they coming out? If you're pulling something...?"

Throughout the semicircle of trucks, bodies rustled, and men slithered up from where they'd hidden. Cobras in baskets. Heads bobbed. Shoulders swayed. Gun metal glinted. One man had a blood-soaked white bandage wrapped around his head, covering one eye.

The hoarse screams out in the forest started up again.

"Shut him up, Goddamit!" another voice knifed through the darkness. The words echoed around the valley like ping pong balls. Bouncing off rocks here, then over there.

Two more rifle shots.

The screaming stopped.

Lauren continued on her unalterable path. She had to get close enough to the LTVs. Had to be able to pitch the grenade right into one of the gunner's laps.

By now, Manford was holding his breath.

Everything depended upon how close she could get. Maybe she'd have a chance to throw the grenade and dive for cover? Yeah, right.

Lauren, you're dead. Just deal, huh?

Curious how the brain worked. Grasping at straws even when they didn't exist.

Megaphone: *"Stop right there!"*

Lauren risked two more steps before she obliged. Close enough? No. But might have to do.

"The rest of you, come out! Right now! This is your last warning!"

"What the hell are you giving them a warning for?" a deep voice called. "Just shoot the bitch!"

"I told you, mother fucker, you're not in charge here!"

Blinded by the lights, Lauren couldn't see who the second speaker was.

She took the distraction to ease forward another step and lower her arms. Felt the grenade slip down the inside of her sleeve to rest in her palm.

Lauren shivered.

Manford must realize she wasn't close enough. He yelled, "We got wounded in here! We're trying to get 'em up!"

One more quiet step forward. Suck in a breath.

No one seemed to notice. *Lucky, lucky.*

At least she'd made it outside into the sweet mountain air, where she could look up at the night sky. Only the brightest stars burned through the haze. The cold wind felt good on her hot face.

Her fingers went tight around the heavy grenade.

"Leave the goddamn wounded behind! We'll collect 'em later."

Just a small step. And then a half step, as if she were nervously shifting. Forward.

"We're sending the horses out first," Manford bellowed angrily. "Don't *shoot* the horses, you hear?"

Good thinking on Manford's part. It bought Lauren another step.

It hit Lauren like a thrown brick: She couldn't remember what day it was? Maybe it was Sunday? The holy day? It made her feel better to think it was. Somehow salvation didn't seem so implausible.

She would die here. She would never get on her bike and ride to the Tappan ranch in northern Wyoming. Never watch the wildflowers from the rocking chair by the big front windows.

Tyrell would understand.

She wrapped her fingers around the lever, freeing its pressure on the pin. All she had to do was reach over with her other hand and pull it. Maybe she could run the last twenty feet to the big guns? Doubtful. Looked like she'd have to try and pull the pin, lift the grenade, and throw it before they shot her to doll rags.

She took one last look over her shoulder, saw movement in the rear, horses maybe, shaking their heads in the shadows behind the tractor.

A curious numbness filled her.

"Listen!" one of the men in the vehicles called. "Hear 'em?"

"'Bout time our birds got here. They'll have fuel and ammo. We're saved."

"Yeah," megaphone agreed. "Guess we don't need hostages anymore."

Lauren's heart sank.

Dear God.

The sound of the helicopters rose. As they cleared the ridge, the thunder grew louder. Nothing more than three dark specters against the haze-black sky, the Blackhawk helicopters came dropping down over the tree tops, sundering the smoke as they cut arcs through the feeble moonlight.

The choppers swung around and dove straight at the yard. Surprised men leaped inside trucks or ran for the trees.

Megaphone: *"What the hell kind of stupid-ass antic is this?"*

Lauren pulled the pin, charged for the closest vehicle. The bullets cracked by her ear. Close. So close. Then she was between the LTVs. Grabbed the door handle and got one foot on the driver's step. Rising as high as she could, she slam-dunked the grenade down through the vehicle's open turret.

The shocked gunner screamed something, clawing at his crotch. She swore she heard the grenade thump onto the floor.

Then her foot slipped off the step. She fell as bullets ripped through the space where she'd been.

On the ground, she scrambled toward the other LTV. Caught a glance as she rolled under the other vehicle: the gunner, leaning out from his turret, a pistol in his hand.

Counting down, ...two, one.

The explosion hit her like the fist of God. Bounced her up and hurled her face-down. In that flash of an instant, frozen, the JLTV above her was blown onto its side.

And then the blow to her head made the world go away. Blasted heterodyne. Floating into a cloudy...

She came to in front of a red Dodge truck. Her first sensation is damning pain in her chest. Excruciating. Hard to breathe.

Darkness.

Lit here and there by burning wreckage.

Hellish images in her swimming vision. Broken trucks.

Fires flickering, illuminating bent and twisted bodies.

Whimpering, she drags herself underneath the truck's bumper and curls up on her side. Cradles her broken and bleeding chest, gasping for breath.

Movement catches her eye.

Horses burst out of the barn and thunder past her with their tails flying. Muzzle flashes. Manford shooting. Methodical, like he had all day now. Taking down any enemy soldier he could.

The endless fucking ringing, like an amp on overload, threatens to split her skull.

Must have turned her brain to mush.

She tries to understand the LTV burning off to the right. The doors have been blown open. The armored windows blasted out and shattered.

The second LTV lies on its side, wheels sticking out. Looking so odd in the jumping and leaping firelight.

Grenade couldn't do that.

Lauren shakes her head hard but can't make sense of what is happening. Worse, she's gone deaf. She can't even hear the helicopter blades cleaving the air right over her head. The downwash is beating at her, rocking the truck above her.

Practically on top of her...

Startled men in fatigues fire wildly at the choppers as the aircraft swing around to make another pass, and the pilots open up, strafing the positions below.

The mini-guns chew the earth to pieces. The air becomes metal-flavored sand, and Lauren feels herself sinking. Her strength leaving her.

Red froth bubbles at her lips. Is she hit? She hasn't felt the shot. In the light, she stares down at the warm blood on her hand. Understands it's from the pain in her chest.

Idly, she tries to determine: Is it just one or both lungs? The macabre debate amuses her. At this point, does it really matter? How long before she suffocates on her own blood?

Lying back on the cold ground, she watches the choppers cut across the face of the haze-choked moon, and elation washes through her. One after another, the Blackhawks sail by. As each momentarily blocks the moonlight, the whirling smoke turns cobalt blue, and she sees the insignia on the helicopter's side.

Wyoming National Guard.

Always ready. Always there.

Oblivion is closing in around her, and she smiles.

The angels have come after all.

CHAPTER FIFTY-EIGHT

***

AN EARSPLITTING SECURITY ALARM RANG, GOING ON AND ON. WHY DIDN'T SOMEONE SHUT that damned thing off? The ringing made Lauren sick to her stomach.

She tried to sit up, but couldn't budge her arms or legs. Was she paralyzed? Strapped down?

Where am I?

She had no sense of time or place. Just floating misery. Breathing was agony.

Struggling, she managed to open her eyes, and the white light in the room felt like stilettos being plunged through her eye sockets into her brain. She closed them again, and fought down the wave of nausea.

Hospital room. Should have known immediately, just based upon the astringent smell.

Why was she in the hospital?

Slitting one eye open, she examined the tubes dangling from hanging bags. What the hell…?

She commanded herself to see. Tubes in her arms, chest. The one in her nose fed her oxygen, which she'd started gulping in great desperate breaths. The blood pressure and heart rate monitor to her right were flashing red.

A woman charged into the room. Tall. Dark haired. Her mouth moved. Lauren couldn't hear her. The woman hurried over to her bed and leaned down close to Lauren's ear.

"Calm down! You…all right. I know…barely hear me." Her voice was so faint Lauren almost couldn't make out the words. "…an explosion," "…hearing…back soon…"

"Explosion?" she asked, stunned by the news. "What happened?" She couldn't hear her own voice. Which meant the woman must be shouting at the top of her lungs.

"Seven days ago... Firefight. ...Shrapnel lodged in your lungs. Chest trauma...four broken ribs. Surgery..."

She frowned up at the woman, not understanding. She had no memory of such an event. "Hurts...to breathe."

The woman nodded. "...Out of danger now. Stable. Keeping you sedated...few more days. Rest."

Lauren sank back into the white pillows and nodded. Okay. She'd been hurt in an explosion. She needed to rest.

While the woman listened to her heart and used a penlight to check her pupil dilation, Lauren fought to recall some shred...

"Manford?" she asked. "Did he make it?"

The woman straightened up, stared at Lauren, then nodded, and mouthed the word, "Yes."

"Okay." Lauren closed her eyes, felt the warm tears drain down her cheeks, said, "Okay," again and drifted back to the sweet oblivion of sleep.

CHAPTER FIFTY-NINE

***

"DAVIS? YOU AWAKE?"

Lauren knew that voice. Had heard it... Where?

"Doc said you were conscious. They did surgery on your ears. You'll be able to hear again."

When she squinted through rheumy eyes, a face drifted out of the ocean of light: Captain Ragnovich. His white hair had a bluish sheen in the fluorescent lights, and his camo clothing had been freshly pressed. A new look for him. She hoped he hadn't done it for her.

"Davis, can you hear me?"

"Yeah. Barely." Made her aware that her ears hurt, like a deep dull ache. It barely stood out against the other pain.

"Good. Don't try and pull the bandages off your ears. They're there to keep them from getting infected and to allow the eardrums to heal."

She roused herself, tried to roll over to face him where he sat at her bedside. Froze and gasped. It fucking hurt too much. "Kids?" she asked. "Make it out?"

"All but one," Ragnovich's voice barely penetrated the ringing and thick bandages. "Little boy. Rest are safe and sound with their families in Laramie."

"Guard lose anyone?"

"Few gunshot wounds...choppers are going to need a shitload of paint. Otherwise...all right."

"Militia?"

His voice had dropped to a mumble.

Lauren licked her dry lips. "Can't hear you, Captain. Sorry."

Ragnovich dragged his chair closer and leaned forward, toward her right ear.

"How are you feeling?" He spoke slowly, enunciating each word.

"Like I was run over by a fucking dump truck and jumped on by an elephant, okay?" she said. When she took a deep breath, her chest hurt like sin, but it was bearable, and this was the first day she could say that. "Thanks for sending the choppers."

Ragnovich's mouth quirked. "Didn't have much choice. I'd have had a mass mutiny if I'd let Lauren Davis, Queen of the Fourth Quadrant, die at the hands of raiders."

A smile touched Lauren's lips. "Some hero."

"Yeah. Some hero. You know what would have happened if they'd turned those two M2 Brownings on the helicopters? I got the full report from Manford. You took them out before they could do any damage. Don't know what they had in the LTV. Mortar rounds? C-4? Whatever it was, your grenade detonated a whole load."

Guilt carved his wrinkled face. "Wish I'd known earlier, I would have…"

He let the sentence dwindle to nothing, and as Lauren studied his downcast eyes and the hard set of his jaw, she said, "What about the Militia? How many did they lose?"

Most of her memory had returned, but not all. Everything between the explosion and waking up in the hospital was a complete blank.

"Twenty-two. Seven more wounded." He hesitated. Looked up at her and took a deep breath. "No easy way to say this. Trevor Phillips died getting the children up the ravine to the ridge top."

Lauren suddenly felt lightheaded. "How?"

"Guess five men were chasing them. Phillips got down behind some rocks and made a last stand. Bought time while his fiancée herded the kids up the trail. Killed every one of the raiders, but they'd shot him up pretty bad. Once Tiffany got the kids to safety, she took a horse back for Phillips. He didn't make it to the hospital in Laramie."

In her imagination, Lauren is in the high mountains with Tiffany, strapping Trevor's body over the back of a horse, and starting down the trail. Being there, she is going to make the difference. She will get him to the hospital in Laramie.

But she wasn't there. Can't go back and change the past.

Her heart breaks for Tiff. Had she and Trevor talked? Gotten to say goodbye? At least been able to hold each other one last time?

If only Lauren could get a deep breath into her lungs…

There is no respite. No pause in the onslaught. Terror, grief, love, anguish. Far horizons. Experience pushed to the outermost limits a human being could stand and survive.

Ragnovich gave her a little while to absorb the news, then he said, "Got more bad news. Mike Vinich passed. Lauren, his heart just couldn't seem to catch up with the trauma. For what it's worth, the cardiologist said he'd never seen such a fighter."

Lauren is falling, weightless, dull-gray and empty. Even the ringing in her ears seems to fade into nothing.

She tries to sob, spears of pain like stabbing agony in her chest.

Closing her eyes, she turns herself into a bird. Stretches her wings to catch the air and rise. Only she just…can't…seem to get off the ground.

CHAPTER SIXTY

* * *

A WHEELCHAIR SQUEAKS AS IT ROLLS DOWN THE HALL OUTSIDE. I HEAR A SOFT VOICE speaking with someone, and I close my eyes to listen. It sounds like Mike Vinich. His voice eases the dark fluttery monster that inhabits my chest. The unbearably heavy thing that relentlessly twists and untwists inside me. For weeks, I've endured its faint motions. Feathery. Malignant. At night, it slithers up and transforms into a cry that I keep locked behind my clenched teeth. Terrifies me. This thing that sleeps coiled around my heart.

When the nurse wheels him into my room, Mike's face lights up with a huge smile. "Hey, you look like hell. How you feeling?"

"Like hell. You?"

"Better now."

The nurse pushes his wheelchair up to my bedside and leaves the room. An antiseptic smell trails after her.

Mike's brown eyes fill with warmth. He exhales, as though relieved to see me. For a while, we just smile at the other.

"Tiff came to see you a few days ago. She sat by your bedside for hours, hoping to talk to you."

The monster moves.

Some part of me knows that this isn't true. I'm just drifting in a misty cloud of drugs and pain. How do I justify this? What does it mean?

"Probably wanted to be the one to tell me about Trev." Pain etches my voice, and I slip away to be with Trevor on the starlit mountaintop, patiently listening to him trying to talk me into staying out of the fight. He was willing to die to save Tiff, but he didn't want me to.

Coiling. Around my heart.

I lie here, waiting for it to end, but it never ends…it never ends…

"How is Tiff?"

"Broken. Grieving, but she'll make it. She's damned near as tough as you are."

Tears burn my eyes. "I wish I'd…"

"Don't. Don't do that." The voice has changed. Deeper, filled with that faint accent. So familiar. It warms my heart.

When I turn and open my eyes, Tyrell leans forward in the wheelchair and reaches out to take my hand in a grip that hurts. "Your friend Trevor knew exactly what he was doing, Lauren. Don't second-guess his decision. He knew it was worth it."

Tyrell pauses, his dark eyes glinting. "Just as you did when you walked out of that pole barn with that grenade."

I have such vast empty space to cross before I find my voice. "Don't even remember that."

Deliverance. This cold forgetfulness. My soul must be certain I couldn't bear to live through it again.

"You don't have to. Hey, chica mia, you're a fucking hero. I guarantee that you'll be hearing different versions of the story for the rest of your life."

"Which means I'm forever condemned to wonder which one is true."

Ty laughs from the belly. I see his teeth, the lights glinting in his coal-black hair. And I remember why I fell in love with him.

He gives me that teasing grin. "Yeah, being a legend will be a curse."

Utter despair hollows out my insides, then slowly bleeds out into the room, giving the white walls a watery sheen. I never wanted any of this.

I have so much to tell Ty, but when I look, my brother Jimmy is sitting in the wheelchair. His tan-brown Davis eyes are taking my measure, an amused smile on his lips. I can see the scar on his chin from where he fell on the sidewalk when he was five.

Jim studies my expression, and quietly says, "Hear that the Tappans have sent word. Heard you were in the hospital. Said you had a place at the ranch. Do you know when you'll be going?"

"I…I… What day is it?"

"Friday."

Shaking my head, I breathe the words, "I don't even know what that means."

"Ragnovich came to see you yesterday, Lauren. Told you that Governor Agar was flying up to Cody, and you could ride along. Special. You know how important it must be. The state jet is too important a piece of equipment these days."

"Okay." My head weakly rolls to the side.

Jimmy rolls his chair as close to the bed as he can. "Sis, Breeze forgave you. I was the one who fucked up that night. I wouldn't have come back to tell you, but you're such a god-damned dense knot-head sometimes. Send word. Tell Agar you want to go."

He glances around. "Besides, I think they wasted enough meds on you here. They probably want your skinny ass gone so they can put someone in this bed who isn't such a pain."

"You and Mike are dead."

"Yeah, sis. I mean, that's the whole point, right?" Odd shadows dance across his face when one of the fluorescent lights flickers.

"Well, for what it's worth…" He lifts my hand and gives my fingers a quick kiss before he lowers it to the bed again. "I love you. But don't make more of that than it is."

"I love you, too, big brother."

I reach out for his hand, desperate to clasp it to my breast. But when I blink and clear my eyes, the room swims into focus.

There is no wheelchair beside my bed. Just the moveable tray on which one of those hospital water glasses with an oversized straw rests.

Vinich? Tyrell? Jim?

They seemed so real.

Or am I just that close to dead myself?

I reach out and press the nurse's call button.

When the tall balding guy in his early forties wearing scrubs comes hustling in the door, I tell him in my gravelly voice, "I need to get a message to Captain Ragnovich. Tell him I'll take the governor's offer."

CHAPTER SIXTY-ONE

* * *

BEFORE THE COLLAPSE—AND WITH FULL WYOMING TONGUE-IN-CHEEK-HUMOR—IT WAS
called the "Wyoming Air Force". The state owned and operated two
corporate jets and a couple of prop-driven planes for conducting official
state business. But, as with the helicopters and C-130s that Agar
"nationalized", the future of the aircraft was a foregone conclusion:
They could only fly until a lack of spare parts grounded them forever.
That Agar was flying to Cody demonstrated just how seriously he took
Edgewater and his power base in the Bighorn Basin.

And I was able to hop a ride.

Wrapped in one of Ragnovich's cast-off old coats, Lauren sat fully
reclined in the Cessna Citation Encore's lush leather seat. She'd been
wheeled from the hospital, taken in an ambulance to the airport, and
painfully transferred to the corporate jet's cabin.

Didn't matter that she'd been given a dose of ever-more-rare
painkiller. It still hurt like blazes.

Watching the world pass by through her window was a revelation.
Everything was familiar and soothing. Like the collapse had never
happened. She could have set the world back to before that terrible
Friday in June as she stared down from twenty-seven-thousand feet.
That was the great thing about flying over Wyoming, to look down
was to see the geological bones of the state.

Enjoy it. You'll never view the world like this again.

Thinking back, the last time she'd been on a plane was flying back
from Baltimore. From that horrible final meeting with her parents:
the general and her mother. Not mom and dad. Which showed how
screwed up her personal life had become after Jim's death. And, yeah,
most of it had been her fault.

We always take it out on the ones we love.

She grunted, which sent a worse stitch of pain through her healing ribs.

Hell of a legacy her family had left her. No chance to heal that rift now.

They're dead. Just like Jim, Mike, Trevor, Randy, and all those people I shot down on The Line.

To the west, the jagged peaks of the Wind River Mountains rose against a red-brown sky. A glistening coat of fresh snow had fallen in the high country, blanketing the slopes and trailing like ragged scarves down the flanks of the mountains. Temperatures for the past few days had been unseasonably cold for the first of July.

She wondered if the nuclear explosions and burning cities had changed the weather patterns. Was nuclear winter descending upon them? If so, the world was about to get much colder. They'd lose days or weeks of growing season. Crops wouldn't have enough time to mature. How could Wyoming farmers and ranchers produce enough to feed people?

And that was probably the least of their worries.

She was dwelling on that when Governor Agar made his way up from where he'd been in the rear, talking with several of his staff. Like usual, the governor was wearing his dandy three-piece suit. Mirror-polished black dress shoes clad his feet.

Somehow, she always thought the Governor of Wyoming should wear a vest, O'Farrell western hat with a high crease and expensive Lucchese boots. Agar always looked like he'd just stepped off Fifth Avenue.

The man seated himself across from Lauren and straightened his tie. Glancing her way, he asked, "How are you doing?"

She gave him a wry smile. "Chest is tight. Hurts."

"I read the reports. The miracle is that you're alive. While they got most of the metal out, they left a few of the smaller pieces as souvenirs. I'm told the scar will be quite the conversation piece. And Dr. Blagovich was able to repair your eardrums. Said you'd have been deaf as a stone otherwise."

"Don't know how I'll ever pay the bill."

"Wyoming will cover it." His thin lips bent. "Think it through, Ms.

Davis. Everything you've done. Buffalo Camp. The Chinese pilot. Marsy Ranch. Now you've survived The Line to take the fight for civilization to the Bighorn Basin."

She gave an uncomfortable nod. "Whatever. Listen, I really appreciate the ride. Would have been a bitch in a car or truck."

Agar's intent gaze remained laser intense. "You still don't have any idea, do you, Ms. Davis?"

"Idea? About what?"

"About what you mean to the state. To the people on The Line. To our future?"

She glanced out at the blue waters of Boysen Reservoir and the narrow cleft that was Wind River Canyon. Beyond, the Owl Creek Mountains rose in rugged humps before surrendering to the jagged and snow-capped summits of the Absarokas farther west. Looked like the top of the world as one soaring peak gave way to the next only to vanish into the distance that was Yellowstone.

What I mean?

Lauren could see now. Really see. Her eyes no longer observed the smooth outsides of things, for she knew them to be a sham, an illusion. She saw only the insides. The dark sharp edges that plunged to the center of the earth. All the questions that had once brought her such wonder in college classes had evaporated into the thin air of terror, forcing her to dwell among the shadows and splinters. Forcing her to live the answers.

"I'm nothing more than a wounded and broken waste of meat, Governor. Nothing I did was smart, brave, or clever. Every mess I got into was because I didn't think, just reacted."

"Isn't that all any of us do in a crisis?"

She stared hotly back into his dark eyes. "The only thing I wanted was to stop the pain. If booze wouldn't do it, maybe a bullet would."

Agar nodded thoughtfully. "You and me, Ms. Davis." He looked down at his hand. Flexed the fingers, frowning as if amazed at how they worked. "We both have blood under our fingernails and know how much that costs. In the process, we have both come to symbolize people that we're not in our hearts. Hell of a price to pay, isn't it?"

"How so, sir?"

"The choices, Ms. Davis. The things we did on the Fourth Quadrant.

You looked people in the eye, turned them back from The Line. But ultimately, it was my responsibility. My order. Am I a monster, for condemning all those people? Sending them back south into the hell that became Colorado? Or am I the only hope for saving just a little sliver of civilization?"

He shot her a questioning look. "Who am I? A savior, or a monster? Or both at once?"

"Like that day at the executions at Frontier Park?"

"Just taking ultimate responsibility."

"So, you're flying special up to Cody to put a bullet into Director Edgewater's brain?"

Agar, looking at his hand again, nodded. "Our mutual friends, the Tappans, have caught him red-handed. Oh, he'll have a trial, tell his side of it. I want that on the record. In his own words. But just because we're entering an age of savagery, doesn't mean we have to promote the practice beyond what it takes for our survival."

"When they were loading me on the plane I heard Edgewater was taking girls and young women. Made them sex slaves."

"He did. And if they didn't satisfy, he shot them in the head and buried them in unmarked graves. He's had people 'disappeared' and put others in a concentration camp. Looted four counties." He glanced at her. "So, tell me. What's your call?"

She winced at the pain in her lungs. "I'd put him down, sir."

Agar nodded. "Ms. Davis. I know you'll be in the Park County Medical Center for a while yet, and then the Tappans want you to recover on their ranch. But should you decide to come back to Cheyenne, you have a place there. In my administration. I want you to know that."

She gave him a sidelong glance. "As a symbol?"

He chuckled under his breath. "Of course. Isn't that all that any of us are these days?"

RESOLUTION

* * *

THIS WAS DISCHARGE DAY. LAUREN SAT ON THE EDGE OF THE BED. SHE'D DRESSED IN HER last pair of jeans; her other pair having been too torn and blood-stained from the fighting on Marsy Ranch. After that she had her riding pants, the shredded remains of her Ralley jacket, and couple of pairs of panties, two bras, and a sweatshirt. Just another reminder that the end of civilization was hard on clothes.

The good news was that Cody had been stocked with T-shirts, sweatshirts, and western wear before the collapse. Local businesses had been expecting a booming tourist trade. The town was awash in clothing. Finding a new wardrobe was going to be a piece of cake, as long as the wearer didn't mind all the Yellowstone park and buffalo images that advertised the "Been there, Done that, Got the T-shirt" tourist image.

Her motorcycle helmet had vanished along the way, although word was that Old Bill Tappan had brought her KTM back from Cheyenne after his last trip down to the capital for meetings with Agar.

She was tired of hospitals. Tired of the owl-eyed looks some of the staff, and too many of the patients gave her.

Turned out that being "a symbol" really sucked the big one.

"You look like shit, Davis," a pinched voice called from the hall.

Lauren glanced up from where she'd been studying her scuffed and bloodstained riding boots. Breeze stood in the door. Ultimate Western woman, she wore a flat-brimmed western hat, long-sleeved red shirt, fitted Levi's, and dusty western boots: the pointed kind with high riding heels. Her dark-brown hair was clipped in a ponytail, and those brown-ringed amber eyes were taking Lauren's measure.

"You ought to feel it on the inside." Lauren tried to smile, felt it fall apart. God, she was tired.

Breeze walked over, glanced down at the boogie bag. "That's all of your gear?"

"Not much to show for, is it?" Lauren eased down from the bed, took a breath to steady herself.

Breeze was right there, offering an arm and asking, "You all right?"

"Just gotta take it slow. Did you know those lazy surgeons down in Cheyenne left little pieces of metal inside me?"

"Serves you right for sticking around to fight when you could have run off with Tiff."

"Aw, I just wanted to be the first person on The Line to blow up a JLTV. You know. I never could turn down a challenge. How far do I have to walk?"

"Brandon's rounding up a wheelchair. Shanteel's got the truck out front."

"Who's Shanteel?"

"Brandon's wife."

"Wife?" She shot a sidelong look at Breeze. "Some buckle bunny finally landed the rodeo Romeo?"

Breeze continued giving her that eerie stare. "Uh, that woman's *anything* but a buckle bunny. Lot of stuff's happened."

"Yeah, tell me about it." Lauren saw the flint-like hardness behind her eyes. "Heard you had a pretty tough time taking down Edgewater." She tilted her head toward the door. "Laying here, you hear things. Not everyone's happy you took the son of a bitch out."

"People died," Breeze whispered, her eyes getting that haunted look.

"You sure this is okay? I mean, you and your family have enough—"

"Shut the fuck up, Lauren." Breeze's smile flashed for the briefest of moments. "We're still sisters. And Mom's looking forward to seeing you. Like you, she's healing. Says she looks forward to sharing the porch with you. According to her, watching alfalfa grow is a hell of a lot better than being dead." Then the haunted look was back.

"What?" Lauren asked as Breeze went distant.

"Old Thomas Star had me do a vision quest. Everything we've done, Lauren, there's more to come. Says we're warriors for the new age."

"Well...screw that."

"Yeah." Breeze smiled, put her arm around Lauren's shoulder.

"Come on. At Tappan ranch, we're always looking for another new-age warrior."

Breeze reached down, swinging the heavy boogie bag up with one arm. "Now, where the hell is that no-good little brother of mine? The kid can't handle a simple job like finding a wheelchair."

"He's a twin. Only, like, twenty seconds younger than you."

"Yeah, but we're in a hurry. They're cooking steaks down at the ranch in celebration of your arrival."

"Then, come on. I'm not waiting," Lauren declared. What the hell were knitting ribs and incisions when steaks were cooking?

With Breeze balancing the boogie bag on one shoulder, and steadying Lauren as they went, they headed for the door.

Steaks? Damn straight!

A LOOK AT: FRACTURE EVENT

Award-winning archaeologists and New York Times and USA Today bestselling authors Kathleen O'Neal Gear and W. Michael Gear bring us a gripping disaster thriller.

The seas flood their banks. Storms devastate entire continents. Fires envelop the world in darkness. The collapse begins…

Anthropologist Anika French makes an explosive discovery: due to climate change, our world is threatened with collapse in just a few years, and humanity will perish. Anika's committee chair published her work under his own name, now powerful people will do anything to obtain Anika's statistical program for their own use.

With murder, kidnapping, extortion, and assassination on every side, Dr. Maureen Cole, a team of specialists, and bodyguard Skip Murphy will do everything in their power to keep Anika safe as they struggle with the implications of Anika's work. For once the "fracture event" occurs, Anika's model predicts the end of the world – and dark powers are already testing the model with devastating results.

Ultimately, it will be up to Skip, Maureen, and Anika as a deadly showdown in the Alps will determine who will profit from the destruction of civilization.

AVAILABLE NOW ON AMAZON

ABOUT THE AUTHOR

W. Michael Gear is the New York Times and international bestselling author of over fifty-eight novels, many of them co-authored with Kathleen O'Neal Gear.

With seventeen million copies of his work in print he is best known for the "People" series of novels written about North American Archaeology. His work has been translated into at least 29 languages. Michael has a master's degree in Anthropology, specialized in physical anthropology and forensics, and has worked as an archaeologist for over forty years.

His published work ranges in genre from prehistory, science fiction, mystery, historical, genetic thriller, and western. For twenty-eight years he and Kathleen have raised North American bison at Red Canyon Ranch and won the coveted National Producer of the Year award from the National Bison Association in 2004 and 2009. They have published over 200 articles on bison genetics, management, and history, as well as articles on writing, anthropology, historic preservation, resource utilization, and a host of other topics.

The Gears live in Cody, Wyoming, where W. Michael Gear enjoys large-caliber rifles, long-distance motorcycle touring, and the richest, darkest stout he can find.

CPSIA information can be obtained
at www.ICGtesting.com
Printed in the USA
LVHW090054310322
714841LV00023B/649/J

9 781639 773015